T0018024

Readers Love
The Girl Whose Luck Ran Out

"Definitely recommended for those who like to follow mysteries, enjoy engaging characters, and second chance romances."

—Nat Kennedy Reviews

"...the story boasts a soothing, balm-like quality that seeks to heal what has been slivered."

—Delphic Reviews

"I can't wait to read the next book in the series. I believe once more people hear about this book, Gayleen Froese will have a hit on her hands."

—Gina Rae Mitchell Reviews

By GAYLEEN FROESE

BEN AMES CASE FILES
The Girl Whose Luck Ran Out
The Man Who Lost His Pen

Published by DSP PUBLICATIONS
www.dsppublications.com

GAYLEEN FROESE

THE MAN WHO LOST HIS PEN

DSP PUBLICATIONS

Acknowledgements

Thanks as always to Ryan and Cori for their advice and support, as well as to the truly wonderful Andi and Gin and the rest of the team at DSP. My deep appreciation also goes out to Sharon, Anne, Dale, and Kim (Go Team Promo!), and to everyone who read the first Ben Ames book and asked to read another.

FOREWORD

I laughed when Ben Ames told me not to give away the name of the killer in my introduction. By now, I don't know who hasn't heard about the murder described in this book. And I think most people know who did it. But it turns out Ben was serious.

Maybe he's imagining someone reading this book in the future, when no one remembers any of the celebrities Ben wrote about here.

For now, his book is a backstage look at what really happened on the night of a famous crime. You could call it an antidote to the conspiracy theories and speculation. It's also a pretty good whodunnit for anyone who hasn't seen the news or been on the internet or left their house at all.

Ben asked me to remind everyone—especially the people he wrote about—that this book isn't court testimony. He says it's a record of how he saw things and "You can't sue a guy for what he thinks of people."

I'm not sure that's true, but if you're a fan of one of the bands or comedians in these pages, please remember that it's just one man's strongly worded, very detailed, sometimes snarky opinion.

And enjoy.

Gayleen Froese
Literary agent for Ben Ames

GAYLEEN FROESE

THE MAN WHO LOST HIS PEN

CHAPTER ONE

A LOT OF people would have loved to be where I was. Standing in the wings of a grand old theatre, watching a rock star do his sound check for that night's show. A secret space where you could see the real Jack Lowe. No filters. Just light, draped like silk over him and the piano, playing up the sheen of his ice-white shirt and the deep blue running through his newly dyed black hair.

I admit, there was nothing wrong with the view.

Where I was, at the edge of the stage, the light was sparse and sliced by rows of curtains. People were milling on stage and gathered around the tech booth at the back. The only person near me was a hedgehog with short hair in spikes, bulky headphones, pens bristling

out of her vest and cargo-pants pockets, and a battered low-end Samsung in her hand. She was texting
someone while she talked to someone else, and I didn't
think she'd noticed me until she said, "You must be the
boyfriend."

"That's on my driver's licence," I said. "Most people call me Ben."

She laughed, quick and sharp. "Sorry. I didn't
mean to treat you like the little wifey. I'm Vic."

Vic offered a fist, and I bumped it. "No worries.
What's your job around here?"

"Assistant director," she said. "Stage manager.
Flunky. Hey, aren't you a detective? Aren't you that
guy?"

I didn't know for sure what she meant by "that
guy," but I'd caught a murderer and made the news the
year before, so I figured that might be it.

"I could be. Do you need a detective?"

She looked me up and down. Mostly up. She was
barely the height of my shoulder. In the dim light, her
face seemed almost as dark as Jess's hair. Or Jack's.
Always the stage name onstage.

"Can you find me a decent sound tech? Your boyfriend's right. The guy does not know how to mic a
piano. They forced us to use the house staff and—" She
stopped abruptly as her phone rang. "Oh shit, excuse
me."

She slipped further into the shadows to take a call.
I could only hear her side, and it didn't tell me much.
A change in the schedule. An unexpected addition. Her
response could have been summed up as "Go to hell,
but fine." She was scowling and fiddling with her horn-
rimmed glasses when she returned.

"Trouble?" I asked.

"Not your kind," she said. I nodded.

"Too bad. I'd love something to do besides stand here."

When I'd said that, I'd had no idea that we were a few hours away from a murder. There was no way for me to know. But I would definitely, before the night was over, feel like an asshole for saying it.

Vic bustled away, onto the stage where she had a word with Jess, then up the aisles to the sound board. Jess tilted his head back and gazed up into the light grid as if it held some kind of salvation for him, then spun the piano stool around and stood. He couldn't have seen me with the light in his eyes, but he smiled at me anyway. He had a lot of practice at that, smiling at people he couldn't see. Also assuming people were where he'd left them.

He gave me a real smile once he was close enough to actually see me. I put my arms around his waist and kissed him. He leaned back against my arms a little, a thing he did when he was tired or frustrated. Like a metaphor in motion: help me. I didn't think he knew he did it.

"Everything okay?" I asked.

"Did it sound okay?" he asked, clearly meaning it hadn't.

I gave him my blankest stare. "Am I a musician?"

"Right. Sorry."

He took my hand, and I followed his lead through the backstage labyrinth to the green room. That surprised me. I'd thought he might want to sulk in his dressing room like a musical Achilles, but apparently he was up for socializing.

The halls did not reflect the glamour of the theatre's foyer or auditorium. They'd never been fancy and hadn't been kept up, because they weren't there to impress anyone. The concrete walls and floors were crumbling in spots, and the off-white paint was further off white than it had been to start with. Bare bulbs overhead were in cages to keep them from being shattered by stacks of amps or incautious double-bass players.

The paint was missing here and there, always in rectangles that I assumed had once been signs holding the theatre's name. It turned out that the fur trader turned entrepreneur and patron of the arts whose family name and money had gone into the place had been, as my friend Luna had put it, "a true ass bag," and the theatre was in the process of finding a less embarrassing title. True Ass Bag Theatre was not under consideration. It was the Calgary Theatre until someone sorted the name thing out.

The green-room door was propped slightly open to save people the trouble of swiping their cards to get in. If I'd been on the security crew, I'd have used the door to go inside, lectured everyone in the room, then shut it myself, but the crew was nowhere to be seen and it wasn't my job. I settled for pulling the door shut behind me and kicking the empty pop can that had been holding it open under the nearest couch.

I'd been in a few green rooms, thanks to Jess, and there seemed to be two kinds. One was everything that wasn't a bathroom or the actual stage. A dressing room, a hangout, a warm-up space. People would be packed in, wearing whatever amount of clothing was convenient for them, and about half would be sitting on the floor because the makeup tables didn't leave room for enough comfortable chairs.

This was the other kind.

It was a big rectangle with a lot of tables and chairs, clutches of small couches scattered around, and a kitchenette at the far end. Real food would show up there later, but for now it was home to a Keurig and a basket of pods, mugs, water glasses, pitchers of ice water, cans of pop, and a bowl each of fruit and granola bars. Not, Jesse had told me, the kind of spread you'd expect at most shows—it was more what you'd see at a cheap convention—but this was a charity show, and economizing was only appropriate. Next to the kitchenette were doors to two unisex washrooms. These, too, had bare rectangles where signs had once been, so I guessed they hadn't been unisex until recently.

The night's lineup was written on a whiteboard next to the door, along with "You are in Calgary, Alberta." If I ever needed that kind of reminder to know what city I was in, I'd hope I was being professionally supervised. Then again, that was probably what road managers were for.

"Oh my God, it's you guys!"

A gangling tower of a person with wavy black hair and a sloppy grin rushed at us, full speed, and hoisted Jess off the ground. Jess laughed and returned the hug. I stood to the side and waited for them to get over their musical-theatre-kid dramatics.

Thom Cross had been in the same music program as Jess in university, and they'd been in the same cast a few times—*Hedwig*, *Evil Dead*, others I'd tried to forget. I wasn't a musical-theatre guy. Now Thom played keyboards for a pop/roots/country/rock band that should have been called We Can't Make Decisions but was instead called the Brennan Murphy Twist. Or the Twist to people with less time to kill.

He set Jess down and offered me a handshake instead of a hug. This wasn't a snub. He'd known me as the criminology student who dated Jess, and killjoy had been my brand. I shook his hand and gave him a friendly smile to show I was both human and happy to see him. Thom had always been a good guy.

"I love the new album," Jess told him. "I love that it's an album, not just a bunch of songs. It's like a concept piece about... I don't know, man. Not rednecks...."

"It's more the whole subsidized housing thing," Thom said. "Brennan and Reiss both lived it as kids. I mean, Brennan was in the UK, but still."

"Not my world," Jess said. He sounded ashamed of it and probably was, though he hadn't touched a cent of his parents' money since high school. He didn't like the corporate raiding they'd done to earn it.

Happily, Thom didn't seem to remember or care what Jess had come from.

"Seriously," he said. "The rest of us are so boring it's boring. But Reiss and Brennan do the writing, so whatever, right? It's their songbook."

If Thom resented this state of affairs, it didn't show. I'd never known him to resent anything for long. He parked his narrow back end on a table—to hell with chairs—and regarded Jess and me.

"It is amazing to see you guys. Like, both of you. Together. What was it? Seven years in the wilderness?"

"We were together for about three and a half years," Jess said, "and apart for about seven. And then together for... about six months now."

Thom raised his hands palms up, like they were the sides of a scale, and moved them up and down.

"Four years... seven years... pretty close. In a few years, it'll be like those seven years never happened."

"It won't," I said automatically. I glanced at Jess to see whether that had stung. He seemed okay.

"It really won't," he confirmed. "Those years mattered. I needed that time to get my shit more or less together."

"And turn into Mr. Big-Time Rock Star," Thom said with a grin.

Jess shrugged like he was trying to dislodge that from his shoulders. Then, as I watched, he pulled some of that rock star to the front. The charisma, the cool, the easy charm. Jack Lowe smiled. "I don't know, you're getting pretty big-time yourself. What did they call you on the Current? Canada's Rock Chroniclers?"

"Yeah, it's cool," Thom said. "It's like we're starting to get respect, you know? Not just sales."

"You deserve it," Jess-as-Jack said. I contemplated his shoes. Expensive, of course, but not one of a kind and not what he intended to wear on stage. I stomped on his foot. Like the pro he was, he did not make a sound. His eyes widened a little, but he didn't look down. Instead, he looked up at me. The glare he gave me was pure Jesse Serik.

"Are you thirsty?" I asked politely. "After sound check? We should grab something for you to drink."

"Oh, yeah, do that," Thom said. "Then I'll introduce you to the guys."

He loped off to said guys, who were on couches around a video game, while Jess and I went to check out the beverage selection. Jess limped a little, which was dickish because I had not stepped on him that hard.

"So, Stompy, mind telling me what I did?" he asked as he picked through the cans.

"Thom wants to talk to you. Not Jack. Most of the people here would prefer to talk to you, I think. Save Jack for the stage."

"Oh, so I was supposed to tell him that I'm not sure about rock star business and maybe I'm downsizing my career or maybe I'm destroying it or, fuck it, maybe I already have? That was small talk. No one wants to know how you really are."

"That's catchy," I said. "They should make that the name of the show, instead of a *Big Night for Mental Health*."

"The name sucks," Jess said.

"It does," I allowed. "Is it me, or is there no booze here at all? I don't care. It's just weird."

Jess laughed, loud enough that a few of the room's scattered artists looked our way. "Oh my God, did I not tell you? What this is?"

"A fundraiser for the Cross-Canada Society for Mental Health?"

"Yeah, yeah, that," he said, waving it aside with a hand. "But we're all… mentally interesting. That's why they invited us. We've all been open about having a mental illness. They're excited about me because I only started talking about it in October. Even if depression is pretty fucking vanilla."

"I still don't see why…."

Jess cocked his head and waited.

"Oh," I said. "Addiction."

"It's not like people couldn't have brought their own poison," Jess said. "But it's a gesture, I guess."

Considering how famous Jack Lowe was for doing all the drugs, preferably in bunches and while drunk, it had taken me a while to concede that Jesse wasn't an addict per se. If nothing else, the past six months of him living with me had shown that he really could take or leave the stuff. What he did was use whatever he could get his hands on to be Jack Lowe, who radiated energy like a forest fire and needed about as much fuel to keep going.

He'd been trying to stop doing that for about two years. The last few months had been easy because his broken arm had kept him off the stage. I was curious how it would go here, at his first show in the new year.

He grabbed a Coke Zero and I found a Sprite hidden toward the back. The logo always reminded me of my mother, who had spent many Saturday nights winning at canasta with a lemon gin and Sprite at her elbow. It gave me a small pang when I realized that I hadn't seen her in a year. I made a note to visit her in Kelowna. Maybe I'd even take Jess along.

"See her?" Jess said, pointing his chin toward the far end of the room. Three wispy women were sitting around a small table with mugs of tea, looking at their phones. They had identical pink cotton-candy hair and outfits made of watermelon-coloured leather, velvet, and tulle. If you put them in a huge chocolate box, they'd be in danger of a giant coming along and eating them.

"I see three hers. Or I'm seeing triple."

"The one closest to us. Ash Rose."

"Is that her name or the shade of her hair dye?" I asked.

"Her name and her band's name," Jess told me. "Anyway, she's borderline. I mean, shit, she's got borderline personality disorder… or… is living with… I need to look this up before I go on stage. Like, am I a person living with depression?"

"Say you're an indolent drama queen. That should be fine."

"You're a riot," he told me. "Never go near a live mic. Also, all mics are live. Seriously, Ben, help me out, here. You've got the psych degree."

"Criminology degree. As you well know."

"You took a lot of psych classes."

I sighed.

"Living with BPD should be fine. If you overthink this, you will put your foot in your mouth. Or you could ask her."

"Yeah, but I need to know what to call myself, not her. I'll say living with depression."

"What kind of music do they do?" I asked. "Ash Rose."

"Shoegazer," he said. "Or dream pop. They're kind of retro. It's really layered, and I didn't see a synth rack that could handle it backstage, so they're probably using backing tracks tonight. I bet they'll just do vocals. It's easier to get them off the stage in a hurry that way too. They've only got—" He peered past me to the whiteboard. "—twenty minutes. Looks like they're on from eight twenty to eight forty. That's not too bad, actually. I've only got forty-five minutes, and I'm the headliner."

"If I were to say the word shoegazer around them...."

Jesse frowned. "Risky. You could say nu gaze... no, better to go with dream pop."

I would have made fun of him over all the linguistic dancing, but I had in fact completed a lot of psychology classes. I knew words could make any situation a lot better or worse than it otherwise would have been.

"Hey, you guys wanna come meet the band?"

Thom was back, already putting an arm around Jesse's shoulders to lead him. Jess went without complaint, though I knew he wasn't wild about being dragged places. I tagged along.

I'd seen enough of the Twist to have an idea about who was who. The two string beans on the couch, both only an inch or two shorter than Thom, were guitarists—one a lead guitarist, the other a bass player. I couldn't have said which was which, and in fact, apart from one having a blond shag and goatee and the other a matching set in dark brown, they might as well have been the same guy. They were playing the same video game as we approached, either shooting reptilian things while wearing battle armour or being reptilian things and breathing fire on the guys in battle armour.

"Connor, Charlie, this is Jesse and Ben. We went to school together."

Connor and Charlie each raised a hand in greeting, without looking away from the screen. One of them said, "Hey." Jess grinned and gave them a "hey" back.

The other two were on a couch sidelong to the screen, one holding an acoustic guitar and the other a notebook and pencil. I wasn't an expert, but it seemed like songwriting to me. They were watching with amusement as Thom slid the fact that he'd turned up with Jack Lowe past their oblivious bandmates.

Brennan, the namesake and lead singer, put down the notebook and stood to offer Jess a hand.

"Is it Jesse or Jack?" he asked, his Geordie accent bending the vowels and chopping off the hard end of Jack.

"Jesse, offstage," Jess told him, shaking his hand. He didn't ask for Brennan's name because he didn't need to any more than I did. I never got used to meeting

"You're having a more exciting life than we are," Brennan said. "I tried a black diamond run yesterday. That's enough for me."

"That's a good thing for you," Jesse said. "My arm has barely healed from my exciting life."

He patted his recently broken arm.

"Ouch." Brennan winced in sympathy. It seemed genuine.

"I can't believe you're allowed to ski," Jess said. It took me a second to remember that it was normal for musicians and actors to get told what they could or couldn't do, like they were five-year-olds and some entertainment conglomerate was their mom. Break a leg, cancel some shows, and a lot of people were out money.

"We're not technically on tour," Brennan said with a shrug. "I could jump out of a plane if I wanted to. Which I don't."

Thom put a hand on Jess's shoulder.

"Man, in university we all thought you must be immortal. You did so much crazy shit."

"You live and learn," Jess said. "If you live. Hey, did you do your sound check yet?"

They hadn't, but they would soon, and everyone talked about that for a while. Most of it went over my head, though I caught the drift that Jess didn't have much confidence in the venue's crew, and no one was happy that the producers hadn't had enough pull to bring in their own people, though of course they supported the venue's union people in principle. Obviously they supported unions, like the artistic friends of the common man that they were.

As they talked, we drifted to another couch cluster, where there was room for all of us to sit and where we wouldn't be disturbed by the video gamers throwing elbows and swearing at imaginary reptiles. Jess wound up next to Reiss, and I could see Reiss watching him silently, with the attentiveness of fear. I didn't think he was afraid of Jess. People, maybe. Or life in general. Jess had once told me that when he was depressed, he didn't need anything to be depressed about. Maybe Reiss didn't need anything to be scared of. Maybe that was why he was here.

"Was your band here for sound check?" Reiss asked Jess.

"He's flying solo," Thom said. Brennan's eyes widened until they looked like shiny blue marbles in his wind-burned face.

"That's a different sound for you," he said.

Jess smiled. His eyes were not involved. "You could sound a little less shocked," he said.

Brennan laughed. "I'm sorry. I'm not worried you can't do it. I just think it will surprise people."

Jess sighed. "Yeah. I don't know. I haven't played anything anywhere since September, and I thought I'd do something simple. Maybe that was dumb. I don't know how to make a sound guy fix the bass for a concert grand. I'm not used to having one on tour, you know? And I play arenas, so it's not like I can borrow the house piano. I asked the label for one last time out, and they were all, what are you, Tori Amos? You gonna want a harpsichord next?"

"You should have said yes," Thom said. "You should have demanded a harpsichord."

I made a note that the next time we were in a bar with Thom, I was buying him a beer.

"You shouldn't have to know how to fix this," Reiss said. "It's their piano. It's their venue. They should be able to work with it."

Thom held up his phone. I couldn't see it clearly, but it seemed like comments, maybe on YouTube.

"This is not the first time they have shit the piano bed," he said, "if reviews and comments are to be believed."

"If," Brennan said.

"But sometimes they are," Thom argued. "Especially if there are a hundred of them saying the same thing." He put a hand on Jesse's back. "Don't worry. We're doing two acoustic pieces, and one of them opens with that piano. If I have to set up the board myself and tape everything down…"

"… then Jesse will know why we got ejected," Brennan finished. "Ah, we'll sort it out."

Jess nodded. He didn't say it, but I could see he was grateful and relieved. That was the other reason he'd opted for a charity show. It was something he could do, one and done, without the manager he'd fired on his last tour and not yet replaced. He wasn't used to being the face of this kind of squabbling.

I hadn't seen any managers around, though there were only three acts in the green room. Jess, the Twist, and Ash Rose. There were three comics booked to perform and no sign of any of them, though they wouldn't have had to do sound checks, so they might have decided to show up later. The other performer was a singer-songwriter type, an enby named Dylan who went around in hoodies big enough to hold three Dylans and all their acoustic guitars. Even I had heard the kid was shy, so I wasn't surprised they weren't socializing. Hanging out in their dressing room most likely.

A pair of skinny shadows fell over us, and a voice said, "Hey! You're Jack Lowe!"

"Sometimes," Jess admitted. He stood and turned to offer handshakes to Connor and Charlie.

"Thom always said he knew you," Charlie said. "But he never said he called you Jesse."

"I've been called worse," Jess said. "Did you win your game?"

"There's no winning," Connor told him. "We live and die in the struggle. I think we've got sound check, fellows."

Brennan checked his phone.

"Yes, we do. We'll catch up with you guys later," he told Jess and me.

Once they'd left the green room, I put a hand on the nape of Jess's neck and pressed lightly. It was like trying to pinch the side of a mountain.

"You want me to try to loosen this?" I asked.

He shook his head. "It'll go when I do my warm up."

I nodded. "So," I said. "Reiss."

He grinned. "What about him? Do you need directions to the inside of his pants?"

"Why? Do you have some?"

He laughed and leaned against the back of the couch. "I met him at exactly the same time you did. You did a lot of staring, friend. You gonna try to draw him from memory?"

"I'm not planning to try anything," I said. "I have a boyfriend, and he might not like it."

Jess sobered and regarded me in silence. It struck me then how quiet the room was. No music playing. Unlike the thinner walls between the dressing rooms, this room had thick concrete walls that blocked out noise from the stage. Jess held out his hands to me, and I took them, allowed him to reel me in.

"You and your boyfriend do not have any kind of agreement," he said. "If you want one, he's willing to talk about it. Anytime."

It was unfair and I knew it. I looked at guys sometimes, and I thought, *That might be fun.* Or, *That is a living work of art.* I knew full well that I could have spent some time with those guys and it would have been exactly that. Some time. Some fun. Maybe, on the rarest of occasions, something like art. If anything so minor could have evicted Jess from my heart, it would have happened a long time ago.

As for Jess, if he were capable of jealousy, I didn't know about it. It probably helped to be gorgeous, talented, successful, blah-blah-blah. But I'd known times when Jess had been in a vicious depression, hating himself so much that he'd have killed himself if he could have gotten out of bed. Even then he hadn't cared about other guys. It was a piece he didn't have.

But damned if my fists didn't itch when someone brushed their leg against Jesse's on purpose or made some other little move. That was ugly. I needed to get over it. And it was way too much for Jess and me to take on a few hours before he had to do a show.

"I love you," I told him.

He smiled. "I know."

I raised my brows and waited. He laughed.

"Okay, okay. Jesus. I love you too."

I put a hand on the back of his head and kissed him. He smelled like his soap and shampoo, the day-to-day things that would soon get buried under hair spray and stage makeup.

"How long is the couch in your dressing room?" I asked, our foreheads still pressed together.

"Long enough."

It wasn't, but we made it work. Then Jess grumbled about having to get back into his regular clothes, the dress shirt and slim black pants he'd spent an hour casually throwing on that morning so that we could go to the green room and eat, only to have to come back to the dressing room and put on his stage clothes.

"You could always—" I started.

"Don't. Don't say I can change and then eat. You're a barbarian. You do your hair before you pull on a sweater. You will never understand."

"I brush my hair," I told him. "I have never 'done' my hair in my life. Can we go eat before you get crabbier?"

We could and did.

CHAPTER TWO

WHEN WE got back to the green room, the guys from the Twist were back from sound check, and we pushed two tables together to make room for everyone while Jess grilled them about their run-in with the sound crew. The piano was sorted out, Thom claimed. When Thom wasn't looking, Reiss gave Jess a skeptical face and made a so-so gesture with his hand.

A buffet had been lined up by the kitchenette, and we picked through it. It wasn't too bad. Rouladen for the carnivores. Lentil loaf for the vegans, with the ingredients noted on a card. Roasted potatoes and a few salads and squares for dessert. Jess scowled and took salad. He'd made comments to me before about not wanting to eat a brick before performing, so it made sense that he wasn't impressed with the selection. The Twist piled their plates like mountain ranges.

The three pink-haired singers remained in place, studying their phones. Once we were all back at the table, Jess waved to them. Ash took out an earbud.

"Yes?"

"You gonna eat?"

The other two shrugged at each other and took out their earbuds. Ash pointed at the whiteboard. Her nail polish shifted from pearl to rose and back as the room's fluorescent light moved across it.

"We're up at eight twenty," she said.

"That's hours from now," Jess said. "I don't eat a lot before a show either, but come on. You've got to eat something."

"You're not our real dad," one of the others told him.

Jess looked startled, then laughed. "That's true. I'm Jesse."

She made a little huff of annoyance. "I'm Izzy."

The third glanced up from her phone. "Kayla."

"I'm Ashley," Ash said. "We're Ash Rose."

"Yeah, I know," Jess said. "You're good. Kind of Au Revoir Simone? I'm sorry. I know it's annoying to be compared to people."

"I'd say more Cocteau Twins," Thom said. "The whole nineties 4AD sound."

Ash's cool nearly broke for a moment as she realized the famous people knew her. She was one of them, in the room with the rest of the pros.

"Nineties 4AD," she said with longing. "That scene was so romantic."

"We were born too late," Kayla said. Jess shoved salad in his mouth to keep from laughing.

"There's room if you want to join us," Brennan told them. They looked at each other and shrugged again, then moved to our table. Kayla and Izzy went to the buffet and came back with tea and melon cubes.

"Should someone get Dylan and the comics?" Jess asked. "They've got that Vic person doubling up as stage manager and AD, and I haven't seen a gofer around. I'm not sure anyone announced dinner."

"Someone brought the food in," Connor pointed out.

"We did," Kayla said. "Security left it by the door. They seemed really busy."

"Might be because of the surprise guest," I said.

"*What*?"

That word came from several directions and at least four people. From the way everyone was staring at me, you'd have thought I'd heard about a bomb threat hours earlier and not bothered to tell them.

"I overheard Vic talking to the director about a last-minute guest being added to the schedule," I said. "That's all I know. I don't see it on the whiteboard."

"When was this?" Reiss asked.

"Are they on before us?" Izzy asked. "Are we all getting less time?"

"Do we have to cut a song?" Kayla asked.

"It's easier to cut than add," Brennan assured her.

"I heard her talking while Jess was doing his sound check," I said, "so they've known for hours. If any of you had to cut time or change things up, I'm sure they'd have told you by now."

The only good that comment did was cheer them up. They all laughed so hard I was worried it was a choking hazard.

"I'm hilarious. What did I say?"

"We're talent," Connor explained. "We will be the last to know."

"We've had to add songs in the middle of a set," Thom said. "The floor manager held up a sign that said Stretch. Charlie's mouthing, 'How long?' and the manager shrugs, like, 'I dunno, until I tell you to stop.' And it's a live broadcast, so it's not like we can run over."

"We were at a festival and someone told some poet they could recite their poems while we were singing," Kayla said. "Like, stand at the edge of the stage with a mike and they'd make us background music. They told us five minutes before we went on."

The room erupted into a combination of war stories and speculation about the identity and timing of the mystery guest. I took the opportunity to check my texts and found a message from Luna confirming that she and Kent would be dropping by before the show, around seven. Since Jess was the only Calgary-based performer who'd been available to do the show, he'd had no trouble convincing the director to allow his local randos in for a backstage visit.

Luna had finished her text by asking what everyone was like. It was a broad question that deserved a broad answer. I wrote, *Loud.*

I was putting my phone away when the comics arrived. One of them I recognized but couldn't name. He'd been a regular on a sitcom they'd shot in Manitoba, one of those characters that's an audience favourite but too goofy to be the lead. I hadn't known the guy did stand-up, but a lot of sitcom actors had at least tried it. I read the whiteboard and matched him to a name. Duncan Winter. He had a few minutes slotted at around twenty to nine. It hardly seemed worth coming out from Winnipeg for that, but maybe he had other business in town.

Or maybe he'd gone to see the Jets play the Flames the night before. It was probably not incidental for some of the performers that the charity had paid travel costs.

The next one through the door was Emilie Brookes, who bounced around western Canada doing live shows but had made her name mostly on TikTok and You-Tube. A lot of her material was about the funny side of bipolar disorder, which made her a natural for this lineup. She was going on early, right after Dylan, and they were only giving her five minutes. People drove between Edmonton and Calgary for less, though. I'd once gone to Edmonton for a lawnmower off a freecycling board. Yes, I'd spent nearly as much on gas as it would have cost me to get a cheap piece of shit from Crappy Tire, but it was a good mower and I still had it.

Emilie was closely followed by Ziad Samara, who needed no introduction. He'd been a social media wunderkind in his teens and moved smoothly into small parts on American TV shows with hip audiences. A year ago he'd had a Netflix comedy special and the lead in some streaming limited run that had done well for him. The last I'd heard, he'd started acting in films. Though his half hour set was right before Jess went on, making Jess the headliner, it could have been argued that Ziad was a bigger name. If you'd polled a hundred people on the street about each of them, much would have depended on the specific people you asked.

"How come no one told us about the food?" Duncan asked, making himself heard over the din. Everyone turned to look.

"We were going to send out a search party," Connor said.

"We don't think they have a runner," Ash said. "They seem way understaffed."

"But they're understaffed for a good cause," Ziad said. "With the money they saved, they're going to buy the Clarke Institute one of those bicycle-powered generators so they can do green shock treatments."

"The University of Alberta hospital already has one," Emilie said. "Last year the doctor pulled a hamstring, and three guys killed themselves."

"We left food for you," Brennan said, probably trying to forestall any more talk about electroshock and bicycles. "It's still warm."

"Like my career," Duncan said, making his way to the buffet. "Drying out over a can of Sterno."

Emilie introduced herself to the table before heading to the buffet, and Ziad did the same. They both did an okay job of acting as if they knew everyone and this whole name business was a formality. My guess, from their behaviour and from playing the odds, was that they both recognized Jess and Brennan and that Emilie knew Ash.

Jess slipped away from the table to a corner of the room, where I found him scrolling his phone. I stood beside him and nudged him with an elbow.

"What's up?"

"I'm trying to find out what Dylan eats. So far all I can find is gluten intolerant."

"Why do people feel the need to post this kind of shit?" I asked. "You don't do that."

"I'll eat anything," Jess said. "I'm not going to tell people I'm a garbage disposal."

"That's sexy talk," I said. "You're trying to get laid again."

"It is sexy. Okay. Lentil loaf. I think the card said it was gluten free. I'll bring that and salad on different plates, and they can sort themselves out."

I helped him plate some food, grabbed a can of Coke, and followed Jess down the hall and around a corner to a small dressing room with a metal number 1 nailed to the door. It looked like it had been taken from a house address set, weathered and never repainted. Jess knocked.

"What?"

"I brought you food. In case you don't want to come to the green room."

We waited. I heard a shuffling sound like a thousand hoodies rubbing against each other. Then the door opened.

Dylan was in the giant hoodie I'd expected, with a hood so far down their face that it nearly covered their eyes. They seemed surprised to see Jess, as anyone would if a celebrity they had never met showed up at their door with lentil loaf.

"Or you can come to the green room," Jess said. "Or I can get you something else."

"No. Um. This is good."

Their voice was soft and calm, which was how I remembered their music. Confessional guitar folk about lost love and losing in love and their love, who they lost when their love died.

"Okay," Jess said. "Like I said, you're welcome to join us if you want. We don't bite. I mean, the comics might. If they thought it was edgy, they'd probably bite."

Dylan almost smiled. "I might later. I, um. I eat… funny."

I saw their hand holding the edge of the door, nails bitten down to bleeding arcs where they met the nail bed. Behind them, the room was dark.

"I bet you a thousand dollars no one would care," Jess said. "I'd go seven hundred and fifty that they wouldn't even notice. But it's up to you. Oh, I'm Jesse, by the way."

Dylan nodded. I got the impression that they not only knew who Jack Lowe was but also knew that it was really Jesse. Which wasn't a secret, but it was the sort of thing people only knew if they'd spent as much time on his Wikipedia page as I had.

"Thanks," they said.

Jess didn't introduce me, just said goodbye and left. I wasn't put out because Dylan had barely opened the door and might not have noticed me, behind Jess and off to the side.

We returned to the green room, my arm around Jesse's shoulders. Walking side by side, we nearly filled the width of the hall.

Back in the green room, the conversation was loud, and everyone seemed to be having a reasonably good time. Jess was nervous and eyeing his phone, the whiteboard, and then his phone again. I brought him half of some chocolate-and-caramel accident scene from the tray of squares and placed it and a paper napkin in his hands.

"Eat this," I said, "then change. Then you'll be changed and you won't have to worry about when you should get changed. If you get hungry again later, I will drape my coat over you like I'm a hairdresser and nothing will land on your precious outfit. Okay?"

He put his phone in the back pocket of his pants, which surprised me every time he managed to make it fit. Those things might as well have been painted on.

"Okay."

I kissed the top of his head and sent him on his way.

Thom was wandering around with a coffee, so I went over to him and asked after people we'd known in school, since he still lived in Toronto and I hadn't been there in years. That was when the penny fully dropped for Reiss and Brennan that I, not just Jess, had known their bandmate back in the day, which led to questions. What was Thom like in school? Was it true he'd been in a production of *Young Frankenstein* so bad that the college had lied about the cast getting food poisoning in order to buy two more weeks before opening? If I was a criminology student, how the hell had I wound up dating Jess?

"Oh, I love this," Thom said. "Can I tell them?"

"Be my guest," I said.

"Jess didn't have a piano, and he wanted to work on his own music, but the school gave priority to school projects, so he couldn't book a piano room for what the school considered…. Ben, do you remember what that prof called his music?"

"Something about the gutter?" I said.

"Yeah, basically trash. So Jess started breaking into the music building in the middle of the night. And Ben had a job doing security there. That's how they met. I remember Jess told me about this, like, right when they got together, and I was all, 'So you're boning a security guard to use the pianos?' And he said, 'No, I'm boning a security guard *and* I'm using the pianos.'"

"And you're picturing a fifty-year-old man with a beer gut?" Brennan said.

Thom laughed. "Totally. Then I met Ben, and I was all, 'Oh. I get it now.'"

"It really says something that you think Jess would have prostituted himself for a piano," Reiss said. "Like the movie. Only it was a whole piano instead of one key at a time."

Thom made a face. "He might have."

I would have liked to dispute it, but since I'd spent the beginning of our relationship wondering whether Jess was doing exactly that, there wasn't much I could say.

"Would you have?" Brennan asked Reiss. "For a drum kit?"

Reiss thought about it.

"Drums are easier to get than a piano," he said. "You can buy them off Kijiji and throw them in a van. If I didn't have a van… I might have considered a hand job. But that's for the whole night. Right up to when the building opens."

"I want to be clear that I was not running that kind of operation," I said. "Though it's starting to sound like I should have been."

They had some questions for me then about my degree and the time I'd spent as a cop and why I was a private investigator now. There were a lot of weeds I could have gotten into, but I steered around them and said I liked being my own boss. I hadn't been hurting for clients since I'd made the news. I even got some cases that weren't insurance frauds or divorces.

Jess was still getting ready when my phone buzzed and I found a text from Luna announcing her arrival at the stage door. Her and Kent both.

Come get us?

When I get around to it, I answered, but I was kidding. It was minus thirty-five out there and dropping, and that was without wind chill factored in. I stepped on it. The first security person I'd seen in hours was by the stage door, talking to someone on their phone.

"I've got a situation," he told his phone, eyeing me with suspicion. "I'll call you back."

"I'm a situation?" I asked.

"What do you want?" he said. He was about my height and twice my age, with a dark complexion and salt-and-pepper hair. Something about the way he stood suggested a military past.

"I have guests at the door. They're on the list."

Between him checking the backstage pass list, me showing him my access pass, and my offer to get Vic on the phone, we managed to come to an agreement that Luna and Kent could come inside instead of freezing to death in the alley. As soon as they were through the door, they stomped snow off their boots and pretended they were too numb to speak. It might not have taken much pretending. The security guard kept his eyes on them the whole time.

"Friendly place," Kent said once we were through the door to the secure area. "Who are they guarding? The queen?"

"First," I said, "that's not a nice thing to call my boyfriend."

Luna hit me with a black clutch that felt like it had an anvil in it.

"Ow, and second, I have no idea. They weren't like this when we got here this afternoon."

"They're acting like something's up," Kent said.

"I know."

Kent was my ex-partner—in the cop sense, not the boyfriend sense. He was still a cop, with the city police in Homicide. He seemed exactly like what he was, a former high school football player who had gone slightly to seed but had a lot of good years left.

Tonight when he took off his tomato-red OTC parka, he revealed a standard white dress shirt under a blue sweater that Luna had absolutely picked out for him.

He'd been trying to transition from one-night stands to one-month relationships, or better if he could manage it, and Luna was doing her best for the cause. This included dressing him as often as he would allow. It appeared she had also lectured him on the inappropriateness of Sorel boots at a concert because he was carrying a plastic shopping bag with his black dress shoes poking out the top.

Luna was a doctor and a friend Kent and I had made on the job when we'd had to escort a parade of victims and criminals through her emergency room. She'd made an impression on us by being sharper than anyone else in the room and better looking than half the aspiring actresses Kent dated. Unfortunately for him, she was much too smart to even consider dating him.

She'd thrown her pearl-grey boiled wool coat over Kent's arm as soon as they'd gotten inside, showing off her high-necked lace dress, in burgundy with boots to match. The boots were designed to be worn indoors, at a bar or on a runway. I couldn't believe she'd worn them outdoors in this weather. Her coat was a little better, being wool, but it was nowhere near heavy enough for the arctic temperature, and it ended at her throat. No hood. No hat since that might have flattened her hair. Even the short time she'd spent outside had burned the skin above her cheekbones and probably the tips of her ears.

"I didn't think I'd need to lecture a physician on the dangers of frostbite," I said.

She rolled her eyes at me. "We took a cab right to the door."

Luna might have been Indian by way of London but she'd lived in Calgary long enough to know better than that. What if your cab broke down or went skidding into a tree? But she was a grown-up, and she got to make her own choices, which included dressing for the red carpet anytime she wasn't in scrubs and paying for fancy fake nails that snagged on her medical gloves.

I knocked on Jesse's dressing room door before entering and cracked the door for a quick peek before throwing it wide. He was in the bathroom with the door closed.

"Just putting coats in here," I called out.

"'Kay." He sounded distracted. I'd tossed my own coat onto the couch, but it hadn't been covered in snow. I gestured for Kent and Luna to pile their coats and scarves and gloves onto the wardrobe rack by the door instead. Kent also swapped his boots for shoes. None of us spoke to Jess. They'd never seen him backstage at a show before, but they did know him well enough to know he didn't like being distracted when he was trying to get fabric tape in place or put makeup on.

Once we were back in the hall, I gave them another once-over.

"I'd say you look like stars," I said, "but you'll be disappointed by what the stars look like."

I led them around the corner, swiped my card at the green room door, and ushered them in. It was quieter than when I'd left it. Ash Rose and Emilie Brookes were gone, the comic possibly to change and the band to warm up in the practice room. It was a few minutes past seven, and the show started at seven thirty on paper. In truth the plan was for the emcee to go on at seven forty-five with a few people from the charity and talk up the organization before Dylan went on at eight.

The emcee, a local radio morning-drive guy, was spending his time on the other side of the theatre with the director and any media who'd decided to come by.

Since Jess and everyone else had done pre-interviews to promote the show, I was guessing the media turnout would be thin.

I introduced Kent and Luna around. They were a little bit wowed to meet Ziad and the Twist, and Kent had been a fan of Duncan's TV show. Discovering that Thom had known me in university was a thrill for them both, less because their pal Ben knew another celebrity than because this was another guy who could dish about Ben's past. By the time Jess finally turned up, I was considering murdering everyone who'd gone to the University of Toronto at the same time as me and hiding their bodies in Lake Ontario.

Jess had debated dressing down for the show to match the acoustic set but had decided to hell with that a few days earlier and picked up a little black dress by some French designer. It was an interesting thing, severe and flowing, silk and leather, and not too much for someone Jesse's size. He'd told me that it was meant to be worn with flat boots, but he was five six, and no one on God's earth was taking away his heels.

Luna made it to the door before I did and put her hands on Jess's shoulders, holding him in place so she could look him up and down.

"Is that Ackermann? For real?"

"Considering what I paid for it," Jess told her, "it had better be."

"I wouldn't have thought of it for you, but you can really wear it," she said. "Mmm… hold still."

She took a tissue from her purse and dipped it into the ice water she'd been carrying around. Delicately as she would have put in a stitch or removed a splinter, she took a fleck of mascara from his cheek.

"Thanks," Jess said. "I hate doing my own makeup."

"You look perfect."

"Right back at you, lady."

Kent gave Jess his usual guy greeting of a light slap to the shoulder and a hey, but he seemed confused while doing it. I knew for a fact that he found my boyfriend hot in a dress, and he didn't seem to know how to treat Jess on those occasions when Jess broke out something androgynous or straight-up feminine for a night on the town.

I'd asked Jess once if it bothered him, Kent getting weird like that, and he'd laughed and told me it was fine. It was his opinion that Kent was working some things out, and I should leave him alone about it.

"How's the dating project going?" Jess asked.

Kent glared at Luna. "Someone signed me up for swing dance lessons."

Jess turned to Luna, who nodded. "Yes. It's strategic. Those classes always have more single women than single men. It's an opportunity to impress a new woman every week, and it would be going gangbusters," she said, turning her attention to Kent, "if you could bloody well dance."

"If I could dance, I wouldn't need the lessons," Kent said.

"You learning to dance is not the point!" Luna said. "It was never the point!"

Jess appraised Kent. "You played football. That takes coordination. How bad could you be?"

I knew the answer. I'd been at a Christmas party with him when he'd gotten drunk enough to forget he was hopeless. To save my feet, I backed away and went to stand by the kitchenette, where Ziad was giving a disapproving look to the buffet.

"I know there's Sterno," he said, "but things go off. Someone should clear this."

"I think they're low on someones," I told him. He made a fist and rapped his knuckles on the kitchenette bar. It felt decisive, like he was punctuating a sentence with it. Then he went to the buffet and started putting lids on anything that was being kept warm. I covered the salads, and we both considered and rejected the idea of using the kitchenette fridge, which was half-sized and mostly freezer.

"Strange vibe around here," he said. "Very strange."

"Do you know who the surprise guest is?" I asked. He shot me a look of concern, puzzlement, and curiosity, each emotion distinct. I wondered if he'd been born with a face that could display his emotions so well or whether he'd worked on it, spending countless hours in front of his bedroom mirror.

"I didn't even know there was one. Who is it?"

"I don't know either. I heard they were adding someone to the show. Vic was talking to the director about it while Jess was doing his sound check."

"Jess? Oh. Right. You mean Jack. Well, shit. You think this is about the guest?"

"Could be," I said. "Security is really tense. I know they were understaffed to start with, and maybe they're diverting resources? I don't know why. They could send whoever it is in here and let them have a plate of rouladen and salmonella."

"That's funny," he said, his face and tone giving no indication that he meant it. I'd have taken offence if I hadn't once worked with a cop who'd done stand-up in her spare time. The deadpan was something they learned to do, she'd told me, so they didn't laugh on stage.

"The lawsuit would be hilarious," I said.

"Some people you don't throw into the commu-
nal green room," Ziad told me. "I've been learning that
lesson. Some people, man, they might as well be gods
walking an inch above the earth. You accidentally brush
their bottle of fancy water with your arm? They will be
brought *another* one. One your arm hasn't despoiled."

"That's very specific," I said.

"Sure is."

"So maybe this is about the special guest," I said.
"If they're special enough."

"Some of them think they can have everything
their way."

His tone gave me a twinge. Whatever he was
talking about, it wasn't trivia like fancy water or being
too good for the green room.

We each got a coffee and stood in companionable
silence next to the buffet table. Across the room, Jess
and Kent were dancing to an old Sam Cooke number
playing on Jesse's phone while Thom made sugges-
tions from the sidelines. Kent was a mess, but Jess had
more upper body strength than most of Kent's partners
and was using it to keep things in line. They were a
ridiculous pair, badly mismatched in height even with
Jesse's high heels, but they were starting to approach
grace in rare moments when Kent wasn't watching his
feet.

"Hey! Eyes up here!" Jess directed.

Kent froze, bringing the dance to an end, and met
Jesse's eyes with panic.

"What do you think I was looking at?"

I heard a strangled laugh beside me and turned to
see Ziad trying to keep it together.

"Solid. Gold," he choked. I patted his back.

"Kent's working some stuff out."

"Yeah, I get it. I had to work some stuff out myself."

I knew that because everyone knew that. Ziad had come out during that Netflix special.

I heard footsteps in the hall, moving fast. I'd heard them all day as the crew rushed around, so that didn't get much of my attention. What did catch me, and everyone else in the room, was a voice that could have cut through steel, proclaiming at full volume, "Oh my God, this place is *such* a *dump*!"

Jess mouthed "What the fuck?" at Thom. Brennan went past them to the door and shoved it open to reveal the hallway parade. In the front were the stage-door security guard and Vic, the assistant director, both on their phones and looking nervous.

Behind them, a spectacle that I immediately associated with the voice. He was blond and maybe twenty-one. Tall, thin, and sporting a floral silk pantsuit, a silver kimono covered in sequins, and white leather slip-on shoes with at least an inch and a half of heel. He was eyeing the hallway with dismay, as if the very existence of the chipped paint was likely to devalue his brand. What that brand was, I could not have said. Judging by the confused faces of everyone in the room, no one else recognized him either.

Behind the spectacle was a Black man in his forties to sixties. He was wearing jeans, a turtleneck, and a bomber jacket, all of which looked like nothing much. It would have been interesting to know which outfit had cost more, the floral-and-silver nightmare or this guy's pay-no-attention-to-me ensemble. I made a note to ask Jesse later.

The Black guy was also on his phone, and something about him suggested he was in charge of whatever

I was seeing. He didn't look scared, he looked mildly pissed off. My best guess was that he was a manager.

I was so busy watching the hall that it took me a second to see what was happening with Jess. He was breathing hard, and glassy-eyed. From the way Kent was holding on to him, I guessed that Kent had caught him on his way to the floor. Thom was at his shoulder, saying something I couldn't hear. Luna was watching closely.

I was already crossing the room to Jess when the reason for his reaction became clear. I realized that he had recognized the Black guy. I realized it because the person the Black guy was a manager for was coming up behind him in the hall.

Matthew fucking Garrett.

CHAPTER THREE

As I REACHED Jess, I heard something break on the floor behind me. I opened my arms to Jess, who came in for a hug. Then I looked over his shoulder to see what was going on behind us and saw Ziad, standing with both hands on the bar and a broken coffee mug at his feet. He was shaking, and his light brown skin was going green.

"What the *fuck* is he doing here?" Ziad demanded of no one in particular.

Brennan slammed the door shut and stood with his back against it. It was clear from his face that, though he had no idea what was going on, the people in the hallway would have to go through him if they wanted to enter the green room. That or politely convince him they had business in here. He wasn't Rambo.

"You okay?" I asked Jesse. He seemed steadier on his feet. Luna was watching from about a metre away, ready to pounce if Jess seemed shaky again.

"Yeah, I just… was not expecting that."

"Was that Matt Garrett?" Reiss said. "Bren, did you slam the door on Matt Garrett?"

"Seemed the thing to do," Brennan said, his voice higher pitched than usual.

Reiss shook his head. "Jesus."

"He thinks so," Ziad said. He was staring at the broken mug on the floor like it might come back together if he wished hard enough. Jess gave me a light push, wanting to be let go, and I released him. He walked toward the kitchenette until he was a few steps from Ziad.

"I didn't know you knew each other," Jess said.

Ziad gave Jess a dark look, and I realized that he hadn't spoken to Jesse since he'd arrived. Not beyond introducing himself. I stepped forward to do… I didn't know what, but it turned out I wasn't needed. Jess didn't seem bothered. He was calmly standing his ground.

"I know you did," Ziad said. "You were sucking that dick for about six months, weren't you?"

Jess looked like he was questioning reality. Specifically, that he'd heard what he thought he'd heard.

"I… you know, I really don't want to talk about this."

Ziad put his hands in the pockets of his dark blue blazer. Like everything else about him, it was tidy and sharp.

"I heard you parted as friends. What does 'parted as friends' mean? That polishing the royal knob isn't your full-time job anymore, but you're not ruling it out?"

I couldn't remember the last time I'd been in a room that quiet. Everyone was staring at Jess. I knew the real story, and he'd told it to Luna and Kent one drunken night, but the rest of them only knew what they'd seen on the internet. They were gawking like people in a restaurant when a movie star walked in, like they hadn't spent a couple of hours hanging out with Jess that very day. Like Thom hadn't known him for years.

"What exactly is your problem?" Jess asked Ziad.

"Is he here to see you?" Ziad said. "Is that why he's slumming in the dump? You called up your old fuck buddy and invited him?"

"Did I look like I was expecting to see him?"

"You're a performer," Ziad said, clearly meaning that on every possible level.

Duncan made a sound deep in his throat, like a laugh had gotten stuck there. "If he's that good an actor, he should change careers."

Duncan and Connor and Charlie had been watching the scene over the back of the couch, their controllers dropped and forgotten. On the screen behind them, the elves they'd been playing were getting their asses handed to them by orcs.

"Ziad, you seem to have strong opinions about the guy," Connor said. "Do you have some kind of history with him?"

Ziad stared at him. "History? What the fuck is that supposed to mean? You think I used to date that walking ball sack?"

Connor turned to Charlie. "Did I say they were dating?"

Charlie shook his head.

"You know him, though, right?" Duncan said.

"We were on a shoot together," Ziad said. "A couple of months ago. You didn't know about that because I wasn't licking his tonsils in public. Or has he had his tonsils out? Jack, you'd know."

"What the hell?" Jess said. "What are you, jealous?"

Ziad took a couple of steps toward Jess. I would have liked to think he stopped because he saw my face, but actually he stopped himself. He realized halfway to Jess that he didn't know what he was going to do when he got there.

"Fuck you," he said. "You're just like him. You think everyone wants to fuck the movie star. I'd rather fuck a woodchipper."

"I do not think everyone is interested in Matt," Jess said evenly. Knowing what I knew, I couldn't believe how calm Jess was staying. But that was his job. Stick to the story. Manage your image. Don't lose your cool. "If he put some kind of pressure on you, I'm sorry to hear it."

Ziad's eyes widened. "I didn't say that. I didn't say anything like that."

The guy had no problem going off on Jess, who was standing right there in a room full of people who had his back. He also had no trouble badmouthing Matt in the abstract. Say one thing about how Matt might have personally done him wrong, though, and Ziad looked like a kid who was convinced that the boogeyman was coming for him.

Jess's face was unreadable, even to me.

"Okay," Jess said. "My bad."

After about a minute of silence, Brennan said, "Anyway, that solves the mystery of the surprise guest."

"Wait, you guys all knew Matt was going to be here?" Duncan eyed Brennan, then Jess. "Why didn't I know?"

"We didn't know it was Matt. We knew there was going to be some surprise guest, but we only knew that because Ben overheard something," Jess told him. "I thought everyone had heard by now." He spread his hands like a magician pulling a spray of flowers from a hat. "Surprise."

I went to stand next to him and put a hand on his shoulder. He put a hand over mine.

"Jess, do you want to go to your dressing room?" Luna asked. She was using her nicest tone, the one she saved for people who'd gotten a knife in the shoulder or a piece of rebar stuck in their shin. Smooth and sweet, intended to calm people down before they pushed that rebar in further.

"Or home?" Kent said. "And fuck these guys for not telling you that piece of shit was going to be here?"

"He has a point," I said.

"No," Jess said, closing his eyes. "I only have a forty-five-minute set, and it's for charity. I'm doing it."

"Oh, come on," Kent said. "You're not doing heart surgery, Jess. No one's going to die if you bail. Let's all go. Ziad, if you don't want to be here, you can come with us. I'll hold the door."

"That would be a breach of my contract," Ziad said absently. He was looking at Jess. Something was on his mind, and it wasn't that Jess was some kind of extension of Matt. Not after what Kent had said.

"I have a contract too," Jess said. He opened his eyes and turned to Kent. "It's just Matt. He's not... I don't know, Dracula. It won't kill me to be in the same building as him."

"Sure," Kent said. "That's why you went down like a fainting goat."

Jess flipped him off, and Kent did an impression of a fainting goat that wasn't great but was a thousand times better than his dancing.

"All right," Luna said. "If everyone is going to stay and if no one wants to associate with Matt, surely it's possible to arrange that. Could you speak to the director?"

"I would like to associate with Matt," Duncan said. "He's a gold-plated opportunity."

"And I still have these moments of feeling sorry for him," Jess said, more to himself than anyone else.

A beep came from the door, the sound of a card being pressed to the scanner. The lock clicked, and someone tried to open the door. Brennan leaned back and dug his heels in—or tried. The ancient linoleum floor didn't give him much traction.

"What the hell?" Vic said through the inch or so she'd managed to get the door open.

Brennan looked at Jess and Ziad. "You boys all right with me letting her in?"

"Yes, of course," Ziad said. Jesse nodded.

Brennan stepped away from the door, and Vic nearly fell inside, like it was a slapstick routine they'd been working on for days. No one laughed. It was silent in the room again as Vic straightened herself out.

"What was that shenanigan?" she asked Brennan.

"Needed some privacy in here," he told her. She squinted at him as if he'd spoken a foreign language, then shook it off.

"Okay. Well, I hear that you've all seen our special guest for the evening."

"Is there going to be a chance to meet him later?" Duncan asked. "I have a couple of thoughts I would love to bounce off him."

"Um, maybe," Vic said. "Maybe after the show. So in terms of lineup, Matt Garrett will be going on stage last, so he'll have a ten fifteen slot. Shouldn't affect anyone else's set. Carry on as usual, and Matt will do his bit once you've all done yours."

"What is his bit?" Jess asked. "Sorry, but... he doesn't sing, and he's not a comic, so it's not like he's got a tight five."

Vic smiled at him, which raised the hairs on the back of my neck. She was kissing up, something I had yet to see her do with anyone. Why?

"No, no need to be sorry. Fair question. He's going to speak about mental health, like the rest of you. He's got a speech he wants to give about his own struggles."

"His own struggles," Jess said. I didn't think he'd intended to speak out loud.

"It's great for the organization," Vic said. "I know, you're probably all pissed that no one told you we were changing the lineup. I get it. We only found out this afternoon. He had an availability, and he wanted to do this, so we made it work. Sarah wants you all to know she appreciates you helping us to make it work."

Sarah was the director. I dimly remembered seeing Sarah at the bottom of an email to Jess, though I couldn't recall the rest of her name.

"You did say we didn't have to do anything to make it work," Ziad said. He was smiling, and every word was dripping sweet acid, like lemon drizzle on a coffee cake.

"Yeah, true," Vic said. "True. Uh, Jack, could I speak to you in private? For a minute?"

Jess stiffened. I pressed his shoulder, reminding him that I was there.

"Don't you have a show starting in a few minutes?" he asked, with a smile as polite and fake as Ziad's.

"I sure do, so I don't have a lot of time, but I would really appreciate a quick chat, if that's okay."

"Any reason we can't talk right here?" he asked. Vic glanced around the room like she was checking for zombies or ninjas, something coming for her from the corners. Maybe Dracula.

"Uh, yeah, I guess if you're okay with it. One of the things Matt asked for was that you would introduce him."

Jess blinked and blinked again. Behind us, I heard Ziad shifting his stance.

Jess said, "What?"

"He'd like for you to introduce him. He thought it would seem odd for you not to, since you're still friends and you're performing right before he goes on stage. He doesn't want any rumours to start about you guys not getting along or something. He said you'd understand."

"Right," Jess said. "Yeah. I think I understand."

"Great, so I'll tell him you'll do it."

"I won't."

It was Vic's turn to say, "What?"

"I won't, and he'll know why," Jess said. "He has put you in a bad position, and that's not your fault. It's his fault. But I'm still not going to do it, and I don't care who he sends in here. If he backs out because of this, I am very sorry, but it's not happening."

Vic took in a deep breath through her nose and let it out through her mouth. "Phew. Okay. It sounds like the breakup was rougher than you guys let on. I get that. But, you know, it's an introduction. Just say a few words. It's for the charity. You have no idea what a game-changer it is financially if he endorses this organization. Even a tweet from him would make all the difference. No offence, but all this support from the rest of you combined can't have as much impact as a tweet from Matt Garrett. Can you… you know, kind of hold your nose and do it? I mean, don't literally hold your nose on stage. This is going to help a lot of people."

"He said no," Luna said. This was also a tone I knew from the ER. It was the one she used on people right before she called security to have them removed.

"I heard him say no," Reiss confirmed.

"We all did," Connor said.

Vic's phone was buzzing. She took it out and glanced at the screen.

"I have to go. We can talk more about this later. Do the guests want to come with me?"

It took me a second to realize she meant Kent and Luna. And maybe me. Did we want to go out front and watch the show?

"We're good," Kent said. "We'll go out later."

"Okay. Jack has my number, so he can text me and I'll send security for you."

She left, and Brennan pushed the door shut behind her, making sure the lock clicked. Then he grabbed a chair and pushed it under the door handle.

"Does that work?" he asked sheepishly. "I've seen it in movies."

"It's like a wedge," Kent said. "Works okay."

"Locking that door doesn't really solve anything," Jesse said.

"So he wants you to introduce him," Ziad said.

Jess turned to face him. "Apparently."

"And you won't do it? Not even for charity?"

He didn't sound like he thought it was unreasonable. That wasn't his tone. He did, though, sound like he wanted an explanation.

"Right," Jess said.

"That's interesting because I think Matt's right," Ziad said. "People are going to get the impression you don't get along. For example, I'm getting that impression right now."

Jess shrugged. That was the entirety of his response. Ziad started to circle him, very slowly. Getting all the angles.

"You really don't like him. You didn't happen to see him *do* something, did you? Did you see a bad thing, Jack? Did he grope a pool boy? Did he get fresh with a waiter? Did he do a Very Bad Thing?"

Jess leaned forward. "I don't know," he said, his voice low and dangerous. "Did he?"

Ziad moved in quick, before I could react, and shoved Jess. I grabbed Jess and steadied him. Ziad moved back, too far for Jess to reach him.

"Fuck you!" Ziad said. "Did you look the other way? Shit, maybe you got in on the fun. I hear back then you were so fucked up, you could have been fucking pool boys on Mars for all you knew. And then you told everyone you parted as friends. Kicked that dick down the road."

"That'll be enough," I said.

Ziad glared at me. "You think so?"

"I really do."

His shoulders dropped. "Fuck," he said. He moved past me, giving me as much space as he could, and went to the door. Brennan got himself and the chair out of the way, and Ziad left, giving the door a good slam as he went.

I tried to pull Jess in closer, but he shook me off and walked away to the kitchenette. He began to run his fingers over the cans of soda as if he knew a magic trick that would turn them into whiskey. At that point, if I'd had any, I'd have given it to him.

"Okay," Thom said in the following silence, "I don't know what that guy did but… I might be willing to threaten to walk. If we do that, and Jess does… and I have to think Ziad would… maybe Sarah would tell Matt to take a hike. She can't fill all of our slots at this point. She'd be better off cutting him loose than losing all of us."

"Not if they've already announced him," Charlie said. He'd barely spoken all day, and I jumped at the sound of his voice. "It's like Vic said: A tweet from Matt Garrett makes all the difference. They talk it up, they tag him, and donations come in. Donations are the end game. You don't make that much off a show like this. Even with the venue donated and the talent donating their time, you have to pay the crew… feed people… the venue might need expenses covered, like heat and power. We had our expenses covered. You can lose money on a charity show if you're not careful."

"If you think about it," Thom said. "This has been sold out for weeks. So he didn't sell any tickets. I think Charlie's right. It's all about the socials."

The sight of everyone pulling out their phones was another thing that would have been comical under better circumstances.

"They have announced," Reiss said. "And Matt has shared it."

"Oh, this is fun. People are already speculating about both of us being here," Jess said. He showed me his phone, which was full of slang and emojis that I was too tired and irritated to parse.

"Marvellous," Luna said. "Jesse, my love, would you care to give me the passwords to your socials?"

"No thanks. Gia says if you want something to die, don't feed it."

Gia was Jess's inside person at his record label, the one they sent with him on tours. She reminded me of a velociraptor, but her advice to Jess seemed solid most of the time.

"Too bad Matt's out there with a bag of birdseed," Duncan said. "What's the story with him, anyway? He's supposed to be one of the Hollywood good guys."

Luna and Kent both seemed about to weigh in but were stopped by another beep at the door. Then a second beep. Then the door started to rattle against the chair.

"What fresh hell?" Luna said.

"Probably the director," Reiss said.

Jess shook his head. "No, Dylan's up, and Emilie's on right after…. I think she'll want to make sure the first changeover goes well."

"That's grunt work, isn't it?" Thom said. "Can't Vic manage the changeover?"

The door rattled again. Everyone looked at it.

"We can't leave people in the hall," Jess said. "It might be Ziad."

"You decide," Brennan told him. "You're the one who's getting press-ganged."

Jess smiled a little. "Press-ganged. So many jokes I don't feel like making."

Brennan gave him a "really?" look before opening the door to Matt Garrett's manager. Jess stopped smiling.

"Abraham Lewis," the manager said, offering a hand to Brennan. "Friends call me Lew." Brennan shook it with a puzzled expression, like the ritual was new to him. He did not offer his own name. The manager turned to Jesse. "Jack. It's good to see you again. Can I have a word?"

"You can have the word goodbye," Jess offered. Lewis smiled and took a few steps into the room.

"I know you and Matt have some bad blood," he said.

"You get that wording from his PR team?" Jess asked. Lewis sighed, and I could see right there how good the guy was. He came off as sad and a little tired, sorry that everyone couldn't get along.

"Maybe we should talk in private," Lewis suggested.

Jess was drumming on his legs, an anxious habit of his. If I'd been Lewis, I'd have taken it as a sign that Jess might be drumming on his face next.

"I doubt we have anything to discuss."

"Well," Lewis said, "that's why we should talk in private. So I can explain."

"If this is about Matt's idea that I introduce him—" Jess started.

"No," Lewis said "He understands why you'd prefer not to do that. All he wants is a few minutes of your time. Not onstage."

"To do what?" Jess said. It was the same dangerous tone he'd used on Ziad.

Lewis sighed. "Please, can we do this in private? You can still decline to see Matt, obviously, but some privacy would allow us to have a more frank conversation."

Jess breathed deep. "Fine. We can talk in my dressing room."

He moved. I was always impressed by how fast the guy could walk in heels. He passed Lewis at the door without so much as glancing at him. I followed, and Lewis followed me.

As I neared the door, Kent gave me his standard "Do you want me to kidney punch this asshole and leave him in a dumpster?" look. I shook my head. There would always be a chance to take Kent up on that later.

Jess's dressing room was close to the green room and larger than Dylan's, as befit a headliner. It still wasn't that big, but it would hold three people without us standing on each other's feet. Jess put most of that space between himself and Lewis once we were in the room. I locked the door behind us and stood between the two of them, slightly to the side so they could see each other.

"Okay," Jess said. "Talk."

"Matthew wants you to know," Lewis said, "that he feels the need to apologize."

Jess cocked his head. "What?"

"He would very much like to apologize," Lewis repeated. "To you, in person."

"Amazing." Jess studied Lewis's face. "Does Matt know what he'd be apologizing for?"

He did a good job of sounding a little flippant and a lot pissed off, but I knew his voice well enough to pick up a tremor.

"Honestly?" Lewis said. "I don't know. That's a conversation you would have to have with Matt."

Jess didn't move, but he still left the room. His attention was turned inward, and I doubt he was really seeing either of us.

"You don't owe Matt anything," I said. "Or this guy."

"I might owe me," Jess said. I clamped my mouth shut. Lewis didn't say anything either. We all stood there not saying anything.

Finally, Jess said, "He could send a card."

"I don't think he's comfortable putting anything in writing," Lewis said.

"You think? I was kidding."

"As long as we're talking about discretion," Lewis said, "Matt would like to see you alone. He's asked me and Alex to give him privacy for this."

"Who's Alex?" Jess asked, which showed how rattled he was.

"I think he's talking about Budget Leto," I told Jesse. It was tough to be sure in the dark, but for a moment, I thought I saw Lewis fight a smile.

"Alex is Matt's boyfriend," Lewis said. "They've been together for a few months."

Jess frowned. "What's the play?"

In other words, how did this sham relationship benefit Matt's career? I'd never seen Alex before, and I was pretty sure I'd have remembered, but that didn't mean he wasn't famous. I'd gotten to the point in life where someone could have a half-billion followers on TikTok and I wouldn't have had any idea.

"There is no play," Lewis told him. "He's a boyfriend. That's all."

"That guy?" Jess said.

Lewis spread his hands. "Mine is not to reason why. Are you willing to give Matt a few minutes, one-on-one? He wants to be able to speak freely about what happened between you."

"Jess hasn't been able to freely speak about what happened," I said, forgetting for a moment that I was staying out of this. "If he had, Matt would have been talking with the police."

Lewis opened his mouth, and I was sure he was going to say something stupid, like that it had been a scuffle between grown men and no one's fault. Something about my face convinced him to stow that.

"Assuming that were the case," Lewis said carefully, "Matt's need for privacy would be understandable."

"We are not in court," I said. "We *should* be...."

Jess raised a hand. "Ben. It's okay."

It wasn't, but I bit my tongue.

"You know, it's funny because I think this is going to be some bullshit. He wants something, and I don't think apologizing is it. And yet...."

And yet? I raised my eyebrows at him.

"He's not Dracula," Jess told me. "He's not going to do anything here. There's nothing for me to be afraid of."

"That doesn't mean you need to see him," I said.

"I know. I just... I didn't know I would react that way, seeing him. That's fucking ridiculous. I can't go through life being that scared of a guy who looks handsome for a living."

"If you want to do this for yourself, that's up to you," I said. "I'd be happy to get our friends out of here and burn the place down. Whatever you want to do."

Jess smiled. "It's a nice venue," he said. "I'd feel bad about the venue."

He was thinking. Drumming on his leg again. I waited.

"Okay," he said finally. "I'll talk to him. Ten minutes. That's it. And then I don't want to talk to him, like, ever again."

"Thank you so much," Lewis said. "I know Matt will be grate—"

"Matt hasn't been grateful for anything in a decade," Jess said, turning on Lewis. "Don't even try that."

Lewis folded his hands over his slight beer gut and waited politely as Jess turned back to me.

"Will you wait outside the door? In case.... It won't be a thing, but if it is...."

"I'll kick in the door," I told him. "I'd enjoy it."

"If you're ready now," Lewis said, "I'll walk you there and swipe you in."

Lewis's phone buzzed. He didn't look at it. Probably Matt, wanting to know why he hadn't gotten everything he wanted the second he wanted it.

"Where'd they put him anyway?" Jess asked.

"He's in the artist-in-residence suite," Lewis said. "Take the hall past the green room and it's pretty much there. Take a few steps around the corner and you'll see the door across the hall."

Jess nodded. "A suite. Of course. No dressing room around here would have been big enough for the ego."

"Jess, can you and I talk without this guy for a minute?" I asked.

Jess gave me a curious glance, then dismissed Lewis with the kind of "shoo" gesture you'd use on an unwelcome cat. It was exceptionally rude, and I thought he meant it that way.

Once Lewis had gone to stand in the hall, I pulled the door shut behind him and put my back to it.

"You don't have to do this," I told Jess. "You don't have to prove you're a tough guy or you're over it or whatever it is you're thinking."

"I know I don't have to do it. I'm not trying to prove anything. I don't like being scared."

"Fear is supposed to be aversive."

"So you think this is a bad idea."

"I—" I stopped myself. "What I think is not the point. You should do whatever you feel like doing. But you don't have to see him tonight—or ever, if you don't want to— and you don't have to do anything on his terms. He says he doesn't want me in there while you talk to him? So what? That's what he wants. I care what you want."

"I want to not have a panic attack in a grocery store because he's on the cover of *People*."

I wanted to put my arms around him, but even in this state, he would likely have pushed me off. Don't rumple the outfit. Don't touch the hair.

"That might keep happening," I said, "whether you confront him tonight or not. There's no magic cure for trauma."

"It's not like he raped me," Jess said. I flinched at the word. I shouldn't have, but it was hard to hear from him.

"How different do you think it was?" I said. "You said no. He physically overpowered you, and he stopped when he chose to stop."

Jess stared at the floor. He was, as he had been since the night it happened, teetering between taking the whole thing seriously and deciding he'd made a big deal over nothing.

"I don't know."

"Do you really think it's ridiculous or shameful that you're still afraid of this guy?"

He looked up. His green eyes were dark and glittering with fury. "I don't *want* to be."

"Jess, you can't bend reality to your will."

He cocked his head. "Watch me."

He came at me, toward the door, and I moved since he obviously meant to go right through me if necessary. I followed him into the hall, where Lewis was reading something on his phone. Seeing us, he put his phone away.

"Shall we?"

"Two things first," I said. "Jess, do you want me to come with you?"

Jess shook his head. "I've got this."

If he hadn't been trying to prove something before, he sure was now. Good talk we'd had.

"Okay," I said. "You've got this. One other question. Lewis, I know that asshole has a gun. Is it with him today?"

Lewis twitched like his skin was trying to escape. I thought I saw a twitch in his eye, too, as he turned his gaze to Jess. "We have a contractual agreement about sharing confidential information," he said.

"The gun thing came to me in a dream," I said.

"He's psychic," Jess added. "He's a psychic detective."

Lewis rolled his eyes. "If Matt had a gun, obviously he would have found it difficult to bring that to Canada, and he would therefore have left it at home. Can we please go now?"

I followed them to the corner between the green room door and Matt's suite so I could keep an eye on who was coming and going while Jess and Matt talked. I put a hand on Jess's shoulder before he went inside.

"Yell if you need anything," I told him.

"You'll hear me," he said. Lewis took Jess inside and came back out seconds later. I never saw Matt.

CHAPTER FOUR

I SAT ON the floor with my back against the wall and set a timer for ten minutes on my phone.

If things were running on schedule, the first two acts would be off the stage. Ash Rose would be on. Duncan was on after them, and Kent would probably want to see his set, so maybe I'd get Jess to text Vic once he was back from whatever bullshit Matt had planned. Or maybe Duncan would be okay with Kent watching from the wings.

Or possibly I was fixating on things that did not matter so I didn't kick in Matt's door.

Duncan left the green room while I was sitting there. I saw him go the other way, where the dressing rooms and practice room lined the hall. If you went all the way down that hall, it turned and reached the doors to the backstage area. Kent and Luna didn't follow him out, but to my surprise, Ziad did. Instead of turning toward the dressing rooms, Ziad went the other way. Toward me.

He stopped once he was right up next to me and stood there, the tip of one pointy shoe resting below my knees.

"I take it Matt is in there?" he said.

"Yep."

"And Jack isn't with you, so I assume he's in there also."

"Yep."

He crossed his arms and leaned against the wall.

"What's that about? Is he getting his monthly payout for keeping Matt's dirty secrets?"

I tilted my head back so I could see his face. "I have a pocket knife," I said. "I will stick it in your foot if you don't shut up."

He didn't say anything. A solid choice. I opened my eyes to see him eyeballing Matt's closed door. So we did that for a while, two guys in a hallway looking at a door.

When the door finally opened, I stood, and Ziad sprang to action. He saw his chance, the space between Jesse and the door as Jess left the room, and went in before Jess could pull the door shut. I couldn't see Matt from where I was, but obviously he wasn't in a position to throw Ziad back into the hall. Not immediately.

Ziad pushed the door shut with his foot. Jess and I regarded each other.

"Bold move," I said.

"I don't see it going well," Jess told me.

"How badly do you think it'll go? Should we let ourselves in there?"

He shook his head. "I think it'll mostly be yelling."

HIs voice was pitched a notch higher than usual, but there was no quaver, and he didn't seem on the brink of crying or dropping to the ground.

"I don't have anywhere to be," I said.

"Of course not," he said. "You're a hanger-on."

"And star-fucker," I said, and he grinned. I offered him a hand and he took it.

"Is it okay to ruin your outfit?" I asked. In answer he came in for a hug.

I placed a hand on his back, between his shoulder blades, and held my breath for a second. Jess was a little tense, but he wasn't shaking. He was breathing well.

"How'd it go in there?" I asked with my chin on top of his head.

"Weird," Jess told me. "He's lost his fucking mind."

I could hear voices from Matt's room. Nothing distinct, but a loud word came out here and there.

"Lost his mind as in actively dangerous?" I asked. "I can't walk away if you think Matt's going to start swinging. Ziad isn't much bigger than you are."

"I don't think that makes you his bodyguard," Jess said. "For all you know, he has a black belt."

"I'd still feel better sticking around if there's likely to be trouble."

"Matt does not want negative attention right now," Jess said. "He'll stick to psychological violence. Let's talk about it in my dressing room. Maybe bring in Luna and Kent?"

"We can do that," I said.

Jess pulled away from me, went to the green room door, and opened it far enough to stick his head in.

"Luna? Kent? We're having a dressing-room conference. Unless you'd rather go out front and watch the show instead. I wouldn't blame you."

"This right here isn't the show?" Kent asked. Jess flipped him off for the second time in an hour, which was a lot but not even close to the record.

We went to Jesse's dressing room and got comfortable. There was barely enough room, between the couch and two armless leather chairs, for everyone to sit. Jess grabbed my coat from where I'd left it on the back of the couch and draped it over his legs.

"So?" Luna said. "Are you all right? You seem better."

"I had a talk with Matt," Jess told her.

"Did you use a baseball bat?" Kent asked.

"No. It was civil. He claimed he wanted to apologize."

"And did he?" Luna asked.

Jess made a face. "Sort of? It wasn't quite 'I'm sorry if you were uncomfortable,' but it was close."

I sat near Jess so he could lean in and leech my body heat.

"So what did he want?" I asked.

"You won't believe it," Jess said. "It was seriously crazy. He wants the footage."

"What footage?" Kent said.

"From backstage. You know, from my show, when he got grabby."

"He thinks there's footage of that?" I said.

"He knows there was footage of that. There were security cameras. Two of them. His people convinced the venue to delete the files."

Luna gawked at him.

"He told you this? Why would he admit that?"

"It's not actually that crazy for people's teams to lock that kind of thing down," Jess said. "Footage gets stolen and sold. It's not even that the stuff in it is bad. I mean, in this case Matt did something that's legitimately bad, but sometimes the A-listers get footage pulled over things that most people would consider trivial. Like, you can see a bald spot from some angles, so their management doesn't allow anything shot from above to get out. It's all handled."

"It's not crazy," I confirmed. "Caligula made it illegal for people to stand higher than him because he was ashamed of his bald spot. If Caligula did something, you know it's normal."

"Is that true?" Jess asked. I shrugged.

"Maybe. Maybe not. Caligula is like Hitler. The shit he definitely did is so bad that people will believe pretty much anything you ice the cake with."

"Huh. Anyway, my point is that it's a fairly common request. It wouldn't have raised any eyebrows. I don't know if security at the venue even watched that footage. Matt's people probably said, 'Hey, Matt was in the backstage area last night. We see you have security cameras. Could you delete the footage.' Places will do that to make Matt happy. If they say no, a lawyer will call saying they don't have the rights to Matt's image."

"So he could commit murder on camera and sue people for using the security footage?" Kent said.

"I doubt he'd try to push it that far," Jess said. "It's just a threat. But no one wants to fight his lawyers."

"No wonder he thinks he's Jesus," Luna said. Jess gave a dry, angry laugh.

"He doesn't think he's Jesus. Jesus would wash other people's feet now and then."

"If his team deleted the footage," I said, "why would he ask if you had it?"

"He wanted to know if my people talked to the venue first and got copies of the files. Before they were deleted."

"Did they?" I asked. I could see Gia pulling off something like that.

"Not as far as I know," Jess said. "So probably not. I think Gia would have told me."

"Did you tell Matt this?" I asked.

"I told him I had no idea," Jesse said. Kent smiled and offered Jess a fist to bump, which Jess did. Not with enthusiasm.

"Why would he ask you this now?" Luna said. "Is it because this is the first time he's seen you since the breakup? I mean, the fake breakup."

"The fakeup," Kent suggested.

"It's why Matt's here," I said. Jess looked at me sharply.

"What? Do you know that?"

"No, but think about it. He shows up at the last second. Didn't tell anyone he was coming. He gets here, and the first thing he does is tell the director he wants you to introduce him, which is a public show of you being on good terms. Second thing is he wants to talk to you in private. About footage. None of this feels like a coincidence."

"He was in the neighbourhood, though," Luna said. "He's shooting a movie by Pincher Creek. A western."

"I thought that was down by the US border," Jess said.

"What's your point?" Kent said.

"Jess thinks places that are more than an hour away are far flung," I explained. "He needs to adjust to the west."

"I have toured the hell out of this country," Jess said. "Don't you tell me what's far. Matt's not from here, and I doubt he'd consider a two-hour drive a quick run to the store. But maybe he wanted something from Calgary? Like…."

"A decent meal?" Luna offered. "Running water? Electricity?"

"People with all their teeth?" Kent said.

"I love how you all think being from Toronto makes *me* a snob," Jess said. "I don't know. He could have been in Calgary already. Normally he doesn't make spur-of-the-moment changes to his schedule, but he's traveling lighter than usual. He's just got Lew and this Alex character. He didn't say where he was until he was already in the venue, so he didn't have to dodge fans on the way in. Maybe he came here on a whim."

"Because he felt an urge to support a mental health charity?" I said. "We all know better than that. This guy doesn't want people's mental health issues treated. He capitalizes on them. And Jess, less than five minutes ago, you said he doesn't like to go out of his way for other people. You know this guy. Do you really think he felt charitable and stopped by?"

Jess considered that.

"No," he said finally. "I guess not."

"Who's Alex?" Luna said. "Is it that sequined scarecrow in the Chinese lady pajamas?"

Jess's lips twitched. "Uh, yeah, that is apparently the boyfriend. An actual boyfriend."

Luna stared at him. "Surely not."

"I only know what I was told. He wasn't there when I talked to Matt. Lew wasn't either."

"Do you think Matt's manager knew what he was going to ask you?" Kent said.

"I think he did it on Lew's orders," Jess said. "It was not Matt's idea to fake apologize to me and then ask me for a favour. Neither of those things would have sounded fun to him."

"So Lew got it in his head that this footage might be out there, and he saw an opportunity for Matt to corner you," I said. "It would have been easier for Matt to call you, but I bet you wouldn't have taken his call."

"You win that bet," Jess said.

"But here Matt shows up, he's causing drama, he's already put a staff member in an awkward position. You'd feel like you had to resolve things."

Jess looked at me, eyes wide. "You think he manipulated me?"

"I think he knows you," I said.

Luna put a hand on Jess's leg, though really on my coat. She gave my coat a little pat.

"Are you all right, though?" she asked. "Was it awful, talking to him?"

"It was tolerable," Jess said. "He was eating crow and hating it. I told him to get help. Obviously he did something inappropriate to Ziad too."

"You think he does this a lot?" Kent said. "His type usually does."

"I think he does it when he hears the word no," Jess said. "You tell me how often Matt Garrett hears that word and I'll tell you how often he flies off the handle. I don't think he hears it a lot."

"He's been *People*'s Sexiest Man three times," Luna said. "I think that's a record."

"Even if it's not, it's especially impressive for an openly gay guy," Jess said. "He's been great for representation. I'll give him that."

More than once in the middle of the night, I'd wondered how much of Jess not telling on Matt had been about representation. About what would happen if America's gay sweetheart turned out to be a big gay monster. I'd never asked, largely because I didn't think Jess knew the answer.

"I didn't think about the next person who said no to him," Jess said. "It didn't even cross my mind."

"That doesn't make it your fault," Luna soothed. Jess stared at her hand on the coat, the long red nails following the curve of his leg.

"Ziad hates me because he thinks I knew Matt was a predator and did sweet fuck all about it. There are no lies in that."

"But it's far more complicated," Luna said. "When something like this—"

"It's not more complicated from Ziad's point of view," Jess said. "I don't blame him for hating me. You know how much *I* hated me about this? I couldn't stand me. I went into therapy so I could stop being that guy who got so wasted he could… what was it Ziad said? Fuck a pool boy on Mars and not know it?"

"It was Mars," Kent confirmed. "I didn't know they had pools."

"I still kinda hate me."

"It is Matt's responsibility to keep it in his pants," Kent said. "Let's be clear on that. He is a grown-up."

"It's also hard to be him," Jess said. Kent rolled his eyes. Jess missed it. He was looking at the back of his phone, which he'd set on the table before us. Wondering what people were saying about him, no doubt. "It messes with your head when people treat you like a little god. And it's not like they even care about him, you know? He's the money train."

"I'm having a hard time generating tears for the guy," Kent said. He balled up a fist and rubbed his eye. "Nope, still nothing."

"It's a monkey's paw thing," Jess said. "Fame is really weird. Everyone thinks they want it. By the time they figure out how fucked up it is, it's already at the door."

"One could quit," Luna said. "And be less famous, eventually."

"Yeah, you could quit," Jess agreed. "One of my friends did that a couple of years ago. She said it felt like she'd died and didn't even know she was a ghost until everyone started staring right through her."

"So she knew a lot of assholes," I said.

"I said something helpful like, those were never your friends, and she asked how I'd like to wake up tomorrow and suddenly know how many people never really cared about me. Apparently it's demoralizing."

"That *Sixth Sense* kid would still see you," Kent said. "You'd always have him."

"You'd spend the rest of your life not talking to anyone but Haley Joel Osment," Jess said.

"You ever meet him?" Kent said. "What's he like?"

"He's like fuck you, I told you to stop asking me that about people," Jess said, and Kent smiled warmly. "I know you didn't mean it."

Jess checked his phone. "Okay. I'm on at nine forty-five."

"Loads of time," Kent said.

"I have to warm up," Jess said. "And I have to do this other thing."

"Jerk it?" Kent suggested. "Drop acid? Snort cocaine off a prostitute?"

"No," Jess said. "I would prefer not to talk about it. Are you okay with me getting someone to take you out front? You've got good seats."

Kent stood and offered an arm to Luna. "Shall we?"

She stood and took his arm. Then they waited while Jesse texted Vic and Vic got in touch with security and security made their way to Jesse's dressing room. Once they were gone, Jess gave me an expectant look.

"What?" I said. "You need me to get the cocaine? Or the sex worker?"

"I'm throwing you out too."

"Jesus. This thing you have to do really must be embarrassing."

"That and I need to be alone," Jess said. I stretched an arm along the back of the couch and grinned at him.

"You gonna tell me what you're doing?"

"No."

I flicked the back of his head with a finger.

He swatted my hand. "Stop it."

"I'll imagine worse things," I said. "Whatever it is."

"Fill your boots," he told me.

"I'll wake you up at three in the morning for a month," I said. "I'll have a new guess every time."

He studied my face. Would I really do that? Maybe not, but what else might I do? Finally he sighed and threw my coat at me. I caught it before it hit my face.

"I have to meditate."

"Really? You? Have to meditate?"

He was on his phone, flipping through apps. "Really."

"Didn't you used to call that pretentious napping?"

"I still do," he said. He dropped his phone into his lap. "My therapist wants me to try it. She thinks it can replace...."

"Cocaine?"

"Yeah, for example. She thinks meditating can replace cocaine."

I tried not to laugh, until Jess made a "come on, out with it" gesture with his hand. Then I let it out.

"Yeah," he said when I tapered off. "I know. I'm pretty sure she's never done coke. I don't think she *drinks* Coke. But I told her I would try it at this show in exchange for her never fucking suggesting this to me again."

"I'm sure that's the attitude she was hoping you'd go in with."

He pulled headphones off a table beside the couch.

"Right now," he said, "it's the only attitude I've got."

I patted his shoulder. "Have fun with that. I should go find out what Thom is telling people about our university days and maybe kill him to make him stop."

"Good," Jess said. He had his headphones on and some meditation app running on his phone, so I didn't know whether he'd heard me. I put my coat back on the couch beside him, in case he got cold again, and turned off the light on my way out.

CHAPTER FIVE

THE HALL was empty. I could see light under Dylan's dressing-room door and the room the comics had been using. Light didn't show from the backstage doors or the practice-room door, but that was because they were soundproof, like the green room. No cracks for the light to slip through. I could see light under the double doors that separated the loading area, where the stage door was. Someone with shiny security-guard shoes was there, talking on his phone. Sounded like the guy I'd met earlier. I caught enough words to decide he was waiting for a delivery of some kind. Something was a little late but expected soon.

Ziad was at the green-room door when I rounded the corner. He wasn't messed up like he'd been in a brawl, but that didn't mean anything. Jess had told me that Matt was very good about not getting people in the face. Not when they had to go onstage right away.

In the green room, Ash Rose was getting caught up on current events by Connor and Charlie. Thom, Reiss, and Brennan were missing, but they all sang, so I figured they'd gone to the practice room to warm their voices up. I had no theory about where Emilie had gone.

Connor slammed his mouth closed the moment Ziad and I entered the room, as if it were a secret that they'd all be talking about Matt and Jess.

"You might as well keep going," I said. Connor glanced at Ziad, who shrugged. He made it look elegant.

"We were pretty much done," Connor said. "I think I told them everything. Except for the stuff we don't know."

"I can't believe Matt Garrett is… I don't know. I guess I don't know what he is," Kayla said.

"I'm never surprised when an actor is an asshole," Ash said. "I did some kids' shows when I was little, and they were so gross to the older girls. Like, grown men. She's twelve, fucko. One guy got fired because he asked a twelve-year-old girl if… I don't even want to say, but it was disgusting. Even the other gross guys were, like, he has to go."

"Actors are the fucking worst," Izzy agreed. Ziad looked as if he might say something, but nothing came out. I would have been interested to hear it, since he likely agreed and yet was an actor himself. "Except directors. Directors are the absolute fucking worst."

"Except producers," Ash said. "They're worse."

"So… everybody," Connor said.

Ash eyed him. "Pretty much."

"How'd your set go?" I asked, hoping to shut this topic down before Connor made another flip comment and got fed a game controller by the pink-haired furies.

"Okay?" Ash said. She turned to Kayla and Izzy for confirmation.

"The crowd's old," Izzy said. "I don't think they even knew who we were."

"Old old?" I asked, "Or old like me?"

"Like you," Izzy said. That wasn't great for my ego, but it was good news for Jess, since he also didn't go over well with the walker-and-shingles crowd. Early thirties was fine.

"Sarah said we sounded good," Kayla said.

"You met the elusive Sarah," I said. Izzy got a twist at the left side of her mouth that I realized was her smile.

"We met her before the show too. She's tall. Really thin. She's wearing a long blue dress."

"And massive headphones," Ash said. "Not ear-buds. I guess she wants everyone to know she's the director."

"I thought the kids of today liked massive headphones," I said.

Ash stared at me with disbelief. "That's for music."

"Silly me. Did Sarah say anything else?"

"No. She was busy," Izzy said.

"If I were as tall as her, I'd wear miniskirts everywhere," Kayla said. "She could totally dress like a model."

"She probably wants people to take her seriously," Ash said.

"What difference does it make what she wears?" Kayla asked. "Why shouldn't she be taken seriously in whatever clothes she wants?"

"I didn't say it was right, I just said people are like that," Ash said. I took the opportunity, with the three of them focused on each other, to head for the kitchenette. The food had been removed. Ziad had probably been happy to see that, unless he no longer cared about anything but how deeply pissed off he was.

He was next to the coffee, his eyes on the place where he'd dropped his mug.

"Security came in to get the food, and they swept up while they were here," Charlie told us.

"Yeah, they were excited about it," Connor said. "In no way did they consider catering and janitorial work beneath them."

"Matt probably insisted that everyone except crew and security be sent home," Ziad said. "He'd be scared some peon might take a picture of him on the shitter."

"Would the peon take that photo from a hiding place in the shower?" I asked. "Or does Matt leave the bathroom door open?"

"Does he?" Charlie asked. "Is he Connor's long-lost brother?"

"For at least the hundredth time," Connor said, "that is not weird. No one locked the bathroom door when I was growing up. It's a farm thing."

"I also grew up on a farm," I said. "It isn't a farm thing. Seriously, though, is Matt really that paranoid?"

"Is it paranoid," Ziad said, "to think everyone wants to see your dick?"

"Optimistic?" I suggested. "To be fair, a lot of people do want to see Matt's whole package. Maybe he really does get people hiding in the shower. Jess gets people trying to break in to his hotel room."

"Me too," Ziad said.

"Us three," Connor said. The Ash Rose kids said nothing but looked sad and hopeful, like a hotel-room break-in was a rare prize, only to be contemplated in their most ambitious dreams.

I got myself a can of Sprite, reminded myself that Ziad had reasons to be an asshole, and offered one to him too. He shook his head. The can was warm, but I wasn't that thirsty and didn't care. It was mainly something to do with my hands.

"How did your talk with Matt go?"

"That's personal," he said. "Actually personal, not like Matt's dick."

"Right." I was watching to see if he was in pain, guarding a sore spot where a fist had landed. It was tough to be certain, but at least now, mostly standing still, he seemed okay.

"It was a waste of time," Ziad said. "Talking to Matt. Are you surprised to hear it?"

"No."

He didn't ask where Jess was, but he also didn't accuse Jess of being an enabler, a blackmailer, or the president of Matt's fan club, so it was something like progress.

"Will you be okay to do your set?" I asked.

"I'm a professional," he told me.

I flashed back six months to Jess, his walking pneumonia elevated to the kind that people died from, insisting that he could do his show in Calgary that night. If not that, then Vancouver the next night. He was a professional. He'd be fine.

"Let me know if you change your mind," I told him. "At this point, I'd be happy to pull a fire alarm. Or start a fire."

We looked at each other. For a moment I thought there might have been another reason he didn't like Jess. Because Ziad was pretty, and he was smart, but Jess was prettier and likely smarter. And Jess would be the answer if Ziad asked me what I was doing next Saturday night.

"Where'd your friends go?" he asked.

"Out front. They're watching the show."

"Oh shit, the show!" Connor said. "We're up, like… now."

He went over the back of the couch. Charlie went around. Izzy watched, shaking her head.

"They knew Duncan went on after us," she said.

"Duncan only had a ten-minute slot," Kayla said, pointing at the whiteboard.

"The emcee will stretch," Ash said. "He loves his own voice."

"So much," Kayla confirmed.

"He smells like a brewery," Izzy said. "I've been to one. In Germany. It's intense. It gets right up your nose."

I didn't know whether that last bit was about the smell of the brewery or the DJ or both.

"I'd bet they're serving booze in the other backstage area," I said. "Where the charity people and the media are."

"The charity people never even came to say hi," Kayla said. "Don't they usually come and say hi and thanks and stuff? And get autographs or whatever?"

Izzy snorted. "They're probably too good to hang out with crazy people. It's okay to raise money for crazy people, but you don't want to talk to them. Ew."

I suspected that was unfair and that we were separated for reasons of security or logistics, but I wasn't officially a crazy person, so I didn't think my two cents were wanted.

"Well, thank God they stepped in to protect us crazy people," Ziad said, "and got all the devil water out of here. I woke up this morning thinking what I need is someone to save me from myself."

"I thought you didn't drink," Kayla said. Ziad gave her an exasperated look.

"I am saying I don't need anyone else's help to not drink. I've been not drinking all my life."

That might have been true. Or he might have been cranky because he'd decided he deserved a drink and had been thinking about getting one.

"You go on after the band," I reminded him. "If you're wanting to get blitzed, you might want to hit pause on that and come back to it later."

"Are you fucking deaf? I said I wasn't planning to drink."

Not answering that seemed like the smart thing to do. I drank my warm Sprite and stared at the far wall.

"Fuck this," Ziad said. He didn't say what exactly needed fucking, just marched out of the green room. He did not, this time, slam the door. He might have been going back to Matt's room or to the practice room or his dressing room or to a bar up the street.

"He's super pissed," Kayla said.

"Me too," I said. "But you don't know it because I swear less and plan more arson."

"Cool," Izzy said. "Give us a heads-up if you're gonna burn this place to the ground."

"I'll try," I said. "But remember, if you hear the fire alarm, it's not a drill."

Jesse was still on his half hour of mandatory meditation, and he'd be in the practice room after that, so I left him alone. I went backstage and watched the Twist from the wings while Vic moved in and out of the shadows.

They were solid, like I'd expected. Not life-changing. I doubted a Twist performance had ever reached the depths of anyone's soul. But they obviously loved music and loved being onstage, and they pulled the audience along. I'd never seen them be less than a good time.

They didn't know I'd seen them at all, though actually I'd caught part of a show three times. It was hard not to see them in Canada, given how often they toured and how many bar and festival shows they'd done in the early years. As Jess had once said about another band, "Those guys would play the opening of someone's fridge."

I could have let Thom know I was at those shows and gone backstage to see him. I'd even wanted to. But he'd always been bullish on Jess and me as a couple, and I hadn't been prepared for his questions about what had gone wrong and did I think it could be fixed.

At least Jess and I had made him happy tonight.

My mind wandered as their set went on, and I scanned the backstage area, seeing how things were arranged and divining the plan. I realized there was a reason the production team had put comics between the bands, aside from variety. They had a curtain near the front that could be pulled to hide the band set-ups, leaving a comic room to do a set right at the lip of the stage while crews reset the band area behind the curtain. Once the Twist was off, they'd pull everything except the piano and two mics, one at the piano and one mid-stage. Then they'd move in Jesse's acoustic guitars, two of them, and set the mics and the piano bench to his height.

They'd have half an hour while Ziad did his set. He had the second longest time slot of the night. Even so, if Jess had been doing his usual show with a full band and all the guitars and every other damned thing, I doubted the crew would have been able to get it done in time.

I caught myself counting pieces of gear that would have to come off the stage and wanting to start moving things myself.

Apparently I was restless.

The changeover was coming. Soon the Twist would be rushing offstage while Ziad stubbed a last cigarette or whatever he did before walking out under the lights. I'd be in the way. I had to find something else to do.

I traced a path past the practice room and the dressing rooms and the green room to the artist-in-residence suite. Or, as it was known for one night only, the castle of Matthew Garrett. Before I'd really thought about it, I found myself knocking on the door.

There was no response at first, which gave me time to think while I kept knocking. It seemed like I intended to have a showdown with Matt. What did I hope to get out of that? What was I going to say to him? Why did I think he would care what I said or even, frankly, let me in the door? Was I some variation on hangry, where the hungry part was replaced with twitchy and a little bored?

"Who is it?"

That was Abraham Lewis. I immediately downgraded my chances of getting into the room from low to subterranean. But there was no sense pretending I was anyone but me.

"It's Ben Ames. Jesse's boyfriend."

There wasn't an answer, or at least not one I was meant to hear. I could hear Lew's voice, but not what he said, and a second voice that… was Matt. I couldn't hear his words either, but I'd been exposed to that voice so often, over so many years, that I knew it as well as, say, Kent's. It only took a word or two, low and through a door, for me to be certain about who it was. Jess was right about fame being weird. Actually I was starting to find it creepy as hell.

The voices went on for about half a minute. Then Lew opened the door.

"Matt will see you," he said. He didn't say, "Matt makes bad decisions," or "Matt doesn't listen to a god-damned thing I tell him," but it was implied. His eye was twitching again, or really the eyelid. Fluttering over his left eye. He waved me in and shut the door behind me.

CHAPTER SIX

I DIDN'T SEE Matt at first. The first thing I noticed was the room itself and how it was more than a room. The part I was in was a living room with a nice conversation area made of loveseats around a glass table. A dining area and a small kitchen were to the left. My best estimate was that Jesse's dressing room, the nice headliner dressing room, could have fit into this suite four times. But that wasn't everything because there were two doors in the far wall, open to small but comfortable-looking bedrooms. On my side of the room, a third shut door led to what was probably the bathroom. So Matt did close the bathroom door.

The reason I hadn't seen Matt was that he was in the kitchen, as far left and back as he could get and in the shadows. He stepped forward once the door to the hall was closed.

"So you're Ben."

I could not possibly overstate the strangeness of that moment. First was the surreality of facing down Matt Garrett. He was a person I saw on screens, some of them IMAX-sized. That was the universe in which this alien creature lived. Seeing him here, in my world, made me feel a little bit like I was losing my mind.

There were probably people who felt a similar way when they saw Jess in the real world, but even Jack Lowe was more of a real-world kind of guy than Matt. He was someone you saw in live shows and on phone screens and sometimes showing up at the local bar because he could do it and not get fully mobbed. Matt was Other, and it did not seem possible that he was standing in front of me, no taller than I was and taking a further chunk out of my sanity by saying, "So you're Ben" like he knew a lot more than my name.

I said pointlessly, "Yep. I'm Ben."

He didn't come closer than a few metres away, and he didn't offer to shake hands. He was appraising me.

"Jess talked about you sometimes."

I had thought that Jess would be Jack to him. Lew had called him Jack.

"He mentioned you to me too," I said. Matt nodded like he'd expected that. He should have. His manager knew Jess had told me everything.

"I'm sure he did," Matt said. The charming self-deprecation he slathered all over that, the way he ducked his head with embarrassment, was familiar from a dozen roles. The public loved it. For me, it wasn't playing as well.

"What do you think he said?" I asked. Matt made a wide-eyed "wow, that's a toughie" face.

"It could have been any number of things," he said. "We spent a lot of time together. But we did have a misunderstanding toward the end, and I think he's still living in that."

"A misunderstanding?" I said. "You sure?"

He thought about it—or pretended to.

"Ben, would you like to sit down? I feel like this is something we should talk through."

Lew, who I'd nearly forgotten was there, moved between us.

"I think we can all agree to disagree," he said. "Mr. Ames, you have an idea about what happened because of what Jack told you. Obviously, Matt and I have a different perspective. Is there really any point to getting wound up about something that's long over and that we'll probably never see eye-to-eye on?"

I gave Lew an exaggerated shrug. "I'm willing to make time for it."

Matt gestured toward the seating area. His buffed nails gleamed. I pictured someone kneeling at his feet like a Roman slave, gently polishing each nail to perfection while Matt gave orders to the rest of his people or maybe took his cock out.

I made myself comfortable on the loveseat closest to the door. They were leather, or close enough to fool me, and more comfortable by a mile than the couches in the green room. Matt was probably disappointed they weren't covered in endangered-rhino hide, but he took a seat without complaining about it.

"Can Lew get you anything?" he asked. I glanced at Lewis to see how he was taking that, since he was a manager and not a concierge. His face gave nothing away.

"I'm fine," I said.

"So. You know Jess and I dated for a few months."

"I know you were pretending to date," I said. He scrunched up his face. It didn't make him any less handsome.

"Ehhhh… it's always more complicated than that. Yes, we did start to date for promotional reasons. It's not uncommon in this industry. I don't know how much Jess has told you about that."

I didn't care for the way he was talking, like he and Jess were close friends and I was an acquaintance Jess hit up on Facebook every now and then. Worse than his actual words was how good he was at selling it. How real he made it sound. I knew he was a goddamned liar, and still I had to concentrate to see past the overlay, the impression that he was a decent, honest guy with nothing to hide.

Not for the first time or the last, it occurred to me that punching him in the face might be more productive and satisfying than a conversation.

"Jess told me why you were pretending to date," I said evenly. For a second, maybe less, I saw his easy confidence falter. He was used to charming people. It would have been unnerving for him when it didn't seem to be working.

"We spent a lot of time together," he said. "I'm usually in a kind of bubble. A lot of security. It's part of the lifestyle. Anyone on the inside of that, we're going to be spending, you know, a lot of time together."

"Time," I said. "A lot of it. Got it."

"You probably think the life of a celebrity is always exciting."

I didn't. I said nothing. Matt crossed his legs with a hiss from his fashionably slim black pants. They were similar to the ones Jess had worn earlier, maybe even the same label. Poured-on pants were okay on guys Jesse's size but made anyone with broad shoulders seem like they'd stolen their legs off an underfed giraffe. Matt was no exception.

"I'll be honest, it's pretty boring sometimes. Lot of sitting around. Waiting to shoot a scene. Waiting to do an interview. Waiting to go to a party."

"Excruciating," I said.

"It's natural to bond with the people you spend that kind of time with," he said. "It can be a pretty intense bond. I'm sure Jess would tell you the same."

If Matt had really known Jess, he'd have known that Jess would bond with people over a two-minute elevator ride. If Jess had gotten to like Matt over those months, and he probably had, there wouldn't have been anything special about it.

"He's a friendly guy," I said.

"This kind of situation, there's no expectation that it's going to be a genuine romantic relationship, if that's what you want to call it, but obviously if it works out, that's great. It's kind of like a blind date that lasts for months instead of one night."

I pressed my back teeth together, hard, to keep my mouth closed. The first rule of detecting—and talking to assholes—was not to take the shovel away when people were digging themselves into the ground.

"And I don't have to tell you that Jess and I had great chemistry. That's what made the whole thing work. People can tell if there's no spark, no matter how much you play it up in public."

He could have been on a talk show the way he was leaning back in his seat and raconteuring. Explaining the business to the host but really to the rubes at home.

"Is that right?" I said. "I thought that's what acting was for."

If he understood it was a dig, he didn't let on. He shook his head sadly.

"Some things you can't fake."

I crossed my legs, not because I wanted to, but because it would slow me down if I found myself starting to go over the table at Matt. He tugged at the sleeves of his light blue sweater, which was riding up a little on his arms, probably because his shoulders were tense. The sweater looked like wool, and I would have been a walking hive if I'd tried to wear it like that, no shirt underneath. But Matt was a tough guy.

"So we had this chemistry, and you know how it is. We flirted. I'm sure you know that Jess likes to flirt."

"He's always saying sexy things. Like no."

Matt kept smiling, but it clearly wasn't easy. I could see the strain around his eyes.

"It was basically a series of misunderstandings. We were backstage before one of his shows, and we'd been flirting a little and drinking a little, and I guess I misread the signs. Could happen to anyone. It's probably happened to you."

"What has? Slugging a guy I outweigh by a hundred pounds because he didn't want to have sex with me?"

Matt spread his hands to show me he was helpless, confused. Sad that it had all come to this.

"I know Jess sees things a certain way, and that's what you've heard. That's how it felt to him. I get that. To me… I made a pass, and he hit me. He took the first shot."

"He shoved you. But I wouldn't blame him if he had hit you. He told you from day one that he wasn't interested."

"That's what he said out loud," Matt said. "But he gave me a lot of signals. We're both adults. I shouldn't have to tell you that a guy can tell you he's interested without saying a word."

"Sorry if I looked distracted," I said. "I was picturing you saying that in a witness box."

For the first time, Matt's gee-shucks persona slipped. His smile was too big and sharp-toothed as he said, "Jess knows better than to try that."

"Okay, gentlemen, that's enough." Lew was on the move, coming to stand behind Matt. "We've all got different ideas about what happened that night—"

"You're not part of this conversation," I told Lew. "You know how Jess said you and he weren't friends? That goes double for me."

Lew put a hand on Matt's shoulder. I was willing to bet it was a harder grip than it appeared.

"I think it would be a good idea for you to leave now."

"Why did Matt ask Jess about security footage?" I asked Lew. "I'm asking you because Jess doesn't think that was Matt's idea, and I tend to agree. You worried about something coming out? Did this asshole finally mess with someone who's willing to report it?"

Lew's eyes narrowed. "Leave or I will have security—"

He didn't finish that sentence because at that moment the lock beeped and Budget Leto, aka Alex, aka the Boyfriend, swanned in.

"That comedian is a hack," he said as he entered. "An absolute no-talent nobody."

"Told you, babe," Matt said. He held out a hand, and his boyfriend sashayed over to take it as Lew returned to his post near the kitchen.

Everything Alex did was exaggerated, from the sway of his hips to the drawn-out vowels in his speech. Matt made room on the loveseat, and Alex flounced down beside him. He cuddled up against Matt's side. Matt didn't cuddle back or even look at him. I wouldn't have wanted to cuddle with Alex, either, but Matt was supposed to like the guy.

Under the ridiculous getup and the snottiness, Alex had looks. He was lithe and angular, and his light green eyes were large, with a slight uptilt at the outside. His thick, wavy blond hair was either natural or a remarkable simulation.

"Who's this?" Alex asked Matt.

"This is Ben Ames," Matt said. "He's Jack Lowe's boyfriend."

"Ooooh. I heard Jack Lowe was dating a civilian."

I'd heard Jesse use that term before: civilian, for people who weren't famous. Like famous people were part of some overpaid peacetime army. Jess knew I didn't find it endearing.

"You're not a civilian?" I asked. Alex pretended to be amused rather than offended. It didn't work. Whatever he was, he was obviously not an actor.

"I was a blue check when it meant something."

"Sure," I said. "Like Anthony Scaramucci. Or the City of Red Deer."

"Alex is an artist," Matt informed me. "Conceptual. Have you seen *The Gaming Chair*? It takes *My Bed* as a jumping off point for a zoomer confessional. That's how the *New York Times* described it."

"Got past me somehow," I said.

"It's not a redux," Alex said with a disapproving glance at Matt. "It's not razors and bloody underwear. It's the dichotomy between screen life and RL. I nearly called it RL. I should have. *My Bed*? Do I look like an irrelevant hag?"

I didn't answer that, much as I would have liked to. The best response to a tantrum was to wait it out. Matt seemed to feel the same way since he wasn't saying anything either. In the background, Lew's head dipped as if he were about to fall asleep while standing.

Finally, Alex said, "I have an NYFA Fellowship."

I had no idea what that was. I nodded. "Congratulations."

"Yes."

"It's challenging work," Matt told me. "Alex's art. It's not for everyone."

In other words, not for the likes of me.

"Babe," Matt said, "can you check on the food? It's supposed to be here by now."

Alex glanced at me, like he was checking to see whether I'd heard that. Since I was sitting right there and Matt had said it out loud and I was not deaf, the answer seemed obvious.

"Can't Lew do that?" he asked. "Isn't that his job?"

Lew seemed pained. I didn't blame him. It was one thing to be disrespected by your A-list meal ticket and a whole other thing to get sent on errands by your client's… whatever the hell Alex was.

"Lew and I need to talk," Matt said. "Please? I'll make it up to you later."

Alex sighed dramatically and gave Matt a sloppy kiss before flouncing away. He didn't slam the door on his way out, but he didn't ease it shut either.

"I didn't know you were into art," I said. Matt surprised me by throwing his head back and laughing. It sounded, of all things, sincere.

"Art. Fuck me. His masterpiece? *The Gaming Chair*? It's a fucking chair. I saw that *My Bed* thing years ago, and that is some crazy chick's bed. Literally. She packed up her bed and a bunch of trash, moved it to a museum, boom! Now it's art. Alex packed up his chair. You got a chair? Maybe you could be an artist too."

"You sounded like you were into it," I said. He spread his hands and grinned, that same wolfish grin he'd had when he'd said Jess would know better than to take him to court.

"Acting."

"So what are you doing with him if you don't respect his art?" I said. "Are you hoping he'll let you borrow his clothes?"

"He *is* a work of art," Matt told me. "Twenty years old, absolutely no inhibitions. Flexible like a fucking gymnast. You forget what twenty was like. The stamina. And he does whatever I tell him to do."

In the kitchen, Lew coughed. Matt glanced at him so quickly I almost missed it. His face shifted back into the mask of the genial all-American.

"I've got a good thing going, and I don't want some misunderstanding from my past coming around to ruin it," he told me. "Alex gets jealous, even when something is long over. I don't want to upset him. That's why I asked about the footage."

"Because you thought it might upset Alex."

"That's right."

"To see you committing sexual assault."

Matt's shoulders tensed. He made himself lean back against the couch, and he kept his face relaxed. It was a good performance, maybe one of the best he had in him, but I could tell he wanted to come at me. Right over the glass table with the gold treble clefs holding it up at the corners like it was a scarred, beer-soaked table in a dive bar.

I would have welcomed it.

He kept himself under control, though, and I did the same.

"That is an inaccurate characterization," he said. My fists clenched. I took a few deep breaths.

"Can I tell you what I think is an inaccurate characterization? Jess thinks you're a tragic figure. Gaslit by fame. Conditioned to expect gratification. He thinks you can't stand hearing the word no because you're not used to hearing it, like being able to accept rejection is a muscle that atrophies. Does that sound like you?"

As someone who didn't want to be seen as either culpable or pathetic, Matt was on the spot.

"Jess misunderstood the entire situation," he said flatly. No salesmanship at all.

"I agree," I said. "Because I don't think you're incapable of hearing the word no, and I don't think fame has melted your brain. I think you're a skilled predator who convinces people to feel bad for him while he's abusing them. I don't think you have momentary lapses. I think you condition people for months before you make a move. And I think you'd better stay away from Jess, because I will pull your spine out through your chest if I catch you going to work on him again."

"All right, now we are definitely done here," Lew said. He was heading for me, a little unsteady but moving at a good clip. I stood.

"I sure hope so."

Matt was seething. His shoulders were down, eyes narrowed, head ducked, and his back pressed deep into the loveseat like the heat of his rage had welded him to it. That was fine. He didn't have to like what I'd said. He just had to believe it.

Lew swung the door open for my exit, and we were both momentarily thrown by the sight of a food cart blocking my exit. Apparently Alex had tracked down Matt's food order and abandoned it there. That or he'd swanned off and someone else had delivered it. Either way, the food was here, and Alex was nowhere in sight. Lew pulled the cart into the room, and I slipped past it and into the hall.

Jess would be onstage soon. I went to his dressing room, swiped myself in, and took something from the bathroom counter before I went backstage.

When I got to the wings, I ran into a crowd. Reiss, Brennan, and Thom were hanging around watching the end of Ziad's set. The Ash Rose gang were loitering by the fly gallery, and Emilie and Dylan were further back in the shadows. Vic and the crew were working around them. Ziad was delivering his big wrap up, and the audience was roaring. The backstage crowd didn't seem as excited about it, but Thom and Brennan gave Ziad big smiles and back slaps as he strode into the wings.

"Great set," Brennan told him. Ziad gave him a tight smile and kept going through the soundproof doors to the dressing rooms.

"Fuck us for being nice," Thom said. Vic glared at him and put a finger to her lips. The emcee wasn't on stage yet, and it was quiet enough that the audience might have heard him. I checked but didn't see any sign of it on their faces.

The emcee came onstage from the other side, encouraging the crowd's applause with his hands and a drunken grin. Izzy had not been exaggerating about his condition. He went into a spiel about Ziad, wasn't he something, how about him. I felt something against my shoulder and looked down to see Jess there, waiting for the emcee to move on from saying generic overblown things about Ziad to saying generic overblown things about him.

"You ready?" I asked softly. He nodded. I moved to stand in front of him and showed him the lipstick I'd taken from his dressing room. He was confused for a moment, then got it and grinned.

"Nice, Casanova," he told me. I answered that by kissing him. He was nicely warm, and the fabric of his fancy outfit felt luxurious under my hands. When we were done, I handed him the lipstick, and he carefully repainted the scarlet before handing the tube back to me and moving to the edge of the stage.

CHAPTER SEVEN

I COULD HEAR people approaching behind me, all of them trying to be quiet. Reiss, Brennan, and Thom. Emilie and Dylan. The pink-hairs. Izzy saw my face, smirked, and handed me a cloth from her small silver crossbody bag. It looked like an eyeglass wipe, but I got the point, used it to scrub the lipstick off my face, and gave it back.

Jack Lowe was introduced and went onstage to cheers and applause. Of course all the people around me were chasing this kind of work, a job where people went nuts because you showed up. Jess rolled his eyes when I said things like that because "all that cheering comes with *expectations*, Ben," but cops and teachers and even retail clerks had expectations on them too. No one cheered them just because they'd dragged themselves into the office and put on their game faces.

He opened with one of his bigger hits. Not the biggest. His Billboard number one was encore bait in a regular show, and it would be the last number in this show. But he'd picked a first song that everyone would recognize, even though he was playing it slow and quiet and on piano instead of loud and fast on an electric guitar.

It was almost a fairy tale, a story about a guy who had an affair with the monster under his bed because it knew what scared him most. It wasn't so simple in Jess's words. He treated songs like magic shows, all misdirection and flashing lights and a haze of innuendo changing the shape of everything.

People speculated online about what Jesse's songs were about, and there had always been a lot of talk about this one. Who was the monster under the bed? Was it the bassist who'd left the band suddenly between two legs of a tour? The guy Jess had been seen with in both Vancouver and New York? Or that guy he'd lived with in college in Toronto?

I didn't think it was about anyone in particular, and it might not have been about a person at all. Jess had liked Keats in university, the only time in a person's life when liking romantic poets was not a serious character flaw. "For many a time, I have been half in love with easeful death." My guess was that the monster under the bed was an allegory.

Then again, considering Jack Lowe's dating history, maybe some piece of work had insisted on sleeping down there, wearing a Dracula costume and hissing if Jess opened the blinds. Anything was possible. I didn't ask Jess what his songs were about, so I was never going to know.

Emilie and Dylan were sitting on a speaker case and whispering to each other about something. Dylan was making chord shapes with their hand, up and down the neck of an imaginary guitar. Jess did that too, without even knowing he was doing it. More often he'd play an invisible piano on his legs or a table or the dashboard of my car.

Dylan seemed to be trying to figure out what Jess had done with the song. I could have told them he'd moved things from the harmony lines into the melody, since he didn't have a whole band up there to carry those parts. I knew this not because I knew a damned thing about music or even cared, really, but because I'd had a front row seat for months while Jess reworked his back catalogue.

He'd started even before his broken arm was out of its cast, plunking around on the upright grand he'd tucked into the corner of the living room. Adjusting the pacing and the flow, moving the bridge around. He wrote on the piano, usually, so it had been an act of deconstruction for some of the songs. He was bringing them back to the moment of their birth.

Once the cast was off, he'd grabbed an acoustic guitar. For one song he'd picked up an oddball dulcimer guitar and, after struggling with it for a few hours, had done something to it with my hacksaw. Added frets, I thought, though I couldn't be sure.

He'd been frustrated and aching, so much strength lost over those two months of not playing piano or guitar. He'd also been a wreck, thinking the audience might hate the acoustic sound or that he wouldn't be able to make the songs worth listening to. He'd moved them from piano to guitar and back again, trying to get it right.

The only reason he'd been relaxed heading onto the stage was fatalism. It was going to go however it was going to go.

So yes, I'd known he was worried, but I hadn't realized how nervous I'd been for him until he threw his head back—pure performance, because it was bad technique—and sang like he was letting out a breath he'd been holding for years. A breath and some demons and a near death on a mountainside. He'd sounded good in the living room, but not like this. I felt like I could breathe again too.

Beside me the pink crew were misting up. Brennen, Thom, and Reiss were watching intently, with serious expressions. They could see the work and the skill. Jess would have been pleased by that. He pretended that he was too cool for technical music school, but secretly he liked for people to know he had the goods.

I heard a rustling behind me and turned to see Alex, of all people, joining the crowd in the wings. He was at the back of the group, and it was dark enough there that I couldn't make out his expression. He was mainly making his presence known through his white clothes and citrusy cologne. It smelled like Louis Vuitton and probably was, since Matt could afford it.

Jess did a few more songs and some light banter before grabbing a mic and turning on his piano bench to face the audience. This was the contractually obligated mental-illness talk, which he started by telling the audience that he had major depressive disorder and, statistically, so did about one in twenty of them.

Then he talked about his life. About not being able to get out of bed and feeling guilty for not being able to get out of bed. The way he'd forget everything he'd done in the last half hour or the name of someone he'd known for a decade—not forget for a moment but lose it entirely down an infinite well. How he could be fine, having a good day by any reasonable standards, and suddenly, for no reason, be as lost and miserable as if someone he loved had died.

It was genuine, but all I could hear was what he didn't say. Nothing about the toll of playing a role on stage or being famous on social media or what it was like to have a million strangers convinced they knew the real you. Those things would have reminded the audience that he was rich and famous and might have made them feel complicit in something, neither of which would have won him any friends.

So he kept it relatable and threw wry jokes and some self-deprecation into the deal. It was a terrific example of mental illness all around, the people-pleasing and the belief that he didn't deserve genuine sympathy. The only thing missing was a banner at the back of the stage that said, You'd Hate the Real Me. Something to think about for his next tour.

Christ alone knew what Matt would say in a few minutes, standing in front of that audience and making his own speech about mental health. "I'm Matt, and I'm a serial abuser"? And the audience would shout back, "Hi, Matt! You're very attractive, so it's okay!"

He'd probably talk about grief. Something everyone went through that didn't suggest there was anything wrong with the great Matt Garrett and his equally great brain. Audience, I want you to know that I've been sad, but sad like a normal person. I feel bad for all the nut-jobs you've seen here tonight. I am a nice and normal guy. Please give generously.

How he was going to stretch that to several minutes, I did not know. I was curious as hell to see it.

Jess wound things up with two more songs and a gracious farewell, thanking the audience for supporting the charity and the charity for inviting him. He didn't say anything about Matt, and he booked it offstage as soon as he was done, giving the emcee no opportunity to grab his arm and drag him into a conversation. I moved to the side to give him room to get past me before Matt showed up or the director tried one last time to guilt him into an introduction. Everyone else seemed to get the hint, because they moved too.

Jess put his hands on people's arms and backs as he passed, a little thank you for the support, and we closed behind him like the Red Sea once he was away from the wings and approaching the doors.

If the next act up had been a band or comic, I'd have expected them to appear at the wings during Jesse's last song, ready for their cue. Matt, being a movie star, was used to people leaving him in his trailer until the last possible second and then bringing him onto a set that was completely prepared for him. It was not a huge surprise that he'd chosen to take his sweet time instead of waiting in the wings. It was also possible that he didn't want to run into Jesse. Or me. Maybe especially me.

It was weird, though, that he wasn't coming in as we went out. He was seconds away from being actually, noticeably late. Vic wasn't anywhere to be seen, so most likely she'd gone to roust the guy. Gently. With boundless respect.

I saw Alex as we were leaving the backstage area. He'd moved away from the wings to a place further back in the darkness, all the way behind the backdrop. If it hadn't been for his silver-and-white clothing and the flash of sequins in what little light there was, I wouldn't have seen him at all. I assumed he was waiting to greet

his boyfriend and working on some clever remark
about Jess being, oh my God, talentless and old.

Once we were in the hallway, Emilie and Dylan
slipped into the practice room, and everyone else went
toward the green room, down the hall that branched to
our left.

Duncan appeared in the hall, coming from the right,
where the stage door was. He was dusted in snow, and
the tears the wind had drawn from his eyes had frozen
into sharp crystals on his eyelashes. That would have
happened almost instantly. Snow was flying around out
there, not because it was snowing—it was too cold for
that—but because the wind was picking it up from every building and tree and streetlight.

Duncan was breathing painfully and trying to un-
zip his parka as he walked. The air would have seared
his lungs, freeze-drying them with every breath, turning them into astronaut ice cream. As he struggled, with
numb fingers, to separate his jacket's zipper from the
wind flaps around it, one of his thick black gloves fell
from a pocket. Thom, trailing the pack, picked up the
glove and chased Duncan to return it.

"Th-thanks," Duncan said. "Lord Jesus, it is moth-
erfucking cold out there." He noticed Jesse and me and
raised a hand. "Did Matt go on yet? Did I miss it?"

"He's supposed to be on," Jess said. "He's not in
there, though. The emcee is stalling for him."

"Good," Duncan said. "Good. If you see my nuts,
could you wrap them in a blanket and come find me?
They froze the fuck off."

"Absolutely," Jess promised. Duncan gave him a
thumbs-up and went through the doors to backstage.

And with that, we were alone in the hall. Jess
turned to me and gave me a tired but genuine smile.

"What a day," he said.

I went to him and put my arms around his waist. "Want to make a run for it?"

"Do I want you to make a run for it, start the car, come back here, and then twenty minutes later, we make a run for it? Is that what you're asking?"

"That is what I'm asking. Yes."

He moved in for a kiss. Then, with his mouth still close to mine, he said, "I'm leaving you for someone with remote start."

I pulled back enough to kiss his forehead. "I understand."

He pressed his face against my shoulder. I felt him shut his eyes. "I should get changed, but it's too much like work."

"You don't want to stay in the fancy outfit for the media?"

He sighed theatrically deep.

"I was gonna say that there is no media. But there will be now. For him. Fuck it. I dunno." He leaned back in my arms and looked at me. "Did I do okay out there?"

I took one arm from around his back and flicked him between the eyes. "Don't pretend you don't know when you've hit one out of the park."

And yet for some reason, his face lit up when he heard it from me. We stood there and stared at each other. I don't know how long that would have gone on for if Vic hadn't gone down the other hallway at a run, heading toward the stage door.

"What the hell?" Jess said.

We went after Vic, through the doors that separated the dressing rooms and green room from the stage door, and found her asking the security guard how in the hell he could have agreed to something.

"Sarah told me to do whatever he wanted," the guard said. He was talking to Vic but eyeing me and Jess. I ignored him and spoke to Vic.

"Is something wrong?"

"I can't find Matt. He must be in his dressing room. He's not opening the door."

The doors all had programmable card locks, so this didn't seem like it should be a problem. I knew how I would have set things up if I'd been in charge of the place.

"Doesn't your pass work on all the doors?" I asked. "What if you need to splash cold water on someone's face and haul them off the bathroom floor?"

Vic's face suggested she had done that more than once and was thinking she might, very soon, need to do it again.

"Yes, of course my pass is supposed to work on all the doors, but Matt asked this idiot here to reprogram his lock, and this idiot did it. Now I'm locked out."

"Sarah said to do whatever he asked me to do," that idiot repeated. Vic glared at him but said nothing.

"So you program the locks and not the keys?" I asked the guard. "That's not usual."

"It's how we do it." He shrugged. "It's easier to manage the locks than the cards."

"My pass might work," Jess said.

"What?" Vic said. I didn't say "What," but I looked it at him as hard as I could.

"Should work," the guard confirmed.

"Jess?" I asked sweetly. He pressed his lips together for a moment before answering.

"Matt told me he'd given me access to his room."

"What? Why?"

"I don't care why," Vic said. "C'mon." Then she did something I'm pretty sure was a last resort for a floor manager. She grabbed the talent's arm and yanked him down the hall. Jess wobbled on his heels and barely righted himself in time to avoid a fall.

"Hey!"

"Sorry," she said but didn't stop dragging him toward Matt's room. I stayed close in case Jess tripped over his stilettos again.

"Did you try texting him?" Jess asked.

"I don't have his number," Vic said.

"Why didn't Lew answer when you knocked?"

"How would I know?"

The green-room door was closed, so the occupants missed out on the bickering as we passed.

At Matt's door, Vic held her hands out to the lock like she was showing off a prize on a game show. Jess took out his card, hesitated, then knocked on the door.

"Matt? Lew? Are you in there?"

"I already fucking did that," Vic said.

Jess knocked harder. "Matt? It's Jesse."

"Tell him you've got the footage he wants," I suggested. Jess gave me the same baleful glare Vic was giving him. Vic was too angry and frazzled to notice I'd said anything.

"Fine," Jess said under his breath. He held his card to the lock, waited for the beep, and pushed open the door. Then he stepped aside to let Vic charge into the room.

We'd barely entered the room ourselves when Vic froze in her tracks.

"Oh no," she said. "No, no, no...."

CHAPTER EIGHT

I WENT AROUND her and Jess and saw what Vic was seeing. Matt Garrett was lying on the floor in front of one of the bedroom doors, now closed. He didn't look good. His face and neck were swollen so badly that his eyes were slits, and his tongue was sticking out the corner of his mouth. His lips were like sausages. I put my head to his chest to feel for breath, though I didn't expect it. I could smell urine and saw a dark patch on his jeans.

"Jess, call 911," I said. "Vic, that woman who came to visit us backstage is a doctor. Go get her."

You had to do it like that—use people's names or at least describe them. You in the blue jacket. You with the red hair. Otherwise, people assumed you were talking to someone else. Vic was hesitating anyway, but that was understandable since I'd asked her to do something both complicated and strange.

"Vic, what am I sending you to do?"

"Get the doctor," she said.

"Right. Go."

She went. Jess had come around to Matt's other side and was crouched beside him.

"Yeah, we need an ambulance at the Calgary Theatre," he said. "Backstage. He's not... I don't think he's breathing."

"He's not," I said. I pressed my knuckles into his chest bone and rubbed, hard, which will wake nearly anyone except a corpse. I loudly asked if he could hear me and was he okay. The answer to both was no. And that was because Matt Garrett was obviously and completely dead.

He was still warm, but that meant nothing. It took hours for a corpse to become noticeably cool in a warm room. Hours for them to go stiff. He had a look and a feel to him, something I couldn't describe but knew well.

I'd seen a lot of corpses over the years. Not that a Calgary cop is running into a murder every night. But people die in a city, all over the place, and other people call 911, and the first responders go. We stand awkwardly over people who've gotten too hot or cold or fell too far or too hard or took too much of the wrong thing. People who've dropped to the thin brown carpet in a seniors' high-rise, somewhere between the recliner and the TV.

I knew death, but a rule had been drilled into every first responder. If the person is not decapitated or stiff or burned to a crisp and you're not a doctor, you don't get to assume they're dead. You start CPR, and once you start, you don't stop until someone takes over or you physically can't do it anymore.

I pulled Matt's mouth as far open as I could and searched for something I could clear out that wasn't a part of him. All I could see was swelling. I used the flashlight on my phone to get a better view, but it didn't make much difference.

None of this was going to make a difference to the dead man, so there was no point worrying about it. I started chest compressions. Across the body from me, Jess blinked like he'd been startled awake.

"Shit," he said, getting to his feet. "Shit, where is it…?"

"Where's what?" I said.

"His EpiPen. He has food allergies," Jess said. Then he repeated it for the operator. "He looks like he's had an allergic reaction. I'm trying to find his EpiPens. I'm gonna put you on speaker."

He did that and set his phone on a side table near me.

"Is he breathing?" It was a woman's voice, calm and even.

"No," Jess called from the kitchen, where he was poking through a pile of things on the counter, lying next to a brown shaving bag. His brow was furrowed, like he couldn't understand what he was seeing. "We're doing chest compressions. His face and neck are swollen. He's got hives on his hands… up his arms. Tongue sticking out… um… his eyes, ah, they're swollen shut. He's not reacting to anything."

"Keep doing compressions. Are you able to give rescue breaths?"

"The throat is closed," I said.

"Try anyway. And leave this line open. We have an ambulance on the way."

I went back to counting under my breath, playing "Stayin' Alive" in my head to keep the rhythm.

Twenty-one, twenty-two.

Matt did have hives on his forearms and his hands. He'd pushed up the sleeves of his fancy sweater. Probably the hives were everywhere, but those were the most obvious ones. His face was such a mess that it was tough to tell what was a hive and what was swelling.

Jess went into the bathroom and opened drawers in there, then cut across to the bedroom with the open door. More drawers and a closet door opening.

Sixty-four, sixty-five.

Jess carefully edged past Matt to the closed bedroom door.

"Lew? Lew, are you in there?"

He knocked, then slammed his fists into the door. I pictured Matt doing the same as his throat closed up. Desperate for an EpiPen or someone to help.

But why hadn't he called 911?

"Lew! Goddamn it!" Jess kicked the door. I was too busy to give advice, but he did okay, hitting a few inches below the doorknob. A splintering sound said he'd made progress. "Matt needs help!"

"What's happening there?" The 911 operator had heard that, apparently.

"Trying to get a door open," Jesse said. He'd shifted his weight to his left leg, ready to make another kick. Had he done this before? It sure seemed that way. I had no idea when or why. I would have loved to know if he'd been in heels that time.

"Do you have an AED? A defibrillator?" the operator asked. Jess scanned the room.

"No. There's probably one in the building somewhere."

"See if you can find it, but stay on the call."

Jess looked at me. I nodded. Using an AED was next on the list of empty gestures I had to perform on a corpse. Jess took the phone and left, propping the door open with some amorphous glass-and-bronze statuette so Vic would be able to get back in.

If I hadn't been counting, and tired, I'd have told him to find the security guard, who would definitely know where the AEDs were, and to get a first-aid kit for good measure. I hoped he'd figure all that out for himself.

If you do chest compressions right, they're exhausting. You have to do them fast, as many as two per second, and deep. You're supposed to push hard enough to break a rib or the breastbone. If you hear something snap, you keep going. You may think this would be no big deal for you if you're a gym rat or some kind of athlete. But I do my gym time, and take it from me, chest compressions will wear you out. If I hadn't known that Luna was probably on the way, I would have switched with Jess and gone after the AED myself.

I'd only been alone with the body for about thirty counts when Kent and Luna came through the door, Vic behind them. Of course Kent had decided to come with Luna. I hadn't predicted it, but I should have.

"I don't know how to tell you this...," Kent said. Ah, hilarious. The implication that I didn't know I was stuck working on a corpse.

"Shut up and get in here," I said.

"Yeah, yeah."

He came around to my side of the body to spell me out while Luna went to the other side and examined her patient.

"EpiPen," she said.

"Can't find them," I said.

Luna sighed. "It doesn't matter anyway."

"What do you mean it doesn't matter?"

That was Vic, standing at Matt's head. She said every. Word. Very. Clearly. In chaos, we control what we can.

It was then that the lightly splintered bedroom door opened and revealed a groggy Abraham Lewis, sleep mask pulled down around his neck and thick headphones on his ears. He was holding on to the door frame to stay upright.

"What the hell is going on?"

Before anyone could tell him, he saw for himself.

"Oh my God...."

He took the headphones off and threw them back the way he'd come.

"Call 911!" he said.

"An ambulance is coming," I told him. "That's a doctor in the red dress. Jess is getting an AED."

"He needs an EpiPen," Lew said.

He was shaking his head like a dog shaking off water, trying to wake up. I went to the kitchen and pointed at the brown leather bag sitting on the counter. Jess had gone straight to it, and maybe that was because it was obvious or because things had been dumped out, but I thought Jess had seen that bag before and had some idea what it was supposed to hold.

"Are they usually in here?" I asked.

"Yeah...."

He made his way unsteadily to the kitchenette. His back was to the group on the floor, so he didn't see Luna gravely shake her head at Vic, or Vic's mouth make a little O, like a fish gasping at the surface.

I backed away from the pile on the counter so Lew could paw through it. I'd had a decent search and hadn't seen an EpiPen, though it was credible that this was where the EpiPen would have been. I'd seen alcohol wipes, a pair of prescription inhalers, and some over-the-counter antihistamines. The lids had been taken off both inhalers and the pills.

"Wha—" Lew gave me a look of horror. "Did he take them?"

I hadn't seen any sign that Matt had used an injector. No used injector or safety cap lying around. But I hadn't had time to search the place, and Jess, who'd been focused on finding unused pens and not discarded caps, might have missed them.

"I don't know," I said.

Vic took out her phone and left the room. Likely reporting to her boss.

I was about to search the rooms for discarded EpiPens when Jess showed up at the door, carrying an AED and a first-aid kit.

"Sorry," he said, crossing the room to Luna. "They moved this stuff and didn't tell security. We had to hunt for it. I told the guard to watch for the ambulance, and it'll come to the stage door. Lunes, do you want to tell 911 anything?"

She shook her head. Jess went around to Matt's other side and took over compressions for Kent, who tried not to look relieved as he moved away.

"There's no point, love," Luna said as Jess began pressing down on Matt's chest. Jess checked to see whether she really meant it, as if that would be some-thing she'd joke about. She nodded, slow and serious. Jess took his hands off Matt's chest.

I looked at Lew to see whether it had registered with him that the CPR had stopped. It didn't seem to have. In fact, he didn't seem like he'd notice if someone had put up theatre marquees with the words "he's dead" on all four walls of the room. He seemed to be struggling to stay awake in spite of the situation. I took his arm and helped him to a seat

The EMTs arrived as I was getting Lew settled. I wondered whether I should ask them to check on Lew if nothing could be done for Matt.

Jesse stood beside Matt and stared blankly at the scene for a moment before picking up his phone and telling the 911 operator that the ambulance had arrived. Thanked her for all her help. Not that Jess had ever been a rude person, but it was funny how scrupulous he'd become about politeness to strangers since he'd started the rock star gig. Probably worried that the 911 operator would see the news tomorrow, figure out who was dead and who'd been on her call, and hit up DeuxMoi to spill the details. Anon pls! Stranger things had happened.

Luna ceded her place by the patient with a familiar "Hello" to the EMTs. They seemed confused for a second as their brains overlaid the person in front of them with their memory of Dr. Fares from Foothills ER. They were a Mutt and Jeff pair, a tall broad-shouldered guy with a dark military fade and a small blond woman with her hair in one of those slicked-back tight ponytails that had to hurt. I didn't recognize them, but they were young and could have started after I left the police.

"Oh, hey, Doc," the tall one said. "What are you doing here?"

"Catching a show," Luna said. "Got called in to take a look at him. I'm afraid there's nothing to be done here."

They gave Matt a once-over anyway, which was not a slight to Luna. They had a job and protocols. But it didn't take them long to decide her assessment was correct.

"Are we calling the ME?" the blond asked. It shouldn't have been a question. He'd died young, healthy, and unexpectedly. Calling the Medical Examiner's office was not optional.

"I'll call it in," Kent offered. "Hey, Tiff."

Of course he knew the blond. To my relief, she didn't seem angry or mortified to see him.

"Holy crap," Tiff said. "You and Dr. Fares are both here? Are you on a date or something?"

"No!"

Kent and Luna both said it at the same time. I would have been hard pressed to say who sounded more horrified.

"They're my guests," Jess said. He didn't add that he was one of the performers or how he knew them in the first place. Tiff didn't ask. I couldn't tell whether she recognized Jess. Probably, since he was in stage clothes, but she was either too professional or too cool to show it.

They almost certainly didn't recognize Matt. They could have been the coolest professionals in the world, but they would have shown something, reacted somehow, if they'd realized who the dead guy was. I'd only recognized Matt because I'd expected to see him in that room and because he was wearing the clothes I'd seen him in about an hour earlier. That, and the hair. His hair was somehow still perfect.

"Do you want to fill out the certificate?" the tall EMT asked. "We've got copies."

Luna, who was perched on the arm of a loveseat, gave that a *hmm* and a thoughtful expression. I didn't know what options she was weighing. Before she could say anything, a high-pitched voice came from the door.

"Oh my God! Matt? Matt!"

Alex flew into the room, white coat flapping like albatross wings. I had an impulse to get between him and Matt's body—in fact started moving before I caught myself. I didn't know why. Old cop instincts, maybe, to do with protecting a crime scene. Even though this wasn't a crime scene.

Right?

I put a pin in that thought. Alex was intercepted by the tall EMT, who was big enough to stop him easily and able to hold him in place while looking at Tiff and Luna for a steer. Normally you'd ask the guy to stay away from the patient, but we'd all agreed the patient was an ex-patient, so did it really matter?

Luna shrugged in a "fuck it" way. Tiff echoed her shrug, and her partner let Alex go.

Alex threw himself forward and went to his knees. He grabbed Matt by his shoulders and shook him, screaming his name. I didn't think he really believed Matt could be shaken awake. This was denial, sure, but you don't see denial where there's nothing being denied. He kept it up for what felt like a long time, though, before his voice broke and the clear sound of Matt's name became garbled and thick and eventually the yelling was crying.

I was distracted enough by Alex that I didn't notice Lew approaching him. Lew crouched next to him and Matt, a slow move that I didn't think he'd be able to get up from.

He didn't make any move toward comforting Alex, which seemed cold. Hell, I wasn't comforting Alex either, but I barely knew the guy.

Jess had scrambled out of the way when he saw Alex coming and was now standing a few feet away looking awkward.

"He's gone," Lew said.

Alex slammed his fists on Matt's chest. The body absorbed the blow into its stillness.

Lew seemed more alert now, or at least aware. He was staring at Matt the way someone might stare at their flooded basement. It was a disaster, but the only way out was through.

I noticed for the first time that he was in sock feet. Probably took his shoes off when he went to lie down. His wool socks were thin enough that I could see them stretching at the tips from the pressure of his toes.

Tiff glanced at her phone. Checking the time, I thought. They had places to be.

"Dr. Fares?" Tiff said.

"Mmm," Luna said. She checked her own phone. "Time of death, twenty-three oh seven."

That was the best she could do, without a time machine. Matt had been dead when we'd found him around ten thirty-five. But Luna didn't have a time machine, so she had no way of knowing exactly when Matt had taken his last breath. She could only say now, in this moment, I'm here, and I'm officially declaring him dead.

The ME's investigator would get closer to the truth by finding out when Matt had last been seen alive.

"Should I get the death certificate for you?" the tall EMT asked.

"Can someone else put their name on the certificate?" Jess asked Luna. "Can the ME do it?"

Luna's brow creased.

"Someone at their office can," she said. "But why?"

I saw Jess's eyes flick to the EMTs before he answered. Or non-answered.

"Trust me?"

Luna shrugged. "All right. I'll leave it."

I could see she didn't get it, but I thought I did. When someone famous died young, conspiracy theories were sure to follow. Luna did not need amateur detectives chasing her around for the rest of her life, trying to prove she'd lied or didn't exist.

Kent came back into the room. I hadn't noticed him leave. His phone was in his hand, so probably he had stepped outside to call the ME's office without the background noise of Alex.

Alex was quieter now, crying softly and sitting beside Matt with one hand on the perfect hair.

"The ME's investigator will be here soon," Kent told the EMTs. This was relevant to them, as they had to wait for the investigator to show before they could cut out.

Jess looked at Kent sharply.

"How much did you tell them?"

"Why would you ask me that?" Kent returned.

Jess crossed the room to Kent, grabbed his arm, and hauled him back outside. Jess kicked the glass figure out of the way as he went so the door would shut behind him.

I took out my phone and texted Jess. *Something I should know?*

The answer came quickly. *If he said Matt Garrett it'll get out.*

I didn't bother to argue since Jess would only have told me I didn't know what I was talking about. I put my phone back in my pocket and looked around the room.

Lew was lost in thought. I couldn't tell whether he was grieving or in shock or still groggy—I was pretty sure he was on a sleeping pill of some kind from the way he was acting and from how hard it had been for Jess to get his attention. He might not have been grieving or in shock at all but instead thinking very hard about how to manage the derailing of his money train.

Luna was trying to get comfortable on the arm of the loveseat. I didn't know why she didn't just shift onto the seat. Maybe she thought it would be too casual. Or maybe she was scared of sitting on salmon.

The glass coffee table held a plate of salmon stuffed with something, cream cheese and some kind of vegetable, with a spring greens salad on the side. I wasn't surprised to see that Matt had been brought something different from the things we'd been served in the green room. If Matt ate rouladen, it would have gold leaf rolled inside.

A few bites were gone from the salmon. A small piece next to the plate seemed to have been chewed and spat out. If that was what had given Matt his allergic reaction, Luna might have been right to be suspicious about the loveseat. Matt could have sprayed that stuff everywhere.

The main piece of salmon looked as if the top had been prised up, and the fork that might have done it was still stuck in the fish. As if Matt had tasted something he hadn't expected or maybe felt the reaction start and wondered what could have done it. The salad seemed untouched.

Vic came back into the room, which likely meant Jess had swiped her in. With his room access that he had for no goddamned reason I could think of.

For once, Vic was not gripping her phone like it was trying to escape. She stopped in the middle of the room and stared at Matt's body.

"Hoo-boy," she said. It was soft enough that I barely heard it. She turned to Luna. "Is he... is it official?"

Luna nodded.

"Yes, dear. I've made the call."

"Fuckity." The word came out like a breath. She glanced over her shoulder at the door. I saw her hand move toward the phone sticking out from a side pocket on her cargo pants. Then she shoved her hand into the pocket of her vest instead and turned to me.

"You know these things," she said. "What should... what happens next?"

"The Medical Examiner's office will send an investigator," I told her. "If someone dies of old age or they were terminally ill, you can skip that step."

"Right, right," Vic said. "And then they'll, um, they'll take him away?"

"Yes," I said. "Unless—"

I stopped. Everyone was looking at me. Even Alex. The only exception was Lew, who was sitting on the floor with his head in his hands. Despair or sleepiness? I couldn't tell.

"Unless?" Vic prompted.

"Unless they think there might have been foul play. Then they secure the scene and call the police."

There it was, a bully of an idea that no one had invited, taking up all the space in the room. No one said anything. Everyone stared. At me or Luna or Matt's body. Lew had lifted his head. He was looking at the food.

"But you're not saying that," Vic said too loudly. "Didn't someone say he had an EpiPen? This was a food allergy. Right?"

"The ME's investigator will try to determine the cause of death," I said. "Sometimes they don't come if the police have been called, but Jess told 911 we had a patient, not a death. So they didn't send cops."

"His appearance is consistent with a severe allergic reaction," Luna added. "I'm sure the investigator will agree."

"Yeah," Vic said. "My cousin's allergic to shellfish. One time a sub place made a seafood sub on the same counter as hers, and they didn't wash between subs, and she swelled the hell up. From, like, nothing. A flake of shrimp. It happens like that, you know?"

"It does," Luna said. "It can take very little."

The door beeped and clicked open, making everyone but Lew twitch. We were all that tense. Jesse and Kent came in, and Jess pushed the door shut behind them.

"Crystal's on call tonight," Kent said. "Just texted me. She lives close, but she needs to run her car. Should be here in about twenty minutes."

This was one of the more annoying aspects of a minus 40-degree cold snap, minus 56 with the wind chill. Everything took longer because you had to run your vehicle before you could drive it. You couldn't get a cab or a ride share for love or money, not with so many vehicles refusing to start because their owners had forgotten to plug in their block heaters or because their 2002 Accord wasn't having it.

"Is that the investigator?" Vic said. "Can you give me her full name for the guest list? Uh, if you said to go to the stage door. If she's going to come in the front…."

She trailed off, seemingly out of ideas for how to handle the needle of an ME in the haystack of the front-of-house crowd. She wasn't about to grab the intercom and announce that the Medical Examiner should meet her at Customer Service.

"I said stage door," Kent confirmed. "You can tell the guard it's Crystal Shaw."

"Cool," Vic said. "Thanks. The guard is Harry, by the way. If you don't want to call him Guard all night."

She left, pulling her phone from her pocket as she went. Keeping her boss apprised, no doubt. I was a little surprised that Sarah wasn't here in person, but she was probably doing damage control with the charity and, for her sins, the media. Telling them Matt was a little under the weather. Couldn't do his speech and we're all very disappointed, but what can you do?

That left a room full of people with nothing to do but wait. Lew had his phone out and checked it a few times. Not like he was reading socials or expecting anything. More like he had calls to make and didn't feel up to the job.

I wandered the room, doing the detective bit. It was something to keep me occupied.

Near the door, tucked against the wall by the kitchenette, was the food cart that had gone into the room earlier, as I'd left to catch Jesse's set. Someone, probably Lew, had placed it there neatly. One metal plate cover was upside down on the skirted tray. That would have been the one that had held Matt's food. I pictured him helping himself, taking the plate and some cutlery and leaving the cover behind. There was a coffee pot on the kitchenette counter, not far from where the brown leather bag had been dumped out. I didn't see a mug on the table where Matt's food was sitting. Was that normal for him? Did he prefer to have coffee after he ate? Jess would know.

Nothing of this mattered, but I couldn't help breaking down the scene. I'd done it since I could remember, long before I became a cop. Back in university Jess had teased me about the way I went through cupboards and read bulletin boards and calendars every time we went to a party in someone's home.

I lifted the covers from the remaining plates on the tray. Both plates were full, one with a small pile of mixed greens and the other with a beef au jus. Those would have been for Alex and Lew. Respectively, I'd guess.

Alex hadn't been there when the food arrived, but Lew had. Maybe he hadn't felt well enough to eat. He hadn't put it in the kitchenette's mini fridge, though, so had he been distracted by something? Or was he, like Matt, accustomed to being tended by gofers and hangers-on?

Over by Matt's body, Lew was saying something to Alex. Whispering. I couldn't make it out. The two of them got up, went into Lew's room and shut the door behind them. I did not suspect an assignation.

I opened the skirt on the cart to find coffee cups, sugar, stevia, honey, agave, monk-fruit sweetener, cream, small packets of almond, soy, and oat milk—non-GMO, each package proclaimed—and stir sticks made of "pure organic bamboo," according to their plastic wraps. There was no indication of what was special about the coffee, but single-source couldn't have been good enough. Someone had probably gone through the beans and made sure they were all the same shade of brown. A brown bag with extra packets said Vincitore on the side, above a local phone number. The catering company, most likely.

Jess had noticed what I was doing but said nothing. Mostly he was scrolling on his phone. Checking to see whether the word was out. I assumed it wasn't because otherwise he'd probably have said something.

I took a better look at the things that had been spilled from the brown bag but saw nothing I hadn't noticed before. I couldn't tell how much of anything Matt had taken. I could see panic in the way things had been not only dumped out but spread around, by Matt but also by Jesse and Lew. Sifting got more violent when people were desperate to find something, as if shoving things around would make the missing item appear. No different, really, from Jesse trying to shape the world to his will.

The drawers and cupboards in the kitchenette were all neatly closed, and I hadn't seen Lew go through them. Therefore neither he nor Matt had figured the EpiPens could be in there. For whatever reason, Jess hadn't gone through them either.

The EMTs were sitting on the unused loveseat. Right at the edge, awkwardly, like they didn't want anyone to catch them getting too comfortable. They were staring at their phones. Whatever the audience had been told about Matt—that he was ill or couldn't make it—it would have to be running loose by now. Would they make the connection? Tiff was typing something, but she hadn't said anything or done an obvious double-take of the body, so I didn't think it was about Matt. For all I knew, she was on Tinder. Or possible reporting to dispatch about where they were and how much longer they expected to be.

I looked at Matt's food again. I didn't go to it, just eyeballed it from the kitchen. I imagined Matt taking it to the couch. Putting the plate on the table. No glass. Because he'd had both hands full, one with a plate and one with his phone? There was no TV in the room, and if Lew had gone to lie down, Matt would have been alone with his thoughts and probably didn't like that. I could see his phone lying on the floor between the loveseat and the table.

So he'd put some salmon into his mouth…. No. First he'd pushed up his sleeves. They'd been down when I'd visited him, and they'd been up, below his elbows, when we'd found him on the floor. I could see him pushing them up before eating with a sweater that fancy.

And then he'd taken that first and only bite. He probably hadn't looked at his food. He'd expected it to be safe because Lew had ordered it, and Lew was careful. But he'd known right away, by the taste or by the numbness or the itching, that something was wrong.

I went to the table as casually as I could. I was the only person in the room not obsessing over a tiny screen, but that didn't mean they wouldn't notice if I stomped over there and started tossing food around. I slowly took a knee beside the table, picked up Matt's fork, and lifted the top of the stuffed salmon.

What I saw put a chill through me, worse than the wind that was freeze-drying people's skin outside. Smeared on top of the cream-cheese-and-spinach stuffing was a patch of bright yellow mustard.

There was nothing unusual about it, and that was what got me. It was the neon-yellow stuff you'd find in a family fridge or next to a hot dog cart. Uniform and smooth. A little watery. Cheap and bland and ordinary.

I didn't know whether mustard was a usual ingredient in stuffed salmon, but this mustard? From the people who'd sent monk-fruit sweetener and bamboo stir sticks? And smeared around on top of the stuffing, instead of blended in?

I checked out the name Vincitore and found it was a catering company specializing in bringing overpriced food to self-impressed wealthy people. This was not its actual slogan. Nothing about their website suggested they would so much as glance in the direction of hot-dog-stand mustard.

I peered at Jess and found him watching me. His expression was grim. I didn't know whether he had grave suspicions, but he had seen the mustard and was, to put it lightly, not impressed. He raised his chin, gesturing at the door, and I nodded. He got up from the sideboard he'd been half sitting on, and I followed him outside.

The hall was empty. The green room door, which we could see down the perpendicular hallway, was closed. The doors at the end of the hall the suite was on, the ones leading to the stage door, were closed. I'd expected the crew to be buzzing around now that the show was done, and especially considering that their lunchroom was down the hall from Matt's suite, but there was no one in sight.

"It is mustard? I asked once the door had shut behind us and we'd moved a few metres away. "Can you be allergic to mustard?"

"You can," Jess said and then craned his head around, probably checking for eavesdroppers. He looked like the *Sesame Street* puppet who sold people letters in back alleys.

"What is this?" I said. "Are you afraid the Soviets will find out?"

"Funny. It is actually a secret. But I guess it doesn't matter now. Yes, his allergy was to mustard."

CHAPTER NINE

"WHY WOULD that be a secret? Anyone with an allergy that serious should be telling everyone all the time. And they should have a MedicAlert bracelet, which I didn't see him wearing. You can get them in platinum with diamonds."

Jess gave me his "don't be an asshole" look, which illustrated the fine lines by which Jesse lived. You could call Matt a sexual predator because he was one, but how dare you accuse him of petty vanity.

"I can't believe this happened. Lew is really particular when he orders for Matt. He talks to the manager and the head chef directly. And this wasn't a trace amount."

"No, it wasn't."

I let that sit with him. He thought about it. I could see him sorting through ideas, pinning some to a bulletin board and throwing others in the trash.

"You think it was deliberate," he said.

"I think it's weird. I think a lot of things about this are weird."

"You think someone at the restaurant put mustard on his food on purpose."

"That's what I don't think," I told him. "Did you see that mustard? Did that seem high-end to you?"

"Sometimes fancy places cut costs by using cheaper ingredients when they don't think people will know the difference."

"Maybe," I said, "but then they'd mix it into the food, wouldn't they? You wouldn't dump it on top."

He looked annoyed, like I wasn't getting something and he didn't know how to say it.

"Ben, I'm not kidding about this being a secret."

"I think it's ridiculous, but I didn't think you were kidding."

"If someone put mustard in there on purpose, to hurt him, it would have to have been someone who knew he had the allergy. When Lew orders, he tells the head chef and the manager, and he asks them to oversee the food from start to finish. He pays extra for that. Like, a lot. No one in those positions is going to fuck around just to, I don't know, prank Matt Garrett."

"And they would have mixed it in," I told him. "I hear you. I guess what I'm saying is I don't think it was the caterer."

"And what I'm saying is who else could it have been? People do not know about this allergy. You can search the internet all day. You won't find it. The caterers are the only people Lew would have told."

It felt like stubbornness, like he was refusing to get the point. He wasn't remotely dumb.

"Lew," I said. "Alex. You. Maybe Ziad. What do these people have in common?"

Jess folded his arms. A protective gesture. Not always, but for him in this moment it was.

"You can't be serious."

"You knew," I said. "You and Lew knew, and Alex must know. The way he reacted to the body? He wasn't surprised by the swelling. And there's a decent chance Ziad knows. To be clear, I don't suspect you."

"Oh," Jess said. "Well. That is extremely big of you."

"If I didn't know you, I'd think you seemed suspicious as hell."

Jess looked around the hallways again, though there was no way anyone could have entered them without being seen. Also, the worst part of our conversation had already happened.

"That's your professional opinion?"

"Yes. You had a grudge and access to his room."

"So what? First of all, no one knows what he did to me. I mean, hardly anyone."

"They don't have to." I started ticking off on my fingers. "First, you refused to be civil on stage with the guy for five minutes. You did that in front of a room full of people. That suggests that you have a serious issue with the deceased. Then you had a private meeting with him, which could have been an escalation in your conflict. Then you were given ongoing access to his room."

"You think he gave me access because we fought?" Jess pointed out. "Very logical."

I waved a hand. "Fine. Skip that. You had a grudge and you had access. And most importantly, you knew about his allergy. Lew also knew about the allergy, but Matt was his meal ticket, and Alex probably knows about the allergy, but he and Matt were in… something. Love?"

"They were in ego gratification," Jess said. "They stroked each other's egos every night."

"What I'm saying is that they both had a use for him. You had zero use for him. Out of the three people that we know for certain were aware of his allergy, you're the one with an obvious motive."

He leaned back against the wall. He seemed exhausted.

"Any of us could have told anyone. I just told you."

"You didn't exactly volunteer it. And I don't see Lew as a blabbermouth. Alex… sure. I'll give you that. But you still need motive. Ziad is the only other person who had a hate-on for Matt."

"You're saying this like…." He moved closer and lowered his voice. "Like it wasn't a fuck-you gesture. You sound like you think someone was trying to kill him."

"A fuck-you gesture is spitting in someone's coffee," I said, "not triggering a dangerous allergy, which you all knew this was. And where are his EpiPens? Weird that they'd go missing exactly when he needed them. Oh, that's another thing. You knew where his EpiPens were kept. I saw you go straight for that brown bag on the counter."

He took a step back from me and squared his shoulders. I'd pissed him off. Somewhere under the pissed off lay, I suspected, hurt feelings.

"Do I need a lawyer, Officer?"

"Never say it that way to a cop. Any wavering on whether you want a lawyer can be interpreted as you not having asked for a lawyer. Say 'I want a lawyer,' and then shut up."

"Great TED talk, ACLU."

"Let's hope it doesn't become relevant."

"Jesus." He glanced up and down the halls again. "Should we move into a room for the rest of this?"

"No. If you're in a room, someone could be listening at the door."

"Someone could be listening at that door," he said, pointing to the door to Matt's suite.

"We're far enough away. We can take this as it comes, okay? If Crystal doesn't think anything is sketchy, fine. If she does, she'll call the cops, and we'll see what they think."

He was giving me a skeptical look.

"Out with it," I said.

"Aren't you compelled to say something? Like, if you think there's been a murder, don't you have to report it?"

"We don't know there's been a murder. I'm not required to call anyone just because I don't like a situation."

"See, I feel like that's…. If Brennan or somebody died this way and you didn't hate them, you might be calling the cops right now."

"I wouldn't. I have no proof of anything, and opinions are not rare or special. Even mine."

"That's some kind of a record," he said. "You've said two things in two minutes that I don't think you believe."

"Think what you want. But be careful what you eat, and don't be alone with anyone, because there might be a murderer in this place."

I headed for the door, but Jess grabbed my arm before I could get there.

"Ben."

I faced him. "What?"

"I really didn't do anything."

I put my hands on his face and kissed his forehead. "I really believe you."

I did too.

Not because I'd know for sure if Jess were lying. A lot of the time, I did. Often enough that he never played poker with me. But lying was a tricky business, full of curves like how well a person can pretend to believe what they're saying and how much you want to believe the things they say. If there really were human lie detectors in the world, I had yet to meet them.

It also wasn't that I didn't think Jess was capable of murder. Anyone could kill anyone under the right circumstances. But Jess was too good-natured to set up a terrible death for someone and do a show while they suffocated down the hall. Anyone who could do that... well, if there was somebody like that around, I wasn't thrilled to be this close to them.

Once we were back in the room, Jess took a seat next to Luna and leaned against her.

"What do they call this in England? When you have to do your job on your downtime? A bus driver's holiday?"

"Busman's holiday," Luna corrected. "It's fine, love. I enjoyed seeing you."

"You could probably go home," Jess said, "since there's another doctor coming."

That was about as Jesse a move as I could think of. He thought he was being clever, trying to usher Luna out the door before she got murdered or caught up in a scandalous celebrity death. I wasn't sure which Jesse considered a bigger threat.

It wasn't exactly *not* clever, but it was unnecessary. He could have gone into the hall with her and told her, not about my murder theory, but about the inconvenience and awkwardness of being associated with the death of someone famous. She would probably have gratefully agreed to bow out. But for no sensible reason, he wanted to play it cool.

He also wasn't making this suggestion to Kent. Jess liked to think he wasn't sexist, the way I liked to think I wasn't sexist. But here we were facing down a possible murderer and his first thought was that his lady friend should go home.

"I should hand off the patient," Luna told him. "And the investigator will have questions. Though you'll be able to answer more of them than I will, I think."

Jess was unconvinced.

"I don't know anything," he said. "Ben and I came in here with Vic, and we found him… like that."

"Yes, but you know him," Luna said. "She'll have questions about him. And his allergy, of course."

"She can ask Lew," Jess said. That reminded me that Lew and Alex were still absent. Probably still in his room, since that was where they'd gone before Jess and I had ducked into the hallway and there was, as far as I knew, no second door out of the suite. That was something worth making sure of, in a murder investigation. Not that this was one and not that I was on the case if it were.

The door to the second bedroom was still open from when Jess had gone in hunting for EpiPens, so it was easy to casually go inside.

There was one narrow twin bed in the middle of the room with a nightstand crammed between it and the far wall and a shallow chest of drawers at its foot. This was a room meant for sleeping and not much else. There was definitely no second door.

I didn't see any luggage, but that made sense. Matt's outfit was probably what he'd intended to wear onstage, and they hadn't planned to stay here. Calgary had some decent luxury hotels, and they were likely booked into one.

There was no sign that anyone had been in here, aside from Matt's Canada Goose coat tossed onto the bed. He'd probably bought it somewhere in Toronto, for a film set that had suffered a dusting of snow. He was still wearing a pair of Chelsea boots.

"Well, it's out." That was Jess from the next room. I went back into the living room and pulled the bedroom door shut behind me. Jess was holding his phone out to Luna.

"What is this? It says he has laryngitis," Luna said. "Who posted this?"

"It's the charity's Facebook account," Jess said. "This is not good."

"Why isn't it good?" Kent said. "Didn't you drag me into the hall to tell me we needed to keep his death quiet?"

"Matt had lunch in town. He went into some stores. People know he wasn't sick. There's already a post on DeuxMoi saying he was fine this afternoon."

"Lie-yngitis is trending locally," Luna said. "L-I-E-yngitis."

"Yeah, I see it," Jess said.

They were too busy scrolling to notice, but I saw Tiff pull out her phone. Clearly, the dead man lying in front of her wasn't just anybody. Not from the way everyone around her was talking. So it was natural she'd be researching. I would have said something, tried to stop her, but what was the point? She was going to find out eventually. Everyone would.

It took her less than a minute. She had a hashtag to work from, though, so it wasn't that impressive. Her eyes went wide, and she shook her phone a little, like it was an Etch-a-Sketch and the words would rearrange themselves.

"Ty?" she said. The tall EMT looked at her. She showed him her phone.

"What's that?"

"That's *him*," she said, pointing at Matt's body with her free hand.

"No fucking way."

Instead of asking Jess, or anyone else in the room, they went closer to Matt and bent over to study his misshapen face. I didn't know what they were hoping to get from that. I doubted the guy's mother would have known him.

I considered telling them yes, it was him, before they turned him over to check for a name sewn into his underwear. I didn't, not because I'd decided against it but because Lew came charging back into the room, phone in hand.

"Who in the hell posted this?"

"The charity," Jess said. "The real question is, what do they know and who told them?"

"If I were you," I told Lew, "I'd ask Vic. Politely, because none of this is her fault."

Lewis glared at me, and at Jess for good measure, but he was calling someone as he raged back into the bedroom, so it seemed he'd taken my advice.

"I can kind of see it," the tall EMT, Ty, said once Lewis had shut the door.

"It's him," Jess said wearily. "He was supposed to make a speech tonight."

"Holy shit," Tiff said. "Matt Garrett. I've seen *Grains of Pearl* about thirty times."

Ty huffed.

"That's chick crap. The *Scanners* remake was awesome, though."

"Fuck you," Tiff said absently. She was looking at Matt's clothes and hair, the things that lined up with the Matt Garrett she knew. "This is so crazy. This is a huge deal."

"You can't tell anyone," Jess said.

"Okay, so, I wouldn't," Tiff said, "because this is my patient and that would be a breach of confidential information. So don't worry about it."

Going by Jess's face, he clearly expected her to spill it three times before the cock crowed. I also thought it was a good bet. Nothing against Tiff, but it was hard not to spill this sort of thing.

There was a knock at the door, and we all turned. Kent swung it open to admit Vic, Harry the guard, and Crystal Shaw of the Medical Examiner's office.

I knew Crystal from my time on the force. She was neither the sharpest nor the dullest knife in the ME's drawer. She made an impression, though. She was a big girl who liked big, eye-catching outfits. Tonight she was wearing a dark blue cloak with a fur-trimmed hood over a forest-green velvet dress that skimmed the top of her black-and-pink Sorels. Her medical bag was clutched in one white-gloved hand. When she threw the hood back, she knocked down some of the brassy hair she'd piled up with duckbill clips.

"Oh my goodness," she declared. "There are an awful lot of people in here!"

Oh my goodness, that was Crystal. I already knew she wasn't going to greet me, though we hadn't seen each other in over a year, because she was here to do a job and socializing was not part of it.

"We can go," Ty said. "Now that you're here."

Harry the guard took that as his cue and slipped away. He shut the door so quietly that I didn't hear it latch.

"Not quite yet," Crystal said. She held up one finger. The nail glittered silver. "Was the patient dead when you arrived?"

"Dr. Fares was here," Tiff said. "She'd already called it."

Crystal's brows went up, and she followed Tiff's gaze to Luna.

"Oh yes! Detective Hauser mentioned there was a doctor here! You found the patient deceased?"

"Unfortunately, yes," Luna said. "CPR was performed. With the swelling, it would not have been effective."

"And did you attempt intubation?" She turned to the EMTs. "You have a King Tube?"

"He was deceased," Luna repeated.

"We agreed with that assessment," Tiff said. "The airway is blocked. The first-aider found him in that condition."

"He'd been without oxygen for a minimum of seven minutes when I arrived," Luna said. "But likely far longer."

"He was late to go onstage," Vic said. "I started knocking on his door at ten fifteen, and he already wasn't answering, and it was ten thirty-five by the time we got into the room. He wasn't moving at all. He looked like he does now. And then, yeah, probably like the doctor says, about seven minutes for me to go get her and bring her back here."

"*Hmm*," Crystal said. "*Hmm, hmm, hmm.*"

She traded her winter gloves for nitrile and went
to Matt's body. Checked for a pulse. Confirmed the
blocked airway. Flipped his hands over and studied the
hives. Luna watched without much interest. The EMTs
shifted nervously on their feet, as if they were waiting
outside the principal's office.

Finally Crystal went onto her haunches and nodded at the EMTs.

"Please leave your contact information with me.
I'll need to follow up for my report. But there's no
sense in tying you up here."

They made grateful noises and presented her with
business cards, then packed up their things and, with
waves to Luna and Kent, made their exit.

"I won't ask how you know Tiffany," Luna said
as soon as they'd gone. Kent made a show of being
offended.

"We met in the course of business," he said.

"I don't doubt that," Luna said. "What I meant….
Never mind."

Kent gave her a "have it your way" shrug and went
to the food cart. He was regarding it not like it was
exhibit A, but like it was the salad bar at the Keg. I
coughed, and he turned to me.

"What?"

"You know what."

He had to. I couldn't be the only one who saw how
wrong things were at this scene.

His face didn't tell me anything, but he left the
food alone and went back to his spot at the front of the
kitchenette island.

"Do you have any thoughts on the cause of death?"
Crystal asked Luna.

"The same as you, I'm sure," Luna said. "An allergic reaction. The patient's manager—he's in the other room—he was looking for EpiPens. Clearly a pre-existing condition."

"More people in here," Crystal said. "Goodness. Can anyone confirm this allergy?"

"I can," Jess said. "He—the, uh, patient—he told me he was allergic to mustard. I saw him have a reaction once."

Jess hadn't mentioned that to me. He was turned away from me, his eyes on Crystal. I couldn't tell whether he was avoiding my gaze.

"To mustard?" Crystal asked.

"He assumed it was. I don't think he had any other allergies, or didn't know about them. We were in a restaurant, and he talked to the chef, but someone must have screwed up and let his food touch something that had traces of mustard. He could get sick from a trace."

"Was the reaction this serious?"

"Maybe?" Jess said. "I gave him two EpiPens. He didn't want to go to the hospital, so he went home after. But he didn't... he wasn't swelled up like this. He was a little swollen, and he had hives. I gave him the shots right away, and he took his inhaler and some Benadryl, and he seemed okay after."

"Oh no," Crystal said. "You have got to go to the hospital. It's very dangerous to go home."

"Tell him that."

It was snarky, but I didn't blame him. The scolding had been directed at the wrong person and entirely too late.

Crystal let his tone roll off her.

"Do we know if he had mustard? Tonight?"

"It looks that way," I said. "There's a bite missing from the stuffed salmon on that plate. There's also food someone spat out that could be the missing bite. And there's mustard on the fish. Inside. A lot of it."

"*Hmm.*"

Crystal took the fork and lifted the salmon as I'd done. I couldn't tell what she made of the watery mustard beneath.

"This surely does match the seriousness of his reaction," she said. "Was an EpiPen administered?"

"We don't think so," Jess said. "They were usually kept in that brown bag, the one on the counter over there. When we got here, it had been dumped out. I didn't find the EpiPens in there, and I didn't see them anywhere else. I didn't see caps from them either."

"He would have been in no condition to tidy up," Crystal said. "We would see the pens on the floor, near the body."

"He might have taken his inhaler," Jess said. "That was in the bag. It's on the counter."

"It wouldn't have been enough. Not nearly enough. Oh, poor man. If his allergy was that serious, it might not have mattered if he'd had his injectors. His fate could have been sealed from that first bite."

In the silence that followed, Vic's phone buzzed. Everyone stared at her, and she put her hand on it like she was trying to shush it before it could embarrass her further.

"I bet I know what that call is about," Jess said. "You should take it. And check Twitter."

Vic was clearly torn about which of those to do first. Her phone buzzed again, and that decided it. She answered.

"Yes? Uh, no, but I…. Okay, one sec." She turned to Crystal. "Do you need me for anything?"

"I don't know yet," Crystal said. "Don't wander off."

"I'll be right outside."

She left and closed the door behind her.

"This is still a lot of people," Crystal said. "Who do I need? Who found the body?"

"Me and him and Vic," Jess said, pointing at me and then at the door Vic had gone through.

"All right, and you're the doctor," she told Luna, "so you'll need to stay for a bit. Detective Hauser, you said you were off duty? You do appear to be awfully off duty."

"Yes, I'm off duty. You don't need me."

"Then, I hate to ask, but could you step outside as well? But please don't leave the building. Just in case."

She didn't say in case what. She didn't have to, for my benefit or Kent's. Just in case she decided to call the cops. She had to keep the witnesses and the suspects around.

"I'll see how things are going in the green room," Kent told me. The way he said it and looked me right in the eye, it was the first indication that we were on the same page. He had suspicions. He was going to the green room to see who was there and what they knew and how they were behaving. All useful things. I wished I could go with him. On the other hand, I might not have access to the crime scene for much longer, so it was probably a good thing I was allowed to stick around for now.

"And you clearly know the deceased," Crystal said to Jess.

"I do know him," Jess said. "But his manager knows him much better. Abraham Lewis. He's in that room there."

"Oh, good. Thank you. I'll keep you both for now. Is there anyone else here?"

"There's a boyfriend," I said. "The deceased's boyfriend. He's also in that room. I don't know how long they've been dating."

"Can he identify the deceased officially? Or the manager? Or," she added to Jesse, "might you be able to do it?"

For the first time, it occurred to me to wonder whether Crystal knew who the body was. Probably she did. Probably Kent had told her when he called it in.

It was strange to think about identifying the body of someone that nearly anyone would recognize. Not in his current state. He did need to be identified, the way he was now. But what if he'd had a heart attack and keeled over this afternoon? Probably eight out of ten people could have identified him right there on the sidewalk. You'd still have to go through the motions of asking someone who knew the deceased personally. What if it was some nobody who was a dead-ringer—so to speak—for a movie star?

As for Matt's current state, though it was tempting to go by his hair and clothes being the same as when he'd last been seen alive, there was always that one chance in a million that someone had decided to make life more like the movies and pull an elaborate switcheroo, so you had to make sure. Usually there was a tattoo or a scar that would do the job. I'd once been at a scene where a guy had jumped off an overpass and led with his face, and his official ID had been based on a Prince Albert.

"There's a tattoo," Jesse said. "Left calf. It's a guy surfing. He got it after he did that Mick Fanning biopic."

For a moment I thought he'd forgotten his own advice about staying out of the paperwork, but I shouldn't have worried. He demurred as soon as Crystal suggested he check for the tattoo and sign a few things.

"Ask Lew," he said. "The manager. They've been working together for eleven years. He'll know where the food came from too."

"Oh, that is helpful. Thank you. So. If you found the body, can you give me a time for that?"

"Same as Vic said," I told her. "Ten thirty-five. Lew was in here with him, but he was in that bedroom with the door closed, so he wouldn't have an exact time of death. I'd bet he was the last one to see the deceased alive."

"I called time of death as twenty-three oh seven," Luna said. "But you should be able to get something better for your records. The death certificate hasn't been completed."

"Did you need one?" Crystal asked, already reaching into her bag. Luna glanced at Jess.

"Is that something you can do?" Jesse asked. "Instead of Dr. Fares?"

Crystal put two fingertips to her lips as if she were telling herself to be quiet. Then she said, "Yes, but why?"

"Because…." Jess stopped. It wasn't that he didn't know why. He was thinking up something to say that wasn't "better you than her."

"Do you know who the deceased is?" I asked. "Did Kent tell you?"

"He did," Crystal said. "But gracious, the state he's in. I wouldn't have known him."

"And I'm guessing you know who this person is," I said, pointing to Jess.

"I do. But it's important for me to distinguish between what I know officially and what I know personally."

"Well, I can tell you officially that Jess—you'd know him as Jack Lowe, but that's a stage name—Jess used to date Matt Garrett. He's also friends with Luna, Dr. Fares. Matt is… was… very famous. People will be talking about this death on the internet. If the doctor who fills out the death certificate is a personal friend of Matt's ex-boyfriend, that is going to attract attention."

"To be honest," Jess said, "whoever fills out the death certificate is going to get harassed by internet detectives. You'll get some weird phone calls and people throwing your name around too. But it'll be worse if it's someone who's directly connected to me."

"You don't suspect something is wrong here, do you?" Crystal asked. She aimed that at all of us, but mainly me.

"It's irrelevant," I said. "The internet will dig in no matter what."

"*Hmm.*" She took out her phone and searched for something. Celebrity deaths? Death certificate procedures? Jess and Matt's "dating" history? It was about a minute and felt like a year before she dropped her phone, which was encased in silicon and hanging on a lanyard around her neck. "Well. If you're not willing to provide official identification and you can't tell me anything about the food, I'll take down your names and you can go. But don't leave the building, please and thank you."

CHAPTER TEN

ONCE WE were in the hall, I could hear muted commotion coming from the other side of the doors leading to the stage door and loading area. We headed for it, but before we got there, Jess took out his swipe card and offered it to Luna.

"You should wait in my dressing room," he said.

"Why on earth?"

"There might be photographers on the other side of that door," he said. "They already know I'm here, but they don't know you exist. You want to keep it that way."

I didn't ask whether they knew *I* existed. They did. After we'd caught that murderer in the mountains, as soon as Jess was well enough to go out in public, we'd had our picture taken almost everywhere, by media and fans and people who wanted to boost their social media traffic. I'd bitched to Jess about being a public private detective, and he'd parroted something I'd said to him about being a shitty tail if people noticed you at all.

Once Luna was safely tucked away, Jess pulled the door open a crack. The EMTs were in there with Harry, all of them shoving the stage door closed against a mob. Phones everywhere, held up to record. The batteries would die from the cold soon. Ten minutes, fifteen at most. People were yelling, asking about Matt. Some were media, going by their branded jackets and bags. Most looked like stacks of balloons in their puffy nylon coats and flip-top mittens, hoods drawn tight. Their breath steamed the air and hid their faces.

I moved in to help, Jess staying behind me, and that was all it took to get the doors shut long enough for Harry to lock them. My hands stung from the ice that had formed along the inside edges of the door.

"Lord Jesus," Harry said. "What was that?"

I sympathized. Jess had told me about the kinds of scenes that happened around Matt, so I'd had some idea what to expect. That didn't make it less unsettling in person. Though the people outside the stage door were driven by curiosity or a feeling of connection to whomever they thought Matt was, it felt like violence. I remembered how fans could get around Jess, the nervous excitement that was indistinguishable from fear.

"It's logic," Jess said, startling me from my thoughts.

"What is that supposed to mean?" Harry asked.

Jesse took a deep breath. "Fans who are really interested in Matt will have been out here ever since Matt posted that he was in the building. The show was sold out, so stalking him is all they've got."

"They haven't been here," Harry said. "I've been letting people in and out. I would have noticed"—he gestured at the door—"that."

Jess shook his head. "I promise they were here. In this weather, they would have stayed indoors as long as they could. There are places you can park, and there's a coffee shop that has a view of this door from the back corner. They just weren't obvious."

Harry nodded. So did the EMTs. I considered asking him when he'd scoped out the backdoor sightlines from neighbourhood cafés, but it seemed a shame to interrupt him when he was on a roll.

"The charity announced that Matt couldn't go onstage because he had laryngitis, which was obviously a lie. People put that on social media. Anyone interested in Matt has seen it."

"Yeah, it's everywhere," Tiff confirmed.

"Right," Jess said to Ty and Tiff, "and you would have parked your ambulance at the stage door. That means Matt's biggest fans saw the ambulance arrive. They know Matt didn't go onstage, and you don't call an ambulance for laryngitis, so they figure the ambulance is for him, and maybe he's really sick. Some of them shared that on social media."

"They're nuts," Ty said. "Someone tried to steal my iPad."

"Matt has dedicated fans," Jess said, managing to sound neutral. "Meanwhile, on the other side of this theatre, a bunch of reporters have been told that Matt can't talk to them. They were probably told there won't be any interviews at all. So they're at loose ends, and then they check social media and find out about the ambulance. Of course they're going to be outside the ambulance with cameras. They'd be bad at their jobs if they weren't."

"But you can't not let people get to an ambulance," Tiff said. "What if we'd had someone on a gurney?"

"You didn't, though," Jess said. "I think they'd have let you through. I *think*."

"What are we going to do?" Tiff asked. "We can't abandon our ambulance."

"Police?" Harry said. "Get some cops here to escort you?"

"It's faster and easier to misdirect them. They'll be pissed off later, but what the hell." Jess turned to Tiff. "You can either put out some tweets about a second ambulance at another door, or if you really want to sell it, you could roll your gurney out another set of doors and get a bad shot of the tires or something, like you were a fan who took the photo while you were running. Whatever you're gonna do, set it up, come back here and make sure you're ready to run, tweet it, and wait for the crowd to move."

A corner of Tiff's mouth curved up, and I knew for the first time that she absolutely recognized Jack Lowe.

"You've done this before," she said.

"Not as often as Matt," Jess told her. "Good luck."

"Where are you going?" Ty asked. "You can't abandon us."

Jess gave him a "really?" look.

"I make this whole situation worse. Trust me."

He went back into the hall, and I stayed close. He was not in the mood to wait for me.

"Where the hell did Vic go?" he said as we walked toward his dressing room.

"Got called in for a meeting with the mysterious Sarah?" I suggested. "I'm surprised they haven't had a conference yet. Sarah, Vic, theatre management, the charity's CEO."

"Comms," Jesse added. "But these are all non-profit groups, so their comms people are probably fundraisers wearing three other hats. Issues management would not be their bag, baby."

"Does the charity really have an issue?"

Jess didn't answer because he was knocking on the door to his dressing room. "Luna? It's us."

Luna opened the door and showed off the coffee table like it was the prize on a game show. She'd set out three mugs of tea, an oversized chocolate bar, and an alcohol flask.

"I don't mean to sound ungrateful," Jess said, kicking the door shut as he spoke, "but is that your booze, and if so, where were you carrying it?"

"It was in Kent's jacket," Luna said. "Shall I call him in here, by the way? Since we'll be drinking his whiskey?"

"Might as well," I said. "I'd like to ask him about his alcoholism."

"I'll make another cup of tea, then," Luna said. "Jesse, you may as well get changed. That dress is a marvel, but it cannot be comfortable."

Jess didn't argue. He went into the bathroom and closed the door while I texted Kent to invite him to join us. He took long enough that Luna had his tea ready by the time he arrived. He sat, poured a splash of whiskey into the tea, and stared into it, watching the steam rise.

"People sure are getting curious in that green room," he told us. "They did not appreciate it when I said I couldn't tell them anything."

I sat on the loveseat next to Kent's chair and took my tea straight. It was good stuff, strong enough to keep me going if my adrenaline gave out.

"No one likes to hear that," I said. "It implies you have something to tell."

"Oh, they know I do," Kent said. "I don't have to imply fuck all. It was like a goddamned scrum in there. 'Where's Matt? Why didn't he go on stage? Why did the emcee say he's sick? There's no way he's sick. Why is the Foundation saying he's got laryngitis? Oh, this says there's an ambulance outside? Is there an ambulance outside? Should someone go check?'"

I held the tea to my chest. It was warm and comforting, like a puppy, or paper straight out of a photocopier.

"Did someone go check?"

"I pointed out that anyone who went outside would find themselves answering questions for the media. No one seemed eager to do that."

"Not even Duncan?"

Kent smirked. He might have been a fan of Duncan's show, but it seemed he'd formed an opinion of the guy over the past few hours, and that opinion was similar to mine.

"He's not in any hurry to go back out in the cold. I take it he left the building after his set."

"Yeah. Jess and I ran into him in the hallway right after Jess got off stage."

"Ziad is having kittens in there. Keeps saying he needs to go out for a smoke."

"He smokes?" Luna said. "I didn't see it on his hands or his teeth. But he would invest in teeth whitening, and he would have someone see to his hands."

"I didn't smell it on him," I said. "But didn't he say something about needing a cigarette before? I don't know. Something about him reads as a smoker to me."

"He's wearing a nicotine patch," Kent said. "He figured there'd be no smoking in the building, and he didn't want to spend all night by the back doors in this weather. But he's wearing out the carpet pacing the back of the green room, and his fingers are twitching. The guy is all nerves. And I thought I smelled fresh cigarette smoke on him earlier."

"Interesting," I said.

Kent nodded and took a swig of his whiskey tea. "I thought so."

"He's been on edge all day. How was his set?"

Kent shrugged. "Okay. Not my kind of thing."

"Not enough fart jokes for the detective," Luna said. She took the chair across from Kent. "I thought it was sometimes clever. But he likes to set the audience up to think one thing, pull out the rug, and chide us all for being foolish. It doesn't seem to have occurred to him that audiences are going along with whatever he suggests—to be agreeable or kind or to have a good collective experience. I found it arrogant and mean-spirited."

I'd seen him be like that, but I'd also seen him be better than that.

"Could be the mood he's in," I suggested.

Jess came out of the bathroom in the dark pants and white shirt he'd worn earlier. The stage makeup had been scrubbed from his face and his usual make-up—a little eyeliner, tinted sunscreen—had been reapplied. He'd washed the junk from his hair and put it into a short ponytail. That ponytail would only hold until his hair was dry, and then strands of it would start escaping in all directions.

"What's in the flask?" he asked Kent.

"A man with priorities," Kent said. "It's good old JD."

"I'll drink to it," Jess said. He climbed over the back of the loveseat and sat beside me.

"Or you could respect other people's property and sit down like a human person," I said.

He grinned. "Little late for us to start respecting this couch, I would say."

"Oh no," Luna said. "Really, boys? That's disgusting."

"It's clean," Jess told her. "We cleaned up."

"Still gross," Kent said and tossed back more tea. Jess added whiskey to the last mug and drank with his eyes shut, like he was trying to wish himself somewhere else.

"Do they know he's dead?" Jess asked, his eyes still shut. "In the green room?"

"Not yet," Kent said. "There are a lot of theories about what's going on, but I didn't hear that one."

Jess nodded. "It would seem impossible. Especially with his healthy image. If I died tomorrow, no one would blink."

"I might notice," I said.

"Sure," Jess said with a twist to his smile, "but would you be surprised?"

"What do they think is happening?" Luna asked. "In the green room?"

"The leading theory is that someone punched him in the face and he didn't want to go on stage with a black eye," Kent said. "I like that one. Makes me wish I had punched him in the face."

"You'd look pretty sketchy now if you had," Jesse said.

"Not as sketchy as you," Kent shot back. It wasn't as mean as it sounded. This was how they played together, like Rottweilers at the dog park.

"What are you talking about?" Luna asked.

Jess glanced at me. I shrugged. No reason not to tell her what we were thinking.

"Did you see what was on the investigator's phone?" he asked.

"It was *her* phone," Luna said, as if she were above that and had never taken a photo of a drunk girl's text screen in a bar and showed it to me later. "Why? What was on it?"

"Recipes for stuffed salmon."

"Fuuuuck," Kent said. It was impressive how much respect he could convey with that word.

"Yeah, she's on our page," I agreed. "Does anyone know whether mustard is an ingredient in stuffed salmon?"

Jesse was already on his phone. "I'm seeing it a couple of places, but it's either in the sauce or it's powder mixed into the filling. It doesn't seem that common, though."

"His allergy was to mustard," I told Luna. "Lew always talked to the head chef when he ordered for Matt."

"And the restaurant manager," Jess added.

"Is it possible Lew forgot?" Luna asked. "He seemed out of it. From his behaviour, I'd guess that he took a sleeping pill, but he might be ill."

"He is," Jesse said. "And he probably did take a sleeping pill."

"Wait, Lew is sick?" I said. "What's wrong with him?"

"MS."

"Really?" Luna was professionally interested now. "Is he Canadian?"

"Nope. A random thing."

What they meant was that multiple sclerosis was more common in Canada than in the States, seemingly a side effect of being further from the equator. I knew this because I'd had an uncle with it and a friend in high school and a mechanic who'd had to give up the job. People from other places knew one person with MS at most, but on the prairies we usually knew a few.

"He doesn't talk about it, though," Jess warned. "He doesn't want clients to think he's ineffective."

"But they must know he's ill," Luna said.

"Matt did," Jess said. "He was Lew's main gig, so they spent a lot of time together. It would have been tough to hide."

"His eye was twitching tonight," I said, suddenly remembering.

"Yeah. Stress was always bad for him. Sometimes he'd take a sleeping pill and lie down for a few hours."

"It can affect the brain," I said to Luna. "Right? He might have forgotten to talk to the chef."

Luna didn't actually put on glasses and a white coat and pull out a PowerPoint, but she might as well have.

"It is *in* the brain, Ben. It is plaques in the brain and demyelination of nerves. Are you asking whether it has cognitive effects?"

"I'm asking whether Lew might have forgotten to talk to the chef."

"I have no way of knowing what he may or may not have forgotten to do. MS can cause mood disorders and problems with executive functioning."

"You're not testifying at a malpractice trial," I told her. "Tell me what you think."

"I think that I have no way of knowing. MS affects everyone differently, and it can have different effects at different times. He might be having trouble with planning and execution of tasks, or he might not be. If he is, it might be the MS, or it might be simply stress, or it could be that he's been drunk since noon. Which I'm not saying he was. It's an example."

Kent picked up the flask, shook it to see how much was left, and poured another shot into his tea.

"The thing is," he said, "I don't see how Asshat forgetting to talk to a chef gets us this result. That was a lot of mustard."

I nodded. "Yeah. If the recipe usually had mustard in it, or if this was a trace contact... I could see it. But that mustard was all over the place."

"Like someone squirted it out of one of those yellow squeeze bottles," Jess said.

"And exactly that kind of mustard," I added. "Cheap stuff."

"I'm surprised he didn't smell it," Kent said. "I knew a guy who was allergic to shellfish, and he could smell it from a mile away."

"The salad dressing was strong," Jesse said. "I could smell it as soon as I got near the plate. It would have covered up any mustard smell."

"Is that usual?" I asked. "Did Matt typically like strong dressings?"

Jess's mouth curved at the corner. "Yes, Detective. Lewis didn't ask for extra smelly tonight."

"What are you all saying?" Luna said, though it sounded like she knew.

"We're wondering how the mustard got there," I told her. "Because it's hard to see an innocent explanation."

"And Crystal's gotta be wondering the same thing," Kent said. "If she was checking recipes."

Luna looked at us all as if we'd lost our minds.

"Are you really seeing a murder in an allergic re-action? People die from allergies every day. This was a known condition. I think you've got murder on the brain."

"Then tell me how the mustard got there," I said. "Tell me someone sprayed cheap mustard all over an expensive piece of salmon by mistake. And then tell me it's a coincidence that Matt's EpiPens weren't where they are always kept."

"She's gonna call the cops," Kent said. "Crystal. If she hasn't already it's because she wants to talk to Whatshiscock first."

"Abraham Lewis," Jess said. "That's the guy's name."

"He can have a name when he stops covering up for criminals," Kent said. "Until then, fuck old Dicknugget."

I hadn't realized that Kent had thought things through that far, far enough to blame Lew for his part in what had happened to Jess. From the surprised look on Jess's face, he hadn't realized it either.

"I... okay, then," Jess said. "Luna, I didn't want to buy into this murder theory either, but I can't pretend this makes sense any other way."

"Murder by mustard. Truly. You do know this is ridiculous. Allergic reactions are not entirely predictable."

"Neither is a gunshot to the head," I said. "But one of them is quiet, and it can happen when you're no-where near your victim."

"You don't need a licence to own mustard," Kent said.

"There's no background check for mustard," Jess added.

Kent nodded. "I'm surprised more people don't commit murder by allergy."

"Maybe they do," I said, "and we don't catch them."

Kent snapped his fingers and pointed at me. "You could be onto something."

"And you really think this is more straightforward than someone making a mistake," Luna said. "If we're imagining scenarios, why not this one: Someone started working at the restaurant a week ago. Maybe they're a bit of an idiot. They think mustard goes on the salmon and that someone forgot to add it, so they put it on. Ooh, here's another story—imagine someone writing a note to themselves to remember not to add the mustard, but the note only says 'mustard,' so the next person down the line thinks it's a note that mustard goes on the salmon and someone forgot to add it, so they put it on. Ooh, here's another for them to add mustard. I could make up stories like this for an hour."

"And they'd all be convoluted," I said. "'Someone knew Matt had an allergy and decided to use it to kill him' is a lot more direct. Explain why his EpiPens are gone."

"The part where someone knew about the allergy, though," Jess said. "That's the thing that's really bothering me. Matt didn't want anyone to know."

"But you did," Luna said.

"Yeah, because I had to be seen at restaurants with him. And I was around when Lew ordered food."

"Did he not want people to know what he was allergic to, or did he not want people to know that he had an allergy?"

"Both," Jess said. "Okay… this is also supposed to be a secret, but there's no point in that now. Matt used to carry a gun because he was scared of some of his fans. You get a million people really fixated on you and some of that million will be truly disturbed, and a handful of those will be willing and able to do something terrible, and one of them might do it. And one is all it takes."

Luna peered at him over the rim of her mug. "How many people have you got fixated on you, would you say?"

Jess shrugged. "A lot less than a million. I don't carry a gun."

"You carry a cop," Kent said.

Jess glared at him. "First, ex-cop, and second, Ben is not my bodyguard." He returned his attention to Luna. "I keep telling you guys, Matt's world is alien. My kind of fame is nothing like his. I know the stuff he did may sound crazy, but his life was crazy. I'm not sure he was wrong to be that scared."

"What does that have to do with the allergy?" Luna asked.

"He thought someone might try to poison him if they knew what he was allergic to."

CHAPTER ELEVEN

I BLINKED LIKE something had hit me in the face.

"Are you," I said carefully, "fucking. Kidding. Me?"

This wasn't the first time, not by a long shot, that Jess had given me information in dribs and drabs. Everything was on a need-to-know basis. Not trivia. He'd tell me everything about a TV show he liked or a restaurant he thought we should try. But his work? His life apart from me? I'd get that when it suited him, if at all.

Normally that was annoying but fine. This, however, was a serious miscalculation of what I did or did not need to know. And the cagey little bastard was sitting there regarding me like he had no idea who or what had pissed in my cornflakes.

"What?" he said.

"Nothing, I guess. I mean, why would anyone care that someone who probably got murdered in an unusual way predicted he would get murdered in exactly that unusual way? Of what interest could that be?"

"You're not getting the context," he said. "Matt made people open his deliveries and check for bombs. Once he had to hire an exterminator for his cabin in Colorado, and he did a deep background check on the guy first. He wasn't even staying at his cabin at the time."

"Jesus," Kent said. "Are all A-listers that paranoid?"

"I don't know. I only spent that kind of time with Matt."

"Okay," I said, "I get that Matt was a very cautious person who was concerned about a lot of things. But do you not see the difference between that and him thinking he was going to be murdered by his allergy and then him actually dying that way?"

"Everyone dies eventually," Jess said. "So eventually Matt was going to be right about something."

"I think what Ben would ask if he wasn't butthurt that you didn't tell him this earlier," Kent said, "is whether Matt ever said anything about being poisoned that seemed different from his usual paranoia."

Jess shook his head. "I never got the impression that he thought someone in particular was trying to kill him. It was more like he thought anyone might be trying to kill him at any moment. Or not even kill... like, he thought someone might slip him mustard so they could save his life and be a big hero. Or so they could get a good story for their gossip site. Matt Garrett nearly dies from mustard allergy. With photos."

"But that's insane," Luna said. "You can't play around with allergies like that."

"Not everyone knows that," Jesse said. "And some people might not even care as long as they got their footage."

"Why did he care if people knew he had an allergy, though?" Kent asked. "As long as they didn't know what it was, they couldn't use it against him, right?"

"Oh, that. That was image. He told me no one would take James Bond or Jason Bourne seriously if they knew the guy could keel over from eating a hot dog. He was worried he'd miss out on roles."

"Does he really think people think that way?" Luna asked.

"The dollars back it up," Jess said. "Millions have been lost over less."

"And yet people will do anything to work in that ridiculous industry," Luna said. "I will never understand people."

"Everyone puts up with ridiculous things at work," Jess pointed out. "Usually for less money. You live with it. Or quit and work for yourself, like Ben."

"Then you're dancing for whoever will pay you," Kent said. "It's like sex work, but it takes longer and pays worse."

"The real problem," Jess said, "is that Ben's boss expects too much and is tight with money. He's bad for morale."

"My boss knows the meaning of responsibility," I said. "Can we get back on track? You're saying that Matt didn't want producers to know about his allergy, but he must have told… what, craft services?"

"He didn't use craft services. He ate in his trailer. He has his own food brought in. I'm sure some people found out, and he might even have had reactions in front of people, but this was not one of those Hollywood not-really-a-secret secrets."

That wasn't good for my theory that Ziad could have known about Matt's allergy from being near him on set.

"He talked to you about it," Luna said to Jess. "He must have trusted you quite a lot."

Jesse got distant at that.

"I don't know why he talked to me," he said. "He might have been lonely. He didn't get out much."

"And you gave him an EpiPen once," I said. "You told Crystal you had."

"Oh yeah. I knew about the allergy before that, but I did give him, actually, two injections. We were at a restaurant. The head chef's theory was that someone made something with mustard on a food-prep surface, and they wiped it off, but they didn't wash it off, and then they made Matt's food. I don't know if it would have gotten as bad as this that time, but he had his EpiPens then. He got me to give them to him because he was shaking."

"And they were in that brown bag?" I asked.

"No. That's the kit for when he knows he'll have a trailer or hotel room. He has a pocket-sized needle case for when he's out for the evening."

"How did you keep people from noticing?" Luna asked. "People do tend to take an interest when someone is getting an injection."

"He moved really fast. I'm sure it helped that it wasn't very much mustard. I gave him the shots under the table, and he took some antihistamines. Then he went to the bathroom and took his inhaler. I went with him to make sure he wouldn't die in there. People must have thought it was…."

"Sexy toilet times?" Kent suggested.

Jess stared at him. "Never say that again."

"I'm surprised no one followed you into the bathroom to take pictures," Luna said.

"It was one of those A-lister places," Jess told her. "There's two kinds. There are places you go when you want people to take pictures for the internet, only you pretend you don't. And there are places where you go when you genuinely want a quiet dinner. This was one of the quiet places."

Since the entire point of Jess fake-dating Matt had been publicity, I couldn't understand why they would have bothered going somewhere they wouldn't be noticed. But this didn't seem like the right time to ask about that.

"So you were on holy ground where the other Highlanders wouldn't take pictures of you," Kent said, "but he still had you give him injections under the table? And he wouldn't even take an inhaler in front of people?"

"And you didn't call 911?" Luna added.

"He didn't want to. Too many 911 recordings get leaked. I don't think he'd have called them if his house had burned down or a shark had eaten his leg."

"That's why the phone was lying near his food tonight," I said. "Not with his body. He didn't even try to call 911."

"Yeah," Jess said. "If he'd lived and found out I'd called 911 tonight, he would have lost his shit."

"How many people knew that?" I asked. "That he never called 911?"

"Probably more people than knew about the allergy," Jess said. He picked up Kent's flask and poured the rest of the booze into his tea. He gave the flask a few good shakes to get out the last drops. "If he got hurt, he'd get some doctor to make a house call. If he ran into someone's car, he'd give them money to forget it. Lots of people could have seen him do those things."

"So he had a nice quiet medical emergency," Luna said, "and then he went to the hospital? Called a special doctor to his mansion?"

"He went home," Jesse said. "That was it. I tried to get him to call someone if he wouldn't go to the hospital, but he wasn't having that. He said he'd sleep it off. I stuck around all night to make sure he didn't die."

"It's remarkable he didn't," Luna said. "He was lucky not to have died long before now. What an idiot."

She went on a rant about people who ignored serious health problems, but I missed most of it. I was thinking about a victim who didn't call for help. More to the point, I was thinking about knowing that. Knowing about the allergy and where the EpiPens were kept. Knowing that Lew was unwell and would probably take a sleeping pill to get some rest. All those intimate little things that most people wouldn't know.

"Is there any chance Matt would have been wearing his smaller EpiPen kit?" I asked once Luna had wound down.

"I doubt it," Jess said. "He didn't like how it messed up the lines of his clothes. Since Lew had the big allergy kit along, he wouldn't have bothered."

One more intimate little thing. If this had been the final exam for a course on how to murder Matt Garrett, Jess would have gotten 100 percent.

"All right," Luna said. "Let's say I am willing, for the moment, to entertain your ridiculous notion about this being deliberate. Who do you suppose did it?"

She barely had the last word out before a knock at the door took a year off all our lives.

"My heart," Kent said, grabbing his chest.

"Don't even joke," Luna told him.

I opened the door to find Vic on the other side. She craned her neck to look around me at the occupants.

"Oh good, that's all four of you. Sarah wants everyone in the green room."

We could have said we didn't care what Sarah wanted since the show was over and the night had gone to hell, but I was curious to hear what she'd have to say. We followed Vic down the hall, Jesse at her heels and asking about the laryngitis lie. Had it been the charity's idea?

"No, that was Sarah," Vic said. "The Foundation people still don't know he's dead. And neither do these yahoos, so don't go telling them before Sarah gets a chance."

"When did they turn from gifted artists into yahoos?" Luna whispered.

"You haven't been in the green room recently," Kent whispered back, as much as he ever whispered. Which meant Vic heard and shot him a curious glance.

"Nothing," he said. "I won't say a word to the yahoos."

CHAPTER TWELVE

INSIDE THE green room, I did a quick head count and determined that Vic had indeed rounded up everyone. The only people missing were the staff, Crystal, Alex, and Lew. Everyone had returned to their original klatches, comics with comics and bands together. The only exceptions were Dylan and Emilie, who were together in the room's back left corner.

New to the group was a very tall and very thin woman in a long navy-blue wool dress. She had matte black hair, straight and thick and well past her shoulders. Her back was to us when the door opened, but she turned to look as she heard us step inside. Her features were long and thin to match the rest of her. She was wearing a simple chain and chunky ring that both looked like gold, and her hair was kept back by a thin band lined with black crystals. The impression was that she was trying to appear self-effacing, which was not the same as being self-effacing.

The headphones lying around her neck and the black toolbelt around her waist were the only things that would have distinguished her from a wealthy member of the charity.

"Thank you, Victoria," she said to Vic. "I think this is everyone?"

"Unless you want his mana—"

"No," Sarah said quickly. She had a crisp voice that would cut well through the headphone chatter during a show. "They don't need to be here. Everyone, please make yourselves as comfortable as you can."

There weren't a lot of chairs left, so I leaned against a wall. Jess joined me there. Kent and Luna pulled a pair of chairs from the table to a clear spot in front of the coffee machine. Vic stayed by the door, seeming far from comfortable.

"First, I would like to thank you all for your generous donation of your talent this evening. I apologize that I haven't been able to come here sooner. In addition to the sold-out event, the Foundation has received an unprecedented number of donations for a single day. They are over the moon and very grateful to you all. You have truly made a difference tonight."

She clapped softly a few times, delicately patting the palm of one hand with the fingertips of the other. Her nails were like inverted teardrops, painted pale gold.

The idea seemed to be that we all give ourselves a hand, but no one was up for it. Brennan and his crew served up neutral expressions, while the ladies in Ash Rose gave one another "did she really do that?" looks.

I thought I saw a phone being held up in Emilie and Dylan's corner. Probably Emilie's phone. If I'd made a living off pitch-dark comedy, I might have been recording this too. I was going to have to say something if it was still there when Sarah got to the point, though, because this was the last thing any of the other artists needed captured for all time.

"I ask that you please do not let what I am about to tell you take anything away from your achievement here or from the rest of your experience with the Foundation or, indeed, the production company."

"Indeed," Jess said under his breath. Happily I was close enough to elbow him without it being seen.

"Before I go any further, I have to ask for discretion in the short term. It's very important that we respect the seriousness and privacy of this situation for both personal and legal reasons."

"For what fucking reasons?" Duncan asked from an armchair near the door. Despite the words, his voice was pleasant and a little beery, like he'd had a few during his trip to the outside world. "Personal and what now?"

"Please." Sarah held up a hand, flat and palm out like a traffic cop. "I will get there. Before I do, and I do hate to ask you this because I know you are all professionals who don't need to be told, but I must ask anyone who may be recording this to please turn off your phones."

Emilie's phone lowered, which was no guarantee that it was off. Anyone else who was recording had the sense not to reach into their pockets or purses. I wasn't entirely reassured, but my main interest was in keeping reaction shots of people's faces—Jesse's in particular—off the internet. I trusted that Jess had enough sense to keep his mouth shut once Matt's death was revealed.

"Some of you may be aware that Matt Garrett did not give his speech at the end of tonight's show," Sarah said.

"I think they're all pretty aware," Kent said. "I wouldn't worry about that. Except maybe those two." That was accompanied by the long arm of the law pointing at Dylan and Emilie.

"It's on everything?" Emilie said. "Even, like, the news-news."

She made it sound like conventional news outlets got their information delivered once a week by Pony Express. To be fair, it could feel that way sometimes. Especially when things were moving fast.

"No one's buying the laryngitis story," Jesse said, which was a kindness to Sarah and Vic. It answered the question they couldn't ask, which was what, exactly, was on everything and even the news-news.

"We told the Foundation members and the media that Matt had laryngitis and so was unable to deliver his speech," Sarah told the assembly. "That may have been a mistake, but we were under pressure."

"What did you tell the audience?" Izzy asked.

"Nothing," Ziad said "They dropped the curtain in front of Barney Gumble while he was still talking."

Vic stepped forward.

"Okay, no we didn't," she said, "and don't call him Barney Gumble, all right? The man has a problem. You think no one in this room has a problem?"

Sarah gave Vic her traffic cop hand, which was a shame because Vic was doing great.

"He said Matt wasn't able to appear," Sarah said. "We left it at that. I felt the Foundation needed some-thing more, but I didn't feel at liberty to say what had happened, so I gave them a related lie. The truth is Matt really couldn't speak, but it was because he suffered a serious allergic reaction this evening."

"So he wasn't boning Jack," Duncan said. He sounded like this had killed his favourite theory. Given that most people thought Jess and Matt were genuine exes, and considering Jack Lowe's reputation as an alley cat, it was a fair assumption.

"Maybe he's allergic to Jack," Emilie suggested.

"You weren't here when Matt showed up," Duncan said. "It sounded way more like Jack was allergic to him."

"Jack says get bent," Jesse said. "This had nothing to do with me."

"So did he go to the hospital?" Ash asked. "Is everything okay?"

I swear there was a moment when Sarah considered lying again. It would have been so easy. Yes, he's in the hospital, and we're all praying for a quick recovery. But for reasons I was about to find out, she didn't take that path.

"I'm sorry to say that Matt Garrett passed away this evening, shortly after eleven."

"Shut the eff up!"

That was Emilie, a loud voice in the silence. She really said "eff." A few people looked at her. A few others looked at Kent, who had obviously known this while they'd been interrogating him and had told them nothing.

"This is going to be a huge story," Duncan said. "Huge. Like being there when Belushi died."

"I think someone did time for being there when Belushi died," Reiss said.

"There might be better ways to be immortalized," Thom added.

"Do you think his allergy might not have been an allergy, though?" Emilie asked. "Was he on a lot of drugs? Or was he, like, suicidal? It's a mental health night, right?"

"Less so all the time," Jess said.

"It was an allergic reaction," Sarah said. "I have the word of the Medical Examiner."

"She's not the Medical Examiner," I explained. "She's an investigator from the ME's office. But she is a doctor."

"The Medical Examiner came here?" Duncan said, as if I hadn't spoken. "What the shit? Who called them?"

"It's standard when someone dies unexpectedly," Kent said. He did not add that he'd made the call.

"How would you know?" Izzy asked. "Is there some reason you know this stuff?"

Kent tugged at the hem of his sweater, though it wasn't riding up. He was twitchy because he knew what was coming. "I am… a cop."

"Whaaaat?" Ash said. "Fuck off!"

"Is that fuck off, I'm not a cop, or fuck off, I am a cop?" Kent asked.

"Oh my God," Kayla said. "Either. Why is a cop here? This is the last place anyone wants to see one of you, except for, like, a Black Lives Matter protest."

"Or any protest. Or, God, anywhere," Ash added.

"Kent's off duty," Jess said. "And he is a friend of mine."

"Seriously, you're queer and you're friends with a cop?" Emilie said. "What is wrong with you?"

"You know some cops are queer, right?" Jess said. Him trying to defend police, any police, was a fun development since he'd spent our university years trying to talk me out of going into police work on the grounds that changing anything from the inside was a fantasy.

"I don't have my badge or my gun," Kent said. "I do have a therapist. I think my best friend's boyfriend has great legs. Instead of thinking of me as the enemy, try to think of me as your inside source on the local PD, because you're going to need that."

"What does that mean?" Brennan asked carefully. He'd put a hand on Reiss's back, between the shoulder blades and under the thick curls of his hair. Was it coarse or soft? Hair that curly was usually coarse, but I'd been surprised before. And this in no way mattered.

"That will do, thank you," Sarah told Kent. "What Jack's guest has… guessed… is that we will be seeing the police here tonight. Shortly. They are on their way."

"Is that also standard?" Connor asked. "Like the Medical Examiner?"

"No," I said. "That happens when the investigator thinks the police should become involved with the situation."

"I thought you said he died from an allergic reaction," Thom said.

"There's some concern about what precipitated that reaction," Sarah said.

"Is that a fancy way of saying someone doctored his food?" Connor asked. "They put peanut butter in his banana sandwich?"

"It's possible," I told him. "The police coming out here doesn't mean it's been declared a homicide or anything like that. It means the investigator wasn't certain that it was an accident."

"Or criminal negligence," Kent said. "If you told me to tell Luna here not to put hazelnut syrup in your coffee, and I forgot to tell her and she served you up a cup of hot death, I might be considered criminally responsible on some level. That kind of thing isn't for an ME investigator to decide, so they bring in the cops, just in case."

"So it was negligence?" Ash said. "Someone couldn't be bothered to get his order right and now he's dead?"

"We don't know what it was," I told her. "That's why the cops are on their way."

"You guys know a lot about all this," Duncan said. "We tried to find you and we couldn't, so we figured you must be in that room."

"Suite," Ziad said. "We had dressing rooms. He had a suite."

"We happened to be there when Vic went in trying to find him," Jess said. That left out the whole thing about him having access to Matt's room, but I could understand him not wanting to bring that up. "So the three of us found him. Me and Ben and Vic."

"We tried CPR, and we called for an ambulance," I said, "but it was too late."

"Allergic reactions can progress very quickly," Luna said.

"Okay, that's why they were in there, but you were too," Duncan said. "What's that about?"

"I'm a doctor," Luna said. "Ben sent Vic to get me when they found Matt on the floor, and Kent came along."

"And the manager and boyfriend are missing," Charlie said.

"Not missing," I said. "They stayed in the suite when the rest of us left. The investigator would have needed to talk to them. There are details the ME's office needs about the person who died, and they would have been the best source for that."

"And an official ID," Jess said. "They had to do that."

"He's Matt Garrett," Izzy said flatly.

"I know, but recognizing a famous person isn't the same as being able to swear to their identity. And his face was swollen from the allergy," Jess said. "The EMTs didn't recognize him. I might not have known him if he hadn't been wearing the same clothes as before."

"Really?" Ziad asked Jess. "You had no other way to ID him? He doesn't have a mole shaped like Louis C.K. on his dick?"

"I genuinely," Jess said, "would not know."

"I'm sorry to interrupt," Sarah lied, "but the police will be here soon, and I have some things to say. First, I am very sorry that your evening has come to this."

"Could've been worse, apparently," Duncan said.

"Second, I ask that you all remain on the premises so that the police are able to speak with you. I understand this is unpleasant and that some of you may be particularly uncomfortable interacting with police officers, but the quickest and best way to resolve this incident is to help the police do their jobs."

"Oh yes, trust the police and everything will be all right," Ash said.

"Thirdly," Sarah said, "though fans and the media do not yet know what has happened, you have probably seen discussion of the ambulance online. The arrival of the police will not go unnoticed. At some point, the... Matt's body will have to be removed. It is inevitable that word will get out. I am bringing in extra security, but this building will be surrounded by cameras eventually, and we may even have media entering the building."

"Are you saying we're not supposed to talk to them?" Ziad asked. "Is this a gag order?"

"That's what Matt said!" Duncan said.

"Tried to say," Emilie added and made a choking sound.

"You can speak to anyone you like," Sarah said. "You can also use social media. I have no control over any of that. I'm letting you know what will happen and asking that you consider being circumspect. It would be best for all of us if we said as little as possible now. I also think you would be most secure staying inside the building, possibly until morning. We should be able to make anyone who chooses to stay reasonably comfortable. If you must leave and need assistance getting to a vehicle, I will see what I can do."

"Will you be serving food?" Connor asked. "Because I'm not sure I'll want to eat it."

"He wasn't poisoned," Charlie said. "His food was adulterated."

"That would still mean there's someone around here who likes to kill people," Connor said, "using food."

"We do not know it was deliberate!" Sarah said. "Please, do not spread this kind of rumour. It won't help anything, and it may embarrass you later to have spoken in haste tonight."

Sarah hadn't endeared herself to me, but I had sympathy for the position she was in. It was her job to protect the production company and their clients from bad press to whatever extent that was possible. That was her interest, and everyone knew it, which made it sound self-serving when she gave people what I thought was well-meant advice. She was right that tweeting from the hip wouldn't do anyone any good. It didn't change the fact that someone in this crew was likely to start doing it to spite her.

Sarah pulled a phone from the thick work belt around her waist and glanced at it.

"Victoria, with me, please."

She left, with Vic on her heels. Vic pulled the door shut as she went.

"That's it," Ash said, rising to her feet. "We're out of here."

"Can we do that?" Kayla said.

"Door's right there," Ash said.

"We need our gear," Kayla said. "And it's two blocks to the van."

"We can get it tomorrow," Ash said. "They can't confiscate our keyboards just because someone died here. We'll get our coats from the dressing room and we're out."

"But will we get in trouble?" Kayla said. "For leaving? Before the police talk to us?"

"We didn't kill anyone," Izzy said. "We're free to go, and fuck them if they don't like it."

Jess looked a question at me, and I shrugged. The rule was that police could briefly detain people if they had good reason to think that person might have been involved in a crime. The actual term was "reasonable suspicion," and it was one of those legal vaguenesses that could mean anything until it was interpreted by a judge.

There was not any rule that said the police could detain someone by proxy just because said person happened to be in the same building as a possible crime.

"I hope we get in trouble," Ash said. "We're not going to sit here helping the police while they railroad some innocent person. I mean, probably Vic. I'm not going to stand for that. I'm leaving."

She did not explain how leaving would keep anyone from railroading anyone, but I wasn't inclined to ask.

"Wait," Jess said.

"Oh, you want us to stick around and help your cop friends?" Ash said.

"No. Were you planning to stay in town overnight? Did the producers set up a hotel for you?"

"No," Izzy said. "We were going to drive back."

"Lunes, do you have paper and a pen in that bag of holding you're carrying?"

"What is a bag of holding?" Luna asked as she crossed to Jess and produced a small notepad and a leopard-printed miniature pen from her clutch.

"Like a TARDIS, only a purse," Jess said. "Bigger on the inside than the outside. Thanks."

He wrote something, tore the sheet from the pad, and held it out to Izzy. I glanced over and saw my address and the key code to my garage.

"Excuse me?" I said.

"The keycode will get you into the garage," Jess said. "The door from the garage to the house is unlocked. There's a spare bedroom and a decent couch. We had someone walk and feed the dog, but I'm sure he'd be grateful if you'd let him into the yard for a few minutes."

Izzy took the note and read it, then scowled at Jess.

"Are you setting us up to get mauled by your guard dog?"

Jess took out his phone. Getting out pictures of Frank, no doubt, which he would do given any excuse or none at all.

While he was messing with it, I said, "There are confidential files in my office."

"You always lock the door. There. Does Frank look like a guard dog?"

Izzy tried not to smile at the photo of my dog. "Oh my God. Who shrunk the Wookie in the dryer?"

"Give him our regards. Don't leave him outside for more than a minute or two. And try not to spray-paint Fuck the Police on the living room wall because it will make Kent uncomfortable when he visits."

"Nobody asked me," I said uselessly.

"They need somewhere to crash, and they're probably broke."

"We are so broke," Kayla said.

"There you go."

"You wanna come with us?" Izzy asked.

"No," Jess said. "I think we'll stay around and try to keep the railroading to a minimum. Is your van plugged in?"

"Yes, and I already started it," Izzy said, holding up her keychain to show a remote starter. "Are you happy now, Not My Real Dad?"

"Over the moon," Jess said, echoing Sarah's phrase. "Good luck out there."

"Good luck in here."

As they left, I considered telling them that Sarah had probably gone to meet the police at the stage door and that they'd be better off going over the stage to front of house and leaving through the front doors. I decided I was also not their real dad and they could figure that out for themselves. Or not. It wasn't my problem, and I had enough of those without adopting more.

CHAPTER THIRTEEN

"'I HOPE WE get in trouble,'" Ziad said once the door was closed. "I think that's the whitest thing I've heard all day, and I've been around Duncan for hours."

"I'm a sixteenth Dene," Duncan said.

Ziad smiled. "And now that's the whitest thing I've heard all day."

"How bad is this situation?" Duncan asked. "Should we all be calling our lawyers?"

Kent and I exchanged looks. This wasn't a simple question to answer, especially for him.

"Yes and no," Kent said. "You're basically fine until you get read your rights. Nothing you say until that point can be brought into court. But you can still dig your own grave by saying stupid things. You tell me

you were at the movies with Emilie during the crime
and she tells me you weren't, I'm going to wonder
where you really were and why you lied to me. Even
if you're innocent, I might find out things you don't
want anyone to know, or I might get fixated on you as
a suspect."

"So lawyer up and clam up?" Connor said.

"I said yes and no," Kent told him. "If you dis-
approve of murder like I do, you might want to be
helpful."

"It's different once you've been cautioned," I said.
"That's when you lawyer up, no matter what. As soon
as the cops arrest you, they are not in the business of
helping you, no matter what they say. They are in the
business of giving prosecutors enough to convict you.
Unless you really like prison, you and the cops have
opposing goals."

"Does anyone really like prison?" Connor asked.

"Not," Kent said, "as far as I know."

"Right. Well, I don't know anything, so it's all the
same either way."

Behind Connor and Charlie, a scene was playing
out. Reiss had gone pale and a little spacey, the way
he'd been before sound check. Brennan had guided
him to the couches in the back right corner, and he and
Thom were sitting with Reiss between them, having a
whispered conversation. What was that about?

"You don't know whether you know anything,"
Kent was saying. "You might have run into someone
in the hall at exactly the right time to exclude them."

"Any idea who's going to show up here?" I asked
Kent. The odds were good it would be an ex-colleague
of mine, though there were a few new faces since I'd
gone.

"I'm not sure who's on tonight," Kent said. "We might only get one detective. Lots of people on leave right now."

"Injuries?"

"Yeah, and mental health stuff. You know."

"It's still not usual to send a detective alone," I pointed out. Kent shrugged.

"Not really alone. Forensics will show up. There's security staff around. I'm here. Hell, you're here."

"It's high profile, though," Jess said. "Or it will be. What did they call that on *Homicide*? A red ball?"

I regretted making Jess watch my box set of *Homicide: Life on the Streets*. It had brought him to new heights of thinking he knew my job.

"I'm sure they're hoping they can sew this up tonight," Kent said. "Or that it really was an accident."

"You think they'll be eager to make an arrest?" Duncan asked. "Pick someone obvious like Jack or Ziad and hang this on them?"

"Fuck you, what?" Ziad said, as Jess said, "Excuse me?"

"I know you make a living with that mouth, buddy," Kent said, "but you might want to shut it for now."

"You make it sound like I give blow jobs in back alleys," Duncan said. Kent said nothing.

"It's weird to think someone here might have killed someone," Connor said. "Can we all agree that's weird?"

"Not for me," Kent said.

"Can we also," Connor said carefully, "acknowledge that some people are going to seem more suspicious than others? Seriously, Jack—Jesse— no offence. I'm not saying I think you did it. I'm asking what the cops will think."

"What, no one's going to bite his head off?" Duncan asked. "He said exactly what I said."

"Not exactly," I said.

"I notice you didn't say you didn't think I did it," Ziad pointed out.

"Yeah, man," Connor said. "That's not personal. Thom and Jesse go way back, so I figure Thom would have said something if Jesse was, like, murderous."

"He also thinks we both look suspicious," Jesse told Ziad. "If that makes you feel any better."

"Loads. Where is this cop, anyway? I thought Sarah and Vic went to get him. Or her."

"Or them," Dylan said. From Ziad's jumpy reaction, it was likely he'd forgotten Dylan was there. Or hadn't noticed them in the first place.

"Shit, you're that non-binary kid who does the mope folk. Sorry about that."

"Are you sorry they're enby or sorry about the music?" Emilie asked.

"Oh, both," Ziad said, then put his hands in the air. "Kidding. I am kidding. Though seriously, kid, have you ever written anything happy? How often have you been dumped?"

"People relate to it," Dylan said. They didn't seem angry or offended. It was a little weird seeing someone as loud and brash as Emilie bonding with someone who barely reacted to anything, but that might have been the appeal.

"Anyway," Ziad said, "about that cop."

"Talking to the manager and the boyfriend," Kent said. "That's a guess, but it's where I'd go first. And they'll want to see the body."

"Do you think maybe they did it?" Connor asked. "Not the cop. The manager or the boyfriend."

"I have no idea," I said. "On the surface, they don't have motives to harm him. Matt's at the height of his career, so Lew can still make a lot of money off him. And Matt and Alex were… they seemed fine with whatever they were."

"How much does someone make managing a guy like that?" Duncan asked.

"Millions," Jess said. "It would vary from year to year, depending on Matt's projects. But it's projects, endorsements, licensing, residuals, probably a bunch of stuff I don't even know exists."

"There's no way you'd want to cut that off," Connor said. "Even if you hated the guy."

"He doesn't hate Matt," Jess said. "Or at least he didn't when I was hanging around with them."

"It was probably an accident," Emilie said. "No one could have peanuts at my school because this one kid was so allergic he'd die if you breathed peanut butter at him."

"I thought you couldn't have peanuts in any schools," Dylan said. "And I think you have to at least touch food you're allergic to. I don't think just breathing is enough."

"Okay, Dr. Science," Emilie said. "Whatever. I mean it would be really easy to accidentally kill someone who was that allergic. I'm surprised anyone with bad allergies even lives as long as Matt Garrett did."

"Do we still have to be here? In this room?" Dylan said. "It's way too bright."

"It's way too fucking everything," Ziad said. "I need a smoke."

"If your plan is to set off the smoke detectors," Duncan told him, "I approve."

"There's a fire door off the back of the stage that's not hooked up to an alarm," Ziad said. "That I know of. No, the fire engines would be here by now if there was a silent alarm on that door."

"I could use a smoke," Duncan said. "Lemme get my jacket so I don't freeze. I want to live long enough to die of lung cancer."

He and Ziad left. Dylan took a few steps after them, then paused and turned to me.

"Can we go?"

"You could go home if you wanted," I said. "If you want to stay and talk to the cops, go to your dressing room and I'm sure they'll find you eventually."

They nodded. "Thanks."

Emilie went with them, leaving my crew and the Twist alone in the green room.

"You think they'll go home?" Connor asked.

"I doubt it," I said. "Emilie's too curious to leave, and Dylan would worry about getting in trouble. That's my snap judgement of two people I barely know. But if you guys want to make a break for it, now would be the time."

"What if I want to make a break for it?" Jess said.

"You'd have left half an hour ago," I said. "You haven't because you think it would look bad."

"It would look fucking terrible," Jess said. "I already seem guilty enough. You guys, is everything okay?"

He said that to Thom and Reiss and Brennan, who were still a huddled coterie on the couch. Brennan and Thom exchanged glances, and Thom came over to us.

"Reiss had a bad experience with the police," he said. "He was a little disoriented, and they brought him to the hospital. It was dehumanizing. Not that they brought him to the hospital, more the thing where they treated him like a criminal. And the hospital also wasn't great."

I carefully did not look at Kent. He and I had transported a few people who were "a little disoriented" when I'd been on the force and before he'd been promoted to Homicide. Some of those folks had been confused or nervous. Some had been convinced we were there to drag them to a gulag or beam them to the mothership, and they'd fought back the way anyone would if they really believed those things.

I'd never blamed them for fighting, but I'd put cuffs on a few. I didn't feel great about that now.

"You can leave," I said. "I can't promise the cops won't find you and ask to talk to you, but it might be more on your terms."

Reiss sighed and leaned back against the couch.

"Jesse, did you really not kill that asshole?"

"I really did not kill that asshole," Jess confirmed. "Why?"

"Because I want to help the cops not arrest you," Reiss said. "I'll stay. In case I know anything that might help."

"We were mostly here or onstage or in the practice room," Thom said, "but maybe we saw or heard something and we don't realize it. Like your friend said, we don't know what we know."

"It's schizophrenia, by the way," Reiss added. "And I wasn't a little disoriented, I was psychotic. They still didn't need to treat me like that."

"I appreciate the support, and I'm really sorry about what happened to you," Jess said, "but can we all stop talking like I'm about to do life at Kingston?"

"You're in no danger of that," I said.

"Thank you."

"Kingston closed in 2014."

Jess eyed me like he was considering what part of me would hurt most if he stuck an icepick in it. Not that he had an icepick, but he might go to the trouble of finding one.

"You know, they might think it was me," Reiss said. "Because I am cuh-razy."

Brennan seemed uncomfortable, but Reiss was looking better than he had in a while, and he had a wry grin.

"We're all crazy," Jess said. "If you want to stand out, you'll have to do better than—"

He stopped because his phone was vibrating. He took it out, checked who was calling, and showed the screen to me. Gia Nately, his road manager, liaison, and troubleshooter at the record label. She was good to Jess, and I appreciated that, but she wasn't gifted with patience or tact.

"Jesus Christ," I said. "Is the woman psychic?"

"Maybe," Jess said. He sounded like he meant it. He tapped the button, quick and sharp, as if he thought it would try to bite him. "Hello?"

I could hear Gia's voice from where I was, though I couldn't make out the words. She didn't sound happy. It was two hours later in Toronto, so that would be part of her mood, but the rest had to be about Matt.

"None of it was my idea," Jess said. "No… I…. Would you stop? Why would I…? Yes, exactly. I wouldn't. I didn't know he was going to be here. Gia? Gee? Who told you he was—"

He listened and nodded. His eyes got wider. "Gia, I'm gonna call you back."

He hung up and looked at me.

"It's out," he said. "About Matt. They know he's dead. Some people were speculating before, but now everyone seems to know."

Luna was already on her phone.

"It's everywhere," she confirmed. "I don't know how. And they're talking about the cops being here, so Sarah guessed right about that."

"So much for sneaking out the side door," Connor said. "You think Duncan and Ziad will be back soon?"

No one answered that because the door opened and Vic walked a stranger inside. He was a little taller than Jess and a fair bit wider, with a rumpled grey suit and an expression that said he was annoyed to be here. His black hair was half grey and in need of combing. Everything about him said "cop."

He hadn't been on the force when I'd been there. I glanced at Kent, who didn't seem thrilled by the way our dice roll had come up.

"Everyone," Vic said, "this is Detective Lam. He'd like to ask you a few questions."

I looked at Reiss. He seemed relieved for some reason. Maybe because the detective wasn't in uniform. It wouldn't have been detectives who'd taken him to that hospital.

"This isn't everyone," the detective said. He sounded like a diner sending food back because he'd been promised, and shorted, a pickle.

"I'm sure they're around," Vic said. "I'll find them for you."

"Ziad and Duncan are having a smoke by the fire door," Thom said. "Behind the stage."

He failed to mention that Dylan and Emilie had gone to Dylan's dressing room, or that Ash Rose had run for the hills. No one else jumped in.

"If you don't know," Jess said, "it got out that Matt's dead. And that police are in the theatre."

"When you say out…," Vic said.

"The internet," Luna said. "Basically the entire world."

"Phenomenal."

"You might want to pull Ziad and Duncan back inside before the streets turn into a candlelight vigil and media circus," Jesse suggested.

"In this weather?" Thom said. "Do candles even work?"

"If fire didn't work in the cold, I don't think humans would have made it this far," I pointed out.

"There's already a zoo at the stage door," Vic said. "I gotta go. Detective, they're all yours."

"But this isn't all of them," he protested as she left. He said the last word to the closing door.

CHAPTER FOURTEEN

DETECTIVE LAM put his hands in the pockets of his suit jacket. Had he come here in just that suit, dropped at the door by a cab? Or were his winter clothes in Matt's suite, dripping melted snow onto the carpet?

"Detective Hauser," he said. "They told me you'd be here."

He didn't seem any happier to see Kent than Kent seemed to see him.

"Detective Lam," Kent said. "They didn't tell me you'd be here."

"My lucky night," Lam said. He took a notepad and a pen from an inside jacket pocket. "Is that the lineup?"

He pointed at the whiteboard with a ballpoint pen. I hadn't seen him even glance in that direction since he'd come in. He'd taken in more of the room than I would have guessed.

"Ash Rose left," Kent said. "There were three of them. Girl group. I doubt they were involved."

"Are you clocking in, Detective?"

That wasn't a real question. It was a comment about Kent's comments, which were seemingly not wanted.

"Nah," Kent said. "It's my night off. Thought I'd spend it watching a master at work."

"When did the young ladies leave?" Lam asked. He asked it of Thom.

"I didn't check the time," Thom said. "I think right before you got here. Not here as in this room. Here at the theatre."

"I'll get their contact information from Ms. Lincoln," Lam said. It took me a second to realize he meant Vic. "Who do I have here?"

"We're the Twist," Brennan said. "Me, those two, that one and this one."

Lam scratched the top of his head, then put ballpoint to paper.

"I don't suppose you have names?"

Thom politely introduced everyone in his band, the way he had for me and Jess about a century ago. Something about cops made Thom act like he was in grade three, offering to clean erasers for the teacher. Maybe he was trying to keep things civil so Reiss would be more at ease.

"Right. Detective Hauser I know. Who are you?"

That was aimed at Luna, along with the tip of his pen.

"Doctor Luna Fares," Luna said crisply. "I am also off duty."

"You're the doctor they brought in from the audience."

"Yes."

Lam nodded and turned to me. "You're familiar."

"Okay," I said. I wasn't sure what else he wanted.

"You're that detective," he said. "You were on the force. Now you're a PI."

"I am that detective," I said. "Ben Ames."

"Uh-huh. That's you. Okay. A detective, a cop, and a doctor. Is anyone else here a performer?"

"I'm Jesse Serik," Jess told him. "My stage name is Jack Lowe. Ben and Luna and Kent are all here as my guests."

"Funny crowd you run with," Lam said. It sounded like an accusation. Of what I could not have said.

"Wait till you meet the comics," Jess returned without a smile.

That would have been a perfect moment for Vic to return with Ziad and Duncan, but instead the words hung there, framed by silence. Lam looked at Jess, and Jess looked at him. Lam would have known Jack's reputation as a hedonist and troublemaker. I could see him considering it. Finally, Lam broke the staring contest and addressed Thom again.

"What about this Dylan and, ah, Emilie Brookes? Did they go home too?"

"I don't think so," Thom said. "I think they're around somewhere."

Lam made a "more" gesture with the hand holding his pen.

Thom shook his head. "I didn't ask where they were going. One of the dressing rooms, maybe?"

"One of the dressing rooms. I'll have Ms. Lincoln track them down as well. Is there anyone else? Anyone who isn't on that board? Any other guests?"

"Just Matt," Thom said. "Uh, his manager and his boyfriend. No one else had guests."

"And the crew," Charlie pointed out. "There's house crew, the production company staff, security, a bunch of media, and people from the charity on the other side of the theatre."

"The media and the Foundation people all got kicked out before midnight," Jess said. "They'll all be home or at their hotels by now."

"Unless they're staking out the stage door," I said.

"They couldn't get to this side of the theatre anyway," Jess said. "It probably doesn't matter."

That was when the door opened and Vic waved Ziad and Duncan inside. Their faces were red, with lashes and brows frosted from the cold. Vic didn't follow them into the green room. Mostly likely she was on the hunt for Dylan and Emilie. And Ash Rose, since no one had told her they were gone.

"Who do we have here?" Detective Lam asked. He did not introduce himself. He regarded them pissily, with no glimmer of recognition in his eyes. I found it hard to believe that someone would fail to recognize at least one of them, but this guy sold it.

"I'm Duncan Winter," Duncan said. "This is Ziad Samara."

"Four and six," Lam said. He made ticks in his notebook. "What is it you do?"

They glanced at each other nervously. I wasn't sure whether that was because they were talking to a homicide detective or because the homicide detective didn't seem to know or care who they were.

"We're comedians," Duncan said. "And actors."

"We did comedy sets tonight," Ziad clarified.

Lam made a noise that came from deep in his chest and was somewhere between a sigh and a yawn.

"All right. I'd like to talk to everyone in the order they performed, to keep things straight, but it looks like I won't able to do that. Mr. Winter, please accompany me to dressing room two."

"That's my dressing room," Duncan said.

"It's our dressing room," Ziad said. "They put all of us in one room. The comics."

"Now it's my interview room," Lam said. "Mr. Winter?"

"Wait, can I get my stuff out of there?" Ziad said. "What if I need something? Dude, don't walk away from me."

Dude kept walking away from him. He did not so much as pause. Once he and Duncan were gone, Ziad addressed the room.

"Who the fuck was that guy?"

"Detective Samuel Lam," Kent said. "Do not call him Sam. Call him Detective Lam."

"Sam it is," Ziad said. "That's the guy Calgary sent to solve this?"

"That's the guy who was on nights," Kent said.

"And you know him."

"We're not pals."

Ziad had a leather satchel over his shoulder. I hadn't seen him with it before. He eyed the pack of cigarettes in his hand like he was thinking of lighting one up and damn the consequences, then slid it into the bag.

"What's he like?"

"A dick?" Connor offered. "Not like Philip Marlowe. A dick dick."

I could feel Jess wanting to say a dik-dik was an antelope. I gave him a look, and he kept it inside.

"I'm not trying to date him," Ziad said. "I want to know what kind of detective he is. Is he any good at solving crimes? Does he arrest the most convenient suspect? Does he arrest the brownest suspect? Should I be worried?"

"I'm not sure how good he is at solving crimes," Kent said. "I'm not sure how good I am at solving crimes either. I gotta tell ya, we do not get a lot of whodunnits."

Ziad sat on the table, after checking to make sure no one had left a plate of squares there. The cool vibe he was going for would have been spoiled by having to scrape Nanaimo bars off his pants.

"What's his temperament?"

"So you don't want to date him," Reiss said, "but you do want to adopt him from the Humane Society."

"I can't believe I'm the one who has to say this," Ziad said, "given my line of work, but you all need to start taking this seriously. Especially anyone who has a history with Matt."

"We don't," Thom said.

"Me neither," Duncan said. "It's Ziad and Jack."

"How worried should we be?" Ziad repeated, looking Kent in the eye. "Assuming neither of us did it."

"I don't know. He's not a dirty cop. He's not dumb. I think he'd like to get the bad guy, but I don't know if he'll figure out who that is. More than anything in the whole world? I think he wants to go back to bed."

"That is not reassuring," Ziad said.

"You both might need your lawyers on standby," Kent said. "Sorry, Jess."

"I figured. I saw how he looked at me."

"What, that's it?" Ziad scanned the room. He had to put a hand behind him on the table and lean back to glare at the guys in the corner. "You're all going to roll over and let this detective haul in whoever is most convenient so he can get back into his Spider-Man pajamas and go beddy-bye?"

Kent's mouth twitched. Likely picturing Detective Lam in Spider-Man pajamas.

"I hope you're not planning to call the chief of police and the mayor and demand a different detective," I said. "You're not rich or famous enough to get away with that."

"Give me a couple years," Ziad said, "if I don't fuck up here tonight."

"I'm not sure there's a better detective to ask for anyway," Kent said. "There are worse ones."

"I'm not talking about calling the police," Ziad said. "I don't want to leave this to the police. I understand we have a world-class private detective in our midst."

"I sure hope someone else here is moonlighting as a world-class private detective," I said, "because that's not me."

"You solved a whodunnit last year."

"No, I solved a keep-chipping-away-at-it last year. I ran down leads until there were no more. I have no experience with this *Murder on the Orient Express* business."

"Oh, we should have all killed him together!" Luna said. "Why didn't we think of it?"

"Now is the time to stop making jokes like that," I told her. "You know what? You gave your information to Crystal. You and Kent have been together all night, so you wouldn't have seen anything he didn't. It's not the worst idea for you to go home."

"What if someone sticks a knife in you?" she asked. "Who will tell you not to pull it out?"

"Poisoners aren't knife people."

"See, that's what I mean," Ziad said. "That's the kind of insight we need. If someone has to hire you before you can work the case, fine. I'll hire you."

"I'm not working tonight," I said. "And hiring a PI whose boyfriend is a suspect is a terrible idea."

Ziad looked at me speculatively. "Would you cover for him? If he did it?"

"I don't date the kind of people I would have to cover for," I said. It wasn't strictly true, but it was the best Ziad was going to get.

"I trust you to turn in the real culprit," Ziad said. "What are your rates?"

"Eleventy zillion dollars an hour. You can't afford me."

"I can't afford not to hire you," he said. The levity that had slipped in while we bantered was gone. "Duncan's an asshole, but he's right. Jess and I seem guilty. I don't like fifty-fifty odds when the stakes are my life."

They weren't his life in Canada. Just his freedom. And his reputation and his career. I got what he meant.

"It wouldn't be ethical for me to take the job."

"What if we all took the job?" Thom said. Ziad regarded at him with surprise.

"What's that, magic beanstalk?"

"What if we all worked together to try to figure out who did it? That way if anyone has a bias, it'll be cancelled out by someone else's bias."

"We're the Mystery Incorporated gang now?" Ziad said. "Is the guy with the hair Scooby-Doo?"

He meant Reiss. I could tell Reiss had picked up on that by the fact that he was flipping Ziad off with both hands.

"Ruck roff," he said, and Ziad actually cracked a smile.

"Why does everyone think they can do my job?" I asked. "Did you see me on stage tonight trying to do your jobs?"

"You make a lot of jokes," Ziad said.

"Not professionally. Do you know how to question someone to get the truth and not what they think you want to hear? Do you know how the chain of evidence works? Do you know what you are and are not allowed to do during a police investigation? If one person here, other than Kent or Luna, can tell me where Matt's body is going to be taken and who is going to take it there, I will be Doctor Watson to your Sherlock for the rest of the night."

I waited. People looked at each other. Connor started to take out his phone, but I glared at him until he put it away.

"Okay," Thom said. "I guess you're right. You should solve this, and we'll help any way we can. You can give us directions."

That was the fastest I'd ever gone from triumphantly proving a point to getting shivved with it. Jess was raising his eyebrows at me. I took a deep breath in through my nose.

"Fucking… fine. Okay. I'll see what I can do."

Ziad held up a loonie. I shook my head.

"No. I told you I can't ethically work for you. I want to think I'm neutral and I'm after the truth, but I'm human and Jess is my person."

"Can you work for me?" Reiss asked. "I want someone to catch the correct person. Until that happens, I'm going to feel like the cops are after me."

I considered that. As my client, Reiss's goal was that he not be arrested. I could best prevent that by identifying the culprit or learning that it really had been an accident. Since I didn't see Reiss as a realistic suspect,

I could take him on as a client while maintaining my belief that Jess was innocent. Those were not conflicts.

"Okay," I said. "Toss me a loonie."

He stood up and went into his wallet, then laughed.

"Man, I almost never carry cash. Driver's licence… health card… Optimum card… would you take an old fifty-dollar Cineplex gift card? It might still be good. I didn't use it during COVID, and then I forgot I had it."

"They legally have to treat that like money," Thom said. "Doesn't matter how old it is."

"That seems oddly appropriate," I said. "I'm hired."

He threw the card to me edgewise, like a Frisbee. I caught it and put it into my back pocket.

"You going to tell Detective Lam you're on the job?" Kent asked.

"He seems busy," I said. "Maybe later."

Kent snorted. Then he put his hands on his knees and leaned forward until he was on his feet.

"Let's have a talk, Sherlock. Jess, can we borrow your dressing room?"

"I guess. Luna still has my pass."

Luna took the pass from her purse but pulled it back when Kent reached for it.

"Am I invited to this talk?"

"No."

She shrugged and started to put the pass back.

"Luna, I'll have this meeting somewhere else if I have to," Kent said. This was a tone he didn't use often, the one he broke out when he was absolutely not kidding around. "Keep the pass. I'm not going to invite you."

She studied his face, then scowled and handed over the pass.

"It's my dressing room," Jess told her, "and I'm not invited either."

Thom crossed the room and put a hand on Jess's arm.

"C'mon… let's go to the practice room. The cop can find us if he wants to talk to us."

"Yeah, okay."

The two of them headed out. After a moment, Reiss and Brennan trailed after them. Kent and I let them go before we left the green room. We both took a moment to glance in the direction of Matt's suite, once we were in the hall. The door was closed, but there was no tape covering it. Forensics were probably still inside.

Kent slapped a meaty hand on my shoulder and pushed me lightly down the hall toward Jesse's dressing room. I didn't know what he wanted to talk about, but chances were he had things to say about Lam that he didn't want to share with civilians. Once a cop, always sort of a cop, in Kent's eyes. Me and him and Lam were different from the rest of this bunch.

I took a seat as soon as we were inside, but Kent puttered around, putting mugs away and returning his flask to his coat. I knew this behaviour. He was nervous, putting off whatever he meant to say.

"We don't have all night," I reminded him.

"No. No, we don't."

He sat across from me and rested his elbows on his knees with his hands hanging loose between his legs. His head hung down. I saw his shoulders move up and down as he took a few deep breaths. Then he looked at me.

"Ben, please don't take this the wrong way."

"Nothing that starts that way ever ends well," I told him.

"Given the circumstances and everything that happened—the trauma, the resentment of keeping it quiet, the surprise of Matt showing up here unannounced…."

"Go on."

"You'd see how someone might react in a way that would ordinarily be out of character."

Anyone would understand. You were justified. It's not even a crime, really. That was an interrogation technique so old, God had probably used it on Cain.

"Please tell me you're not using 'no one could blame you' on me right now."

"Fine. I'll cut to it. Are you really sure Jess didn't do this?"

My fists clenched, but that was the only move I made. He hadn't known Jess that long. Less than a year. He was a cop. He thought like one. He couldn't assume anyone was innocent.

"This kind of thing," I said, "would not be his style."

Kent smiled a little, without humour. "That wouldn't go far in court."

"We're not in court. Do you think he'd poison someone and do a show while that person was choking to death?"

"I don't know what he'd do," Kent said. "And you don't either. How many times have people told us their kid or husband or whatever would never hurt anyone when we know for a fact they did? You could say I know Jesse better than you do in this situation, because I don't have as many illusions."

It wasn't appropriate, maybe, but I couldn't help it. I burst out laughing.

"Oh my God. You think I have illusions."

"He's your boyfriend."

"Yeah, but he's not some cute guy I've been dating for a month. I'm not infatuated. I am extremely well aware of what Jesse is about. Considering how familiar I am with all his bad points, the fact that I still love him is kind of a miracle."

"The fact that you talk about him that way tells me you're a little infatuated." He put up his hands. "I don't blame you. And this isn't the 'I don't blame you' speech. I mean it. And I was skeptical. When I met him, I thought he'd be fucking precious and no fun. He is neither of those. I am Team Jesse. But I'm also your best friend, and it's my job to keep a clear head about the people you date."

"This is the only person you have seen me date," I pointed out.

"Not helping your case here," he said.

"I know what's wrong with him. I had seven years to think about it. I never once thought, he's probably a murderer. But you know what? Fine. If you're sure you know him better, tell me what you make of the suspect."

"Hmm." Kent leaned back in the chair and put his hands on his knees. "Highly intelligent. Calculating. He's a planner."

"I know that," I said. "I saw him plan his whole career."

"And yet I bet it would surprise you to know that he's had a Calgary realtor since three months before his last tour."

A few thoughts ran into each other at high speed. What came out of the crash was, "How do you know that?"

"Dated a girl who works with Jesse's guy. Jess asked the guy not to tell anyone, but he was trying to impress this girl, so he spilled it."

"I really hope it's a woman you dated," I said, "not a girl. How long have you known this?"

He shrugged. "About a month. I wasn't planning to tell you. It was supposed to be a secret."

I flashed back to Jesse and me in the mountains near Banff, him commenting on local real-estate prices and me rolling my eyes, thinking he was talking about local shit he didn't remotely understand. Apparently he'd been better informed than I'd thought.

Also apparently, he had decided we were getting back together.

"Does he still have a realtor?" I asked. "I told him not to buy us a house. I told him that would be weird."

"He did as of a month ago," Kent said. "That's all I know. Maybe he wants studio space."

That seemed unlikely since there was already a piano in my living room, but he wasn't set up to record from there, so maybe he did need another place. It was too bad that it would be impossible for me to ask him.

"Getting back to the murder," Kent said. "Your boyfriend is smart, he's tenacious, he plans, and he can keep his mouth shut. He knows he's exceptional. He is confident he can outwit and outperform most people. If I met him for the first time this close to a murder... I'd be worried about what I was dealing with."

"In that case," I said, "I'm going to pretend we're talking about some nameless suspect. This guy is a planner. So does he commit a crime of opportunity? Especially a serious crime like murder. Does he decide to kill someone with whatever is at hand a few hours after they turn up in his life by surprise?"

"Sometimes that's the best way to do it," Kent said. "If you don't want to get caught."

"Sure, but that's not how this guy likes to do things. He likes to pick his time and choose what other people see. So does he commit murder a few hours after making it clear to a room full of people that he hates the victim? Does he freely choose to commit this crime in a scenario where he knows he'll be the main suspect? Is that... his style?"

Kent rubbed his mouth. Slowly, the corner of it turned up.

"Okay," he said. "That's a good point. If this guy put mustard in someone's food, it would be a trace. And no one would know he'd been anywhere near the food."

"And," I said, "he'd put the EpiPens somewhere likely when he was done. He'd drop them on the floor next to the counter so it would seem like they fell out and Matt missed them in a panic."

"So this murder was committed by someone who's not as smart as Jess."

"Or not as thorough," I said. "Definitely more spontaneous."

Kent nodded. "I guess it wasn't you, either."

"I guess it wasn't."

He stretched and yawned. I heard something in his back crack.

"Did you think about it?" he asked.

"Not really. I thought about beating the shit out of him."

"So did I. Kind of. It's strange when it's a guy friend."

I could have called him out on that, but the truth was I got it. We'd both been raised a certain way, and there was a feeling that guys could take care of themselves, whereas women needed us to step in. It wasn't that I still thought this was true, but the impulse was there.

And there was the fact that I'd seen Jess slug someone, and he hit harder than people would expect.

"He probably got a few good shots in at the time," I said.

"Makes it worse for him in some ways, I bet. No one expects a woman to win a fight against Matt Garrett. They shouldn't expect it of someone Jesse's size, either, but I bet he's ashamed he didn't."

He hadn't said so, at least not to me, but Jess didn't talk about that night very often, and he'd never given me a lot of detail. The one time I'd suggested it might be good for him to really talk about it, he'd told me he had a therapist for that. Then he'd gone for a walk that had lasted three hours.

"I didn't feel like I needed to defend Jesse's honour or some shit like that," Kent said. "I mean, I'd have to find it first."

"Ha. Ha. Ha. Ha. Ha," I said, each an individual word.

"I don't like people who think they're above the law."

"Even when they basically are?" I said, already knowing the answer.

Kent said it anyway. "Especially then."

I nodded. We sat there for a minute or so. Kent broke the silence.

"He looks fucking guilty, though."

It's worse than you realize," I told him. "The reason me and Jess and Vic all found the body together is that Vic didn't have swipe-card access to Matt's suite. Hardly anyone did. She couldn't get him to answer the door, and she couldn't get in.

"So?"

"So Jess let her in."

I rarely saw Kent gape. He had a not unfounded idea that letting his mouth hang open made him look like a hillbilly.

"What the hell?"

"After his little talk with Matt, Matt gave him access to the suite. Jess says it was a 'come see me if you remember anything about that footage' kind of thing."

"Jess says that, does he?"

I didn't care for his insinuation, largely because I'd been thinking the same thing for about two hours.

"You think Jess is lying to me," I said. "Is that what you're saying?"

"I don't know. Would he have to lie? Or did Matt say 'come see me about the footage' and then whip his dick out? Then it's not a lie. He just left out the visual."

"Jess would have told me if Matt had done that."

"*Mmmm.*"

"What?"

"Would he? Or would he rather not have to bail you out of jail right before his set?"

"He would have told me," I insisted, with more conviction than I felt.

Kent shrugged. "Okay."

"My point is that he had access to that room."

"We should get a list of people who had access," Kent said.

"*I* sure should," I said. "*I* should do that on behalf of the client *I* have."

"Don't be like that," Kent said. "I'm here. I might as well help."

"And if Detective Lam views it as obstruction?"

"He can eat a dick."

"I doubt it, and thanks for that picture in my mind. You could get in a lot of trouble. More than if you were a civilian or a PI. Maybe you and Luna should both go home."

"Maybe we should all go home," Kent said, "and call our lawyers."

"If Gia hasn't already lined up a lawyer for Jess, I will eat this chair."

Kent whistled. "Toronto lawyer. We love that here."

"We seem unfriendly because we're in awe," I agreed. "We don't know what to say."

"It's too bad they mistake that for us wanting them to fuck off."

"She might have hired local," I said. "Actually I bet she hired some international firm, and they'll send in a local rep. Which is great because we do not have enough people wandering around this crime scene."

Kent laughed.

"Do you think Forensics is still working in there," he said, "or do you think they looked around the suite and now they're all sitting on the floor crying?"

"Probably crying," I said. "Once I realized it might be a crime, I thought about securing the scene, and then I realized it was way too late. At one point we could have taken everyone in there and fielded a baseball team."

"I almost feel bad for Lam."

"Why is it you don't like him?" I said. "Aside from his sunny personality and charm."

"Heh. The guy is… I dunno. He's not a shitty enough cop to call out for it, but he could do a better job."

"Most people probably could," I said. "Current company included."

"He could be a good detective instead of an okay one."

"So the wasted potential is pissing you off."

Kent pushed his chair back and put his feet up on the coffee table. "Phew. That's better."

"Knee bothering you again?"

"Again. Still."

It was a football injury he'd made worse one night by chasing an agile sixteen-year-old burglar out of a pharmacy and over a few fences.

"It's also," he said, "that he has me figured for a big dumb hick."

That was something Kent would only say to me. Maybe, *maybe*, Luna, if he got drunk enough. Most of the time, he was happy for people to think he was a hick. Good guy. A little thick but salt of the earth. Easy to put one over on if you were a criminal. He did a lot of good work by making criminals think they'd been lucky enough to land the dumbest cop in town. When another detective really believed he was dumb, though, that put a thorn in his pride. "So he's unobservant," I said. "That's on him, not you."

"He observes fine."

"We'll see. What do you think his plan is? Tracing movements? Good luck with that."

"Yeah, I don't think he brought a big enough notebook. He'll be wanting someone obvious."

"And someone who was set off tonight," I added, "since it's a crime of opportunity."

"Everyone will tell him that Jesse and Ziad had beef with the guy."

Being sure I could rule Jesse out put me ahead of Lam. That and having a good idea where people were most of the time. Only an idea, though. I'd assumed singers were in the practice room before they went onstage, but I didn't know that for sure about any of them. I'd never gone in that room. Ziad had apparently taken smoke breaks at the fire door and I hadn't known. I didn't even know where that fire door was. Hell, I hadn't even known Duncan had left the theatre until I'd seen him coming back inside.

And I could only hope the crew weren't involved, because they'd been all over the place all night. They probably didn't know Matt. But what if, somehow, one of them did?

"I don't envy a guy walking in on this," Kent said, as if I'd spoken out loud.

"What do you think of Ziad?" I said.

"I think you could pull if you wanted," Kent said with a twisty little smile. "He's not too far off your brand either."

"Not funny or helpful. Do you think he could have done this? Did I tell you he went into Matt's suite to yell at him?"

Kent's thick blond eyebrows shot up. "No shit? When did that happen?"

"Ziad slipped in the door as Jess was coming out. I don't actually know that Ziad was planning to yell at Matt."

"Might've been planning to cock punch him."

"Or blackmail him. It's one of the many things Ziad accused Jess of. Not telling anyone what Matt did so he could blackmail Matt."

"Poor little rich boys," Kent said, shaking his head. He made more as a detective than he had as a regular cop, but it was still chump change compared to Jess and Ziad. And he had to work a lot of overtime to get it.

"It wouldn't be for money. They'd blackmail him for connections. Roles. Shout-outs. But Jess wasn't doing that, and Ziad doesn't seem like he wanted anything from Matt except for Matt to drop dead."

"But he went into Matt's suite to talk to him."

I nodded. I'd have to ask Ziad what that was about. He might refuse to answer, or lie, but even that could tell me something, depending on how he did it.

"I think he's a facestabber," Kent added. "Not a backstabber. Not a blackmailer."

"Yeah, he's like Jess that way," I said. "If he hates you, you've been told. But that doesn't mean Jess won't ruin your life behind your back. Maybe Ziad will too."

"Will he poison your food?" Kent asked.

I'd been asking myself that, somewhere in the back of my head, since I'd seen the mustard.

"He might. I like the big showy smear for him too. Lots of mustard everywhere, like a big yellow fuck off and die. Actually, I could see him spelling that out in mustard."

"He wants credit for the things he does."

I agreed, and it was a good thing. If Ziad did it, he'd be bursting to talk.

"What's your next move?" Kent asked.

"I need to talk to Lew. This all hinges on the food. The food and the EpiPens. I want to know how and when each of those things got in here and where they were between then and now."

"The pens," Kent said. I nodded. We didn't have to say it. The food had been in the hall, unsupervised, for a few minutes at least. Those pens had likely been in the suite the whole time. Doctoring the food was open to everyone, but unless Lewis had left that allergy kit in the open somewhere, stealing the EpiPens took access only a few people had.

"I'll see if Jess has Lew's number in his phone. He probably does. He might be able to talk Lew into meeting with me. I have to get him to come out here somewhere because there's no way I'm getting back into that suite."

"There is," Kent said. "But not right now."

"I sure hope you didn't suggest to a PI that he break into a sealed crime scene," I said.

"I must not have," Kent said. "That kind of thing could get a guy fired."

We left Jess's dressing room and went our separate ways, Kent back to the green room and me down the hall to the practice room. It was across from the entrance to the backstage area, convenient for warmed-up performers who wanted to go straight onto the stage.

As I walked, I twitted myself for not making a better search of Matt's suite while I'd had the chance. In the chaos, I hadn't confirmed that there was no second exit. I hadn't found the EpiPens, which had to be somewhere. Were I the killer, I'd have ditched them in the suite.

Kent had given me Jesse's pass, so I didn't need to knock. I swiped myself in.

It was a big room, nearly as big as the green room. The lights were mostly off, apart from a safety light over the door and a few small pots over the piano—a black beast that took up most of the back left corner. It was a concert grand if I remembered my pianos correctly.

Jess was sitting at the piano with Reiss standing beside him and, to my surprise, Dylan standing on Reiss's other side. I'd thought they'd be hiding out in their dressing room with Emilie. She was here too, sitting cross-legged a few feet beyond the piano's pool of light. Thom and Bennett were beside her.

The crew at the piano was singing something mournful, slow, and multi–part. Jess and Dylan were swapping the background and lead vocals, and Reiss was filling in with harmony. They sounded like they'd been working together for years. I'd never understood how musicians did that. I'd asked Jess, and he'd shrugged and said everyone did their bit, as if that were an answer.

I hadn't heard the song before, but the gist of it seemed to be that someone wanted to know if something was all right with someone else, and also something about a gun. Very much not Jack Lowe's usual thing, or the Twist's, but they were making it work. Dylan was right at home with regret in a minor key.

Emilie had her face upturned to Dylan. She looked adoring and five years younger, which is to say she looked her age. It was nice to see. She needed more people in her life who weren't comedians.

I waited until the impromptu band was finished, because it was polite and because I liked listening. It would have been nice if I could have stood there listening to them for hours. But it was not that kind of night.

"Turn my back for ten minutes and you form a supergroup," I said. Dylan gave me a huge smile, much broader than I'd thought they had available. It probably meant something for someone so young and barely starting out to sing with people who'd been touring and making records and winning Junos for years.

"Were you looking for me?" Jess asked. His hands were still on the piano, fingertips on the keys and wrists dropped. He played a lot of instruments, mainly guitar, but I never saw him meld with anything else the way he did with a piano, like he was plugging into a port that had been made for him.

"Yeah. Sorry. I need to talk to Lew, and he's in with the cops. Do you have his number?"

He didn't even have to think about it. He kept everyone's number, always, just in case. Even if he would have paid ten thousand dollars not to have to talk to them again.

"Yeah. I've got his cell. What did Kent want?"

"Bull session," I said. It was mainly true. "I can catch you up in your dressing room."

I could see he was considering making a joke before he remembered that someone was dead. Instead he pulled his hands from the keys, pushed the bench back, and stood. Dylan reached out to tug at the sleeve of Jesse's shirt.

"Jesse? Can I talk to you first?"

"Yeah, sure. What's up?"

Dylan shuffled their feet uncomfortably.

"Did you want to come to Jesse's dressing room with us?" I offered.

"Yes, please."

He didn't invite Emilie, and she neither assumed nor asked. She did seem lightly crushed and shuffled backward into the darkness as we went to the door.

CHAPTER FIFTEEN

I PUT AN arm around Jesse's shoulders as we walked, and he leaned into me. He felt a little cold, no longer heated by the stage lights or the effort of the performance.

"You okay?" I asked.

"I'm tired."

"I believe it."

In his dressing room, I got him settled on the couch and threw my coat over him before I handed him back his pass. Dylan took the chair next to him.

"Do you want tea or coffee?" I asked. "Either of you?"

Dylan shook their head.

"I'd take more of Kent's whiskey," Jess said, "if we hadn't already drunk it all."

"You should ask Duncan," I said as I took a seat next to him on the couch. "There's no way that guy doesn't have a flask on him somewhere."

"Or airplane bottles," Jess said, shifting over slightly so he could press in against my side. "He flew here. Dylan, seriously, is there anything we can get you?"

"No. Thanks. I want to tell you about something."

Jess nodded. "Go ahead."

"I heard something tonight. In the bathroom. The one beside my dressing room. Emilie and I were in my dressing room, and I needed to put water on my face, so I went into the bathroom for a minute. I turned on the light when I went in, but someone was in there already. In the dark."

I felt a shiver run through Jess and put a hand on his arm.

"What did you hear?"

"Voices. I think someone was listening to something with earbuds. In the back stall with their feet off the ground. So no one would know they were there."

People never seemed to understand that earbuds were audible from outside their ears. I could imagine someone hiding in a dark room, listening, believing they were perfectly concealed.

"Could you hear what it was?" Jess said. "Was it a show or something? Maybe someone wanted alone time. In the dark."

"This being mental health night," he did *not* say. It hung in the air regardless.

Dylan nodded. "It was Ben."

"What?" Jess and I said as one.

"I was not in that bathroom," I added.

"It was you on the earbuds. You were talking to someone. I think it was Matt Garrett."

"No, it wouldn't have been Matt," Jess said. "He and Ben have never talked."

Well. I had not been planning to tell Jesse about my meeting with Matt. I was certain he wouldn't approve, and more than that, I didn't approve. I shouldn't have gone in there. It had been a thuggish thing to do, and as Jess had been kind enough to tell me once, I was not a thug.

But there was no getting around it now.

"We did," I said.

Jess sat up straight and gawked at me. "You what? Who did what?"

"We talked. Matt and I. Tonight."

His eyes went from wide with surprise to a little narrower than usual. Dylan probably didn't notice that slight narrowing, but I knew it well. It wasn't a good sign.

"Did you?" Jess said pleasantly. "How on God's green earth did that come to pass?"

"I wanted a word. Can we put a pin in this? Please? I promise we can come back to it."

"I can stick a pin in something," Jess said, but he leaned back and pressed his lips together. I turned to Dylan.

"About what time did you hear this? Do you remember?"

"A little after nine. For a few minutes."

Jess and I looked at each other.

"I was in the practice room," he said.

"Yep."

"And you were in Matt's room? Around that time?"

"Yes. It could have been me and Matt. Dylan, did you hear anyone else in the room? The boyfriend? He has a high voice."

"I only heard you and Matt. But it was quiet."

"Okay." I considered that. "There's no way anyone would have had time to record our conversation at, I don't know, five minutes after nine, and then listen to it in another room a minute later. Whoever was listening to it would have been hearing it live."

"Holy shit," Jess said, forgetting for the moment that he was furious with me. "Is that room bugged? Who the hell would do that?"

"Could have been audio and video," I said. "There could be cameras all over the place. Wouldn't Vic have said something, though, if we could watch some footage and sort this whole thing out?"

"Don't count on it," Jess said. "She's not used to people dying at her shows. Anything could have slipped her mind."

"Lam would have asked," I said, but what if he hadn't? Maybe he hadn't thought of it or meant to do it later. Maybe we could get in there first.

"You have Vic's number in your phone?" I asked Jess, as if there were any chance he wouldn't.

"Yeah." He'd started scrolling for it before I'd even finished talking. Dylan was up and circling the dressing room, hunting for cameras in the corners and on the kitchenette shelves. They were an organized and thorough searcher, dividing the room into chunks and carefully going over each before moving on. It wasn't the fastest way to search a room, but it was the best if you wanted to be sure not to miss anything, or if the thing you were searching for was small.

"Good technique," I told them.

"I play a lot of hidden object games," they said without pausing their search.

"Hey," Jess was telling his phone. "It's Jack." He paused, then repeated that, much louder, followed by, "Yeah, I can call you back."

"Is she still having the best night of her life?" I asked.

"Sounds like she's at the stage door," Jess said. "Could they be taking Matt away this soon?"

"No reason not to," I said. "Where he died isn't that important. They're not going to learn much from seeing him in situ."

"So they'll be trying to get him into… not an ambulance. That would be a waste of an ambulance."

"Basically a hearse," I said. "The ME's office has a few of them. And there'll be an autopsy since it's a possible crime. So there'll be some delay before the body is released to the family. Does he have family?"

"He wasn't sent here from Krypton," Jess said. "He has a sister and two nieces that he sees sometimes. Twins. They're nice kids. The sister is a decent person. His dad is dead, and I don't think he's close with his mom at all. He never talked about her."

Jess was still mixing up his tenses, bringing Matt back to life in one sentence and killing him in the next.

"The sister is probably his next of kin," I said. "Crystal would have asked for that information, which I assume Lew gave her. I'm also assuming Lew called the sister to tell her Matt was dead. Am I assuming too much?"

"No, you're not. He probably called," Jess said. "Do you still want me to see if Lew will come in here and talk to us? Or do you want me to keep trying to talk to Vic about security cameras?"

He was doing an admirable job of moving on from the topic of why I'd met with Matt and what had been

said. But that was Jesse. He was good at putting something in his pocket and leaving it there until it was time
to give it a good airing.

"There's nothing in here," Dylan said. "Unless
they put it somewhere really hidey." I wasn't sure hidey
was a word, but I got their point. In buildings like this,
public or semi-public places, they put cameras in for
security. That kind of thing was a deterrent as much as
anything. The cameras wouldn't be hidden.

"There might not be anything in the dressing
rooms," I said.

"I'll check the halls," Dylan said.

They slipped into the hall. I remembered that Jess
had asked me something.

"Ah… talk to Vic first. I want to know about cameras before I talk to Lew. Did you ever call Gia back?"

"No, but she's been texting me. She says I need to
make a statement."

"What? Why? You're not, I don't know, Lew. Or
Alex. And didn't you quote Gia tonight, her whole
thing about how you shouldn't feed something if you
want it to die?"

"Yes to all of that," Jess said. "But I knew Matt,
and as far as most people know, we were on good terms.
He died here tonight, and I was also here tonight. I can't
get away with not saying anything."

"What are you going to say?"

"She's working on that. It's delicate. Obviously I
can't drag him, because he just died. Even if I think he
deserves that, no one wants to hear it right now, and it's
not fair to his sister and nieces."

I wasn't sure I cared what was fair to them, but that
was petty. It wasn't their idea to be related to Matt.

"Does that mean you have to be nice to him?" I said. "Write a nice two-hundred-and-eighty-character eulogy?"

"Kind of? I need to seem nice enough that it's not weird, but I can't go all in on praising him because I know what he was really like. I mean, it seems pretty obvious he also did something to Ziad. Who knows how many people he's at least creeped on, if not worse? If I talk about what a mensch he was and then the truth gets out, I seem like I was providing cover for him."

"So what the hell can you say?"

He shrugged. "Gia will figure it out. Actually no. She'll probably wake someone up and make them figure it out. She knows experts."

It was hard to imagine someone being an expert in giving a backhanded non-eulogy to a sexual predator, but it was a funny old world.

"They've probably taken Matt away by now," I said. Jess nodded and called Vic again.

"Is this a better time?" he said. After a pause, "Okay. Good. Was that the body leaving? Yeah, I figured. Hey, the detective was wondering, are there security cameras around here?"

That was a neat way of putting it. They detective he meant was me, so he wasn't lying, but she would think he meant Lam, and Jess intended for her to think that. If she called him out later, gosh, what a funny misunderstanding.

"Right, but in the hallways? Or over the doors? Backstage?"

He listened and raised his eyebrows at me.

"That's pretty normal for Matt. Did you do all of them? Is there anywhere there would still be… yeah. No, I can imagine. I've heard him do it. Right. Thanks."

"Okay." He set his phone on the table, facedown as always. Even when it was just him and me. "They don't put cameras in the dressing rooms because that's objectionable and people would object. That includes the suite Matt was in. They also don't have them in the practice room, I guess because no one is going to steal a concert grand, and if they did they'd have earned it."

"And you paranoid freaks think someone would sell footage of you singing scales?"

Jess shrugged. "They might. Especially if you were a shit singer and you had backing tracks and backup vocalists keeping you afloat on stage. But, okay, none there, not in the dressing rooms, and not in the bathrooms. Everywhere else back here, usually yes. Dylan will find them, no problem. They're not a secret."

"You don't sound as excited as you should about us finding the solution to the case. And I didn't hear you asking to see anything."

"Yeah. We've solved fuck-all, and there's nothing to see. The cameras are turned off. All of them."

"Is that usual?" I asked.

"Not for this place. But it is kind of usual when Matt is going to be somewhere. Lew called this afternoon and asked them to turn their cameras off."

"I keep thinking I have a handle on the gall of Matt and his crew," I said, "and then I'm surprised again."

"He wouldn't have done it to a big theatre or a big production. You don't call up the *Grammies* and ask them to shut off a big part of their security system. But Lew knows who he can boss around, and he does it."

"He was probably worried because you were here," I said. "And Ziad, if he knew Ziad was here."

"Oh, he knew. He's not in the business of not knowing things."

"Imagine you or Ziad running into Matt in the hallway and deciding to get into it. You guys were both bombs waiting to go off."

"I've been a pretty stable bomb," Jess pointed out. "It's been years."

"Yeah, but Matt was going to ask you for the footage of the assault. That's both weird and offensive. Even I couldn't have predicted how you would react to something like that."

"You'd think Lew would be especially averse to having a recording device in Matt's suite," Jess said. "Matt actually asked me to put my phone on the table so he could see it wasn't recording before we had our conversation."

I stared at him. "And after you said no and broke a chair over his head, what did he say?"

"You know I did none of that. I agree it was a ridiculous ask, considering, but I wanted that conversation to be over, and arguing about the phone would have dragged it out."

"Unbelievable. I'm sorry you didn't kill him. I'm tempted to cover up for whoever did."

Jess considered that for a moment, then sighed. "You have a client. You'd have to give back the Cineplex gift card."

"I don't watch a lot of movies."

"And then Reiss will want to know why you quit."

"Might be worth it," I said.

Jess grinned. "Are you sure? You'd have to stare right into his pretty blue eyes and tell him you weren't going to work for him."

"I'm capable. I've said no to you often enough."

"I don't have luscious curls. Maybe, if you asked nice, he'd let you comb his hair and tie it up with a ribbon."

"Thank you for making me want to talk about murder instead," I said. "If it wasn't Lew who was recording things in that room—and I agree it wasn't—who was it?"

"Matt? So he could have his own copy of the conversation and edit it however he wanted?"

"Too risky."

Jess nodded. "He liked to keep things simpler than that. No recording at all is simpler."

"Who had access? Before nine?"

"Me, Matt, Lew, Alex, Ziad, I guess you. And staff. Whoever set the suite up for him."

"The staff thing is possible," I said. "What I like about it is, say you got something interesting, and you thought you could sell it, or even if you wanted to send it to a gossip site… you could do that without losing your job. It could have been anyone on staff. There's no way to trace that to one person. Unless the recorder is still in the room."

Jess sat up. "I wonder if my pass still works."

It was an interesting question.

"If they moved Matt's body out, they probably cleared out their gear and left. They wouldn't have left Lew and Alex in there. I don't know where they are now. That suite might be empty. And there should be someone out front guarding the crime scene, but it's probably all hands on deck at the stage door because of the… I want to say, mob?"

"Then let's go."

"It'll have barrier tape on the door," I told him. "You know, bright yellow, Police, Do Not Cross?"

"What does that make it, then? If we go in? A crime?"

"At least one, depending on the circumstances. We don't have to break and enter because you have that pass, but an argument could be made that we were trespassing. And then there's obstructing justice, which has broad applications. In this case, if we touched or moved anything, that's bad. But even if we didn't, how would they know that? We've contaminated a crime scene by being there. Normally they'd have to get our DNA and fingerprints to exclude us but—"

"We've been all over that room," Jess said. "Hell, I tossed it hunting for those EpiPens."

"It's an unusual situation. What are you going to do, dust the salmon for prints?"

"Can they do that? I mean, not dust, but spray something on it and use different lights or... I don't know. Science."

"I have no idea," I said, "but there were forks right there to lift the fish with, so I doubt anyone touched the fish itself."

"Anyway, does being a huge inconvenient pain in the ass equal obstructing justice?"

"Don't ask me," I said. "Ask the judge at your trial. Or if we do catch whoever did this and they have a trial, we can explain what we were doing in the room, and the defence attorney can say that we framed their client by putting their prints on the salmon."

"This is a genuinely very bad thing."

"Yes."

"Are you saying we shouldn't do it?"

"Not necessarily," I said. "I am saying let's not get caught."

Jess considered that. "I can't imagine it would be good for a licensed PI to get caught. In particular. I think I should go in alone."

That was the kind of thing that, if you were inclined to think Jess was a good suspect, would make you worry about what he had in mind. Like stealing back the

camera he'd hidden, for example, or tossing a few EpiP-
ens under the couch. I genuinely trusted the guy, at least
on this, and even I got a twinge when he said it.

"There's not any more risk for two people to sneak
in," I said.

"Yeah, but you need to be able to make a living.
What am I looking for? A camera or a phone, maybe?
Anything else, as long as I'm in there?"

"If the bedroom doors are open, see whether
there's a back door out of Lew's room. If the doors are
closed, don't open them. Don't touch anything. Don't
pull down your shirt sleeve and start touching things
like that makes it okay."

He nodded thoughtfully. "So the list of things I can
touch is—"

"Nothing, you punk. Look for a camera or a phone
or somewhere somebody might have put one. If dust
has been disturbed, that might be the spot. Get in, see
what you can see, get out. Or you can stay out of the
suite, and we can try to work this another way. We can
try to figure out who was recording in there and get
them to admit it."

"If I see a camera or a phone, do I take it?"

"Is it a thing, Jess? Is it a physical object in this
world?"

"Sure."

"And," I said, "how many things did I tell you to
touch?"

"Okay, but don't we want to know what's on it?
Even if it was transmitting to somebody somewhere
else, which I guess it obviously was because someone
was hearing your conversation in real time, there'd still
be footage on the camera or the phone."

"Yes, and that'll be important footage for the police to use in their investigation of this crime. So we will leave it there. You will take a photo of whatever recording device you find, and we will use that as leverage to get whoever left it there to take out their phone and show us whatever they've got."

Jess cocked his head. "If that's the plan, why don't we tip off Detective Lam that someone was monitoring that room and let him deal with it?"

It was, in a lot of ways, the sensible thing to do. The problem was that I was on the case, and I wanted to see that footage. There was no way I would get that if I left it in the hands of the police. I wanted to find the person doing the recording before Lam did so I'd have a chance of getting them to show it to me.

"Lam won't share it with us," I told Jess. "I can't let him get to it first."

"Then let's do this," he said. "You can be a lookout by the stage door."

"If you're sure. Because we can—"

"Okay, enough," he said. His voice was sharp, and his eyes were suddenly dark. All the anger he'd slipped into his pocket was back. "I don't want to get into details right now, so I am going to ask you one question, and I want a short and direct answer. Is there a recording out there of you threatening Matt's life?"

Kind of. It had been conditional. But Jess's directions had been clear. I said, "Yes."

"Then I'll go into the fucking room and see what I can see."

CHAPTER SIXTEEN

AS WE got into position, me by the stage doors and Jess down the hall, I considered what his plan might be. I'd been clear about not even touching a camera or a phone, let alone deleting anything on there. Even if he'd toyed with that idea, he would have realized that it had been transmitted to someone in that bathroom, who would have recorded it from there. We had to assume there was that second copy. The only value in going into that room was leverage to get to view the footage, if we could find the person who had it. That wouldn't change the fact that I had, somewhat arguably, made a death threat to someone who had shortly thereafter died.

He might have been on board with my plan, where I needed all the clues I could get so that I could find out who really had done it in the interests of proving Jess hadn't done it. Except Jess would be wanting to prove I hadn't done it.

Unless he thought maybe I had. But I doubted it. If I'd decided to kill Matt Garrett…. I wouldn't have, probably. I wouldn't have done that. Like Kent, I generally disapproved of murder. But if I had decided to kill the guy, I'd have done it when Jess had an alibi and was nowhere near the situation. And Jess would, if nothing else, know that.

There was commotion behind me, on the other side of the doors to the stage door entrance. Reporters yelling questions. Fans crying. Some of them yelling questions. Cops telling everyone to get back. Crystal had probably tried to haul Matt outside without security, not knowing that the word was out about his death, and been forced to rethink that decision. Jess had already figured out this was going to happen even before word got out, so it could have been avoided if anyone had asked him and believed him and made some plans.

But if they had, they wouldn't be flailing now, and there would be someone guarding the door to Matt's suite.

Down the other hall, I saw Dylan coming out of the practice room. Still hunting cameras. I waved them over and, once they were close enough for a quiet conversation, told them what Vic had said about the cameras.

"Oh," they said. "That sucks. There are cameras all over the halls."

"Yeah. It would have been convenient. Would you be interested in a new mission?"

"Can I bring Emilie?"

"Sure. You think you can track down Matt's manager and boyfriend for me? Do you know what they look like?"

They shook their head. "I never saw them."

"The boyfriend is about my height, very thin, blond. He's young. Not much older than you. Last time I saw him, he was wearing a silver-sequined coat over white silk pajamas."

Dylan gave me a disbelieving stare, and I shrugged.

"I don't know how else to describe that getup. The manager is older. Might be fifty? He's Black, and he was wearing jeans and a sweater the last time I saw him."

"I'll get Emilie, and we'll find them," they said.

"Thanks."

I almost told them to be careful, but what would that even mean? Stay away from condiments?

Dylan had barely left when Jess reappeared in the other hallway, coming my way and walking fast. He went past me into his dressing room, and I followed.

"There's nothing there," he said, turning to face me as soon as I was in the room.

"There has to be," I said. "Unless Lew was wearing a wire—"

"No, I mean there's nothing there now. But there's a spot on the back table where things have been moved to the middle like someone was trying to hide something about… this size?" He used his hands to limn a small rectangle in the air. "There are things boxing in the space, and there's a gap at the front the right size for a lens."

"That's not something you could do while someone else was watching," I said. "That's not the same as casually dropping your phone behind a chair."

"Yeah. If it was staff, like you said, they'd have had time. I wouldn't have. You only have my word for this, but I was never alone in that room. I doubt Ziad was either."

"I wasn't alone in there," I said. "Matt and Lew were both in the main room with me. And Alex came and went."

"Do we have time for you to tell me what happened when you were in there?" Jess asked. "I won't ask why you were in there because I have a feeling I know."

"We don't, and I'm not just saying that because I don't want to talk about it," I said. "Maybe we can carve out some time later to talk about what Matt and I said to each other, and why Matt gave you swipe-card access to his room. Knowing that there's footage out there, are you going to tell me again that you have no idea why Matt gave you access?"

Jess said nothing.

I nodded. "Anyway, the interesting thing here is that there's a camera missing."

"Yep. Do you think someone has it on them, or would they have ditched it?"

"I have no idea. If I had the footage somewhere else and the camera couldn't be traced to me, I'd have ditched it, but that's me. Me and this murderer make different choices."

"And, if it's gone, someone took it out. After you were in there. So that's another thing."

Somehow, I hadn't thought of that.

"You're right," I told him. "Someone else could have found it and put it somewhere, but let's assume whoever placed it also took it away. That's another time when they would have needed access and privacy."

"Almost everyone was backstage when my set ended," Jess said. "Do you remember who was there when you got there? And whether they were there the whole time?"

"Good question. I'll think about it. And we should find the camera, in case it was ditched around here somewhere."

"Maybe we could divert Dylan," Jesse suggested. "Get them to stop looking for cameras, since there's no point in that, and ask them to look for… a specific camera."

"I sent Dylan and Emilie off to find Lew and Alex. But it's probably still worth you giving Lew a call and seeing whether he'll meet us."

Jess took out his phone and after some hunting got the number and made the call.

It took a few rings, but Lew did answer. Jess was close enough to me that I heard Lew's voice, tired and scratchy, saying, "Yes?"

"Would you be willing to meet me and Ben for a talk?" Jess said. "Shouldn't take too long."

"He's not going anywhere," I said under my breath. Jess gave me a "shut it" look and moved toward the bar.

"I'd rather discuss it in person," Jess said. "I can meet you wherever you are."

Another pause, then he added, "I know you have a lot to take care of. Calling Paige, the PR team, the director, the caterer… what? Why wouldn't you?"

His phone buzzed to announce an incoming text, and he winced and held it away from his ear for a second.

"Okay," he said, "maybe not, but don't you want to talk to them anyway? I would if I'd—"

He made a "beak, beak, beak" motion with his free hand.

"It's your call," he said. "Obviously. I have some-thing I have to deal with, so come by my dressing room or call me, whichever."

"Is he willing to talk to us?" I asked once Jess was off the phone.

"Not sure. I think he doesn't want to, but he also doesn't want to not know what we have to say. The curiosity will get to him eventually. But he did confirm that he ordered Matt's food like always."

"I guess that's something," I said. "What was that about him phoning the caterer?"

"Oh yeah. He doesn't want to. He says he knows what he told them, and if they fucked up, they'll lie about it."

"Huh." I took the mugs from the table and brought them to the bar. "Does he think they fucked up?"

"He didn't say. He's acting like it was an accident, but I don't know if that's really what he believes. He's kind of… he wants to see how the wind is blowing before he does something. If he can ride this whole thing out like it was a random accident and there's no tantalizing murder, that's what he'll do."

"Even if that's not what he believes."

Jess half sat on the back of the couch, his phone cradled loosely between his hands. He bounced the phone a little like he was testing the weight of it. Testing the weight of what I'd said.

"You know, I actually think so? Even if he was convinced someone had murdered Matt, if it was better for the legacy…."

"And by legacy you mean residuals. Because Matt wasn't Olivier."

"No, but he was Lew's greatest accomplishment, you know? He was Lew's legacy. Not that…. Lew has time and other clients. I mean, his legacy is still a work in progress. But he'll always be associated with Matt."

"And he'd rather be associated with a tragedy than a crime."

"Yes."

"And," I added, "he's used to burying things that might embarrass him."

Jess sighed. "There is also that."

"You have a text," I reminded him.

"I have several dozen," he said. "But that last one might have been Gia."

He checked his phone, and his shoulders dropped in relief.

"Good news?" I said.

"Good tweet," he said. "I'm in shock. This doesn't seem real. Thinking of his family tonight."

"Believable," I said. "Commits you to nothing. They should give Gia a raise."

Jess eyed me with suspicion. "You sound like you approve," he said. "But you don't."

"I think your job is mind poison for you," I told him. "You know that."

"You have mentioned it," he said. "Okay. Tweeted. I'll stay off everything else. People will share it across anyway."

"What are they saying?" I asked.

He scrolled for about half a minute, frowned, and slipped the phone into his pocket.

"Fucking… everything. I did it because he dumped me, you were jealous and you did it, he wanted to get back with me and I said no, and he killed himself."

"People seem very focused on you."

"It's my Twitter feed," he said. "It skews heavily toward me. But you can see people making the connection. Matt and I aren't seen together for years, and then we're in the same building for one night and he dies? Do you really expect people to believe that has nothing to do with me?"

When he put it that way, it made sense. A little too much sense.

"Do you?" I said.

His brow creased in confusion. "Do I what?"

"Do you believe this has nothing to do with you? Because you're right that it's a hell of a coincidence."

He laced his fingers and let his arms hang, an exaggerated portrait of unconcern. "Are you working your way around to accusing me of murder?"

He was surprisingly quick to think I would assume the worst of him. Or maybe not surprisingly.

"No," I told him. "I meant exactly what I said. Do you think this had something to do with you?"

"Something to do with the footage he asked for," I *didn't* say. "Or the access he put on your card."

"No. Except—"

"Except?"

"Except maybe someone thought now would be a good time. Because I'm here. Because it would seem like it must have been me."

I hadn't thought of that. I'd thought it was a coincidence that Jess was here when it happened. Even though I had a personal rule that crime-related coincidences were suspicious at best. The truth was if someone had been thinking of doing Matt in, this night might have felt like the perfect opportunity. With Jess here, and Ziad. And a food cart left alone in the hall.

"If that was someone's idea," I told him, "it was a very stupid one. Because we're going to get them."

"Okay," he said.

He'd barely had time to force a smile and pretend he believed me when someone knocked at the door. We both turned, but calmly, like we'd expected it.

I admitted Dylan and Emilie. She was bursting, and they looked fondly amused as she finger-gunned to her right and blew imaginary smoke away.

"The manager and boyfriend are in Ash Rose's dressing room. They left the door open when they fucked off, and now the door is closed."

"So you shot them?" Jess asked politely. I thought I saw Dylan hold back a laugh.

"What? No. This is my PI gun. I'm a badass private detective."

"Did you knock on the door?" I asked.

"We thought we should tell you first," Dylan said, where "we" clearly meant "I."

"Great work," I told them. "You're earning your way into part of a movie pass. Ready for another assignment?"

"Anything other than talk to the pig," Emilie said. "No offence. I mean, you're, like, an ex-pig. You're a ham roast. With pineapple all over like in those old magazine recipes. And potatoes on the side. And pie after. I think I'm hungry."

"I wouldn't eat anything around here," Jess told her. "Unless you brought it in yourself and it's in a sealed container."

"This place turned into the Howler so fast," Emilie said.

The Howler was a yearly Halloween party thrown by a radio station in Edmonton. The jocks were of the "political correctness will kill us all" stripe, and the music was mostly hair bands, so it drew the sort of crowd you'd expect.

"The food wasn't poisoned, though," Dylan said firmly, as if trying to convince themself. "It was an allergy. I don't have allergies."

"It was an allergy," Jess said. "What we had for dinner was fine. We're all fine. You should just be careful now. Okay?"

Dylan nodded. They had drawn their hands close to their chest and balled them into loose fists. Not getting ready for a fight. More a curling inward, like an armadillo.

"What's the next assignment, boss?" Emilie asked.

"You're searching for a camera."

"We already did that," Dylan said.

"Yeah, but this is different. It's not a security camera. It's a small one. Jess, how big?"

Jess described it with his hands again.

"About that size," I said. "It can transmit to another device, like a phone."

"What do we do when we find it?" Dylan asked.

"Don't touch it," I said. "It'll have prints on it, probably. Come back here and tell us where it is. Actually… one of you should stay near it, somewhere in the line of sight, and send the other one back here. Don't be obvious that you're guarding the camera, but make sure no one could take it without you seeing them."

"Is that a good idea?" Jess said. "What if the person who owns the camera goes to get it?"

"If they think it's being watched, they'll leave and come back later," I said. "As long as they're not sure the camera has been found, they won't draw attention to it."

"We're on it, Captain," Emilie said with a salute. It was the British army salute, and no one in Canada used it, but I wasn't a captain either, so I let it go.

"If you don't mind," I added, "I'll get a number from one of you so I can text you."

Dylan offered their number. I put it into my phone and texted Dylan to give them my own number. In case of trouble. Which there wouldn't be.

When I turned back to Jess after letting them out, he had an imaginary phone to his ear.

"Hi, Employment Standards? I'm calling about a child labour situation. Yeah, I don't even think he's paying them. I think he's planning to buy them theatre popcorn."

"Cute," I said, swatting at his arm to make him lower the pretend phone. "Those kids are well over sixteen. Or... over sixteen."

There was another knock on the door, and I flung it open, expecting the kids to be back with questions. Instead it was Vic. She came into the room, and I moved fast because it seemed like she was willing to go over or through anyone in her way.

"Did you tell Ash Rose they could leave?" she demanded.

"I told them they weren't legally compelled to stay."

"Jesus Christ. Detective Lam is super fucking mad. Why did you tell them that?"

"Because it's true?"

Jess rubbed the bridge of his nose. He did that when he was getting a headache, or when he already had one and the headache was me.

"They were on a tear about the police," he told Vic. "I agree with them in a lot of ways, but the difference is I'm not going to call the detective a fascist while I'm a murder suspect. Ben thought they'd be better off elsewhere, so when they stormed off, he let them go. We know where they are."

I hadn't said any of that, to him or anyone, but he wasn't wrong. I also hadn't realized he'd had a motive for offering Ash Rose our house to crash in, aside from helping out starving artists. He'd thought it might be nice to know where they were.

"Sarah told everyone to stay," Vic said. Jess shot me a look before I could say anything, such as that I did not work for Sarah and she was not my real dad.

"We can get them back for you if you want," Jess said, "but I don't think they had anything to do with this, and it's going to be ugly for everyone if they get arrested for throwing something at a cop."

"Fuck. Okay, where are they?"

"The moon," Jess said. "Can't Lam talk to them over the phone? That way all they can do is call him names and hang up on him."

"Oh, that is the other thing. I gave him Ashley's number and now she's fucking furious with me."

"I would be too," Jess said. "You should have given his number to her instead."

"Yeah, but you're you and she's...." She made a piffling gesture with her hand.

"You don't give out the phone numbers of the talent," Jess said. "We give you our contact information in confidence. Our privacy is not valued by a sliding scale of fame."

Vic looked away, and her shoulders pulled in. She'd felt that.

"Well," she said. "Anyway. They want to talk to you. Ashley wants to talk to you. Or Ben. She said to give you her number."

She gave it, and Jess and I both put it into our phones. Then we regarded each other.

"Rock, paper, scissors?" I said.

His scissors cut my paper, and I placed the call while Jess had a quiet conversation with Vic at the back of the room. I heard "food" and "delivered" while the phone rang, so Jess was making good use of the time.

"Hello?"

"Ashley? It's Ben."

"Oh my God. You said we didn't have to stay at the theatre. You said we could leave!"

"You didn't have to stay," I told her. I couldn't be sure, but I thought I was on speaker at her end.

"That's not what the cop said."

"Cops say a lot of things," I said. "I'm surprised that's news to you."

"So we don't have to come back? He can't, like, arrest us?"

I heard something in the background that sounded like "Told you so."

"He can arrest you if he wants," I said, "but he'd have to find you to do it, and he'd have to come up with a reason. I doubt he'd do any of that. He's pretty busy here."

"He keeps calling."

"So?"

I definitely heard someone laughing in the background. My money was on Izzy. She'd probably already said everything I was saying to Ashley now.

"So he's a cop!" Ashley said. "I can't not answer."

"You can," I said, "if you want. If I were you, I'd talk to him. You weren't involved, and I doubt you have useful information. He'll exclude you and move on."

"I saw on YouTube that you should never talk to a cop."

Hadn't I already had this conversation with them? No. They'd left by the time I told the Twist. But I'd gone over it enough for one day.

"You know Google? It's this thing, you ask it questions…."

"I think I heard of it one time."

"Look up your rights. Or call a lawyer if it makes you more comfortable, but that won't be cheap. You might as well start with Google."

"And we don't have to come back."

"It's up to you," I said.

"Okay."

"Your dog is super cute," another voice said. It sounded like Kayla.

"Feel free to brush him," I said. "His brush is in a basket by the patio doors. I forgot to do it today."

"What do you pay dog sitters?" That was Izzy.

"Room and board," I told her. "Do you have everything you need? Will you be going to sleep soon and not doing God knows what in my home?"

"Who knew Jack Lowe would be the nice one," Izzy said.

"Touch his guitars and you'll find out who the nice one is."

"We can't sleep anyway. Your phone won't stop ringing. Do you have a landline, Grandpa?"

"That would be my work cell," I told her. "It's in my office."

"Well, it's blowing up."

Of course it was. When I'd solved the murder in the mountains and word had gotten out that Jess had helped me do it, my phone had rung non-stop. Not because people were offering me jobs, although my star had definitely risen in that respect. I was brought more work, and more interesting work, than I had ever imagined could come my way. But the main reason my phone had rung ceaselessly was that people had realized I was usually steps away from Jack Lowe.

Media, fans, a parade of opportunists who wanted a piece of Jess for one reason or another. Thousands of people who'd hit a wall trying to connect with him had been delighted to learn that my office number was not only public but advertised. A lot of uncomfortable changes had come with Jess when he'd moved into my house. I wasn't famous, not even as well-known

as someone like Ashley, but I wasn't anonymous anymore, and when I was with Jess, I might as well have
been him. I did not enjoy the attention.

The work phone thing, though, had been the most
annoying. Clients and potential clients and people with
information all needed to be able to reach me. I didn't
want to give them my personal number, and advertising
my personal number as my new work number would
only have resulted in a thousand people calling that
number too. Jess had offered to pay for anything from
an answering service to a receptionist, and I'd snapped
at him—unfairly since it hadn't been his fault. I'd said
he couldn't throw money at every problem. As if he
didn't know that.

I'd taken jobs by referral only for a while, and
eventually the calls had tapered off. They never went
away completely, but Jess and I had told our story to a
few big players, like Strombo, and that had made it less
valuable. People who'd thought they could get to Jess
through me had learned from their disappointments.
Things had become tolerable.

Until, apparently, tonight. If what Jess said about
Matt and his fans was accurate, I was going to have the
same problem, the way "I'm Henry VIII, I Am" had a
second verse—a little bit louder and a whole lot worse.

Not to mention having every nosy parker on the
internet scouring the details of my life.

"You're lucky people aren't calling you," I told
Izzy. "They'll probably start calling everyone you've
ever been seen with."

"Cool," she said without sincerity. "Cool cool."

"Yeah." As I spoke, I had a thought. Jess wasn't
the only person with fans watching his every move.
It might be easier to get information from the internet

than from some of my fellow suspects. And anyone the age of the Ash Rose crew ought to know how to do it. "You know what? If you're not going to sleep, there's something useful you could do."

"I like your dog, but I'm not brushing him."

"Not that. I want to know what happened between Matt and Ziad."

"So ask Ziad. He's right there. Unless he left too."

"He's here. But he doesn't want to talk about it."

"Then it's not your business, man."

In many ways, Izzy was a lady after my own heart. Until Matt died, what happened with Ziad hadn't been my business, and I would have agreed that I should leave it alone. Matt was dead, though, which changed things.

"I'm with you right up to the point where it might be a motive for murder."

"Is it everyone's business what happened to Jack? Whatever that was?"

"It will be," I said. "I don't think there's any pre-venting that at this point. But he's not going to post about it on the night Matt died where Matt's sister and nieces can see."

There was silence for a few seconds, or near si-lence. I could hear Frank's nails clicking on the floor.

"Fine," Izzy said. "We'll start digging."

"Thank you."

Jess and Vic had finished talking by the time I hung up and for lack of entertainment options were watching me.

"Are they coming in?" Vic asked.

"I doubt it," I said. "They may talk to him on the phone. Or Lam could spend his time talking to people who might be good for this crime instead of harassing teenagers."

"Sure. I'll go tell the cop what to do. Should I go do that? You want me to boss the cop around?"

"Maybe over the phone," Jess said.

Vic gave him a deadly glare. "You're not funny at all."

"You're not the first to say so."

"Go fuck yourselves," she sang out, three ringing notes, like a doorbell. And left.

"This might be a reach," Jess said, "but I don't think she's happy that you informed those people of their rights."

"And I only barely did," I said. "They have rights I never even mentioned."

"She's testy anyway. She saw someone steal one of Matt's shoes right off his body."

"That's pretty bold," I said, "considering how many cops were out there. But I guess they were busy."

"They might get caught later when they put it up for auction," Jess said. "Unless they keep it and build a little shrine around it."

I studied his face. "You're not kidding, are you. You really think that's possible."

"It wouldn't be one of the craziest things I've heard about fans doing," he told me. "Not even top fifty. If they hadn't taken the shoe off his dead body in front of the cops, it wouldn't make the top one hundred."

"I hate your job," I said. It was becoming a refrain for me, something I said as often and casually as "Remember to take a coat" or "Did you lock the patio door." Jess shrugged and said nothing, so I decided to change the subject.

"Did I hear you talking about the food delivery?"

"Yeah. Her only part in it was bringing Harry the guard to Matt's suite so that Lew could give him instructions. She wasn't around for the instructions, so we'd have to ask Lew or Harry what was said. Or we could assume it was the usual. I've heard this spiel a few times. Basically, don't touch the food. Don't

uncover the food. Don't let anyone else touch or uncover the food. Confirm the name on the order with the
delivery person so you know it's correct."

"And she doesn't know what time the food showed
up, can't confirm that Harry received it, and doesn't
know whether it was brought directly to Matt's suite or
what time it was left outside his door?"

Jess smiled. "To think I went to the trouble of asking her when you knew the answers the whole time.
How are our houseguests?"

"We have not actually discussed whose house it
is," I said.

"I'm kicking in rent," Jess said.

"You have a funny idea about how much my rent
is. Even for Calgary you are overpaying by a lot."

"I barely notice the money," Jesse told me. "Mainly because you don't accept the transfers."

That was true, and it was equally true that he stocked
the kitchen, and I kept finding little things like a set of
new tires on my car. If he'd thought he could get away
with it, no doubt it would have been an entire new car.

"I feel that you invited people to stay in my house,"
I said, "without asking me."

"I would have invited them to my house," Jess
said, "but I would have had to get them plane tickets to
Toronto. If you'd let me buy a house for both of us, this
wouldn't be an issue."

"Should we fight about this another time?" I asked.

"I'll pencil it in for next week. Unless one of us has
relocated to prison."

"Great. Our houseguests were getting calls from
Inspector Lam saying they had to come to the theatre or
they would be in big trouble. I don't know exactly how
he worded it, but that seems to be what he implied."

"Did you straighten that out for them?"

"Sort of," I said. "I told them they didn't have to go anywhere, and I recommended the law firm of Google, Wikipedia, and YouTube. I also suggested they brush Frank because neither of us did that today. They mentioned that my office phone won't stop ringing."

"Oh. Damn it. I'm sorry."

"It's not your fault," I said. I even mostly meant it. He did go along with the plan to date Matt, and he had decided to become famous in the first place, so I couldn't forgive him entirely, but he couldn't have known it would result in this.

"Maybe I'll let you hire me an answering service for a few months," I said. "In lieu of rent."

"I'd be delighted."

"I asked our guests to do something for me," I said. "I want to know what happened between Matt and Ziad. I doubt they can find the whole story, but if they get enough of it, I can probably get Ziad to give me the rest."

"Does it matter?" Jess said. "We know Matt did something and Ziad hates him for it. Isn't that enough?"

"It's always better to have more if you have to convince a cop that you're onto something," I said.

"So what do we do now?"

"You could go back to the practice room," I said. "Play some music with your friends."

"I'd feel bad about doing that while so many children are working so hard for you."

"I'm keeping them occupied with useful work," I said. "I don't know what they'd be doing if I didn't give them something to keep them busy, and I don't want to find out."

"I'll talk to Harry about what happened with the food," Jess said. "If you think up something better I can do with my time, text me. Unless I'm too old to work for you."

I felt like I should follow him out the door and spring into investigative action, but on what? It was easy when caught up in a case to want to keep moving. Sometimes, though, it was better to stop and think.

I knew some things. I knew the person who had listened in on me from that bathroom had been in there at a certain time. Nine o'clock or close to it. The Twist had been on stage at that time. Kent and Luna were in the audience. The crew had been mostly backstage and busy. That included Vic, who I was nearly certain had not had time to plant a camera, let alone hide in a bathroom listening to it.

Matt and Lew and I had been in Matt's suite together. Alex had been too, but not the whole time and not at the start. Was it strictly possible for him to have been the person in the bathroom and to have made it to Matt's suite in time to join our conversation? Maybe. Dylan had only been in there for a few minutes, they'd said.

It couldn't have been Emilie because she'd been with Dylan in Dylan's dressing room when Dylan went into the bathroom. Getting around them and into the bathroom without being noticed was flat-out impossible.

Dylan could be lying about the whole thing, but that was unlikely as they knew I'd been talking to Matt shortly after nine and I had not advertised that. So. Ziad. Ash Rose. Duncan, though he'd been out of the building for a while, and I'd have to see if I could time stamp that with Harry. Duncan must have used the stage door because he hadn't known about the fire door until Ziad had mentioned it a few minutes ago.

I took out my phone and texted Jess.

Ask when Duncan left

He sent back a thumbs-up.

So that was covered, unless Duncan was lying about not knowing there was a fire door he could use. But to be honest, I'd seen his acting, and he wasn't that good.

The thing was, as far as I knew, Duncan and Ash Rose hadn't had access to Matt's suite. Maybe before Matt had shown up, but they hadn't known Matt was coming, so there was no reason for them to go in there and plant a camera.

If it wasn't Jess—and it wasn't—I was looking at Ziad, who wasn't likely to have been left alone in that suite long enough to plant a camera and probably couldn't have gotten back in to take it away, and good old Alex.

Alex, who had been in the suite when Matt arrived and wouldn't have been watched closely. Who had his own swipe-card access. Who had come in late when I'd been talking to Matt and had showed up backstage after Jesse's set had started, giving him time to both listen to my conversation and take the camera away.

Why would Alex have planted a camera? I didn't know, but that was okay. For something like this, planting a camera, there could be any of a dozen motives. It was plausible, and that was enough to know.

What I did need was leverage. Did I have enough to confront Alex? I had logic, but I doubted he'd stand there and listen to me laying the whole thing out. He'd dismiss me and walk away. I could describe the size of the camera and where it had been, but that wouldn't prove it was his.

Lying was an option. I could say someone had seen him in the bathroom or had seen him going in. That was risky. He might cave, thinking it was possible he'd been seen, but he might brazen his way through it. If he'd been really careful, and he probably had, he might be confident he hadn't been seen. Because it was hard to control all the variables and because you lost a lot of power when you got caught, lying was never my first choice.

I could tell Lew about the camera, assuming that he'd be horrified and would help me lean on Alex, but what if Lew had been part of it? What if he'd wanted that footage for some reason and he and Alex had been in on that together? Also, even if Lew wasn't involved and helped me get the camera from Alex, would he let me see the footage? Most likely he'd delete it before anyone could see it. It was safer not to make that play.

What to do.

I stood and stretched. My legs felt so crumpled and knotted that I didn't know what it would take to pull out the tension. I would have been willing to have a dungeon master stretch them on a rack.

I left the dressing room and strolled up the hall toward the stage. No one was in view, but just in case, I stayed casual. I was a guy who needed a washroom. Nothing notable about that.

The washroom was unisex, not because it was at the forefront of social change but because it was crammed into a narrow space between the practice room and the first dressing room and there wouldn't have been room for a second. It could have been argued that there wasn't room for one.

The light switch was outside the door, a thing I associated with old buildings. It had been the same in the farmhouse where I'd grown up. Inside I found a cracked white sink set in a counter so narrow that the lip of the porcelain nearly hit the edge. A plain rectangular mirror was set above it, held up with clips at the corners. It didn't match the age of the room, so it had been added later. Maybe the original had been broken at some point. I could imagine an actor coming offstage, unhappy with their performance, smashing the mirror with a prop sword. That felt suitably dramatic and not like what had probably happened—a janitor hitting it with the end of a mop while trying to clean a ridiculously narrow room.

There was one stall at the back, and I could see why Dylan hadn't been able to tell who was in it. Unlike a modern public bathroom with gaps on each side of the door and space to crawl under it if you dared, this stall had a floor-to-ceiling door that was snug in its frame.

I reached for the door, then stopped, my hand frozen above the latch. I was nearly certain there was no one behind the door. It didn't matter. I had these little moments every time I was investigating a murder.

Not that I'd done it often since becoming a PI, but as a cop I had. At least I'd had to talk to witnesses and neighbours, collecting information for the Homicide cops. I was fine most of the time, doing the job, following one lead to another. But there were moments when I'd feel a rollercoaster drop in my stomach and a buzzing in my head.

When I'd told Luna about it, she'd tried to sell me on something psychic, a warning from the universe. That was horseshit for two reasons. One was that there was no such thing as psychic warnings from the universe, and the other was that there was no connection between the "warnings" and any danger I was actually in. I'd told Luna all of that, and she'd replied that if I didn't want a mystical connection with the universe, I could have panic attacks and like it.

I shook my head and opened the stall door to find, horror of horrors, a toilet. An old one like the one in Jesse's dressing room. They had to have upgraded some things for the theatre to still be operating. The wiring for example. To run even a few of the lights they used on stage, they would have had to upgrade the wiring. And a lot of the front of house had been overhauled, making a patchwork of a few things that had been left over the years, some things that were redone in the '70s and not since, and some that had been replaced recently but with faux antiques that seemed original if you didn't inspect them too closely.

Backstage, though, they hadn't bothered to spend that kind of money or time, so a lot of things seemed to be the originals. This toilet was a fine example. The sign above it warning people not to flush anything that hadn't come out of them or off the toilet-paper roll, was newer.

Had the person sat on the closed lid of the toilet, or accustomed to doors with gaps, had they automatically put their feet on the lid and crouched there, trying not to be seen? I looked at the lid, even took out the credit-card-sized LED I carried in my wallet. I couldn't see any prints.

I stood and read the sign until the letters crossed and blurred. What was I doing in here? What did I hope to find? I turned and sat on the toilet lid, imagining I was sitting there in the dark, listening, maybe watching… on my phone? Most likely that. Lots of cameras would transmit to an app. Earbuds in. Staring at the bright screen.

I looked at the back of the door. They should have put the poster there, not on the wall behind the toilet. Down at the floor, the same black and white tiles as in the rest of the room, laid out in a checkerboard pattern. Real lino, not vinyl, so they could have been original. There was a speck on one of the black squares, next to the toilet. A piece of toilet paper? Tissue? I leaned down and pressed the pad of my finger to it. I knew what it was as soon as I touched it but brought it up to my face to confirm with my eyes.

A silver sequin.

CHAPTER SEVENTEEN

ALEX AND his sequined coat. I should have realized he'd been leaving breadcrumbs all over this place. I'd never seen a sequined jacket or bag, no matter how pricey, that didn't shed like a husky in the spring.

This didn't mean that getting the footage from Alex was a sure thing. He could say he'd needed the bathroom and used it, so the sequin proved nothing. It sure didn't hurt, though.

I took a picture of the sequin and texted it to Jess. A few seconds later, he texted a question mark back. I waited. It didn't take long, a few more seconds, before he texted, *Where did u find it?*

I told him, then asked him to meet me at his dressing room. He was waiting for me by the time I got there and opened the door to wave me inside.

"You've cracked the case!" he said as he shut the door behind us. "The sub-case. The mini-case."

"The camera case," I said, and he grinned.

"So what do we do now?"

"I'm not sure," I admitted. "Tell me what you've got first."

"The food? Harry received it at the stage door. The person who delivered it was from the restaurant. They didn't use a delivery service."

"How do you know?"

Jess pulled a business card from his back pocket and handed it to me. It was a promotional card from the restaurant. There wasn't anyone's name on it, just the name and address and phone number.

"They gave this to Harry," Jess said. "I'm not surprised. Lew would always ask for that. Otherwise Matt's food could have been in the back of a delivery driver's car with other people's food, and some of that food could have had mustard on it."

"Okay. That's good, actually. What time did the food show up?"

"Nine thirty. And Harry brought it to Matt's suite right away. He left it outside the door and texted Lew because Lew asked him to do that instead of knocking. That's pretty normal too. Lew doesn't want Matt interacting with random people. And if Lew was backstage or something, he'd get a text and know the food was there."

"But he sent Alex to find it?" I said.

"Well." Jesse gave me a wry smile. "Are you saying you can't imagine why Lew would keep quiet if Matt was getting Alex to fuck off?"

"Fair point," I allowed. "Okay. I found the food outside when I left at twenty to ten, and Harry says he dropped it outside the door right after it showed up, which would be supported by a text from him to Lew. That's a window of ten minutes for someone to adulterate the food in the hallway, and an unknown amount of time for someone to adulterate it inside the room."

"That's not bad, though," Jess said. "Right? It's not that much time, and it's only two places. We can exclude people."

"I'd like it better if the food hadn't sat around unguarded in an empty hall," I said, "but yes."

I took out my phone and texted Dylan, asking them to come back to Jesse's dressing room.

What are you doing?" Jess asked.

"I have a plan for dealing with Alex," I said. "Kind of two plans."

Dylan and Emilie couldn't have gone far because they were at the door in under a minute.

"In, in," I said, waving them to the couch. "Any luck finding the camera?"

"I mean, it'd be easier if you didn't haul us back here," Emilie said.

"True. But I think I'm about to make it a lot easier for you. Jess is going to talk the manager into coming in here for a conversation—"

"Am I?"

"Yes. And I'm going to confront Alex about the camera."

"Wait, confront Alex? What?" Emilie said.

"The camera you were looking for was planted in Matt's suite by Alex. His boyfriend."

"Ooooh!" Emilie said. "Sister don't trust her man!"

Drag Race had a lot to answer for. I chose not to get into it.

"We don't know why the camera was there, but we're sure Alex put it there," I said, "so I'm going to tell him so, and I'm going to ask to see the footage. Maybe he'll give it to me. If he doesn't, I'm going to leave."

"How will that help?" Dylan asked. It sounded like a genuine question.

"I'm hoping that if I rattle him enough, he'll want to check on his camera. It's not the smart thing to do, but when people get nervous, they don't always do smart things."

"And we follow him?" Dylan said.

"Yes. Stay far back. Don't let him see you. But I don't want you to take this on if you're uncomfortable doing it. If you're worried about it, say so, and I'll put Luna or someone on it."

Dylan shook their head. Little wisps of brown hair caught air, making a halo for their face. "I don't mind."

"It's so cool," Emilie said. "Seriously, you have the best job."

"Are you sure this isn't dangerous?" Jesse asked. "What if Alex really, really doesn't want people to know where that camera is?"

"He doesn't seem too dangerous to me," I said, "but they don't have to get close to him."

"What if he's, like, trying to make off with the camera?" Emilie said. "Can I tackle him? I bet I could tackle him."

"Don't make me regret involving you," I told her. "Stay away from him. If he seems like he's going toward some kind of hiding place, text me. If he does anything threatening, start yelling and run away."

"We could ask Kent and Luna to do this instead," Jess pointed out.

"They're more noticeable than these two," I said. "And they're associated with me."

"We can do it," Dylan said. "He won't even see us. I can stay in my dressing room and watch for him under my door, and Em can stay around the corner by the green room and pretend to be on her phone if he goes by."

"Easy peasy," Emilie said.

"Easy peasy," I told Jess. He didn't seem impressed.

"Oh, before you go," I said, "Emilie, do you know where Duncan went earlier? When he left the theatre? Did he mention anything, like going for a drink?"

"I didn't know he went outside," she said. "He never said. When did he go?"

"Nine thirty," Jess said. "And he came back right after my set. He was probably planning to hang around backstage and buttonhole Matt when Matt got off the stage."

"What?" Emilie said, a laugh curling around the word. "Holy cows, I do not think so."

Jess frowned. "He sounded like he wanted to talk to Matt pretty badly," he said. "When Matt walked by and we were all in the green room, Duncan went on a whole thing about this being his opportunity to... he didn't say kiss up, but that seemed to be the idea. He wanted to elevate his career."

"He might have wanted to kiss up," Emilie said. "But it would be more like begging for forgiveness. Do you not know about this?"

"I guess we don't," I said, glancing at Jess. He shook his head. "Why would Duncan have to beg Matt for forgiveness?"

"He made a bunch of jokes about Matt at Juste Pour Rire a couple of years ago, and then he was going to be cast in a small part in some movie that Matt was starring in and Matt said no. Duncan was totally shocked because who thinks Matt Garrett knows what they're up to, right? Like, who would think Matt even knew who they were?"

I remembered my own disorientation at realizing Matt knew who I was, even though I was sleeping with his ex fake boyfriend.

"I can see it being a surprise. So Matt did him out of a role?"

"Not just one. Matt didn't, like, totally blackball him, but there were a bunch of people who wouldn't take Duncan's calls because Matt told them not to. Duncan tried to apologize and sent gifts and stuff, but Matt wouldn't talk to him. Maybe Duncan thought he'd, like, drop to his knees and grovel? I would have totally liked to see that. Nothing against Duncan, but that would be fucking funny."

"Sounds like we should have a talk with Duncan," Jess said. He kept his voice even, but I could see in his eyes that he'd latched on to this new possibility. Someone else with a motive. Someone else who'd been around the food at the right time. Did Duncan know about the mustard? We had no proof of that, but it wasn't impossible.

I glanced at my watch. It had been a while since Duncan had gone in for his interview with Lam. He was probably done now. Back in the green room? He didn't have a dressing room anymore. I texted Kent.

Is Duncan in there

He must have had his phone in his hand because the answer came right away.

Yep

I texted back, *Try not to let him leave the building*

Kent didn't ask a lot of questions when he was in work mode. He assumed I'd brief him when I could. All he sent back was *Will do*

"Okay," I said. "Emilie, Dylan, if you want to get into place, Jess will get Lew in here."

The kids left. Jess was scrolling on his phone.

"Are you worried about being alone with him?" I asked. "We can do this another way."

"No, I'm good," Jess said. "I mean, I'm not good. But I can talk to Lew."

"If you're sure," I said. "I'm sorry. I should have asked."

He shrugged. "I invited people to your house."

"He shouldn't be dangerous."

"Yeah. Poisoners. Like you said, they're not shooty or stabby. Okay. I'm doing this."

He went into the small bathroom and shut the door. I didn't know why he wanted his call to Lew to be private, but I didn't feel like I could complain. I spent the time searching for clips of Duncan's comedy routines so I could see what he'd said about Matt. I couldn't find anything from Just For Laughs, and that was odd because they usually posted at least a clip from damned near everything. Maybe Duncan's routine was one more thing Lewis had arranged to have deleted. His routine and, apparently, his career.

The guy was a better actor than I'd thought because I'd believed him when he'd said he wanted to network. Hitch his wagon to a star. I hadn't seen any resentment or nervousness, and he had to have felt both.

If Matt Garrett had blacklisted you, or close to it, what happened when he died? It might stick, if other people were also offended by whatever you'd done. But if all Duncan had hurt was Matt's pride, people had likely agreed not to hire Duncan in order to stay in Matt's good graces. That wasn't the same thing as not wanting to hire him because he was incompetent or unruly on set. Now that Matt's good graces had died with him, the blacklisting would probably go away.

Was that enough reason for him to kill Matt when he saw a chance? As revenge, or to get his career back, or both? Only Duncan would know.

Jess stayed in the bathroom until someone knocked on the dressing room door. He came out and crossed the room, past me, to open it and invite Lew inside. Jess looked next-level tired, like someone had hollowed him out and the husk of him could crumple at any moment. I hesitated, but he gave Lew a thin smile and said, "Ben was just leaving."

I wasn't a professional performer, but that seemed like a cue.

CHAPTER EIGHTEEN

THE HALL was empty as I went to the next dressing room and knocked. I was willing to bet most people were in the green room, having sociable conversations and trying to guess which of them was a murderer. In a brightly lit room full of people dealing with a killer who was cruel but not violent, it would have been like going to see a horror movie or getting on the free-fall ride at the exhibition. A delicious blend of scary and safe. Even Luna was probably enjoying herself.

Kent, on the other hand, would be fuming that Lam had not yet asked him for his take on the situation or his opinion of the suspects. Lam wasn't obligated to ask Kent, and it might even have been considered a little off since Kent was clearly personally involved and could even, if you stretched a point, have been considered a suspect himself. But most of his colleagues would have asked him anyway.

There was no response to my knock, so I did it again with more force. That time, after a moment, Alex's reedy voice came through.

"Who is it?"

"It's Ben Ames. I was wondering if I could ask you a few questions."

"I'm grieving!"

He sounded indignant, but I was sure that was nothing new for him.

"I'm sorry for disturbing you, but this is important," I said. "I only need a few minutes."

I had leverage to apply if he didn't open the door, but I waited instead of using it. When I needed someone to open a door to me, even if it was against their interests, curiosity usually did the job.

Sure enough, he swung the door open after less than a minute.

"Make it quick," he said.

For whatever it was worth, Alex looked like he was grieving. His eyes and nose were red, and his face was puffy. There was nothing glamorous or theatrical about it. I could see balled-up tissues on the table at the back of the room.

Some of Ash Rose's things were still crammed into the room, which was smaller than Jesse's and much too small for three people to share. A loveseat had been shoved against the back wall, and I hoped no one ever needed to move it because it would be a struggle. The wooden arms had dug into the walls on either side.

Chairs, a low table, and that loveseat took up most of the room. There was no door to a bathroom and no kitchenette. I hadn't realized how deluxe Jesse's room was by comparison. Matt's suite was pie-in-the-sky luxury. The stuff of kings.

Alex and I made our way to the seating area, stepping carefully to avoid makeup train cases and sparkly sneakers and someone's stuffed pink unicorn. He flounced onto the loveseat and grabbed another tissue from the battered half-empty box on the table. Single-ply, bargain brand. I was surprised he hadn't gone to Vic demanding something better. Or insisted on access to Matt's suite, where all the good stuff was.

He was having trouble making his long arms and legs fit into the narrow space. I pictured him in the bathroom, hiding in the stall. His arms would have brushed the sides, knocking that sequin loose. Here, he sat with his limbs at odd angles, like he was striking a pose for a high-fashion shoot.

"Well? What is it?"

"I wanted to talk about what you were listening to in the bathroom down the hall."

He blinked slowly. The rest of his face didn't move.

"Why on earth would I be listening to anything in a bathroom?"

"Exactly," I said. He wrinkled his face, like he'd smelled something bad.

"What?"

"Why would you be listening to something in a bathroom? What would you be listening to? I should say, watching. I kind of think you were watching a camera feed."

He stared at me. He didn't seem at risk of bursting into tears again, but his eyes were still watery.

"I don't know what you're talking about."

"You do," I said. "If you're confused, it's because you don't know how I know or why I'm here. But you know what I'm talking about. Right? I'm talking about the camera you planted in Matt's suite."

I could try to make myself sound cool by saying I could see some kind of tell on him, like a flinch or a twitch or a narrowing of his eyes. If I did say that, I'd be kidding everyone, including myself. Sure, I thought I could see deception on him, first the surprise that I really was onto him and then the cover-up, but of course I thought that. I knew he was lying. I was primed to watch for signs of the lie, and once you're primed for that kind of thing, you'll see it. Even if it isn't there.

"This isn't funny." He sniffed. He held the tissue to his nose and dabbed gracefully. "I'd like for you to go."

"I don't doubt that," I said. "And I really am sorry to do this right after you've lost someone you cared about, but you have to see it from my point of view. You have footage from Matt's suite on the night he died, and that could be relevant to what happened to him. Maybe it was an accident. Maybe not. Either way, you could have vital information, and you don't seem to have mentioned it to anyone."

That was his chance to say that yes, actually, he'd mentioned it to the police officer, and it was none of my business. Or to say he hadn't thought of it like that, and he'd go tell Detective Lam right away. He did neither of those things. He sat and he stared and said nothing.

I wasn't really surprised. I didn't know whether that camera had been his own little secret or something Lewis and Matt were in on, but I did know being able to keep a secret was a prerequisite to entering Matt's inner circle. My cagey boyfriend would have fit right in.

"Okay," I said, "I guess I'll tell you some more about how I see this. I don't know whether Matt or Lew knew about your camera. I could ask Lew. You'd probably rather I didn't do that. If you planted a camera and he didn't know about it, I don't know specifically what he'd say, but I bet it would be a threat. Something about turning you into a pariah."

"I didn't plant any camera," Alex said. This time the denial was stiff and mannered, a line from a Perry Mason villain on the stand.

"You did," I told him. "If this was something the others didn't know about, I'd bet you planted it when you and Matt first got here. You and Matt and Lew would have been bustling around, putting things away, maybe using the washroom... you could have done it without being seen. It would have taken you a little time to move the knick-knacks around and hide it, but I think you'd have had the time. I mean, Matt trusted you. It's not like he'd have been watching you the way he'd watch someone like Jess."

Weirdly, that was when I did see something odd cross his face. I thought it really was there, not something I'd imagined, because I hadn't expected it. It wasn't quite a flinch, but that was the best word I could find for it. His head pulled back and his brow pulled in and down. Like a reaction to a slap.

"I don't know why you would want to record Matt without Matt knowing," I said. "For all I know, you needed footage for some kind of art project. If you tell me that's what it was, I'll go ahead and believe you. You can also tell me Matt and Lew knew about the whole thing, and I'll believe that too. I won't say a word to Lewis because why would I if he already knows?"

I leaned forward in my chair, chummily, my hands loosely clasped and my elbows on my knees.

"The best thing you can do is show that footage to me. If it has nothing to do with Matt's death, I don't see any reason Detective Lam or Lew or anyone else needs to know about it."

That was a total lie, of the sort I'd learned to tell while with the police. Both cops and reporters, like mean kids in school, will tell you things can stay between you and them. It's never true. Mean kids want to share your secrets on the playground. Reporters want to put your secrets into their story. And cops want to see someone put up on charges, which means laying all of your secrets out in front of some lawyers, who will proceed to lay them out in front of a judge and jury and any reporters who are willing to listen.

The best thing for Alex to do was to sit mute and pretend I wasn't even there. But I wasn't obligated to tell him that.

"I can't show you any footage because I don't have any," Alex said. That was the next smartest thing he could do after refusing to speak to me at all. Tell a simple, straightforward lie and cling to it like a baby orangutan clings to its mother. He could have gotten dramatic. How did I know someone had footage? Why, they'd filmed him too, and he would like to know who they were! Who, oh, who might it have been? Given his style and his profession and, frankly, his outfit, it was what I'd expected from him. But he was a cooler customer than that.

"I know that you do," I said. "Oh, that reminds me. I have something of yours."

His eyes widened slightly. I could see a moment's panic as he wondered what I had. The camera? Had I found the camera? He was visibly relieved when I showed him the sequin I'd picked up from the bathroom floor.

"This came off your coat while you were in the bathroom," I said. "You know, watching the camera feed."

"Oh," he said airily. "Those get everywhere when I wear this coat."

"I have a hard time believing one would waft past two closed doors into a bathroom stall," I said.

"It didn't," he said. "I used that washroom. I needed one, and I didn't want to go all the way back to the suite. I didn't realize that was a crime."

"That wouldn't be the crime," I said. "Do you know what single party consent is?"

He pursed his lips and said nothing.

"It says as long as one person in a conversation knows they're being recorded, it's legal to make that recording. If all the people know, obviously that's okay too. When no one in the conversation knows, then you've got a problem. That's another reason why you're better off showing that footage to me. If you don't, I'm obligated as a private investigator to inform Detective Lam that you're withholding potential evidence. That could get you charged with obstruction, and then you've got an illegal recording on top of that?" I shook my head. "It's not good, Alex. You don't want to be in that position."

Then I leaned in closer and did something that would require a bleach shower when I got home.

"Alex. We both know how it is. When you're a gay man dealing with the police—"

Alex sat up and glared at me. "Who the fuck said I was gay?"

"I—"

"I'm pansexual."

To be fair, I had assumed.

"Right. My apologies. No matter where you are in the community, can you really trust the police? They're not going to give you the benefit of the doubt. They could be looking for excuses to pin something on you. I don't want to hand another queer person over to the police. If you show me the footage, I can see whether you've got anything relevant, and I can show you how to stay out of trouble. If you don't, I can't help you."

I'm like you, in other words. We're in the brother— and sister—and otherhood of queerdom, and you should trust me because of that. Never have we in the community, this one big and undivided community, done each other wrong. It was unforgivable bullshit, and I was almost relieved when he narrowed his eyes at me.

"Fuck you," he said, each word clipped and precise. I completely agreed, but I told my face that I was disappointed and saddened by his foolhardy response.

"I can give you a little time to think about it," I said. "Not a lot of time. Even if I don't go looking for Detective Lam, he'll come looking for me. At that point I won't have any choice. I'll have to tell him about your camera."

"There is no camera," Alex said.

I shook my head. "That's not smart. I was hoping you'd be smart. If you come to your senses and realize this is your best offer, I'll be next door in Jesse's dressing room."

The movement of his lip was so quick that I almost missed it. A slight tenting of the upper lip, just past the midline. A quirk that, if it had lasted longer, would have been a sneer.

If I'd still thought he might give in and show me the footage, that would have put an end to my delusion. The guy didn't merely dislike and mistrust me. He had contempt for me. He didn't think there was anything of value I could offer, or any threat I could bring to bear.

That was fine. I'd done my job, coming at Alex like a cop, trying to manipulate him in a few ways, searching for a place I could knock in a wedge. I needed it to seem like I'd sincerely tried. He had to believe it.

Now all I could do was leave and hope that, despite appearances, I'd gotten under his skin.

Alex did not show me to the door. I left in silence and shut it behind me. I couldn't see Dylan, even though I knew they were watching through the crack at the bottom of their dressing room door. I couldn't see Emilie directly, but there was a glint, a tiny bit of light moving around in the hall, and that had to be her. If I looked very carefully, I could see something jutting past the edge of the wall at the end of the hall. A phone, I decided. She was probably using the camera to watch around the corner without being seen.

Would I have seen the phone if I hadn't known she was hiding there? I didn't think so.

I knocked on Jesse's door. It took longer than I'd expected before he opened it. Seeing his face, I got a surprise.

Jess wasn't as weepy as Alex, but he had been crying. His eyes were slightly red, and the eyeliner was smudged. I looked over his head to the couch, where Lew was sitting with a hand to his forehead, seeming exhausted. He would be exhausted. Never mind the stress or his illness or the sleeping pill he seemed to have taken before Matt died. He was an older guy, and it was damned near the middle of the night.

I might have almost felt sorry for him, in a limited way, if Jess hadn't been teary. I put a hand on Jesse's shoulder.

"Jess? Are you okay? What did he say to you?"

"Nothing," Jess said. "He didn't do anything wrong."

He had, as recently as a few hours ago and in this very room, but I didn't say so. We were talking about now.

"Leave him with me," I said. "You can go to the practice room or the green room."

I would have liked to offer to kick Lew out, but I needed to keep him and Alex apart for now.

"No," Jess said. "Actually… could you give us a few?"

It was a hard job, trying not to gape.

"You want me to leave you alone here with him."

"You didn't mind when it suited you," Jess said, quietly enough that Lew might not have heard him. Between the words and the temper in his eyes, I thought this wasn't the right time to ask what the hell Jess wanted with Lew, or why he'd been crying. I put my hands up, palms facing him.

"Okay. I'll be in the green room. Text me if you need me."

"Yeah."

He shut the door on me. Not aggressively. Aside from that flash of irritation, I didn't think he was mad at me. Not exactly. He just had something eating him.

On my way to the green room, I passed Emilie. She was giving a very natural performance as "girl sitting in hallway obsessively checking her phone" and didn't even glance up as I went by. At the end of the hall, in front of Matt's suite, a cop sat on a chair. No one I recognized, but this was the kind of crap detail you got when you were brand new, so that made sense.

He was wearing his coat, open, probably for lack of anywhere to put it. I could see a rip in one arm. His hat was askew, and the reddish-brown hair sticking out from it was messy. I raised a hand in greeting or sympathy, and he stared through me. I didn't take it personally.

The green room was unusually quiet. Duncan was in there by the pop and coffee, talking to Luna and Kent. Ziad was in the opposite corner, texting rapidly with a grim expression. Handling his social media? Telling his manager about the shit show he was starring in? Engaging a lawyer, just in case? There were any number of unpleasant tasks he could have been digging into.

Kent strolled over to me and stood against my shoulder, where he could speak in a near whisper and still be heard.

"The Twist are talking to Lam," he told me. "He got Vic to wrangle the two that were in here and the other three from the practice room."

"She must love being his border collie," I said. Kent shrugged.

"It's a lot of her job anyway. Getting people to where they're supposed to be."

"Yes, but she doesn't work for him. Anyway. You think Lam will cut the Twist loose after he gets their statements? They don't have motives as far as I can tell. They were backstage watching Ziad when the food showed up. And we have too many people wandering around this crime scene."

"Yeah, he'll probably send them to their hotel and tell them not to leave town."

"What's up with Duncan?"

"Lam told him he could go, so he was trying to do that. Luna had to intervene."

"Looks like she's still intervening."

Kent grinned.

"Yeah. She told him there's some mark in one of his eyes that's a sign of... I forgot what. Big words. She's got him terrified that he's going to die, and she's doing all kinds of doctory shit. Making half of it up, I think."

"That is some excellent work," I said.

"It's not the first time she's had to talk a guy out of leaving. People try to crawl out of the ER on their three remaining limbs all the time."

That was an exaggeration, but I knew what he meant. On the force, he and I had brought in a lot of people who had held their stab wounds while heading for the door.

"Lam's not much of a detective," I said.

Kent's face brightened. "What's that you say?"

"Duncan had opportunity, and he has a motive. Lam shouldn't have told him he could go."

"Oh," Kent said "Oh my. Tell me what he missed."

"Apparently Duncan insulted Matt in one of his routines years ago, and Matt has kept him from getting roles ever since."

Kent cocked his head.

"Seriously? He was talking like meeting Matt was his lifelong dream."

"It seems he's a better actor than we thought."

"Than you thought," Kent said. "I always thought he was pretty good."

"He probably wanted to meet Matt so he could beg forgiveness," I said, "but murdering him would also have solved Duncan's problem."

"And Lam told him to go to his hotel," Kent said, shaking his head. "Disgraceful. An embarrassment to the force."

We both knew that murder suspects got sent home all the time. If you weren't sure who did it or you weren't ready to charge someone or you were confident your suspect wasn't going anywhere, you could cut them loose.

But it was fun to pretend Lam had fucked up, and I was pretty sure he hadn't realized Duncan had a motive.

"And he was by the stage door when Matt's food was delivered," I said, "because he went out for a while after his set."

"Really?" Kent said. "You sound like you're taking him seriously."

"I might be. I need to talk to him and see where his head is at."

"I'd do it now," Kent advised. "Luna can't stall him forever."

"I would, except I've got something else…. Actually, I'll hand that off to you if I can. Alex has a camera stashed around here somewhere with footage from Matt's suite, and I just rattled his cage, so I think he'll go check on it eventually. I've got Emilie and Dylan hiding so they can follow him when he moves."

Kent's eyes were wide. "Holy shit. What else have I missed?"

"Not too much. I don't think. I forget. But can you keep my phone and watch for texts from Dylan or Emilie? If you get one while I'm talking to Duncan, feel free to go terrify Alex and get that camera away from him."

"It would be my pleasure."

"I thought so." I gave Kent my phone and my PIN and wandered over to Duncan and Luna.

"There's really no telling," Luna was saying. "You'll need to get tests—"

"Stand down, Lunes," I said. "I can take it from here."

"Oh," she said. "All right. In that case, Duncan, I should tell you that everything I've said to you tonight has been bullshit. I was asked to keep you here, and I did. You shouldn't worry about the mark in your eye, but genuinely, if you haven't had a checkup in years, you really should have one as soon as possible."

"I… what?" Duncan said. "What is happening? I'm not sick?"

"You could be," Luna said. "I don't know, and neither do you. Get a checkup."

"What?"

I put a hand on his arm and tugged on it, gently. "Come on. We need to talk."

I led him to the couch in front of the TV screen and gestured for him to take a seat. He did, his face letting me know that he was suspicious and put-out.

"You told your buddies to keep me here?"

"Yeah." I sat beside him. "Sorry about that. I realized I would need to talk to you before you left."

"Okay," he said. "Start talking so I can get out of here. These people put me up in a hotel with sheets that cost more than my whole bed at home. I would really like to sleep on them."

It wasn't completely unfair that the charity had covered a hotel for Duncan and not Ash Rose, since he'd come from Winnipeg and they'd come from Edmonton, but somehow it still felt like favouritism. Or that usual thing where the people who have the most and need the least get everything for free. Not that Duncan was a yacht-owning billionaire, but he was better off than the people currently crashing in my house.

"Did you have any idea Matt was going to be here?" I said. "Did you hear a rumour? You know people in the film industry."

"You are barking up the wrong tree in the wrong forest on the wrong planet. You think I get that level of industry gossip? Trust me, if your boyfriend didn't know, I didn't know."

I caught a waft of beer when he spoke. This was the closest I'd been to him all day, so I couldn't have said for sure when he'd gotten his drink on, but it gave weight to my theory that he'd hit a bar on his mid-evening field trip.

"You never know," I said. "There are probably some locals on the crew down at Pincher Creek. Anyway, doesn't matter. You left the theatre at one point tonight."

"I didn't know I was supposed to be under house arrest. The guard let me go, no problem."

"Easy," I said, raising my palms the way I had to Jesse. "I don't have a problem with you taking a break. I just thought you might have seen some things that could be helpful. That's why I asked Luna and Kent to stall you a little bit."

"Did it occur to you to ask me to stick around? Instead of having your doctor friend tell me I was standing on the lip of my grave?"

"I thought about asking, but I didn't know if you'd be up for it. You know how it is, man. It's late, and we're all cranky. I apologize again."

He closed his eyes. There were dark circles beneath them, visible through his stage makeup. He hadn't taken it off, but the snow and wind had removed some of it for him.

"Whatever." He opened his eyes and pulled a crumpled tissue from the front pocket of his black jeans. Once he had it out, he didn't seem to know what he wanted with it. He let his hand rest against his leg, the tissue held loosely in his curled fingers. "What do you think I saw?"

"You left around the same time the food was arriving," I said. "Harry keeps a log."

"Good for Harry," Duncan said. "Give that man a raise."

"Did you see it being delivered?"

"No. But there was a cart of food there when I got to the door. Must have just missed the delivery guy."

"Okay. And did you see what the food was? Did you notice anything about it?"

"It was all covered up with those… you know, the silver lid things. Like in a hotel. It smelled like fish. I noticed that. Smelled like salmon."

"It was," I said. "You have a good nose."

"I was a bloodhound in a past life."

"You didn't take a peek? To see how the other half eats?"

I could see him thinking. This wasn't a question that required thinking, unless you were trying to figure out whether you could get away with a lie. Whether you'd left fingerprints somewhere, for example.

"Okay, one little peek," he said. "Harry was telling some fans to get away from the door, and I lifted a couple of lids."

That would have given him time. Not a lot of it. And where would the mustard have come from?

"Did you see any condiments on or around the tray?"

"Condiments? Who the hell says condiments? What, do you manage a grocery store in your spare time?"

"Ketchup," I said, keeping my voice even. "Mustard. Relish. That kind of thing."

"I never saw any of that. But I never looked either."

"Did you see anyone take the food anywhere? Move it somewhere?"

"The food was still there when I left. I don't know what you're picturing, but I wasn't hanging around the stage door trying to get someone's autograph. I went *to* the door to go *through* the door so I could fuck off."

He illustrated the last bit with his hands, dropping the tissue into his lap and walking two fingers up to and through a doorway, then flipping his hand over to give me a British up yours.

"There were some of Matt's lunatic fans hanging around. They asked me if I'd seen him, gave me things to give him, blah-dee-blah. I took their shit, and I tossed it as soon as I was around the corner. Then I was gone until I came back, which is when you ran into me in the hall."

I could have said something about him throwing the fans' gifts away, but what? He wouldn't have been able to get them to Matt, and I doubted Matt would have cared even if Duncan had managed to pass it along.

"And can you tell me where you were?"

"You sound like Inspector Ham. Lam. Hammy Lam a Ding-Dong."

"How about sticking with Inspector Lam," I suggested.

"Fine. Why don't you ask Inspector Lam what I said so I don't have to say it all twice?"

"I could do that," I said. "But I do have one thing to ask you about that the detective probably didn't."

From the corner of my eye, I saw his fingers twitch. Might have been a meaningless cramp.

"What's that, Gay Maigret?"

"I was wondering why you sounded so eager to meet Matt."

His eyes widened. I saw red around the edges.

"Jesus Christ, buddy, was I unclear? He's a star. He was a star. I thought he could help my fucking career. I was planning to lick his asshole until it gleamed like the Koh-i-Noor."

I was nearly certain he meant that figuratively.

"I see the misunderstanding here," I said. "It's my fault. I'll clarify. I'm wondering why you sounded so eager to meet him, considering that you insulted him and he's spent the last few years keeping you from landing any decent film roles."

Because everything seemed to happen at once on this enchanted evening, as Duncan reacted to my bombshell, I saw Kent taking out my phone like it had buzzed to alert him to a text. Kent glanced at me, and I raised my chin toward the door. Go get 'em, tiger.

Duncan's face was shifting from one expression to another as he tried to decide on a response. I watched it settle into resignation as he realized the receipts had to be out there somewhere, and evidently I had found them.

"Fine. I wanted to beg forgiveness. It's not that different. I was still planning to kiss his ass for as long as it took."

"This can't have been the first time you've tried to beg forgiveness from Matt."

He raised his brows. "No? Okay. It's not. What's your point?"

"You've tried this before, and it didn't work. What made you think things would be different tonight?"

He leaned back and laced his hands behind his head. An open position, meant to display confidence and candour. The salesmanship was good, but I still wasn't buying it.

"I didn't. But a guy's gotta try, right? I don't know. I figured, face-to-face might be different. I never got past his people before."

"And you were going to stop him on his way onstage?"

Duncan stretched and yawned. That I believed. It was late, and he was a little drunk.

"Coming offstage. He'd have time to talk to me. He'd have just said a bunch of high-minded shit. You halfway believe that stuff when you say it. I thought he might be in a forgiving mood."

"What if it didn't work?" I said.

"I didn't plan that far ahead."

"You would have been stuck not getting roles," I said. Pushing on the bruise a little.

He responded with a glare. "That brings us again to what's your point?"

"You must have thought about it. If he refused to forgive you or walked right past you… then what?"

He flicked something I couldn't see off his jeans. A bit of lint—or an idea he didn't like.

"I wasn't going to kill him. Is that what you're suggesting? Am I the special guest star on the episode of *Columbo*?"

"Matt dying would have solved your problem. It did solve your problem."

"It's my lucky day. Is this all you wanted?"

"Nearly," I told him. "Did Liam ask you about any of this?"

"No. I don't think he's heard about my big Matt drama. Are you going to tell him?"

"I don't know," I admitted. "I don't know whether it's relevant to this case. It doesn't look great that you had a motive and you were right there with the food cart."

"You think I put something in his food? With the guard standing right there? You're a lot of assumptions deep, my friend. You assume I knew what he was allergic to and that I had it on me and that I knew he had an allergy in the first place. And then you assume I knew it was his food, which I didn't. I guessed, but I didn't know. And that I have the coconut-sized titanium-plated balls to try to doctor his food with the security guy standing two feet away. That's flattering, but my balls are not gilded and they are a regular size."

"I only have your word for all of that," I said. "And please don't take that as a request to show me your balls."

"I wish I could say you were missing out. You only have my word, all right, but come on. Two feet away. And there were, what, three different meals on that tray? Which one was Matt's? See, I don't know that either."

I blinked, hard, like he'd tried to stick a finger in my eye. He was right. Yes, there was some way he could have found out which dinner was Matt's, but that was piling something extremely unlikely on top of an already teetering pile of pretty unlikely things. Whoever had doctored the food had to have known what Matt's order would be. Maybe by the strong salad dressing or because he always ate salmon a few times a week. Maybe because they'd been there when Lew had placed the order. That or... was there mustard in everything? Had anyone checked?

If there was, I still didn't see Duncan as a good suspect. Not with the few seconds he'd have had to doctor the food. One dish? A quick zigzag of mustard in the stuffed salmon? Maybe. It seemed possible. But all three?

No way.

"You're right," I said.

"I know," he answered.

"Huh."

"Yep."

"So," I said, "I guess the only other thing I'm wondering is, what did Lam ask you?"

"Where I was at which times," Duncan said. "When I left. Where I went. Why. Before you ask, I went for a drink at the pub around the corner."

"I thought maybe," I said. He gave me a half smile.

"No one told me this was a Prohibition event."

From the way he said it, I got the sense that having a drink was less something he'd decided he wanted to do and more something he really needed to do. But that was irrelevant to the case and fundamentally none of my business.

"If you still want to go to your hotel," I said, "I won't sic any more physicians on you."

"Fuuuuck," he groaned. "I have to call a cab in this fucking weather. What's the wait time on that? An ice age? And I have to get up and put my coat and boots on and get into the cab and get out of it at the hotel… fuck me, that list is way too long. I don't know if I can do it."

"So sleep in here," I said. "Or go back to your dressing room. Lam doesn't own the place. Make him use the security office."

"He should use the stage," Duncan said. "That would add some drama."

Drama was added to the green room a moment later when Luna's phone went off. Her ringtone was some kind of Bollywood surf disco thing, and it did its job well because it was impossible to ignore. Duncan and I both looked at Luna as she answered her phone with, "Yes?" listened for a while, then signed off with, "I'll tell him."

"Am I him?" I asked.

"You are. Kent wants you to meet him in the practice room."

I thanked her, and Duncan, and went to meet Kent. On the way, I passed Jesse's dressing room. There was light coming from under the door. I wanted to knock, but

Jess had been pretty clear about wanting to be left alone
with Lew to finish whatever the hell they were doing.

A tableau awaited me in the practice room. Kent
and Alex were sitting on a couch against the back wall,
with Dylan and Emilie on the floor at their feet.

"Come on in," Kent said heartily. "Have a seat.
Alex has something to tell you."

He sounded like a father setting his child up for
a forced apology, and Alex fit the part. His head was
down, and he was picking at his nail polish. He gave
me a hooded glare without lifting his head, then went
back to ruining his manicure.

There were still chairs around the piano from earlier. I pulled one close to the couch and sat.

"Alex?" I said. He raised his head and looked me
in the eye.

"Be fucked."

"I see." I turned to Kent. "Maybe you should tell
me."

"Your Baker Street Irregulars followed this charm-
er backstage. They saw him reaching behind the fly gallery for something, so Emilie here told him to freeze,
and Dylan texted your phone."

"Good work," I told the kids. Emilie beamed.
Dylan nearly smiled.

"When I got there," Kent said, "Alex here was still
trying to pretend he was stretching his legs and didn't
know what a camera even was, but it took me maybe
thirty seconds to find it."

"Not even," Emilie said.

Kent reached into his pants pocket and pulled out
a small camera. It was similar to a GoPro, sturdy and
small on the palm of Kent's meaty hand.

"Well whadda ya know," I said. "Alex? Still pretending you don't know anything about this? Because we're going to watch it, and there's probably footage of you setting it up and walking away."

That wasn't necessarily true because Alex could have triggered the camera from his phone, but I could see that it hit home. Alex swallowed audibly. His fingers were entwining and separating like thin white worms with lives of their own.

"Fine," he said. He sounded close to tears. "I set up a camera. Are you happy?"

"Not especially," I said. "But I am professionally satisfied. Would you like to tell us why you put a camera in Matt's suite?"

Alex sat up and raised his chin. "It was my suite too. I'm a guest too."

"Do you routinely set up a camera when you're staying somewhere?"

"Maybe I do," he said. "It's really none of your business."

"Skip it," I said. "We can talk about that later."

"Never," Alex said. "Am I being detained?"

"Nope," I said. "You've been free to go the whole time. And if you're upset about how any of this was handled, or if you're mad about Kent finding this neat little camera backstage, we could get Detective Lam in here and talk about it."

"*Hmf*," Alex sniffed. He stood and strode from the room with a flash of sequins and a rustle of silk. I might have to talk to him later, depending on what the camera showed, but I doubted Alex would leave the theatre. If nothing else, Lew had probably told him to stay put.

I took the camera and turned it around in my hands. It had a viewscreen on the back, small but good enough to see what it had captured. To actually watch it, I might need to convince Alex to give up his phone. Or at least hunt down some headphones so I could get the audio.

"You'll need this," Kent said. He was pulling something else from his pants pocket. An SD card. "I didn't know if he could erase the camera from his phone. Figured I wouldn't take any chances."

My stomach tensed at the thought that Alex might have deleted the footage before Kent arrived, before he even went to look for the camera. I put the SD card in, or tried to, with a slight tremor. Backward. I flipped it and it went in smoothly. The camera had a menu I could get into if I wanted to be confused, but the basic controls were simple. I did not have to go through the humiliation of asking the younger generation to help me get the playback working.

I almost laughed at the sight of Alex doing exactly what I'd said, peering blurrily into the lens from a few inches away, then standing up, turning, and walking out of the room. It was empty, no Matt or Lew in sight. It was still possible that one, the other, or both had known about the camera, but it was unlikely if Alex had picked a time when they were both away to set the thing up.

Matt walked into view from the bathroom at the left side of the room. He went to the kitchenette and opened the mini fridge. He stood there for a while, staring at the bottled water and juice but not reaching for it. On the counter, the brown bag that should have held his EpiPens was upright and closed.

Lew came into the shot from what seemed like his bedroom. He was reading something on his phone. Matt went around him to the couch. Lew went to the door and stood next to it. Matt checked his phone. Nothing happened for so long that I thought the video might have paused, but then Lew said something, and Matt looked up. From the expressions on both of their faces, Lew's frustration and Matt's pissiness, I was definitely going to want the audio. For now, I decided to fast forward through the thing and watch for comings and goings.

Lew left and Matt sat, looked at his phone, paced like a sped-up cartoon character, sat down, stood up, paced some more. Jess came in, and I suddenly realized, as I should have before, what the camera thing was about. Why Alex had put it there. I'd forgotten that Matt and Lew had kicked Alex out before Matt talked to Jess.

Alex had been curious. Who wouldn't be? He'd have known that Matt and Jess had dated. He might have known it was a big put-on, but maybe not. There wouldn't have been any particular reason for Matt to tell him. Either way, anyone who spent time in that camp would have figured out there was something strange between Jess and Matt. If nothing else, Matt driving all the way up from Pincher Creek to talk to Jess would have been a ten-foot-tall neon clue that something weird was going on. What boyfriend, knowing all of that and then being told to make himself scarce, wouldn't have been tempted to eavesdrop somehow?

Why Alex had carried that camera on him in the first place was another matter, but he was an artist. It could have been as simple as him needing to pick up footage for whatever piece he was doing next.

Jess and Matt talked. It didn't seem like an argument. They sat and stood in turn. Matt moved closer. Jess moved away. Was Matt trying to threaten or bond or seduce or… I couldn't tell at this speed and on such a tiny screen.

"Holy fucking shitballs," Emilie said. She was looking at her phone and had an earbud in one ear. Dylan and Kent had been watching their own phones, but they both moved toward Emilie when she spoke. She held up a hand, still staring at her phone. She was chewing on the end of her long blonde hair.

"Look on TikTok. Ash Rose posted."

Dylan got that video up and running long before Kent or I managed it, so we gathered around their phone. It wasn't Ash Rose so much as Ashley and a silent background Kayla, with Izzy nowhere to be seen. Dylan turned up the audio, and we watched Ashley outline the harassment she had suffered at the hands of the Calgary Police Force. She called Lam out by name, dropped at least one f-bomb for every ten words, and left no doubt whatsoever that Matt Garrett's death was being investigated as a murder. She never used his name, but she didn't have to. They were at the same event in the same venue. Matt was dead. Now Ashley was getting calls from a homicide detective? It would not take clamps and industrial glue for people to put things together.

"Hoo-boy," Kent said. If he was trying to look sad about this, he wasn't doing a great job. "What brought this on?"

"Lam got her number and implied that she had to come back to the venue and report to him. She called me, and I explained that she didn't have to do that. She doesn't like cops in the first place, so I guess she found it particularly annoying when a cop tried to jerk her around. This isn't what I would have done about it, but I can see her point of view."

"Pressure's on Lam now," Kent said. "The whole world knows he's investigating Matt's death."

"Yeah, that's one of the reasons I wouldn't have gone about things Ashley's way," I said. "I know you don't like the guy, and I can see you think this is funny, but he is going to get hounded until the end of his days."

"It's a little funny," Kent said.

"What's going to happen to her?" Dylan asked.

"What, Ashley?" I shrugged. "Nothing probably. Maybe he could charge her with something like obstruction, but it's a stretch. Lam's boss will already have memos from Communications and Legal saying Lam needs to sit down and shut up, so that's probably what he'll be directed to do. Oh, and solve the murder. Kent's right. Lam is going to be under a lot of pressure to solve this, fast."

"Like he wasn't already," Kent said. "I almost feel sorry for him. Actually no. I'm just relieved it's not me."

"You need more high-profile friends," I told him. "That way every time there's a high-profile case, you'll have a conflict of interest."

"I'll ask Jesse to introduce me to more people. He'll love that."

"So much."

"You guys," Emilie said, "like, I'm glad you think this is funny, but won't the cops be, like, unofficially up Ashley's ass forever? She's kind of a bitch, but she doesn't deserve that."

I hadn't noticed any friction between Emilie and Ashley, which showed what an expert I was in the social cues of today's young ladies. It had probably been like skywriting to everyone under twenty-five.

"She's got BPD," Dylan said. It was a gentle but unmistakable scolding.

Emilie reddened, and her face tightened around her jawline. "She has BPD and she's a bitch."

They launched into a debate over something that I knew from experience was a no-win. Could you blame someone for something if it might be part of a disorder they had? As a corollary, how could you tell whether it was the disorder or just... them? It was the kind of thing my criminology classmates and I had drunkenly yelled at each other about back in university. We'd never come to any useful conclusions, and I doubted Emilie and Dylan were going to sort it out tonight.

Kent and I slipped away with the camera before either of them dragged us into the conversation.

CHAPTER NINETEEN

WHEN WE got into the hall, the Twist was coming out of what had been the comics' dressing room before Lam had commandeered it.

"Interrogation over?" I asked.

"We didn't give him nothin'," Connor said in a mafioso accent so terrible that I almost didn't recognize it.

"We gave him everything," Brennan said with fond exasperation that probably came out a lot when he was dealing with Connor. "No reason not to from what I can see."

"What did he ask you?" I said.

"A lot of where and when," Thom said. He was standing next to Reiss, who was wary and pale. Thom had a hand on Reiss's back, right below his shoulder.

"And did we know Matt," Connor added. "Because that's the kind of guy we'd know."

I snorted, which sounded like a response to the idea of Connor knowing an A-lister.

"Sorry," I said quickly. "That wasn't…. Last year I told Jess that I'd better not run into Matt on the street, and Jess said I wouldn't because I didn't winter in Dubai."

Connor surveyed the hallway. "Shit. I would never have known we were in Dubai right now."

"It's not what I expected," I agreed. "Did the detective ask if you saw any hostility toward Matt?"

"Yeah," Thom said. "Duncan obviously told him about Jess and Ziad. We tried to downplay it, but everyone knows Jess has issues with Matt, and Ziad hasn't been subtle, so…."

"Not much point trying to hide it," I agreed.

"Did he ask you to stick around?" Kent asked. The band looked at each other.

"He didn't actually say get the fuck out…," Charlie said.

"…but it was implied," Brennan finished. "I suppose it's understandable."

"It's busy around here," I said. "I can see him wanting to thin out the herd."

"Yeah," Thom said. "But we don't want to abandon you and Jess."

I looked at my client. Reiss met my eyes, and I felt something in my spine, a little buzz of excitement that woke me up like espresso. In spite of how tired and stressed he seemed, he smiled.

"We'll do whatever helps," he said. "Do you need us to stay?"

Jess and I had Kent, and Luna, who should also have gone home. And the Irregulars. And I could see the toll it was taking on Reiss to stay here when being around a police investigation pushed one of his deepest Don't buttons.

"Nah," I said. "I appreciate the offer, but I could also stand a little less chaos around here. I have a case to solve for my client."

"You're sure being paid enough," Reiss said, his smile broadening.

"It's the main reason I'm taking this so seriously," I told him.

"All right," Brennan said. "If you're sure, we'll head to the hotel and get a few hours before we come back for the gear."

"Call if you need anything," Thom said.

"Hey, if you're going, can one of you leave a key card?" Kent asked. "I don't have one, so it would help me out. And it might be good to have access to your dressing room. We're trying to have private conversations, and we're running out of places to do it."

"Sure." Thom handed his pass to Kent. "Let us get our stuff out of there first."

We stayed in the hall while the Twist got their winter clothes and bags. As we waited, Vic and Ziad came around the corner, Vic moving fast and Ziad slouching along behind her. So he was up next.

Seeing Ziad reminded me that I had that camera and might, depending on how much Alex had recorded, be able to see what Ziad and Matt had said to each other. Though there was almost no chance that Ziad would notice the camera or know what it had recorded, I turned and moved my arm so it was tucked behind me as he walked by.

He didn't acknowledge me or Kent, but it didn't feel like a snub. He seemed to be nearly out of steam and grimly focused on putting one foot in front of the other to get down the hall.

"He seems fine," Kent said, once Vic had delivered Ziad to Lam's makeshift interrogation room.

I imagined what it might have been like for Jess if Kent and Luna and Thom and I hadn't been there and if he hadn't spent the start of the night making friends like usual. Lonely, I thought, and scary.

"Not the best night of his life," I said. As Vic passed, I said, "Does the detective know he's an internet star?"

"He's a what?" she said.

I showed her the TikTok, and she pressed her lips together. She clearly had a lot on her mind, but when it was over, all she said was, "Wouldn't see me trying that."

"Me either," Kent said brightly. She barely worked up the energy to glare at him. Everyone was showing the strain of the situation.

"Any idea how Lam's investigation is going?" I asked. "Have you heard anything? Did he say anything to you?"

"All he says to me is do this and bring that," she said. "It's going slow, I think. He's only talked to Duncan and the Twist so far. And Lewis and that Alex guy."

That made sense, in a way. Lam had a lot of disadvantages compared to me. He had to get a sense of things—who was who, what they were like, what the flow of the evening had been. He could have used Duncan for some of that and the Twist to fill in any gaps. Now as he spoke to someone who actually looked good for the crime, he'd have a pretty good idea of who had been where and with whom, when. He'd have some chance of knowing a lie when he heard one. And he'd be able to ask Ziad about his hate-on for the murdered man.

"He'll want to see me and Jess next," I predicted. "Separately."

"He asked to see you already," Vic told me. "About the Ash Rose thing. I told him I couldn't find you."

"Really?" I said. "You're running interference for us? Why?"

"I want you to solve this so it goes away and doesn't shit all over my career."

"That's a big ask," I told her. "People will be talking about this for years. Decades."

"It's still better if it gets solved faster."

I couldn't argue with that. What I did say was, "You can't keep pretending not to see us forever. The theatre isn't that big."

"I can drag it out longer than you think," she told me. "It's a core skill in my line of work."

"Right. Well. Let me know when you need us to appear out of nowhere."

Vic left, and Kent watched her go. I didn't think he was eyeing her up—she was a little solid for his tastes, with broad shoulders and strong limbs. He preferred the waifish type.

"Who do you think she'd want it to be?" he said. "If she could pick?"

"What, the murderer?" I shrugged. "No one. A tragic accident."

The Twist emerged from their dressing room and flowed past us with back slaps and arm squeezes and hang-in-theres. They didn't stop at Jesse's dressing room on the way out. Likely planning to say their good-byes later. Not being on tour, they were free to stick around for a day or two.

"Okay!" Kent said. "Let's watch Alex's *Funniest Home Videos*."

He sounded like he genuinely thought this would be entertaining. Kent also liked a good combine crash.

"There's no speaker," I told him. "We'll need headphones."

He gave me the pass card Thom had given to him.

"Go get settled. I'll be back right away."

It wasn't right away. It was long enough that I had time to watch most of Jess and Matt's conversation again, at regular speed. I rewound over the part where Matt had moved in on Jess. Watched it again. Rewound again. Watched it again. Fuck me if it didn't look like a pass.

A knock at the door was Kent, with a hand outstretched and a small speaker on it. The other thing he had returned with was Luna.

"Duncan's asleep, and there's no more coffee," she explained, as if she were sleepy, bored, and not at all curious about the video.

"You could take a nap on one of the other couches," I said. Her upper lip arched in disgust.

"I know what happens on couches around here."

"Not in the green room. Probably." I gestured at the speaker. "Did that come from your bag of holding?"

"I got this from Harry," Kent said, "if you can believe it. No one else was carrying anything except those wireless air things. Harry keeps this in the security office."

"Give the man a raise," I said, an echo of Duncan's words.

"I also scouted popcorn," Kent said. "No luck there."

The Twist's dressing room was reasonably comfortable. A little bigger than Jesse's, which made sense as it had held a whole band. The seating area was a scuffed wooden table that was the twin of the one in Jesse's room, surrounded by slouchy chairs with curved wood frames and corduroy-covered cushions. Burnt orange fabric against clear lacquered pine. I couldn't tell if they were from the sixties or the eighties, but I would have bet they were cast-offs from the other side of the theatre. They'd held important guests once, people with a cheque book in one hand and a champagne flute in the other. Now the chairs were fraying and a little dusty, sagging under my weight and especially Kent's. The chair under Luna was bearing up well.

I set the camera on the table between us and plugged in the speaker. It was battery operated and connected with a thin cord. Not as tinny as I'd expected, though. Once I got everything running and started the playback at the beginning, it reproduced the sound of Alex fussing and rustling and swooshing away pretty well. I could even hear the click of the door as he shut it behind him.

"Those two guys have nothing to say to each other," Kent said as Lew and Matt ignored one another with synchronized grace.

"They do eventually," I said. I fast-forwarded until Lew was by the door and let it play.

"Are you ready to do this?" Lew asked.

"No," Matt said. "It's a stupid idea."

Lew folded his arms in front of him.

"That may be. That may very well be. But you have put us in this position. It was not my stupid idea to harass that young man. Or the other one."

Matt shifted around on the couch like he couldn't get comfortable.

"Jess doesn't have anything. Even if he did, he wouldn't use it. He knows his career is over if he messes with me."

"I'm not prepared to bet everything on that. You need to apologize properly and thoroughly and then make it clear it's in his best interests to turn over any recordings. And for God's sake, make sure he's not recording you while you do it."

"I'm not an idiot."

"History suggests otherwise," Lew told him and left. Matt screwed up his face and mouthed "History suggests otherwise" at his back.

"He's confessed to harassment!" Luna said. I paused the playback

"Not really," I said. "It's a conversation, not a trial. It would look pretty bad on social media."

"Maybe it belongs there," she said. "Has Jess seen this?"

"He's in his dressing room, talking to Lew. He told me to leave them alone."

Luna sat up straight. "Did he? Strange. What's going on in there?"

"No idea."

"And you're not curious?" She was edging forward, about to leap to her feet and charge down the hall.

"Leave it," Kent said. It was his very serious voice. I'd learned to take it very seriously because he only used it when he thought someone was about to do something very wrong.

"Let's see what else is on this camera," I said. "Jess can watch it later if he wants."

CHAPTER TWENTY

I STARTED THE video again. Matt didn't say anything or do very much, alone in the room. He kept looking at his phone and at the door and around the room and at the floor.

"He's nervous," Luna said. "I didn't think he'd be nervous."

Jess came into the room, and Matt stood, took a step forward, and stopped. He seemed confused. How did you greet someone when the last time you'd seen them you'd threatened to ruin them? A handshake would have seemed weird, and a hug was out of the question. Matt stood there with his hands hanging at his side, slouching like they were pulling his whole body down.

By the door, Jess was frozen. He didn't seem scared or angry or anything. His eyes were the only thing moving, taking in Matt and the room.

"It's good to see you," Matt said. His voice was tight and too high. Jess breathed deep enough that, even on the small screen, I could see his chest move.

"What do you want?" Jess said. He sounded tired.

"I wanted to say that I'm sorry about how things ended up with us," Matt said. "I always—um, before we do this, can I see your phone?"

Jess smiled without his eyes. "Nope."

"Come on, Jess. You know the protocol."

"Fuck your protocol," Jess said, not unpleasantly. "This isn't your camp."

"Can you show me it's not recording? I can't do this unless I see that it's not recording. Lew would throw my balls in his piranha tank and make me watch."

"Do you think he'd cut them off first?" Jess asked.

"If I was lucky."

That landed with me like a punch to the gut. It was banter, or something like it. Matt had made a joke about a guy they both knew, and Jess had gone along with the script. I could see him soften. Not a lot but more than he should have.

Jess got out his phone, unlocked it, and held it up for Matt to see. Matt leaned forward without moving his feet. It was almost far enough to be comical, like he was in a black-and-white slapstick scene with his shoes nailed to the floor. Matt nodded, and Jess set his phone, facedown, on the stand near the door.

"Thank you," Matt said. He warmed those words with a soft smile and kind eyes. I'd seen exactly that face in a half-dozen films or more.

"I don't want to stand around here fighting about it," Jess told him. "I said you could have ten minutes, and I meant it. Tell me what you want."

Matt frowned and drew back a little. The poor man was wounded. A victim. I'd seen that one in his films too.

"I told you. I don't like how we left things."

Jess cocked his head. "I think that might be true."

"It is true!"

"But that's not why you had Lew haul me in here. You have nine minutes now."

Matt gazed at the ceiling. Because Jess was so difficult. God grant him patience.

"All right," Matt said, looking at Jess again. "You've got me. Lew wants me to ask you something. I told him I wouldn't but… you know. My balls."

"Their sheer size," Jess said. "The piranhas will choke."

Matt laughed. "I told him you'd say something like that. Can we…? Do you want to sit down?"

"Oh, we're asking what I want now?"

I smiled a little. Jess hadn't forgotten he was angry. Matt looked stung.

"I told you I was sorry about how that went," he said.

Jess nodded. "Then I guess we're all good."

Matt was performing tolerance now, patience for Jess's crankiness.

"Please, Jess, can you sit for… eight minutes?"

Jess sat on the loveseat across the table from him, the same one I'd sit in later. He stayed near the edge and canted forward, ready to spring up and leave in an instant.

"I am really sorry, Jess," Matt said. "I read things wrong."

"I can see where 'I do not want to have sex with you' could be ambiguous," Jess said.

"I never got a chance to say this," Matt plowed on, "but it was nice spending that time with you. You were a good friend."

Jess relaxed a little. "It was fun," he said, "until it wasn't."

"About that night," Matt said. "You know there were security cameras."

"Lew didn't have them turned off?" Jess said.

"He didn't know I was going to be there," Matt said.

"Oh," Jess said. "No. Of course he didn't. You wouldn't have told him what you were going to do."

Anger passed over Matt's face, a moment of real emotion. "I'm thirty-seven years old. I don't need my daddy."

"No comment," Jess said. "But there's no way Lew didn't call the venue the next day and bully that footage out of them. You have nothing to worry about."

"It wasn't until the next day," Matt said. "We were wondering—Lew and I—did someone from your camp call first? Maybe Nia got a copy before it was deleted?"

Couldn't even get Gia's name right. Jess was shaking his head.

"Unbelievable."

"I know you have too much sense to use it," Matt said. "And I know you think I bullied you into dropping this, but you don't understand. I'm in a machine I can't control. There's too much money riding on me. There are huge corporations that would need to ruin you if you threatened my bankability. It wouldn't be up to me, Jess."

"Are you just as much a victim here as I am?" Jess asked. I knew that tone. Jess had used it on me once, for reasons, shortly before he'd pitched my phone off the balcony of a friend's twentieth-floor apartment.

"It's reality, Jesse. And you know that wouldn't even be the worst of it. You know how my fans can be."

Knowing how Matt felt about his fans, I wasn't certain he'd meant that as a threat. It might have been more of a warning, the sort of thing Jesse would call a public service announcement.

"I'm familiar," Jess said. "Did you seriously drive all the way from the ass end of nowhere to pretend to apologize, ask me about evidence of your assault on me, and make threats?"

"I went shopping this afternoon," Matt said, and I could see Jess almost laugh at that. It was easy to think of Matt as a well-constructed dolt, forgetting that he'd built an empire on that audacious charm.

"Cowboy hat?" Jess asked. "Pair of boots?"

"No comment," Matt said. "Jess… I wasn't pretending to apologize."

Jess sighed. "That's probably true. It would have been more convincing."

"I hate how things ended." Matt stood and went around the table to Jesse's chair. Jess stood as well and took a step away. This was the bit I'd noticed in fast forward, Matt moving closer and Jess moving back. Matt said, "I miss you."

"Oh my God," Jess said. He sounded sorry, genuinely sad for Matt. "You are such a mess."

"No one else says things like that to me," Matt told him.

"Lew does."

"Not like that."

"You have a boyfriend," Jess pointed out. And Matt laughed.

I wouldn't have guessed I had it in me to truly feel bad for Alex, but apparently I did. That laugh. It wasn't

contemptuous—that would have been better. It was the
way you'd laugh at something so ridiculous, so silly,
that you couldn't help it.

"Oh, come on. Like you don't know what he's doing
here? Okay, yes, I say boyfriend. It makes him happy. I
don't talk to him. You wouldn't either, believe me. He
thinks he's an artist. Fuck. I don't know. Kids these days."

"I'm not sure he's representative," Jess said. "Stop
chasing me around the room."

Matt looked at his feet for a moment, like he'd forgotten they were his.

"Sorry," he said. "Really. I didn't realize I was doing that."

"Your bullshit with your boyfriend is your business," Jess said. "If you're lonely, date someone you
can relate to."

"I'm trying to," Matt said, without artifice or even
charm. Next to me, Luna winced. Jess looked sad again.

"I don't owe you anything," he said, "but I know
you're really fucked up, and no one is honest with you
because they can't afford it. I've thought about you way
too much."

Matt started to move forward again. Jess raised a
stop-sign hand.

"Not like that. I have one piece of advice for you.
That's what I have that I'm willing to give you. Do you
want it?"

"Yes."

"Go online and get some random therapist. Not
a shrink to the stars and not a fucking life coach and
definitely not anyone endorsed by Oprah. Some normal
person. If you don't like them, get another one until you
feel like you can talk. Then you do that. Don't tell Lew.
Don't tell anyone. Do it all online and on the phone so

you can go hide in your trailer for an hour, tell everyone you're taking a nap, and talk to your therapist. Keep doing it until you feel different or until the end of time, whichever comes first."

"And if I get therapy, you'll—"

"There's no 'and,' Matt."

"I gave you access to this room," Matt said. "On your card. So you can come in whenever you want."

"I don't want that," Jesse said. He looked exhausted. "Not that you care. That's kind of a theme with us. Try to have a good life."

I paused it as Jess was opening the door to leave since I knew Ziad's invasion would immediately follow.

"So that's why Jess has access to Matt's suite," I said. "Funny how he told me he didn't have any idea."

Luna put two fingers on my wrist. Not checking my pulse. Holding me in place.

"Benjamin."

"Earlier tonight, we all sat there listening to Jess describe that conversation. Did he say one word about Matt making a play for him?"

"Maybe he thought it was more of Matt's bullshit," Kent said.

"I don't think he did," I said. "I don't think it was."

"He may have thought you'd be like this." Luna suggested.

"Like what? How am I the only one who's pissed that he lied?"

"It wasn't our business," Luna said.

"He told me he didn't know why Matt had given him—" My phone was ringing. "Fuck, hold on."

I checked the screen. An unknown number with an Edmonton area code. That pretty much had to be a houseguest. "Yes?"

"Hello to you too," Izzy said. "I've got some stuff about Ziad. Nothing too secret. I just put some pieces together."

"It's more than I have," I told her. "Go ahea—" There was a knock at the door. I couldn't get a god-damned moment. "Oh, hold on."

"It's me," Vic called. Kent opened the door while Luna turned the camera sideways to hide what was on the screen.

"Something we can do for you?" he asked.

"Yeah. You can talk to Detective Lam. You and you," she added, pointing at Luna.

"Not me?" I said.

"Saving the best for last," Vic said. "He told me to definitely not let you or Jack leave."

I wanted to say that I'd leave if I wanted, and I'd like to see her try to stop me, but that would only have gotten me scolded by Luna again. Instead I said nothing as Kent and Luna left and as Luna turned in the door-way to give me a warning glare. For some reason.

"Sorry about that," I told Izzy.

"No worries. Sounds like you've got your own problems."

"Sounds like you've found the kitchen," I said. She was eating something. Not crunchy. Could have been a sandwich.

"Detective work is hungry work," she said. "Is that a problem?"

"Nope. Put the tie back on the bread bag and don't drink straight from the milk carton."

"Right-o, Dad. Is it okay if I eat on the phone with you?"

"Why wouldn't it be?"

"I don't know." I could practically hear her shrug. "My sister has misophonia, and she loses her shit if you eat around her."

I didn't know what that meant and did not ask.

"Tell me about Ziad."

"He and Matt were both cast in a film that shot last summer. It's in post-production now. It's called *Prince of Bah-koo*."

"Of what?"

"*Baku*. It's the capital of Azerbaijan."

"If you say so."

"Did you fail geography in your one-room school-house?" she asked.

"I aced it," I told her, "but everyone lived in one city in Mesopotamia at the time."

"Nice," she said. "Okay, so, *Prince of Baku* is a romantic thriller where Matt's character meets some reporter in a bar, and she goes missing, and he has to find her and rescue her. Typical sexist crap."

"Pretty standard Matt stuff," I said. "Where does Ziad come in?"

"It was supposed to be a big break for him," she said. "There was a lot of talk about it in industry trades before shooting started. He was the bartender, and Matt's character hires him as a local guide, so he's the comedy sidekick, which is typical racist crap."

"Also pretty standard Matt stuff," I said. "This movie sounds like a dog."

"It'll probably make tons of money, and the world is garbage."

"Can't disagree. Did you find anything about trouble on the set?"

"Not really? But it got a rewrite a few weeks in. Ziad's character became, like, nothing. He's the bartender. And there's some other guy, Olly Abadi. I guess he's a British comic. He's the sidekick now. Did you know all Arabic people are interchangeable? You can swap them out."

"Is that so? I bet Ziad isn't too happy about it."

"No, he's probably in a mood, and we probably heard about his mood all day," she said. "But that's all I can find. Nothing about Matt doing anything to him or them fighting or anything. There's one rumour site where someone says that Ziad was hard to work with and he got fired, but no one seemed that interested, so it died. Matt's people could totally have planted that."

"They totally could have," I said. "Okay. This helps."

"Does it? I feel like I found a lot of nothing."

"You've given me a conversation starter," I told her. "Finish your sandwich and go to bed."

"I would, but my socials are out of control," she said. "Which reminds me, Ash kind of—"

"Seen it," I told her. "I hear Lam is thrilled."

"Maybe he should get a job not defending structural inequity," she said.

"He probably won't do that before he runs my boyfriend in for murder," I said, "so I'm going to get back to work. Turn off your phone and go to bed."

I hung up before she could tell me it wasn't a school night.

The camera might have been safe where it was, but I preferred to be certain. I took it and the pass card and went down the hall to Jesse's dressing room.

"Am I allowed in now?" I asked as I knocked. Jess opened the door and waved me inside. Lew wasn't there, unless he'd folded himself up and crawled into the bar fridge. Jess looked the way he usually did after a cry: red eyes and a freshly washed face and patches in his pale skin where he'd held ice cubes under his eyes trying to make the swelling go away. I could see the remains of the ice cubes in a glass on the table.

"Did I miss Matt's funeral?" I asked. Jess shut the door harder than he needed to.

"It's not fun telling people someone died," Jess said. "Lew was feeling a little rough."

"And you felt bad for him."

"I can feel bad for someone even if they weren't always good to me," Jess said.

I set the camera down on the table and said, "So it seems."

"Holy shit. Did the kids find it?"

"Alex led them to it. Would you like to tell me again that you have no idea why Matt gave you access to his suite?"

"I would, actually." Jess stayed by the door, his face stubbornly set. "I didn't tell you because I didn't want to get into it and there was no reason you needed to know."

"You didn't just not tell me. You lied."

"That was because I didn't think you'd let it go if I said I didn't want to talk about it."

"I give you space when you say you don't want to talk about things," I objected.

"Cool. I don't want to talk about it."

"Well, now you don't have to, because I know," I said.

"Cool," he said again. And waited. We stared at each other. He could wait me out. I knew it.

He won.

"Do you really," I said, "have nothing to say about any of this?"

"Any of what?" he said. "Matt is—was—a mess. He made a pass, and I told him no and to see a therapist, and he ignored everything I said. Same as last time. Only this time he didn't hit me before he let me leave."

I stood, and Jess took an instinctive half step back, which did nothing for my mood.

"Really?" I said.

"Not really," he said. "I'm jumpy. But can you stop taking whatever the fuck is bothering you out on me?"

"Why did you stay in there talking to him? Why didn't you leave? Why didn't you tell me what he said?"

Jess's hands curled like he was trying to grab the air with talons. "I didn't… it… it was embarrassing!"

"You don't have anything to be—"

"Not for me. For him."

"Why the fuck do you care if something is embarrassing for him?" I asked, forgetting for a moment that Matt was well past embarrassment now. "Did you have a thing for him? Are you a little hung up on the guy?"

"You are not your best self right now," Jess told me, his voice dangerously even. "You're overtired. You should know I did not at any point have a thing for him. I felt sorry for him. You don't know what his life was like."

"That was stupid," I said. "You're not usually stupid. He was manipulating you. That whole conversation, the way he talked to you, how did you not get it? Him saying he misread the situation, like you'd done something he could misread. Playing the poor lonely rich boy. Playing to your ego, how much better you are than his current boyfriend."

"To play to my ego," Jess said with his darkest glare, "he would have to raise the bar."

I sat down again and looked at my coat, still lying on the couch beside me. If you counted all the time Jess spent curled under it when we were indoors, he wore it more than I did.

"I'm sorry," I said. "I don't withdraw any of that, but it's not your fault. He was manipulative. He knew how to get to you."

"Is this National Shitty Non-Apology Day?" Jess asked. "Do you really think treating me like I'm pathetic and stupid is mollifying?"

He seemed more miserable than angry. My chest felt tight.

"I didn't say…. Okay, I did, a little, but I take that back. You aren't stupid. You aren't pathetic. Anyone can be manipulated by a guy like that."

"He was manipulative," Jess said. "He was also sincere sometimes. But you need him to be a villain. What do they say about pressing charges for rape? You have to be a perfect victim? Ideally you'd have a perfect villain too. If he had no good intentions toward me or anyone, ever, that's so much fucking easier for you."

"I'm a bad guy because I don't feel sorry for the guy who assaulted you?"

"No, you're being an asshole because you can't stand that I felt sorry for him. I don't even get how that threatens you, but clearly it does."

"I guess," I said, "I would rather see you save your sympathy for people who deserve it. I wish you could at least feel relieved that he's dead."

Jess did something I hadn't seen since our days in Toronto, and only once then. Slowly and deliberately, he picked up the water glass on the table where he'd dropped the ice cubes…

… a mug of cold coffee left on the kitchen table

… and threw it at the back wall of the dressing room.

… the bathroom door

His eyes burned, but his expression never changed as it flew and hit and shattered. Then, just as calmly, he went to the broken glass…

… ceramic

… and picked it up, carefully, a piece at a time. I thought of his therapist telling him he needed to meditate when he'd always done it, in his way.

I didn't offer to help. This was his thing. But I dampened some tea towels and set them beside him for the bits of glass too small to pick up with his hands.

I was back on the couch, staring at my jacket some more, when he spoke from his spot on the floor.

"I am relieved he's dead."

"There's nothing wrong with that," I said. I didn't turn around.

"There is," he said. "No one is all bad. Maybe a few people. Not him."

"You have every right to hate him," I said. "If you did, you would have every right. You don't have to forgive him because he's dead."

"Yeah, well," Jess said. "I don't have to hate him because he hurt me either. It's okay if you do."

"It's all I know him for. That and the worst Bond movies."

I heard the towels going into the trash and the rustle of the bag being pulled out and tied off. Jess wouldn't want anyone to try to rescue the towels and get a nick. Truly, he was the baddest boy of rock and roll.

He washed his hands and joined me on the couch. I offered him my jacket, but he shook his head. He was looking at his hands, at a few small cuts that had stopped bleeding already.

"He's never going to get any better," Jess said.

"It's probable he never was," I told him. "He had a long time to learn, and he doesn't seem to have tried."

"But now he never will," Jess said, raising his head. "There's no chance at all. I will never hear him say he's sorry for real."

If I hadn't already been certain Jesse wasn't the killer, that would have sealed it for me. Jess had been living with a tiny piece of hope, as small and sad as one of Alex's sequins, that Matt might repent his sins one day. Maybe even in public so Jess didn't have to treat it like his own dark secret anymore.

I opened my arms, and he curled up against me, bringing the jacket with him for warmth. I kissed the top of his head. He didn't cry or say anything.

"I'm sincerely sorry," I told him after a minute or so. "I came in here with my stupid issues, and you didn't deserve that."

"It's okay," he said into my chest. It sounded more like, "Ish oku." It occurred to me that I might want to take Jesse's advice to Matt for myself.

CHAPTER TWENTY-ONE

"DO YOU want to see what happened with Matt and Ziad?" I said. "When Ziad went into the suite after you?"

It was a weird thing to offer someone as a pick-me-up, but Jess sat up immediately.

"That's on the camera?"

"Did you think it was just you and me?" I said. "It was in there all night."

I set the camera up, and Jess got comfortable against my side, like we were watching a movie at home.

On the screen, Ziad tumbled into the room, off balance from shoving at an open door, but recovered with the quick grace I would have expected from him. Matt backed away speedily to a spot behind the couch. Ziad turned back to the door and slammed it shut.

"Take it easy," Matt said, holding out a hand with his index finger outstretched. "Stay right there and we can talk."

"We can?" Ziad said. He did stop, though. "That is so funny, because every time my manager tried to get in touch with you or your people it was impossible."

"My schedule's pretty crazy," Matt said. "But we can set something up right now and—"

"Fuck you," Ziad said. "Fuck you so very much. You can get me kicked off that shitty movie, but you can't end my whole career. I really don't think so. I think maybe you should be more afraid of me. Harvey Weinstein's in maximum security. Kevin Spacey's not getting a lot of work."

"I apologize for the misunderstanding between us. You said some things I misread, and I acted on that, and obviously I shouldn't have."

"Misread," Jess said softly.

"What did I say that sounded like 'be naked in my trailer'?" Ziad said. "Was it 'Hey, bro, can you hand me my script? Sorry I touched your water bottle'? When did I say I wanted to see your whole production?"

"I said I was sorry," Matt said. "We're both adults. No harm done."

"Unless you count killing my breakout role," Ziad said. "That was, financially, some harm. Yeah. Not just the role, but every other role I didn't get because word got out that my character got cut down to, like, two minutes of screen time."

"It's still in editing," Matt said. "We could extend that. You weren't right for the supporting role, but you could still get a nice piece for your reel out of this."

"Fuck you some more. First, I don't even trust you. Whatever you say, it's because I walked in here all pissed, and you're worried that I'm going to cut your dick off."

Matt stood up straight, demonstrating his full height. His overly friendly expression had gone cold. "You can come at me and try."

"I'm not going to do that. I came in here to let you know that I am done sneaking around about this like I'm a criminal. I didn't do a fucking thing. You got into my trailer, got naked, and waited for me. I could not have been more surprised when I opened the door and there you were. And then you tried to get past me to the door when I went to leave, like you were, what? You were gonna get in my way? Lock me in? What did you have in mind, Harvey?"

"We obviously remember that day very different-ly," Matt said.

I wondered why he was trying so hard to sell the party line to someone who clearly knew better, but then it hit me. Ziad hadn't been stopped at the door and asked to demonstrate that he wasn't recording the conversation. Matt was protecting himself in case there was a phone in Ziad's pocket capturing the whole thing. It was something like actual irony that he hadn't real-ized his boyfriend had been recording him all along.

"You know exactly what you did. And your fuck-face manager, he knows too. Does he love his job? I bet he got into this business to work with talent, not cover up for a weird pervert."

"You're obviously not well—" Matt started. Ziad put a stop to that with a loud, cutting laugh.

"You're a hack. You're an obvious hack. See how that goes for you when Ronan Farrow calls."

Matt shook his head. He was trying to appear unconcerned about his future and deeply concerned about Ziad's mental health. It was not his finest performance.

The door opened and there was Lew, maybe three feet behind Ziad and loaded for bear. He grabbed Ziad's arm and flung him toward the doorway. Ziad was surprised enough that Lew was able get him most of the way with one fling and the rest of the way with a shove to his upper back. He shut the door on Ziad and turned around to give Matt the hairiest of eyeballs.

"Goddamn," Matt said approvingly. "You could have been in the Secret Service."

"Don't get cute," Lew said. "It's your fault we couldn't bring security along today. If you didn't have so many secrets, we could have had bodyguards at that door."

"Blah, blah," Matt said. "Blah."

Lew glared. "What happened with him?"

"What, Ziad? Nothing. He made accusations, but I didn't admit anything. If he was recording, it should be okay."

"Oh, you think it will be okay?" Lewis said. "It won't just *be* okay. It will be okay if I make it that way, and I don't know how much longer I can do that, Matthew."

Matt scowled. He seemed younger when he did that, but not in a good way. More like a stroppy six-year-old.

"It's not my fault people are so oversensitive."

"You assault people. I suppose you get some kind of kick out of it. I am not here to judge, but I cannot keep making this go away. It's too many young men, and these aren't gofers. You are going after people who have fans and management teams. They have platforms and resources. If they decide to bite back, they might sink their teeth in."

"I'm open about what I want," Matt said. "It's not like with women. You don't understand gay culture, Lew. We don't do all that flowers-and-chocolates crap."

"It would seem several of the gay men you've approached also do not understand gay culture."

"They're too sensitive," Matt said. "I told you. I have a thing for tortured artists, but come on. What are Jess and Ziad both doing here tonight? What do they have in common? They're both fucking crazy. No offence, but they admit it. They're going to go out on that stage tonight and talk about how out of touch with reality they are."

"Maybe they aren't believable," Lew said, "but eventually you will do this to someone impeccably credible and you will be finished. Then I will be finished because every person you have done this to will crawl out from under the kitchen cupboards and it will be known that I have been covering up for you."

"You want me to be a monk? No sex for Matt?"

Lew's eye twitched.

"See, now, that worries me, Matt. Because I am not sure you can stop. You may not have that kind of self-control. I am very afraid that you are going to drag us both into the fire."

"You're getting emotional," Matt said. "What did your doctor call it? Emotional liability?"

"Lability," Lew said. "This is not that."

"Maybe you should go lie down anyway."

"Maybe I should."

Lew went to his room and shut the door. Matt stared at the closed door, then at his phone. He put his phone on the couch, facedown, and stalked off to his own bedroom. The main suite was empty, both Matt and Lewis behind their respective doors. The screen went dark.

I reached out to turn the camera off.

"Alex must have stopped recording there," I said.

"And started up again when you went in to see Matt?"

"I guess so. Do you want to see that?"

It was only fair to let him, since I'd watched his meeting with Matt, but I was relieved when Jesse wrinkled his nose and said, "I'd rather not."

I wanted to ask whether he still felt sorry for Matt, but that would have been petty and mean, and also he probably did. Before I could think of something different to say, there was a knock at the door, and Kent's voice came through.

"We're back from the interrogation."

Jess let them in, and we arranged ourselves around the table again. Luna's hair was out of place. It wasn't that I'd never seen that before, since I had seen her at work in Emerg and things happened, but generally she fixed it the second she was able.

"Luna, you're wiped out," I told her. "You should go home."

"Don't be ridiculous," she snapped. "Jesse, how are you doing?"

"I have no idea. Who does Lam want to see now?"

"Ben's up," Kent said. "Vic will be here any second to escort him."

"What did he ask you?" Jess asked.

"Same things he seems to be asking everyone," Kent said. "When did we get here, where were we at particular times. He asked a lot of questions about Matt's body because we saw it. We were in the room. He wanted to know who was in the room with the body and what they did."

"He asked about Jess and what happened with him and Matt," Luna added. "Where the conflict came from. We said we didn't know."

"Lying to the police," I said, shaking my head.

"Kent said it was fine." Luna glared at Kent. "You did! You said it was fine!"

"I'm messing with you," I said, "I don't know if I'd say it was fine, but you weren't under arrest or under oath."

"It's maybe obstruction," Kent said. "But what isn't?"

"Cooperation," I said. "But seriously, I'm not going to tell him what happened between Jess and Matt either. And I'm definitely not telling him about this camera until I have to."

"Should I tell him about me and Matt?" Jess asked. "I have to say Matt wanted to talk to me and that I was in his suite. What should I say that was about?"

"Say he hit on you," I suggested.

"Are you guys sure this isn't obstruction?" Jess asked me and Kent.

"Maybe a little," Kent said.

"It won't matter," I said, "because I'm going to get the actual person who did it. While I'm in with Vic, maybe you could all watch Matt and Lew on the video and see what you think."

"Wait, you think Lew did it?" Jess said.

"Why do you sound so surprised? I'm not completely sold on it, but he had access. He knew everything he needed to know. And he was worried that Matt was going to ruin him by getting Me Tooed. I can see where the guy might have wanted to take action."

Jess shook his head. "Matt was like a son to him. A disappointing son. Or maybe not a son, but at least a nephew or a protege or something. You don't work with someone like that for so long and not have some kind of feeling about the other person. Lew is broken up."

"Murderers are as complicated as anyone else," I said. "They can have mixed feelings about the victim and mixed feelings about what they did."

"You find a lot of people standing over the body holding a knife and crying," Kent said.

"This was colder than that," Jess argued. "You think Lew sat in that bedroom listening to Matt banging on the door while he choked to death? That is very fucking cold."

I didn't get to hear where that argument went because Vic showed up to escort me to my one-on-one with Lam.

"Bon courage," Jess said.

CHAPTER TWENTY-TWO

VIC AND I walked down the hall slowly because she was in front, she was dragging, and it would have been awkward to go around her.

"You've been here since yesterday morning, I'm guessing," I said. "Can't someone else take over for you?"

"Lam only has a couple more people to talk to."

"Has he talked to you?" I asked.

"Yeah. I told him stuff. Like how Jess didn't want to be on stage with Matt and what I knew about the food and… I don't know. There's mustard in the staff kitchen. Little condiment packs, like when you get a hot dog at the 7-Eleven."

Jesus. I needed a damned nap.

"Mustard," I said.

"Sometimes love itself becomes a lethal weapon," Vic said. "Sometimes it's mustard."

That first part was a song lyric. Some late eighties hair band. Maybe from the movie soundtrack. Well before Vic's time, and mine.

"Deep cut," I said. "Two things before I go in there."

She stopped and turned to face me. Her eyes were red. Maybe crying, but I doubted it. More like contact lenses being in too long.

"Go on."

"Was the staff kitchen accessible to everyone or just crew?"

She gave me a little grin. "You sound like Lam."

"I probably stand upright and breathe like him too," I said. "Some things everyone does the same way. What did you tell him about the kitchen?"

"It's not even a room, man. It's like, the hall narrows, and on the other side there's some kitchen stuff."

"Would it have been easy to find the mustard?"

"Would have been harder to not find it," she said. "All that stuff—salt and pepper and napkins and whatever? It's on a table. The cops were all over that. They dusted it and took pictures. The whole hallway. They've got it blocked off now. You never noticed that?"

"I haven't been down that way since we left Matt's suite," I told her. Jess had, of course, and had not mentioned that the hall had been taped off. The guy was never going to make the homicide division if he kept leaving out pertinent details.

"You probably don't even know about the mustard packs!" Vic said. She was immediately brighter at the prospect of telling me something I didn't know. "Whoever did it ditched them in the toilet."

"What, in Matt's suite?"

"No, next door. They were floating in the toilet bowl."

Did that change anything? Logistically? There were too many moving pieces, and I was too tired to stop them and drag them into place.

"Thanks for telling me that," I said. "Sincerely."

"Does it help?"

"I don't know. One more thing. Were you in the room when the cops were going over the food tray?"

"Yeah. Sarah had me watch to make sure…. This will sound fucked up."

"Try me," I said.

"She was worried they'd take things."

"The cops."

"Sarah is a weird lady."

"So while you were guarding an acrylic award for best set dressing in 1993, did you see whether there was mustard on anything except Matt's food?"

Vic thought that over.

"I didn't see any. I think I would have."

"Okay," I said. "Thank you. That definitely helps."

"I don't see how, but you're the big-time detective." She gestured at the door to the comics' dressing room. "In you go."

Lam looked magisterial seated in an easy chair at the far end of the room. The room was large, almost half as big as the green room. Probably meant for troupes of one kind or another because there was nothing luxurious about it. Cafeteria tables and chairs in the centre of the room, and a few bags—Emilie's, Ziad's, Duncan's—on the floor around the edges. The room didn't even have its own bathroom. It did have a few full-length mirrors on the wall, which made it seem both bigger and dingier under the fluorescent strip lights.

"Ben Ames," Lam said. "Private detective."

Two cafeteria chairs were set up facing Lam. I took a seat in one of them and was reminded why I didn't spend a lot of time in cafeterias.

"What can I help you with?" I asked.

"I have a few questions for you," he said, taking out his notepad. He made a big production of it. He could have kept it out the whole time, since he knew he'd need it again, but apparently he liked to put on a show.

"I hope I have answers," I told him.

"I'm sure you will. I'd be worried if these questions were difficult. First, can you confirm when you arrived here today?"

I told him. He walked me through the day, and I told him what I knew without speculation or editorial input. I was here. I was there. These people were in the room. I knew how to deliver a succinct report, and I gave him that. He didn't take notes for most of it but instead flipped back and forth in his notebook, making check marks. It seemed my story was lining up with everyone else's.

I didn't add anything he hadn't asked for. About Matt's arrival, I said that Matt and Alex and Lew had come down the hall with Vic and Harry and another security guard. I didn't add how Jess or Ziad had reacted or that I'd found out later who Lew and Alex were. It's trickier than you'd think to only answer what was asked because we hardly ever do it. We're always trying to answer what we think the other person intended to ask or adding details we think are relevant. Cops love this because they can say any of those frills were "volunteered."

I saw him wince a few times while I described the finding of Matt's body and the chaos that had followed.

Here he got particular. Instead of asking who was in the green room or who was backstage, he wanted to know where people had been standing in Matt's suite. What they had touched. What they had said, if I could remember. I could, but he didn't need to know that. I gave broader strokes: Luna said he was dead. Kent said he'd call the ME's office. The EMTs said they didn't recognize Matt. Not that they didn't recognize him, which they'd claimed and I believed based on their behaviour. Just that they'd *said* they didn't recognize him, which was what I knew for sure.

I could sense Lam getting frustrated. He got in a few chews on the end of his pen.

"Let's go back to Ms. Lincoln asking Jack Lowe to introduce Matt Garrett," he said.

"What about it?" I said.

"My understanding is that Jack refused. Do you know why that was?"

"No," I said. My first lie.

"I find that hard to believe," Lam said. That wasn't a question, so I said nothing. He glanced at his notepad.

"Later, Abraham Lewis came to speak with Jack Lowe in the green room, and that conversation moved to Jack's dressing room. You were there."

Also not a question. I kept still, with a politely open expression.

"Did that discussion cover the reason why Jack did not want to introduce Matt Garrett?"

"No," I said. He'd surely asked Lew the same thing, but that was okay. I had a feeling Lewis would have given him the same answer.

"*Hmm.*" He made a note. I doubted he needed to. The note probably said something like "A note to make Ben nervous."

"After the meeting with Lewis, Jack went to Matt's suite to talk with him. Why did he choose to do that when he didn't want to introduce Matt on stage?"

"I don't know," I said. Lie number two.

"*Hmm*," Lam said again. "Do you know what Matt and Jack discussed in Matt's suite?"

This was going to come out because I would have to hand over the camera. That meant saying I didn't know could bite me.

"I understand," I said, "that Matt made a pass at Jess, and Jess turned him down."

I'd committed to that now, so I hoped Jess would back me up.

"I see," Lam said, making a note. Could have been a real note. He probably hadn't heard this from anyone else. "And was that a heated exchange?"

"I don't think so," I said.

"After this, Ziad went into Matt's suite. Do you know what that conversation was about?"

"Probably about Ziad breaking into his suite?" I said. "I don't know."

"And of course your conversation with Matt," he said. "Why did you go to speak to him?"

It was funny. I couldn't get away with saying "I don't know" about that question, but it was kind of the truth.

"I wanted to meet him," I said. "Everyone's curious about big stars. And he used to date my boyfriend, so that made me curious about him too."

Lam seemed skeptical, but what could he say? There was no way to prove I was lying.

"What did you and Matt talk about?"

"Jesse," I said. "It's what we had in common."

"And what was the, ah, tenor of your conversation?"

"How do you mean?"

"Was it friendly? Antagonistic? Aggressive?"

"Polite," I said. Lew could have said otherwise, but he wouldn't have because that would have opened a can of worms he'd rather keep closed. "I don't think Matt really wanted to talk to a stranger, but he was polite about it."

"I have heard from several people," Lam said, "that Jack Lowe had a dramatic reaction to seeing Matt Garrett this evening, and that Abraham Lewis characterized their relationship as having 'bad blood.' What was that about?"

"Did you ask Lewis?" I said. I expected Lam to refuse to answer that, and he did not disappoint.

"I'm asking you."

"I wouldn't know why another person said something," I told him. "As for Jess being dramatic, that's subjective."

Lam checked his notes, making a big show of it. Flipping pages.

"Objectively," he said, "I have a number of people telling me the same things."

No question still meant no answer. It was difficult not to jump in and say that Ziad had said far, far worse things about Matt than Jess had. But that would have sounded exactly like the deflection it was, and I didn't need to say it anyway. Anyone who had mentioned Jess having a redout at the sight of Matt would definitely have mentioned Ziad calling Matt a ball sack.

"All right," Lam said when it became apparent that I was going to wait him out. "Thank you for your time. I have one last question for you. Do you know why Matt and Jack broke up?"

Tricky, tricky. Had anyone told Lam that Jess and Matt's relationship had been a sham? I decided to go with my usual.

"No. I do have one question for you, if you don't mind."

He raised his brows. I saw a bead of sweat roll when his forehead moved. It wasn't that warm in the room.

"I may not be able to answer."

"I'm wondering if anyone has talked to the crew," I said. "I know it may seem like there's no motive there, but people do weird things around celebrities. I hear someone stole a shoe off Matt's body."

"We're talking to the crew," Lam said. "I have several officers on the other side of the theatre and some at front of house. This is a delicate situation, as you know, so I thought it was best if I looked after this side of the theatre on my own. Does that answer your question?"

"Yes."

It also answered my question about where Sarah had disappeared to. Tending to the mess on the other side.

"Then that's everything," Lam told me. "Please send Jack Lowe in."

Part of me wanted to do exactly that. Send in the "fuck if I care" goth who lived for drama and might be on cocaine at any moment. But Jess would handle this better.

Jess and Kent and Luna were in Jesse's dressing room where I'd left them. Kent let me in, and I offered Jess a hand to pull him up.

"Your turn," I said.

"Can't wait," he said while I helped him to his feet.

"So he talked to you," Kent said, "and then he sent you back here, unsupervised, to collect the guy you're probably colluding with?"

"It's not optimal," I said. "But I don't think he cares too much what Jess and I say at this point. I think he's torn between Jess and Ziad as his top suspects. He's not going to arrest anyone tonight because it could be either of them. He wants to talk to everyone and make notes and see where it takes him. You know the guy and I don't, but that's my read."

"That's probably close," Kent said. "Takes some pressure off you if he's not going to arrest anyone tonight."

"No, I'm still going to solve this thing," I said. "I think I can. Jess?"

"Still here," Jess said. I gave him a kiss on the forehead. "I told him Matt made a pass at you in his suite. He asked a lot of questions about the history between you and Matt and where the hostility was coming from. I said I didn't know. If he says something that isn't a question, don't answer it. Don't elaborate on anything."

"He's a hostile journalist," Jesse said. "Got it."

Put that way, he probably did have it. I sent him off and went to the bar fridge to see what was left in it. A can of Coke. It would do.

"What now?" Luna asked as I tossed back the soda.

"I want to talk to Ziad," I said. "I want him to know that I'm pretty sure he couldn't have done it."

"He was in the green room the last time I saw him," Kent said, rising from his chair. "I'll go round him up."

That left me with Luna. I had decided not to talk and see if she might fall asleep in the silence. She was bearing up the best she could, but she worked hospital hours, and I wasn't sure how long it had been since she'd slept.

Instead of going along with my plan, she slung an arm over the back of the couch and looked at me.

"Please tell me you didn't get accusatory with poor Jesse."

"I did," I said. "But I got over it. I've apologized."

"Better than nothing," she said. "Have you considered talking to someone about your feelings? Someone who isn't Kent?"

"It has crossed my mind."

She laid her head on the back of the couch and closed her eyes. I set the empty Coke can down as gently as I could. It didn't make any noise, but when I turned back in her direction, she was awake again.

"Who do you think did it?" she asked. "The manager, really?"

"I don't know," I said. "He's got a strong motive, and it would have been easiest for him. The boyfriend is still in this too. I thought he didn't have a motive, but he saw how Matt talked about him when he wasn't there. Maybe he didn't like that."

"Do you kill someone because you don't like something they said about you?" Luna asked. "Maybe if they said it on the evening news or a big social media account, but just because they were rude about you in private?"

Since Luna was awake and it wouldn't bother her, I picked up the Coke can and rinsed it out before putting it back on the counter.

"I really don't know," I said. "You hear about these quote, unquote funny reasons for murder, like the guy who shot his friend because they were arguing about James Brown's height. But that's not really why that murder happened. That guy would never have gone home and thought about it and planned a perfect crime with an alibi. They were mad at each other about probably a few decades of built-up resentments, and they started yelling about something stupid, and one of them had a gun, and it was a southern state so it was probably muggy... do you know what I mean?"

"I would never discount the effects of heat. Or pain. We can only tolerate so much."

"That's the thing. People lose it. But getting mustard and stealing EpiPens and waiting... what did Jess say? It's a fucking cold thing to do. But I don't know. I don't know what else has been going on in that camp. And it still could maybe, at a very outside chance, have been Ziad or Duncan. Though it's very unlikely when you add everything together."

Luna yawned and pulled my jacket onto her lap. "Like what?"

Before I could launch into everything: How you'd have to know what food was meant for Matt and how Duncan would have needed a monster set of balls to doctor Matt's food with Harry standing right there; how Ziad had a motive but he also had a plan to try Matt in the court of social media, so why kill the guy; how getting the EpiPens, above everything, seemed nearly impossible unless you had access to the room.... Before I could go through it all, Kent knocked on the door.

"Did someone order an angry comedian?"

CHAPTER TWENTY-THREE

"I WAS MORE specific," I said as I swung the door open. "Otherwise you could have brought back any comedian I've ever met."

Ziad did seem like he could have been the model for an angry comedian emoji if the world needed such a thing. Also a tired comedian.

"Nice digs," he said as he went past me into the room.

"Comparatively," I said. "I'd offer to get you something, but we don't really have anything."

"There's tea," Luna said and yawned again. "I could make tea."

"No, thank you," he said. To Luna, he was polite. To me, he said, "What do you want?"

"I wanted to tell you that I don't think you killed Matt," I said.

He took a breath so deep it might as well have been a yawn. "I already knew I didn't kill Matt."

"Jess didn't either."

"So you say."

"He didn't," I said. "For you… I don't think you had a good opportunity to steal Matt's EpiPens. And I think you might have known what Matt liked to eat, but I doubt it because I've learned that Matt always ate in his trailer on film sets. To avoid allergens. You probably never saw him eat."

"That's true," Ziad said. "We all thought he was stuck-up. Who knew that was only one of the things wrong with him?"

"And you were planning to sic Ronan Farrow on him," I said. "Or something like that. So you already had your revenge planned out."

That got the guy's attention. He went from a slouch to sitting up straight, and I could see calculations behind his eyes. What were the odds that I'd have guessed he was going to expose Matt? He'd been vocal and obvious about hating Matt, like he was working up the nerve to tell the whole story… maybe I'd assumed it. But mentioning Ronan Farrow, could that be a coincidence? I waited while he chewed that over.

"How," he said finally, "the hell? Were you outside the door?"

"For a while," I said. "I could hear a little bit. But it might interest you to know that Matt's boyfriend planted a camera in that room at the start of the evening. I assume it was so he could see what Matt was doing behind his back."

"Could have been for blackmail," Kent said. "He's got that skeezy blackmailer vibe."

"Fuck me with a wrench," Ziad said. "Where's the… oh."

He looked at the camera on the table in front of him, very much not hidden or in disguise. He reached for it, and I scooped it up before he could do something stupid, like taking the SD card or hitting Delete.

"Give that back!" he said. "That's private!"

"I'm on here too," I reminded him. "So's Jess. You can watch those clips if you want. We've seen yours. Fair's fair."

"Fair's fair," he repeated. "Fucking hell."

"Do you want to see the clips?" I said.

"Do I… yes."

I set it up, and we had movie night again, less cozy than when it had been me and Jess. Ziad rolled his eyes a few times watching Jess talk to Matt, and I considered the ethics of slugging him, but I could see him softening toward Jess by the end.

"Buddy's too nice," he muttered with a sideways glance at me.

"Kind of," I said. "Sometimes."

As if we'd spoken of the devil, Jess swiped himself into his dressing room. He barely registered Ziad's presence as he sank into the nearest chair.

"You got your card back," I said. "I lost track of who had it."

"Yeah, me too. But it was in my pocket when I got to the door. What's going on in here?"

"I was about to explain to Ziad why he needs to be on our team," I said. "But first you might as well tell us how it went with Lam."

"Okay," Jess said. "I guess. He clearly suspects me. I don't think I gave him anything he didn't have before."

"Did he ask you about me?" I asked.

"Not really. I don't think he thinks you poisoned anyone yourself. You're just complicit."

"Oh, well. That's fine."

Jess smiled a little and sang a line from Zevon's last album, something about unindicted co-conspirators. His voice had the smoky fragility it got when he was exhausted.

"He thinks I did it too," Ziad blurted, startling everyone. "Lam. I thought he was going to arrest me. And I thought you were going to pin it on me."

"I don't pin things on people," I said. "I realize you have no reason to believe that. But it's a point of pride with me to get the right person."

"It is," Kent confirmed. "It's annoying."

He was standing behind the couch, within swatting distance of Luna, who took advantage of that.

"You care just as much. Stop trying to seem cool."

"Yes," Ziad said. "If that's what you think cool is, please stop trying to look cool."

"Feeling a little ganged up on," Kent said. "People have been ganging up on me all night."

"Shut up, Mitch Miller," Ziad said.

Jess's eyes brightened. "What did you say?"

"Mitch Miller was a singer in the sixties."

"Oh, I know that," Jesse said. "I'm a music nerd. But you're not, are you?"

"My great-grandmother had a roommate in her nursing home who loved Mitch Miller. Mitch Miller and the sing-along gang."

"Follow the bouncing ball," Jess said.

"For some reason, he decided to do his own version of 'Give Peace a Chance.' It's fucking awful. A lot of 'right on, brother' from some white guy in a sweater vest who got rich teaching other white people to sing 'The Yellow Rose of Texas.' And at the end, he starts yelling 'Hassle the man!' He has no idea, *no* idea that he is himself the man. Hassle yourself, Mitch."

"And I'm Mitch Miller?" Kent said.

"If the sweater vest fits, Officer."

"See, once again," Kent said, "I am feeling the slightest bit—"

"Hush now," Luna said, patting his arm. "You hush, Mitchell."

"Can we get back to solving a murder?" I said. "I hate to bother all of you when you're clearly so busy."

"Right on," Jess said, deadpan. I saw Ziad quickly raise a hand to hide a smile.

"Okay," I said. "First, Ziad, for the reasons I explained earlier, I don't think you killed anyone. You've seen Jesse's conversation with Matt—"

"He has?" Jess said.

"Fair's fair," Ziad told him.

"So," I went on, "you know that Jess wanted Matt to get help, not get poisoned."

"He was never going to do that," Ziad said. He glanced at Jess. "He had you fooled."

"It's pointless to talk about that," Luna said. "We can never know, so you'll be arguing forever."

"I accept that Jesse is too naive to be a murderer," Ziad said. "Good?"

"I'll take it," I said. "We have a detective in the other room going through his notes, and I don't think he's going to arrest anyone tonight, but he'll be under pressure to do it soon. If we don't point him at the correct person…." I looked at Ziad. "I said, the correct person."

"I heard you," he said. He'd leaned far back in his seat and had crossed his legs the way only skinny young guys did, with the ankle of one leg resting above his knee on the other.

"Chances are Lam will take the easy route and arrest one of you. Your motives are very understandable. Ziad, I know you haven't talked publicly about what Matt did, but it didn't take long to dig up the history of the film you shot last summer. Even without the footage of you talking to Matt tonight, there's the movie. That was supposed to be a big deal for you. You were supposed to have a major supporting role in *Prince of Baku*, and your management team was playing that up as your springboard into leading roles."

"They were overexcited," Ziad said. "It was crap, even compared to regular Hollywood crap."

"It would have been a good role, though," I said. "Wouldn't it? Lots of eyes on you. You'd get to be funny, which is a strength. But then you got written almost entirely out of the movie."

"They said I didn't pop on screen. What the hell does that even mean? I've been popping on screen since I was fourteen. And do you really think they didn't screen test me before they cast me?"

"Between your comments about Matt in the green room tonight and the fact that they halted production on an expensive movie to essentially write you out of it, I think it's clear what happened. This video clinches it, but the story is clear enough without that. Lam wouldn't have much trouble selling his bosses on the idea of you as a killer."

"Or Jesse," Ziad said. "I don't know what Matt did to him, but it's got to be a sex thing."

I looked at Jess. He was doing slow breathing, in and hold it, out slow and hold.

"I'll tell you," he said. "Not because of some quid pro quo thing. Because I know… I never told anyone what happened. I mean, I told everyone in this room except you, and I told my therapist and my rep at the label. But that's it. I never told a reporter or a cop, and I never posted anything online. So this all went downstream to you, and obviously you're going to feel some things about that. And I don't blame you. I'd be mad too."

"Would you, though?" Ziad said. "Go on. What's your story?"

"It sounds like nothing," Jess said. "I was backstage before a show—one of my shows—and it was this weirdly quiet gap where everyone else was off doing other things, and Matt grabbed me somewhere personal."

"As boyfriends do," Ziad said.

"Matt and I were never boyfriends. It was set up by my label and his management team. He wanted to be offered more complex roles, but everyone thought he was too, I don't know… four-colour comics. So his manager thought pretending to date me would make him seem edgier. And it would get people talking. What's Matt Garrett doing with that weird guy?"

"People generally used your name," Ziad said. "You're not as obscure as you seem to think."

"Yeah, well, I'm not Matt Garrett either. Which is maybe okay. Anyway, my label thought it might soften up my image if I was in some domestic photo shoots with the all-American gay boy, so they agreed to it, and I got told I was going to be hanging around with Matt Garrett for about a year. Like, that was my job for a year. Do not look at me like I'm the biggest sellout you've ever met. I know people you've worked with. I'm far from the biggest."

"So the whole thing was a scam," Ziad said. "And he grabbed you anyway."

"Yep. And I was really pissed off because he'd made a few passes before and I'd been clear every time that it wasn't going to happen. Genuinely, I was clear. I didn't say, 'Not right now' or 'I don't think so.' I said, 'No. Not ever.'"

"Matt probably thought he was losing his hearing," Ziad said. "Because you couldn't possibly have said what it sounded like you said. No one says no to him."

"Who would?" Jess said. "Handsomest man of the year, multiple times. And that's part of the problem, right? People would cut off their right arms to nail him, so they think you're lying if you say you weren't into it."

"Unless you're a lesbian," Ziad said.

"Nah," Kent said. "People would think he could turn them."

Ziad nodded sagely. "True."

"But I knew he knew that I'd said no, and I had a show to do, so it was both sexually predatory and inconsiderate, and both of those things pissed me off. I realize that sounds crazy, like they're equivalent."

"It doesn't," Luna said softly. "It really doesn't, Jess."

"Anyway, I shoved him. And he hit me. And I hit him."

Ziad actually, fully smiled.

"What? Mr. Butter Wouldn't Melt hauled off and slugged the guy? Did you do any damage?"

"Some," Jess said.

"He's a scrapper," I confirmed. Ziad held out a fist to bump, and Jess obliged.

"Thanks, but it complicated things. Matt likes to call it that time we got into a fist fight, and he always mentions that I 'swung first.'"

"Always the same bullshit," Luna said. "Either you were in a fight between equals and what are you complaining about or you didn't even try to fight the guy off so clearly you wanted it."

"I never had any hope of winning a fist fight with Hercules," Jess said. "But people think when you're a guy, somehow you should be able to. No matter what."

"That's purely stupid," Luna said. "If you ever go public with this, please let me take over your social media."

"I'd let her do it," Ziad said.

"You don't know her like we do," Kent said.

"Eventually what he did...." Jess paused. I went to stand beside him and put a hand on his shoulder.

"You don't have to," I said.

"No, it's... nothing happened. That's the whole thing. It was nothing. He, uh, he slammed me down face first on a table and, uh, I was wearing a skirt and fishnets, so he pushed the skirt up and he started to pull.... Anyway he... he stopped."

"That's not what I expected," Ziad said quietly.

"Me either," Jess said. He laughed a little. His voice was shaky. "Matt said... he said, 'I want you to know this is my choice.' And then he walked away."

"I still think he realized someone was likely to show up backstage and catch him," Kent said. "He didn't decide to teach you a lesson or whatever the fuck he wants to pretend it was."

"Hundred percent," Ziad said. "If he'd gotten past me to the door of my trailer.... I've thought about that. I think he likes it. He's followed through with people before. Guaranteed."

"Liked it," I said. "He doesn't like anything anymore."

"That's why I should have reported it," Jess said. But I thought… we were two guys, I swung on him, he walked away… and I had this reputation as an alley cat, you know."

"No one would have believed you," Ziad said. "I didn't know all the details before. It would have been hard to report it no matter what, you being you and him being him, but the way it went down, you had no chance of anyone taking you seriously."

I wanted to say that it was absolutely illegal to do what Matt had done, and that it was always worth reporting, wasn't it, because how else was anything ever going to change? But I was pretty sure Ziad was right, and it wasn't like Jess didn't know it.

"It would have been a warning to others," Jess said. "For anyone who believed me. You could have used that information."

"I'm not sure I'd have believed you," Ziad said. "I hate to admit it, but last summer was an eye-opener for me."

"So that's Jesse's motive," I said. "And also mine."

"It would have been my motive for punching him so hard his lungs came out his throat," Kent said. "I'm sorry I didn't get a chance to do that."

"Lam doesn't know what happened to me," Jess said. "It's funny he's latched onto me anyway."

"He knows there was a falling-out," I said. "And that Matt was laser focused on talking to you and that you wouldn't even suck up whatever the problem was long enough to give him a quick introduction on stage. He's aware of your reputation as a drug fiend. If I were Lam, I'd be focused on you too."

I didn't mention that Kent had suspected Jess himself. Kent didn't volunteer that either.

"It's not the end of the world if you do get arrested," I said. "You can both afford good lawyers, and I assume you've got them lined up. Jess, would I be right to think that Gia wants to send someone from Toronto? Because she has no idea how much we love that out west?"

"I tried to talk her out of it," Jess said sheepishly.

"Mine's local," Ziad said.

"Ideally, though, can we all agree that no one in this room is eager to get charged with murder?"

"As much as I'd love a dozen YouTube videos analyzing my body language to show why I absolutely am a psychopath," Ziad said, "I think I'd prefer to give it a pass."

"It seems simpler to hand over the actual murderer," Jess said. "Can we do that?"

"I hope so," I said. "I think we're down to two people."

CHAPTER TWENTY-FOUR

ZIAD TAPPED his fingers on his leg. Impatient? Nervous?

"Which two people?"

"The manager and the boyfriend."

"Those two?" Ziad said. "Why?"

"Alex's motive is tenuous," I said. "He planted this camera, and he overheard Matt shit-talking him. Dismissing him and their relationship."

"And trying to pick up Jesse," Kent added.

Ziad made a scoffing noise. "You can't convince me that Matt and Casper the Bedazzled Ghost were such a serious item that his boyfriend would murder him over a little infidelity. Or some smack talk."

"Oh, Casper. That's so much better than Sequined Skeleton," Luna said.

"But you have to wonder why he planted the camera in the first place," I said. "That says trouble in paradise to me."

"What about Lewis?" Ziad said.

"He's worried about his reputation," I said. "Hang on."

I showed the video of Matt and Lew arguing after Ziad left the suite.

"We're crazy people," Ziad told Jess. "Did you know that?"

"Completely out of touch with reality," Jess agreed.

"Convincing Lam that the manager's a good suspect could be a hard sell," Kent said. "Yeah, he's worried about his rep, but Matt makes the guy a ridiculous amount of money. He's not going to try to find some other solution before he jumps to poisoning?"

"Maybe he felt like Ziad was going to escalate things too quickly. He was probably listening outside the door before he came in and shut things down."

"Then why not kill Ziad?" Kent said. "No offence, buddy."

Ziad, for possibly the first time in his life, opened his mouth, thought for a second, and closed it again.

"Too obvious?" I said. "Too difficult? Doesn't get to the root of the problem?"

"He could have been planning to do it for a while," Jess said, "and tonight looked good all of a sudden. Because there was so much confusion and they were using a new caterer for Matt's food and Ziad and I were around with our big sexy motives."

"That could apply to Alex too, though, couldn't it?" Luna said.

"It's one or the other," I said, "if you eliminate the improbable."

"Pretty sure that's not how it goes," Kent said.

"It should be."

"What's after that argument?" Ziad asked. "Is there more video on that camera?"

"Just me," I said. "I think."

"Yes," Luna said. "We watched to the end when you were talking with the detective. It goes to black after Matt and his manager go to their rooms, and then it comes on again as you're sitting down. It doesn't have you coming in from the door."

"Alex probably saw me going in there and wanted to wait until he was somewhere private before he started the camera. I'm assuming he could control it remotely."

"It stays on for a while after that," Luna said. "Alex comes in, and then he leaves, and then you leave and push the food into the room, and then Matt says something about Lewis looking like shit, and Lewis takes a pill and goes to lie down."

"And then Matt eats dinner?" I said.

"No. It ends there."

"It doesn't have the death?" Ziad said. Luna shook her head.

"No, thankfully. I would have felt obligated to watch it, and I didn't want to see that."

"Why does it go to black between when Ziad leaves and when you come in?" Jesse asked.

I shrugged. "Alex probably went back into the suite. He might not have wanted to be on camera."

"Not if he was helping himself to some EpiPens," Kent said dryly.

I remembered the first thing on the camera, the bag on the counter while Matt scrounged in the fridge.

Visible in the frame, then and probably always, unless someone was standing right in front of it.

I grabbed the camera and backed up to the start.

"Does anyone have a ruler?" I asked. Kent produced a multi-tool from his wallet with centimetres and millimetres etched along one side. Everyone pressed a little closer as I placed the ruler against the screen and measured the distance from the edge of the brown bag to the tap of the sink. The sink wouldn't move. The camera probably didn't move. But what about the bag?

I followed it through the rest of the video, played back at two times normal speed. Whenever someone entered or left the room, I measured again. The bag stayed put as Jess and Matt talked, as Ziad and Matt argued, as Lew told Matt off. The image went to black. When it came back up....

"Am I imagining this?" I said.

"Did it move?" Jess said.

"Maybe?"

It wasn't obvious, a few millimetres, but this was the first time the measurement had changed at all.

"It did," Luna said. "It's farther to the left."

"That's it," I said. "That's where the EpiPens got swiped. When it went to black."

"Right after Alex turned the camera off," Jess said, "in other words."

"Could still be a coincidence," Ziad cautioned.

"Someone could have bumped the bag," I said. "And the pens could have been taken out later. Or they could have been taken out before that bag ever left their hotel in Pincher Creek."

"I bet none of that happened, though," Kent said.

"So it was Alex?" Jess said. "Is that what this means?"

"Still could have been Lew," I said. "With that camera off, it could have been anyone with a pass. Could've been Harry, or you."

"But he turned the camera off," Ziad said.

I nodded, still looking at the screen. "He did."

"For reasons we don't know," Jess said.

"Yep."

"Like he was planning a blistering row with Matt," Luna suggested.

"It's like Nixon's eighteen minutes," Jess said. "Except we don't even know how long it was turned off."

"Maybe we do," I said. "Ziad, you're the TikTok guy. Are there time stamps on this thing?"

"Yeah, I'll take a look at it while you read my IMDB page and realize I'm a professional, not a four-teen-year-old who does the swim to the 'Wreck of the Edmund Fitzgerald.'"

"Please tell me that's real," Jess begged.

"It's not," Ziad said, taking out his phone and typing something into a notes app. "But it will be before the month is out. Okay. Give me that camera."

He pressed buttons and opened menus and came across very much like a guy who knew what he was doing.

"The clock on this thing was never set properly," he said. "So I can't tell you what time it really was. But it was off for about five minutes. Do you need that in seconds and frames?"

"Minutes will do. Thanks."

"Where does this leave us?" Luna asked.

"Kind of the same place as Lam, I think," Jess said. "He doesn't know whether to arrest me or Ziad, and Ben doesn't know whether to accuse Alex or Lew."

"Could it be both?" Luna said. "Like *Murder on the Orient Express*?"

"That would be all of us," I said. "I guess in theory it could have been both of them, but that feels unlikely."

"Collaboration is rare," Kent said. "I'm a homicide detective too, remember? I know these things. The only time I bring in multiple people for a murder is when someone got a beatdown from a bunch of rednecks or it's organized crime. Badly organized. They're not soccer moms."

Ziad took out his notes app and started typing again.

"Soccer moms as organized criminals has been done," Jess told him. Ziad ignored him and kept typing.

Luna stood and rolled her shoulders. "Where's my purse? I thought I left it on the couch."

I grabbed it from the floor and handed it to her. She went into the bathroom and shut the door.

"Remember not to flush that," Kent said, loudly enough that they could have heard him in the green room.

"Shut up," Luna called back.

"It's Shark Week," Kent said. "The Red Army invasion. The Crimson Tide."

"Oh my God, shut up," Luna said from behind door.

Kent nodded sympathetically. "Very emotional. She might be the murderer."

"Only if you were the victim," I said.

Then it hit me.

"Jess, what were you saying about your earbuds the other day? Remember, you were ranting about how much they cost, and people couldn't get the simplest things right? You sounded like an overpaid douche?"

He looked confused. Not about the rant but about why I was bringing it up.

"They have too much high end?"

"Perfect. I need to borrow them."

"They're in my coat pocket. Left outer chest." He did a regal wave at the coat he'd hung up so many hours ago.

I retrieved the earbuds and connected them to the camera, smoothly enough that I would have felt okay about doing it in front of children.

I went into the corner of the room with the camera and took my jacket with me. Sat on the floor and draped my jacket over my head. I played the video again and again, sometimes with my eyes open and sometimes with them closed. My shoulders were hunched forward. They'd hurt for that later. I was trying to squeeze into the camera and into the scene, to be there again and catch what I missed the first time.

The first time I heard it, I thought I was imagining it. It was so faint, and I'd thought I'd heard it a few times already, only to go back and listen again and find nothing there. But this was there every time I checked. And it sorted out everything.

I pulled my jacket off my head. Everyone stared at me. Luna, who was back on the couch, silently offered me a comb from her purse. While I put my hair back in place, I said, "I've got it. I want to talk to everyone who's here, including Lam. In the green room. I need to use that TV."

No one moved for a few seconds. Then Kent went to the door and opened it.

"You heard Poirot. Let's get set up for the big reveal."

I felt ridiculous when Kent put it that way, like I was play-acting at being a detective instead of doing the job. But everyone else got up and filed out like this made sense. The fact that they'd seen it in a hundred movies made it seem more realistic to them, not less.

I let them go without comment and stayed behind to put my thoughts together. I'd need someone to guard the door. Kent would be best. There was only one door out of the green room, which was probably against the fire code but worked for me.

Would Lam go sit in the green room just because I'd sent someone to fetch him? For that matter, would Alex and Lew go where they were told? I didn't even have the shaky authority of Detective Lam. But I had people's natural curiosity and their FOMO, and that might be enough.

I pulled up Google Maps and made a few quick phone calls, cleaning up a loose end.

That done, I took the SD card from the camera and put Jesse's overpriced earbuds back into his jacket. Then I got up and fussed around the room, killing time. It would take a few minutes, at least, for everyone who was willing to move into the green room to get there. So I put things away. Pulled the next garbage bag from the bottom of the trash bin and snapped it into place. Wiped the counters in the kitchen and bathroom.

Jess had offered to have someone come in and clean my house for me and had teased me about my paranoia when I'd demurred. I'd let him think that was it, that I didn't want some stranger going through my things. The truth, though it was painfully on the nose, was that tidying up a room helped me tidy up my head.

Once the room was in order, I went down the hall to put on the last act of the big charity show. I paused outside the green room door, gazed down the hall and nodded to the guard again. Again, he ignored me. It was comforting, though I couldn't have said why.

The room was set up perfectly. Someone had moved chairs and couches so they were in a semicircle facing the TV, and they'd pulled back the table and couches that had been in front of the TV to make a kind of stage for me. More room for pacing or gesturing or whatever it was I needed to do.

Emilie and Dylan had chosen the chairs farthest from the stage, like schoolkids who wanted to appear delinquent but had still shown up before the bell. They were whispering to each other.

Duncan was standing by the kitchenette, clutching a can of Barq's. A true Canadian, he'd known to avoid the uncaffeinated Mountain Dew. He looked worse than he had when I'd last seen him. That made sense if he'd been sleeping. Twenty minutes of sleep could help, or eight hours, but an hour or two did no one any favours.

Ziad and Luna were standing to the side of the seating area, talking about something. Kent was standing behind the chairs with Vic beside him. Lam was on her other side. They didn't seem to be talking to each other, which was not a surprise.

Jess came to stand next to me and pressed something into my hand. A remote control.

"There's an SD slot on the TV," he said. "Use the Auxiliary button on the remote to access it. Or I could run the AV for you."

"I can do it," I said. "I see you got Alex and Lew here."

They were sitting next to each other, right in front of the stage. Looking at their phones. I didn't think they'd even said hello to anyone they didn't have to all evening. Like reality-show contestants, they weren't here to make friends.

"Yeah. I said you were going to name Matt's killer. I didn't mention that they were your prime suspects."

"That's for the best," I said. "That kind of thing puts people on edge."

"Tell me about it."

I put an arm around his shoulders, and he leaned against me.

"We can go home soon," I told him. "And you won't go to jail."

I felt him sigh. "I'm glad you were here."

"Me, too."

I left Jess and went to put a hand on Kent's shoulder. He turned, and I gestured for him to follow me. Once we were near the door, I said, "Can you stay back here? In case someone tries to make a run for it?"

"The role I was born to play," he said. "You ready to tell us who murdered Roger Ackroyd?"

"I guess I am."

I went to the front of the room prepared to ask for silence, but I got it without having to say a word. All the standing people, except for Kent, awkwardly found chairs or couches while staring at me. There were ten of them in all. Add me and Kent to get twelve.

"I won't drag this out," I told the assembled, "but I want to explain what I've learned and what I've been thinking."

"I would prefer," Lam said, "that you tell me in private, and I can decide whether to act on it. This is not your role."

"Someone hired me to investigate Matt's death," I told him. "You weren't in the room at the time. I have a retainer. I'm doing my job."

"You're stunting," he said. It was a refreshing change from obstructing justice.

"You're not obligated to arrest the person I'm going to identify," I told him. "But I'm hoping that once I've laid everything out, you'll see things my way. I really will only need a few minutes."

"Fine," Lam said. "Get this over with."

I faced everyone and said, "Matt Garrett was murdered tonight. The murder weapon was mustard, to which he was fatally allergic. It was in his food, and that was not an accident. It was put in his food by one of you, and you didn't stop there. You also took his EpiPens so that he wouldn't be able to save himself. You may even have known Matt well enough to know that he was paranoid about people finding out he had that allergy. He had a history of not calling 911."

"It wasn't me," Duncan said groggily. "You already said it wasn't me."

"I'll get there," I assured him. To the others, I said, "No one realized Duncan was a suspect because he put on an excellent show of being a craven opportunist who wanted to get in good with Matt. We all fell for it, except one person who knew that Duncan had history with Matt. This person told me that Duncan had made some jokes about Matt and word got back to Matt about it. Was it your Just For Laughs show, Duncan? A lot of industry people go to that."

"I don't know," Duncan said. "Probably."

"Matt started telling people not to cast Duncan. He got frozen out of a lot of roles. His life got easier tonight when Matt died."

"You didn't tell me this," Lam said. Duncan turned in his chair to look at Lam.

"You didn't ask, bud."

Lam scowled and took out his notebook. Duncan faced the stage again.

"Duncan also handled the plate covers on Matt's food tray," I said. "Detective, you may find his fingerprints on them unless the murderer wiped everything down. Duncan went for drinks after his set, outside the theatre, and Matt's food was coming in as he was going out. He told me he was curious and checked out the food. I'd bet he did something more. Maybe spit on it?"

"No comment," Duncan said.

"But he wouldn't have had time to hide mustard in every meal with Harry standing right there. Harry's the guard, for anyone who hasn't met him."

No one said anything. I pressed on.

"To put mustard in just one meal, which he might have had time for, he would have had to know what Matt liked to eat. But one of the things about his allergy was that Matt liked to eat in his trailer on sets, and he didn't like to eat during interviews, so no one knows a lot about his food preferences unless they're part of his inner circle."

I could see people glancing around and trying to seem like they weren't. Eyeing Lew and Alex and Jess.

"He would also," I said, "have had to be carrying mustard, and he would have had to have known about Matt's secret mustard allergy. He would have had to get into Matt's suite and steal Matt's EpiPens, but he was out of the building for most of the night. I checked a map for any bars within two blocks of here. Duncan wouldn't have wanted to go far in the cold. Took me three calls to get a bartender who was closing up. He remembers Duncan being there from about nine thirty-five to ten thirty. It was about five minutes later that me and Jess and Thom saw Duncan in the hall with snow on him."

"I saw him too," Vic said.

"And Harry has notes in his log about when Duncan came and left. It's barely possible that Duncan found some other way in and somehow doctored Matt's food and stole those EpiPens without anyone seeing

him, but I think it's a lot more realistic to think that
Duncan mostly told me the truth. He was drinking. He
did not put mustard into the food. He was planning to
talk to Matt. Maybe he was planning to beg for Matt's
forgiveness, like he told me, or maybe he was planning
to punch Matt in the face. It doesn't matter because neither of those things is murder."

"Thank you," Duncan said, "for your vote of
semi-confidence."

"If we all agree about moving on from Duncan," I
said, "the two most obvious suspects we've got are Jesse and Ziad. I won't tell their stories, but I will say they
both had reasons to want Matt dead. They were also,
unlike Duncan, both in Matt's suite tonight. That's important because the suite is where Matt's EpiPens were
kept. Unlike Matt's food, which was left unattended in
the hall for several minutes, those EpiPens were behind the suite's locked door. Detective Lam, have they
turned up yet?"

"That's part of an active police investigation," he
informed me.

"I'm going to take that as a yes," I said, "and I have
a pretty good idea where you found them. But I'll put a
pin in that for now."

I could see people looking around the room like
they thought they'd see the missing EpiPens under the
nearest table or tucked in with the pop. But the green
room was the last place they'd be.

"It comes down to those pens," I said. "And to one
other thing. But I'll get to that later. Like I said, the
food was accessible, but the pens weren't. In fact, there
were only two times when someone could have taken
them. One is before Matt's allergy kit ever arrived at
the theatre. There are two people here who were staying

with Matt in Pincher Creek who knew about the bag the EpiPens were kept in and who could have planned far enough ahead to remove them at their leisure. But I don't think that happened. I think Lam did find those pens here tonight, which he couldn't have done if they were discarded a few hundred kilometres away."

"What's the other time?" Emilie asked.

"That's something I'll have to show you." I scanned the room and did a quick calculation. There were far more people who knew about Alex's camera than didn't. Even if someone did freak out when I started to play the footage, I wasn't likely to get mobbed. I decided to go ahead. "What not all of you know is that Matt's boyfriend, Alex, for unknown reasons, decided to place a camera with remote access in Matt's suite tonight. He was watching on his phone from a hiding place by the dressing rooms, and he recorded onto this SD card, which was in the camera."

Lam got to his feet.

"That is evidence! Turn that over immediately!"

"I'll turn it over in a minute," I told him. "If you sit down, this will go faster."

He did. I plugged in the card and used the remote to show the opening, Alex setting the camera up and walking away, in case anyone doubted who'd put it there. Then I pointed out the brown bag on the counter.

"There," I said. "That's where the pens were. When Vic and Jess and I found Matt's body, that bag had been dumped out on the counter, and it was lying on its side. I'd say Matt did that in a panic when he realized he was having a reaction. For most of the evening, the bag was exactly here. Do you see how the end of the bag lines up perfectly with this cabinet edge behind it? Keep your eyes on that."

I fast-forwarded from there. Not full speed but better than double. Lam popped up again when he saw Jesse enter Matt's suite, and again when he saw Ziad. Both times, I reminded him that he'd get the card in a minute. He didn't like it, but he knew he was outnumbered with his usual retinue stuck on the theatre's other side.

"Okay, here the feed goes dead for about five minutes. Could be a glitch, but it was working fine otherwise. I'd say Alex pressed pause on the camera because he was going back into Matt's suite and he didn't want the camera to capture him. Before you jump to any conclusions, there are a few reasons Alex could have turned the camera off. That doesn't prove anything. What I want you to see… is this."

Emilie gasped when the picture came back and the bag was obviously in a different place. It was so much clearer on the big screen. I paused the footage.

"Holy shit," Vic said.

"Who was in there when the camera went off?" Emilie said, leaning forward to get a better look at Alex and Lew. "Was it you guys and Matt? Did you two do it together?" She turned to me. "Did they do it together?"

"I'll get there," I assured her. "I don't know who was in the room at that point, but it wouldn't have been enough just to get in there. You'd have to be alone in that main part of the suite long enough to open the bag, steal the pens, close it, and put it back more or less where you found it. There are only three people here that Matt would have given that kind of access. One of them was Jesse, and he was in a room with me, Kent, and Luna while that camera was shut off. The other two are sitting right there."

"You'd better watch yourself," Lew told me.

"Are you worried I'm going to get into motives?" I said. "Good call. You and Alex both had them. Alex forgot that blackmailers never overhear anything they want to hear. When he watched Jesse and Matt's conversation, he got an earful. Matt didn't take him seriously. Matt didn't respect him. Matt made a pass at Jesse. Are any of these things enough to make someone murder their boyfriend? They have been before."

"I loved him," Alex said, on the verge of tears. "I would never have hurt him. You can't say those things about me."

"And you," I said to Lew. "You knew that Matt had a habit of being… let's call it sexually inappropriate. You argued with him about it. That's in this footage."

"I could see that," Lew said. He sounded like his jaws were wired shut.

"You said Matt was going to drag both of you down and that you weren't sure he could stop."

"We argue with people we are close to," he said. "We do it when we believe they can be better."

"Maybe," I said. "You didn't sound convinced."

I let the footage continue.

"Here's where I came in," I said. "I wanted to eyeball Matt, get a sense of the guy. We talked for a few minutes. Alex comes in here… stays for a few minutes. Matt sends him out to look for the food delivery. Then I leave, and the food is right outside the door, so I hand it off to Lew and he takes it inside. The camera turns off again. At this point, Lewis has had access to the food. Did Alex? Apparently he did, because Harry has a note of when he put the food outside Matt's door and it was before Alex left. Alex didn't knock on the door to say the food was there, but he was a little pissy about being sent for it, so maybe that's why."

"So it's still either of them," Vic said slowly.

"Or both!" Emilie said.

"I was stuck on that for a while," I said. "There was no way to know who had done it. Not only did they have access to the food and the EpiPens, Matt's suite was down the hall from the staff kitchen where the mustard packets seem to have come from. Both Lew and Alex were wandering the halls while Matt talked to Jesse and Ziad. Either could have found the mustard and pocketed it. I later heard that the empty mustard packets had been found floating in a toilet in the bathroom next to Matt's suite."

"That could have been either of them too," Vic said.

"It bothered me that the packets were floating in the toilet," I said. "If I hadn't been distracted by the chaos around here, I would have dug into that right when you told me. Why do you take something you really want to get rid of, throw it in the toilet, and not flush?"

"It was yellow, and they were letting it mellow?" Duncan said. When no one laughed, he swatted an imaginary bug out of the air. "Fuck all of you. I'm tired."

"Then I was reminded of something. This building has gone through a lot of renovations, but one thing back here that seems original is the toilets. And the plumbing, I guess. Old lead stacks? Getting narrower every year? There are signs up saying not to flush anything except toilet paper. I bet people ignore those sometimes. Vic, you've worked here a few times. Do people obey the signs?"

"It's like people don't think it applies to them. A sound guy flooded half this floor one time."

I nodded. "What would happen if they flushed something small? Like a mustard packet or two."

Vic's eyes widened. I could see her getting it.

"It would come back up."

"That toilet was flushed," I said. "They flushed the evidence away and walked off thinking it was taken care of. Except it came back up. I apologize for the volume here, but the sound is quiet."

I played it for them three times, until I saw on everyone's face that they'd heard it. Matt was on the couch, talking to me about the endurance of his young boyfriend. Lew was in the kitchen, watching us with a twitching eye. And faintly, next door, a toilet flushed.

I turned off the TV to break the spell it had cast on the room. Everyone turned to look at Alex. He stood up.

"You're accusing me?" Alex said to me. "Because someone flushed a toilet?"

The last word rose to a shriek.

"Were the EpiPens backstage?" I asked Lam. "Maybe near the fly gallery? That's where Alex hid his camera after he took it out of the room."

Slowly, Lam got to his feet.

"I'd like to talk to you," he said to Alex, "down at the station."

"Get me a lawyer," Alex said to Lew, as if Lew still worked for him or ever had. Lew was stone-faced. Only his eyes moved up to regard Alex briefly before he looked away and said, "Get one yourself."

Alex turned to Jesse. Lam was between them, or he might have stepped forward. Not that he'd have gotten far.

"Stupid old bitch," he said. "Matt only wanted you because he never fucked you."

Jess blinked in surprise. "That could be true."

Alex sneered and turned away.

Lam reached a hand out to me. To shake, or… no. Of course not. He wanted the SD card. I got it and put it into his palm. He slipped it into a pants pocket, went to Alex, and took his arm. Alex shook him off with a shudder.

"I'll go. I'll go."

Kent opened the door but stayed nearby as Lam and Alex went into the hall. Once they'd gone, he shut the door and stayed in front of it. In case Alex knocked Lam out with a high kick to the jaw and came back for me, I supposed.

"Holy shit," Vic said into the silence. For what seemed like the first time since I'd arrived at the theatre, no one was on their phones.

"You're gonna need your own lawyer, Lewis," Ziad said. "It's all coming out now."

Lew said nothing. That was a guy who could keep his mouth shut. He'd be the same in police custody, if it ever came to that. Alex, on the other hand, would confess inside of an hour. He'd been cool with me, but that was before we'd all seen the video. Before we'd heard him try to flush the evidence away.

Jess came up and gave me a hug. It was nice, the appreciation and the contact and the help of another body to keep me upright. It had been a goddamned long day.

"You should all go home or to your hotel and get some sleep," I told the crowd. "You'll be hearing from the cops again tomorrow."

"I gotta go talk to Sarah," Vic said, standing and taking out her phone. "She'll be pretty relieved."

"I gotta get an Uber or a cab or something," Duncan said. "Anyone else want in?"

Dylan raised their hand, and Emilie followed. It was strange to see Emilie with nothing to say.

I let Jess go and went over to the pair of them.

"You should have this," I said, offering the movie card I got from Reiss. "You earned it."

Up close, I could see that Emilie was a little teary. She shook her head.

"I don't want it," she said softly.

Dylan seemed steadier, but they shook their head too.

Vic left first, and that broke the dam. Everyone else drifted out in a slow daze. Most went to their rooms to pick up their things. Luna linked her arm through Jesse's as we left. I offered my arm to Kent. He grinned and slapped my back instead.

Lam was standing in the hall next to Harry. The double doors leading to the stage door were propped open.

"Where's Alex?" Jess said. "Did the uniform cops take him?"

"He's getting something from the rehearsal hall before we go," Lam said.

My brain was taking a moment to translate rehearsal hall into practice room as Kent, apparently more awake, said, "What? Why aren't you with him?"

"This is the only door," Lam said, gesturing at the stage door. His face and tone were smug. "Work smarter, not harder," they said.

"No, it's not!" Luna and Jess said. Kent was already running toward the practice room and the fire door beyond. I went after him.

It wasn't that I thought Alex was going to get away. He wouldn't blend into most crowds. He might have been clever enough to have called an Uber before we all went into the green room, but that was an easy thing for the cops to track.

The thing that had me moving fast was the weather. If Alex had a coat aside from his shiny robe, or boots, I hadn't seen any sign of them. He was from the States, and I didn't know whether he'd spent any time in real cold.

When you first went out in it, without the right clothing, it felt painful and shocking. Your lungs protested every breath. Your muscles tensed, and things like your ears and fingertips felt like you were holding them against a hot stove. Your instinct was to get warm any way you could. All of that was unpleasant, but you could live with it.

The problem was that you were already on your way to hypothermia. It snuck up on you. You got tired. Everything felt heavy; it became harder and harder to move. You could be standing a few metres from a warm building, well aware you had to get inside and not able to talk your legs into it. You'd get sleepy and confused. All of these things happened faster than you'd expect. I couldn't remember a year on the prairies where no one had died from an urban walk in the cold, trying to get to a gas station a few blocks away when their car ran out of gas or thinking they could make it home from the bar. You found those people in the morning, sometimes on doorsteps with keys in their pockets.

Even the fans and reporters at the back door, dressed for the cold, had to have been going back and forth to all-night drug stores or indoor ATM nooks or warm cars.

Kent and I were also going out there in indoor clothes, like idiots, but at least we knew what we were getting into.

"Christ!" Kent gasped when the cold air hit him. I saved my breath.

The sun wouldn't be up for a while, but it was overcast and we'd had a recent snowfall, so the city lights were reflected up and down in a soft glow. The ground had been trampled around us but not cleared of snow. If I crouched low enough, it was possible to see Alex's footsteps, the smooth, pointed front and square heel of his slip-on shoes, leading from the door to the lane beside the theatre.

Kent took off toward the street while I stayed low and kept my eyes on the prints. I tried my phone's flashlight, but it didn't help with the light bouncing off the snow.

The fire door opened behind me, and I realized Kent and I had failed to prop it open. Jess was there with my coat and Kent's, both of which he threw to me. His eyes widened as the cold hit him. He was thin and lean, and the shirt he had on was about as warm as a Kleenex.

"Get back inside," I said.

"I'll stay at the door," he managed to say before his teeth started to chatter. As I was pulling my jacket on, I saw Luna's purse being slid into the doorway to keep the door about two inches open. I hoped she'd run back for Jesse's coat if he was going to stand next to that draft.

Kent was standing where the lane met the street, marching in place and rubbing his folded arms. I gave him his jacket, and he shrugged into it, already clumsy. With jackets and hoods, even without boots or gloves, we'd easily be able to outlast Alex. It still remained to be seen, if he was hiding outside, whether we'd find him in time. Here, where the road and sidewalks had largely been cleared, his footprints were gone.

The street in front of the theatre was quiet. It was the middle of a cold night. The audience and charity members had gone home, and the mob had decided all the action was at the stage door. The bars had shut down. The only motion was from windblown tree branches and awnings and the occasional passing car. Our footsteps were muted crunches on the snow, which softened the edges of every sound.

"Hey!"

The cry sounded faint and distant, but when I turned, I saw it had come from someone a block away, standing in the back parking lot. One of the stage-door crowd. The voice was high and young. I couldn't tell anything else because all I could see was a lime green blob, closer to the outline of the Michelin Man than that of a person. Coat, snow pants, big arctic boots. Other Michelin Men started appearing behind them. I heard them talking but couldn't make out the words.

They started to run toward as, or as close as they could get to running in the cold and in their colourful space suits. Kent went further into the street and started searching between buildings and behind vehicles, like he was hunting for a stray cat. I waited for the mob.

"You're Jack Lowe's boyfriend," one of them breathlessly informed me. "Where is he?"

"Inside," I said. "But Matt Garrett's boyfriend is out here somewhere."

More of the fans caught up, and I found myself surrounded, the way Jess usually was when he left the venue after a show. Some of them were shouting questions at me about Matt and Jess and even Ziad.

"Okay!" I yelled. "Listen up! Matt Garrett's boyfriend came out here in a silver robe and white pantsuit. The guy is not dressed for this. He needs to be found before he dies."

Someone deep in the fur-rimmed hood of a Canada Goose jacket asked if I was kidding. I assured them I wasn't and pointed out the last few footprints leading out of the lane.

They went around me like water and fanned into the street. I followed. Kent didn't notice, at first, that he had company. It could have been concentration, or it could have been the tunnel vision people got when they were struggling, physically, to keep going. When he finally looked up, he noticed a nearby pair of Alex-hunters and watched them for a moment, then peered up and down the street and finally back at me. I'd moved onto the street and was keeping an eye on the crowd for a sign that they'd spotted Alex. Pacing a little to keep warm, I waved Kent back to me.

"What's going on?" he asked.

"Fans," I said. "I told them to find Alex."

He stared at me in disbelief, then shook his head and smiled.

"Damn," he said.

We kept walking, mostly in circles in the middle of the street. Alex could have gone either direction. It seemed like we were there for hours, but it had to have been minutes instead. No more than ten. My legs were numb, and my feet were burning. I kept my hands in my pockets and wished for gloves.

Someone wearing a purple full-length coat over white Baffin boots jumped back from a doorway in surprise, then yelled something and started waving at everyone nearby. Kent and I glanced at each other and got moving.

There was a small crowd by the time we got there, but we were both taller than average and could see over them to the white-and-silver pile pressed into a corner of the shoe-store doorway. Alex's face was hidden under the robe, which he'd pulled up over his head, but I could tell how he was doing by the amount of shivering. His clothes were moving like they were filled with bees. You shivered like that at first, when you got seriously cold. Then, when it got worse, you stopped.

Kent had his phone out to call 911. I took off my coat and pushed through the group to place it over Alex. I leaned in, and he shoved his body close to mine. He was crying, but not dramatically like before. It sounded like wind blowing through reeds on the edge of a frozen pond. As I tucked the coat around him, he said, "Matt?"

I stopped for a second. He tried to push closer.

"Matt, I'm cold. Can we go home?"

"Not Matt," I said. The words were thick and my voice was hoarse, but I made them clear enough. He stopped pushing and tried to clutch at my coat with waxy fingers. Slowly, he raised his head and opened his eyes.

For that moment, he was clear on everything. Where he was. What he'd done. That Matt wasn't coming to take him home. That he wasn't going to be going to galleries and stylish New York parties for a very long time.

"You did this," I said with a rattling cough at the end. The air got so dry in the cold. I could see the difference now between genuine misery and the act he'd put on before. He dropped his head again and said something. It was muffled and clumsy, and I'll never be certain I heard him right. It sounded like he said, "He would've left me anyway."

I should have been a good first responder and stayed with him, close, sharing body heat. I couldn't. I backed away, and a couple of fans pressed in instead.

"I'll stay," Kent told me. "You go back inside."

I was too logy to move for a second. One of Alex's shoes had fallen off, and there was a chip in the store window above it. He'd kicked it, trying to get inside. I kept staring at the shoe like I'd never seen one before.

I had a strange floaty feeling, like there was nothing between my hips and the ground. I couldn't stay out there any longer. I went back to the theatre as fast as I could. It wasn't that fast. A couple of fans trailed me. I would have resented being followed under normal circumstances, but they were probably sticking with me to make sure I didn't fall over and die, so I let it go.

I was shivering like Alex when I got back into the theatre. Luna put a blanket around me and shoved a hot cup of tea into my hands. I had no idea where she'd found the blanket. Lam and Vic were both at the door, and they helped Jess to shove it closed against the fans trying to get in.

"Where is your coat?" Luna demanded. I had to down most of the tea before I had enough control back to explain where my coat was and where Kent was and where Alex was and that an ambulance was on the way.

Jess leaned against the wall and sank to a sitting position. He was wearing his coat. I hadn't noticed.

"Tell me when you're ready to go," he said.

"You're going to have to start the car," I told him. He shook his head.

"I've got a cab waiting out front. We can come back for your car… some other day."

After a second cup of tea I felt okay to make it to a warm cab. I napped on the way home, which wasn't so much a choice I made as a thing that happened. We were sitting outside the house when I woke up, and a glance at my phone told me we'd been there for half an hour or more. Jess had paid a cab driver to sit there and run the engine while I slept.

Chapter Twenty-Five

THE SKY had a different light as we headed into the house. Not morning yet but thinking about it. Frank greeted us at the door in his usual way, which was to slobber all over Jess and welcome me by bumping his side against my leg.

"You'd better not be a burglar," Kayla yelled from the kitchen.

We trudged in there to find Kayla, Ash, and Izzy making pancakes and bacon.

"Jack texted us that you were coming home," Ash explained. "We thought you might want breakfast."

"Before bed," Izzy said. "As you do."

"Bless you all," Jesse said. "Have you been following the news?"

"About that Alex guy?" Izzy said. "Yeah. It's everything. There's, like, official stuff and fan stuff, and Duncan pretty much play-by-played your whole reveal on Twitter. That guy is a next-level attention whore."

Ashley moved some pancakes to a plate while she said, "You guys, like, took over the internet. They're probably talking about you on the space station."

"For real, though?" Kayla said. "Did Alex seriously kill Matt because Matt said mean shit about him?"

"I get it," Ashley said. "You trust a guy and he does you like that?"

I got a prickling sensation in the back of my neck. I believed her when she said she got it.

"I can't believe you can die from mustard," Kayla said. "How would you even think of killing a guy that way?"

"The awful thing...," Jess started. "No. Let me.... There are many awful things. But Matt was paranoid that someone was going to find out about his allergy and use it to hurt him. I kind of wonder if Alex would have thought of it if Matt hadn't been so obsessed with that idea."

"Did you see Alex's posts tonight?" Izzy said. "Before you exposed him, he was on a weeping tour of social media. My boyfriend, Matt Garrett, the famous Matt Garrett, he's dead and I'm heartbroken, and did I mention my boyfriend was Matt Garrett? It looked pretty tacky to begin with, but now that everyone knows he killed Matt? Hoo-ee."

"He was posting?" I said. "He was putting on a show of being too broken-up to do anything."

"Get those views," Izzy said with a shrug. "He was doing crazy numbers. I've never seen someone's subscribers jump that fast. Hey, since you guys are here, you can set the table in the dining room. The one in here is too small."

I hardly ever used the dining room table, or in fact the dining room, but Izzy was right. It was the only table of the correct size. Jess and I cleared the table of recording equipment and a book of crossword puzzles and some camera lenses I'd been cleaning.

"We're animals," Jess observed. "We don't deserve a dining room."

"We don't deserve a werewolf butler either," I said, "but Frank has to earn a living somehow."

"I really love you," Jess said. "Just so you know. Keep clearing this off and I'll bring in plates and… I don't know, whatever the hell else you set a table with."

Alone in the dining room, I thought about Alex. Not freezing in a doorway but sitting in a bathroom, listening to Matt talk about him. Knowing how tenuous his place in the inner circle might be. How soon he might stop being an A-lister's boyfriend and return to being an obscure artist fighting to be noticed.

But not now. Even if I hadn't called him out as a murderer, he'd have been forever famous for being there, being the boyfriend, the night Matt Garrett died. For crying on social media while the subscriptions went up and up.

Maybe Kayla was right to think hurt feelings weren't enough of a motive. Not compared to clout and money and immortality. The hijacking of Matt Garrett's fame.

I shivered as Jess was returning with the plates, and he gave me a hug after he set them down.

"Go put on a warmer sweater," he said. "I'll get you some tea."

It was easier to comply than to tell him why I'd really shivered.

Breakfast was a blur of food and talk. I felt like I kept missing little things, like I was taking five-second naps while sitting up. At one point I felt the movie card digging into my leg and offered it to Izzy for services rendered. She gave me an odd look but said nothing. Shrugged and tucked it into the little backpack she'd been dragging around.

Eventually the food was mostly gone, and we all agreed to leave the mess where it was, lock Frank out of the dining room, and go to bed. I was tucked in, nearly asleep under a pile of blankets, when Jess put an arm around me and said, "It was nice of you to pay Izzy."

"Emilie and Dylan didn't want it," I said through a yawn.

"You're good at telling a bunch of people what to do."

I was too tired to figure out whether that was a dig.

"What do you mean?" I asked.

"Maybe you should hire some people, Mr. Pinkerton."

He kissed the back of my neck, and I let myself sink into the pillow. I was already mostly asleep as he said, "We can talk about it in the morning."

Keep Reading for an Exclusive Excerpt from
Lightning Strike Blues,
Book #1 in an Exciting New Series
by Gayleen Froese!

HE'S GOING west. To Edmonton, maybe, if he keeps it up, but for now he has the travel plans of a bottle rocket. That way, as far as the pressure will carry him.

The sky seems bigger than usual, with extra rows of stars. The night is that clear. The casino's spotlight sweeps past, and he wants to get beyond it. Everything will be better the moment he can't see it anymore.

What he knows is this: he is as cold as he has even been, and as hot. He has been struck everywhere at once. Every nerve is shivering, and every muscle hurts.

And then he's lying on the highway, his bike far behind him, and his clothes have been burned away.

CHAPTER ONE

Gabe

IT WAS a warm night, even for June, but it wasn't warm enough for Gabe to feel comfortable standing bareassed on Sandy Klaassen's front porch. Not that he ever would have felt comfortable about that, but now he was cold besides.

He knocked on the splintering door, casting nervous glances over his shoulder at the street. It was so far from a main drag that it wasn't even fully paved—it merged from crumbling pavement into gravel and dirt about halfway along the row of ill-used duplexes. Still, those duplexes were crammed to the rafters, and the residents came and went without regard to time, so there was no telling when a beater would roll by on its way to the nearest 7-Eleven.

To Gabe's relief, he heard Sandy's footsteps approaching the door. He placed himself to the left side of the porch, assuming Sandy would use the chain, and waited until the door opened the two inches or so that the chain allowed. Then he leaned in so that his face would take up most of Sandy's view.

"Hey," he said. Sandy shoved a dark blond curl out of her face and scowled at him.

"What happened to your key, Gabe? I had to put my book down to be your fucking butler."

"Sorry," Gabe said automatically. A pissed-off Sandy always merited a sorry, in Gabe's opinion, regardless of his culpability. "About that, though, don't open the doo—"

In the silence that followed the door's opening, he said, "It's not my fault you're seeing the goods. I told you not to open the door."

"Oh my God!" Sandy said, one blunt-nailed hand pressed tight across her eyes. "I am not seeing the goods! I see nothing! Get into the bathroom, and I'll bring you some clothes."

"Deal," Gabe said, waiting until Sandy had moved aside before heading for the only bathroom. He was relieved beyond words to find it unoccupied—almost as relieved as he'd been not to see either of Sandy's roommates in the living room as he'd scurried by.

He gave the door a good slam, just to let Sandy know she could uncover her eyes. The sound of her cursing him as she searched for clothes that might fit let him know the message had been received.

"Jesus fuck!" drifted through the air, and Gabe smiled. The bathroom door wasn't the one that had come with the place when it had been built in the sixties. That door had been replaced at some point by the cheapest thing Home Hardware had to offer, and it let bits and pieces of Sandy's rant reach him.

"...naked in the middle of town... your brother is going to... in the horse-raping Christ is wrong with you... will never know...."

"Horse-raping?" Gabe asked the door, as if it might have an answer. He knew better than to expect one from Sandy. Not that it mattered. He had more important things on his mind.

He turned to face himself in the mirror.

Gabe couldn't have said exactly what he'd expected to see. He was together enough to know that he was likely in shock. He didn't have a sense of how badly hurt he might be, but he knew what kind of shape his bike was in and how far he'd slid down the road. So pretty hurt, he figured.

Which was why he stood perfectly still and stared into that mirror for a good long time.

He saw nothing wrong. No bruises. No scrapes. His left hand had a healing cut from when Colin had been chopping up ham to throw in the scrambled eggs that morning and Gabe had put his hand too close to the cutting board. But from a motorcycle accident that he knew, in the dusty sixty-watt light of the bathroom, ought to have killed him, there was nothing to see.

There had to be, though. As he searched himself for a sign that he'd been body surfing a highway for some indication that the friction and fire that had stripped him of clothing had done some damage to the flesh beneath, he came to the uncomfortable conclusion that he must be crazy. Or concussed. He'd hit his head, and he was seeing things. In the sense that he *wasn't* seeing things that absolutely had to be there.

He had an appropriately crazy thought then—that it was good they were all lazy at Sandy's place. Because it had been almost a year since Jerry's birthday, when Sean had knocked out the porch light with a bokken and no one had replaced it. Which meant that Sandy hadn't been able to see how fucked up Gabe clearly had to be. She would have lost it if she'd seen that. Score one for lazy roommates.

Seconds later, Gabe found himself laughing again, in a spiky way that suggested he might be about to cry. He was laughing because Sandy had knocked on the bathroom door, and the surprise had almost killed him. His heart had stopped for a moment. And then Sandy had shoved a pile of clothes at him and asked what was so goddamned funny. She'd wasted no time in pulling the door shut once the clothes were in Gabe's hands.

"I'm just proud of you," Gabe told her, raising his voice a little to be heard through the door. "Someday swearing will be an Olympic event, and you'll represent Canada."

"Fuck yourself," Sandy suggested in response.

The clothes were probably Jerry's, Gabe determined. They were too long but not much oversized in any other way. Jerry was the tallest in the house, and far slimmer than Sean. And Sandy usually dated burly guys. So.

It was nice, really, dealing with a problem that he could solve using logic and basic laws of nature. It was a breath of fresh fucking air, as Sandy might say. Which reminded Gabe that he wasn't exactly cold and hadn't been since this incident had started. He'd noticed the temperature while standing outside. But he hadn't shivered or longed for a cup of coffee. He'd just known that it was cold, the way he knew that it was a clear night or that Sandy's neighbour's ancient pine tree had a tilt to the left.

It had been the excitement, he decided, of the accident. And running from the highway to Sandy's house. And hey, maybe even some of the friction that had worn his clothes away.

And he was probably concussed and crazy.

"I'm coming out," he told Sandy. "With clothes on."

"Waiting with bells on," Sandy answered.

Sandy

OBJECTIVELY, THERE was no reason for anyone with an interest in young men to prefer Gabe with clothes to Gabe without clothes. Sandy wasn't blind, so she knew that. She even knew he was, technically, legal and then some.

It was just that she'd known Gabriel Reece since he was in diapers, and somehow he was always in diapers, as far as she was concerned. Which looked surreal on an eighteen-year-old, but there it was. He was always tottering, his baby blue eyes about to darken and black hair coming in thick, grabbing at the supposedly adorable patchwork jeans her parents had seen fit to dress her in and pulling himself up to stand.

He wasn't swimming in Jerry's clothes. They were the right width for him. The impression was that these were his rightful clothes, but someone had taken a few inches out of his legs and arms when he wasn't looking. Before Sandy could ask whether that had happened, Gabe shot her a nasty glare with those disconcerting Reece eyes and said, "Cram it."

Sandy extended an arm toward the living room.

"Who was it," she asked, "that said a 'guest is a jewel on the cushion of hospitality'?"

"Percival C. Crammit," Gabe said. "I'm not sitting on that couch."

Sandy tried to run a hand through her hair, but it got caught in curls about halfway back. She had to relax her fingers and pull her hand up to disentangle it.

"Then don't," she said, trying to make her voice suggest the height to which she had had it with Gabe's shit. "We have other chairs."

Gabe sulked past her to the nubby green armchair Sean favoured, and curled up in it as if he were an orphan girl from a Victorian novel. Sandy's mouth twitched. She told it to stop that. Laughing at Gabe was not a good start to getting information out of him.

Naturally, when Gabe opened his mouth, he said nothing useful.

"You know a cat pissed on that—"

"Oh my God!" Sandy said. "Will this be the millionth time I have told you this? Should we have fucking balloons falling from the ceiling? No cat has ever pissed on that couch. My grandpa had it before me, and he never had a cat."

"So a stray got in one day," Gabe said. "Just own up, Sandy. It's not that shameful. A lot of trashy people's couches have been pissed on by cats."

Sandy pressed the heel of her hand to the bridge of her nose and counted, silently, to five one-thousand. Gabe was picking her ass. He was picking her ass because something was upsetting him. This was what Gabe did. Had been since the diaper days.

Funny how knowing that made it no less annoying.

She crossed the room to sit on the couch. It did have a faint cat-piss smell on damp days, along the back on the right side. But the kid would see her eat a live cat, fur and all, before he heard her say so.

"Who," she said as calmly as she could, "actually said it? About a guest being a jewel?"

Gabe gave her a half-hearted smile. "Nero Wolfe," he said. "I lent you that book"

"How'd you wind up naked on my front porch?" Sandy asked as her follow-up.

"Um...." Gabe got a strange look on his face at that. "Do I... do I look normal to you?

Sandy looked at his eyes. They didn't seem off. She'd seen Gabe chemically altered before, and he wasn't now.

"You always strike me as kind of abnormal," she said. Gabe didn't smile or glare. He just blinked at her in confusion, like he was a curious dog.

"You look like you," Sandy assured him, since assurance seemed to be what he was after. Gabe nodded, and the confused look cleared.

"Good to know."

"So," Sandy said. "Naked. Porch."

"Oh, thereby hangs a tale," Gabe said.

Sandy nodded.

"Get on with fucking telling it."

"Well," Gabe said, "it started when Colin threw me out of the house."

Gabe

THE GUY'S okay looking. Just okay. But okay is okay, as far as Gabe is concerned, because this guy is about to give Gabe head, and no one has ever done that for Gabe before. North Battleford, Saskatchewan, isn't a place where guys generally offer. And Colin's at the job site until at least nine and probably out with the guys after, and Gabe has the house, so obviously the cosmos wants Gabe to get a blow job at long last.

Gabe's on the living room couch, and he's pretty sure Colin wouldn't like that, but it's not as if Colin is going to know about any of this.

Mr. Okay's a kisser. Gabe could do without that. He barely knows the guy, and it seems weird. The blow job should seem weird too, in fairness. Gabe's probably just over the weirdness in that case because he would really like to have a blow job, and his brain will do whatever it has to do to make that work for him. What's more, thinking about any of this crap while a guy who's about to blow him is prospecting for his larynx is not what he should be doing. It is not seizing the day. He should just be going with it.

So he slaps his stupid brain into thinking nothing except, *Go with it. Go with it. Go with it.* Until his brain is saying it so loudly and persistently that Gabe almost doesn't hear the sound of Colin's truck crunching gravel on the drive.

And then he does. Nothing could ever be important enough for him not to hear that truck.

Mr. Okay is surprised to be shoved back and lands on the floor ass first, his hands still reaching toward Gabe. It is, objectively, funny. Probably the first time someone has shoved him like that before he could even get down to business. Gabe tells him to put his goddamned clothes on and leads by example. Not that they're completely undressed, but it's obvious what they've been doing, and obvious is not what Gabe's going for. One hundred percent evidence free is more the look he has in mind.

"Hey, Gabe, we broke off early," Colin says as he walks in the front door. That's Colin all over, starting the conversation before he even sees Gabe. Drop whatever you're doing, kid. Colin's home. Not that Gabe generally objects.

Now Mr. Okay is showing some hustle. He's got one of his shoes on, and he's already scouting for a back door. Gabe doesn't have the heart or the time to tell him the place doesn't have one.

"You wanna see a movie or something?"

Colin says this over the sound of the fridge door opening and a beer bottle chiming softly. Regular old night at the Reece house. Movies and beer. Gabe is looking for a place to hide Mr. Okay. Behind the couch, maybe? In Colin's room? That one's risky, but Gabe could get Colin out of the house on the way to see a movie and then—

"Jesus Christ!"

That's the sound of the jig being up. Gabe would know it anywhere.

"How old are you?"

Colin has Mr. Okay's shirt in his hands as he asks this, and Mr. Okay is wearing said shirt, so that's awkward. It's a weird question too. Gabe is still trying to figure out why it matters how old the guy is when Colin shoves Mr. Okay toward both the floor and the archway to the kitchen. Kind of an angled shove. It gets the job done, because Mr. Okay lands on the kitchen floor before spinning from lying on his back to being on his hands and knees and then scrambling out the door with no dignity but a pretty good rate of speed.

Gabe, who has always been dazzling with words, looks at Colin and comes up with one for the ages. He says, "So now you know."

He doesn't wait for a riposte. He heads for the kitchen and out the front door, pausing only long enough to put on his shoes and grab the keys to his motorcycle. No jacket or helmet, an omission Colin would not like, but Gabe figures Colin will have to catch his gay ass if he wants to beat Gabe to death.

Which, who knows, he might.

Sandy

"OH GOD, Gabe…."

Sandy had her eyes not just shut but screwed tight, her forehead resting on her hand. As if Gabe had given her a migraine by talking.

"I know," Gabe said softly. "He's never gonna talk to me again. I'd better hope he doesn't. If he's close enough to talk to me, he's close enough to kill me, right?"

Sandy raised her head and squinted at him. "You are—could you explain to me again the part where Colin actually threw you out of the house?"

"Well…. "Gabe shrugged. "He didn't, like, physically throw me out. But—"

"He didn't vocally throw you out," Sandy said. "He didn't, whatever, figuratively throw you out. There was no throwing of you out."

Gabe leaned his head against the back of the chair and stared at the stippled ceiling. It had little gold and silver flecks in it. Someone, at some time, must have thought that would make it more attractive. Gabe did not understand that person.

"Okay, fine," Gabe said. "I got while the getting was good. Happy?"

"Lord no," Sandy told him. "Why would—look at me, punk."

Gabe rolled his eyes before lowering them to bring Sandy into his field of vision.

"Okay," Sandy said. "Why would you think you'd need to run from your brother?"

"Because," Gabe said, raising a hand and mimicking sign language as he spoke, "he caught me with a guy. Now he knows I'm gay."

"That's obnoxious," Sandy said, stabbing an index finger in Gabe's direction. "You picked that up from Sean, didn't you? That fake-deaf thing? Don't let me catch you doing it again."

"The problem," Gabe said evenly, "remains."

"There is no problem," Sandy said. "Gabe. You idiot. Your brother knows you're gay. I mean, before tonight. He knew."

Gabe put his hands on the arms of the chair and leaned forward, his heart pounding the way it had when Colin had manhandled his date.

"He what? You told him?"

Sandy gave him a look he couldn't read and seemed about to say something when the front door opened and Jerry came in. He looked beat, his orange-red hair messed up and his face unshaven, which always made Jerry look as if he'd been eating spaghetti and was slipshod about washing up.

Gabe shot Sandy the best "shut the fuck up" look he could manage. From the corner of his eye, he could see Jerry looking him up and down.

"You wearing my clothes, Younger?"

Gabe had never found Jerry's habit of calling him Reece the Younger endearing, but it sucked in a special way on this special night.

"I'm trying to pick up your sweet style," Gabe told him, still looking at Sandy.

"Good luck," Jerry said. He walked past the living room and veered into the kitchen.

"Long day?" Sandy called after him.

"There was a busted hard drive in Meadow Lake," Jerry called back. "Four hours of driving for a fifteen-minute fix."

"They couldn't get it done local?" Sandy asked. Jerry appeared in the living room entrance with a beer in his hand.

"It's expressly not my job," he said, "to point that out to clients."

"Yeah, really," Sandy said. She looked at Gabe. "I didn't tell him anything. I didn't have to."

"Tell who what?" Jerry inquired, entering the living room and taking the far end of the cat-piss couch.

"Nothing," Gabe said distinctly, glaring at Sandy. She gave him a sweet smile, and Gabe's stomach dropped. Whatever was coming, he was going to hate it.

"Jer," Sandy said, "what would you say Gabe's sexual orientation is?"

"Sandy, shut the *fuck* up!" Gabe said, launching himself out of his chair and then not knowing what to do, because it wasn't as if he could hit her. She could take him.

He just stood in front of her, wishing he were dead. Or she were. Or everyone.

"He is gay," Jerry said. Gabe stared at him, speechless. He felt cold again, frozen clear through, the way he had on the highway.

"You sure?" Sandy asked.

"I would say he is less gay," Jerry said, "than Lady Gaga doing an impersonation of Liza Minnelli on a float in the San Francisco Pride parade. But gayer than David Bowie."

"Oh, my God," Gabe said. He could barely hear himself. The words felt heavy, almost impossible to push out. "You told everyone."

"Sweetie."

Gabe felt something, a touch to his hand, and looked down to see Sandy holding it. Pressing it, even. It barely registered.

"Sweetie," she said, "I didn't tell anyone."

Gabe kept staring at Sandy's hand. And his. Seeing the touch made it easier to feel.

"How do they know?" he asked. "I've been really careful."

"We know you," she said softly. "And we don't care, honey. Colin doesn't care. I promise."

Slowly Gabe pulled his hand from Sandy's and backed into his chair. He could believe, maybe, that Sandy hadn't told anyone. She'd promised. She had never broken a promise to him before.

But that was one thing. Colin not caring was something else.

"He threw the guy out," Gabe said, looking now at the way his hands rested in his lap. Was it a gay way of holding his hands? Did he sit gay or something? Or was it all over his face?

"Guy?" Jerry asked.

"Colin caught Gabe with some guy," Sandy said. "Older guy."

"Ah," Jerry said. "Colin gave him the bum's rush?"

"You're a funny man," Sandy said, biting off the words. There was silence for a second or two, and then Gabe heard Jerry taking a pull on his beer. Giving up on his career as a comedian, it seemed.

"Gabe, come on," Sandy said. "If you were Colin's little sister and you'd come home with some skeezy older guy, what do you think Colin would have done?"

"If you were a chick," Jerry said, "Colin would have castrated the guy on your kitchen table. So this actually went better."

"You have to eat on that table," Sandy agreed. Gabe raised his head and looked from one to the other of them, their earnest expressions, the way they were leaning forward slightly to give their words that extra push in his direction. And to his great surprise, he laughed. Right through to tears, and Sandy laughed with him. Jerry was too damned cool to laugh, but he smirked while he finished his beer, which was effusive for him, and Gabe appreciated it. Because he knew the guy, and knew what he was like, and he was okay with that.

"I'll make coffee," Sandy said, getting up and patting Gabe's knee on her way past him to the kitchen. "And then you can tell us how you wound up naked on the porch."

IT HAD to be a practical joke. Some terrible fucking joke that Gabe had cooked up, maybe with help from Sean. Definitely with help from Sean, because where else would he get a bike he could do this to?

"Fucking *Sean*!" she blurted, and this, going by the look on Gabe's face, was about the last thing he'd expected her to say.

He was standing at the side of the highway, stars for a backdrop and wind tossing his hair around and, even in Jerry's too-long clothes, he looked like a goddamned movie star. Or rock star, which he would likely have preferred, considering what a freak he was for music. Sometimes it was stupidly obvious that he didn't belong around there. Sometimes Sandy wanted to slap him for it.

"Was this Sean's idea?" she asked. "Get an old bike and fucking, I don't know, melt it to the highway, and cook up this whole story about Colin finding you with a guy? And haul me and Jerry out here so you can see the look on our faces?"

Gabe had his head tilted a bit to one side. Everything about his expression said that Sandy had lost her mind.

"Your hypothesis," he said carefully, "is that I outed myself to Sean and invented a story that's pretty much my worst nightmare just so I could tell you a bullshit story about my bike getting wrecked?"

"That's your worst nightmare?" Jerry asked mildly. "Colin walking in on you?" He was still looking at the bike, or the bike-like pile of melted plastic and metal... metal... stuck to the road. He nudged some of it with the toe of his shoe and shrugged when it failed to move. "It's on there pretty good."

"Careful you don't melt your shoe," Gabe warned. Jerry shook his head.

"Mostly cooled off now."

"What am I supposed to think?" Sandy asked Gabe. "How else could this have happened, and you still be... standing here?"

Gabe took a deep breath. A trio of cars passed, not slowing at the sight of three people and scrap metal. People were always in a hurry on that road.

"I think," Gabe said once the cars were gone, "I got hit by lightning."

That got Jerry to stop looking at the ex-bike and start looking at Gabe.

"Out of a clear sky," he said.

"Yeah, I know," Gabe said. "But it's the only sky I've got, and I'm thinking lightning came out of it. Look, you guys, something knocked me off my bike and down the highway, burned off all my clothes, and did that to the bike. What else could it have been?"

Jerry looked at the sky.

"Meteorite?" he offered.

Sandy's stomach lurched. "Come on. Gabe did not get hit by a fucking meteorite. Or lightning. He'd be… he'd…. Jesus, Gabe, you're telling us you skidded how far?"

"About even with the windbreak," he said, pointing out a row of scraggly trees.

"Without leathers or a helmet," Sandy said, staring down the highway. "You didn't even have a jacket?"

"T-shirt and jeans," Gabe said.

Jerry walked around Gabe in a tight circle, looking at him. "No broken bones. No sprains."

"Nothing," Gabe said. "Not even a scrape."

Jerry whistled. "Somebody up there likes you."

Gabe smiled. "Somebody up there has a love/hate relationship with me," he corrected.

Jerry barked out one of his rare laughs. Sandy thought she might throw up. It wasn't funny. This was so not funny.

"Sandy?" Gabe asked softly. She looked at him and tried on a smile as another group of cars sped past.

"Whatever happened," she said, "no harm done, I guess. Except to your bike."

"Yeah," Gabe said. "I don't think even Sean's gonna be able to fix it. That's fucked. How am I gonna get up to Cochin next week?"

It took Sandy a moment to remember that Gabe had a summer job lined up at Cochin, teaching people to windsurf on Jackfish Lake. He'd learned like the rest of them, tooling around on Sandy's dad's old board, and he was certified in exactly nothing, but somehow he'd talked his way into the gig. The owners probably thought teenage girls would line up for lessons with the hot guy. The owners were probably right.

"Maybe Sean can lend me a bike," Gabe said.

"We'll figure it out," Sandy said. She put a hand on Gabe's shoulder and steered him toward Jerry's dull red Geo. "You can bunk with us tonight. Tomorrow you can see a doctor and make sure you're really okay."

Gabe stopped, pushing back against her hand. The motion had more force than she expected, and she had to take a step back to keep her balance.

"I don't need a doctor."

"See a doctor," Sandy said, "And I'll make Sean lend you a bike. Don't see a doctor, and you're hitching."

Gabe's shoulders dropped as his face fell, giving a general picture of things rushing toward the ground.

"Sandeeeeeeee...."

"You're tall for a six-year-old," Sandy observed. "That's the deal. Stay at our place tonight. Tomorrow morning Jerry will run you by your house so you can talk to Colin before he leaves for work. And then Jerry will drive you to a Mediclinic."

"Wow," Gabe said. "This deal keeps sucking bigger and bigger balls."

"Nobody consulted Jerry," Jerry pointed out.

"Or I could phone Colin right now," Sandy said, ignoring Jerry. "And, I remind you, you will be hitching to Cochin."

"Colin's probably at the bar," Gabe said, as if that won the game for him.

It was bad enough that Gabe and Colin refused to carry cell phones for some bullshit reason, but so much worse that they were obnoxious about it. You can't pin us Reece boys down. Sandy stepped closer, so that Gabe had to tilt his head back to look her in the eye.

"I will call him at the bar," she said. "I will call all the bars."

She and Gabe stood there for a while, a few more groups of cars' worth of time. One even honked as though the whole freaking road wasn't enough for his ugly-ass sedan and he resented them taking up the shoulder. They did not, either of them, so much as twitch.

"Have it your way," Gabe said finally.

Sandy smiled and put a hand on his cheek. "Thanks, kiddo."

She stepped back and to his side, then put an arm around his shoulders and led him to Jerry, who was looking irritated and leaning against the side of his car.

"Your chariot," Jerry said, as they approached. "Apparently."

"Just until Sean gives him a bike," Sandy assured him. "And I will owe you."

"Story of my life," Jerry muttered, and something in his eyes told Sandy not to ask what he meant by that. Instead the three of them said little as the tiny car full of hard drives and towers and cables bounced from the shoulder to the highway and back into town to take them home.

GAYLEEN FROESE is an LGBTQ writer of detective fiction living in Edmonton, Canada. Her novels include The Girl Whose Luck Ran Out, Touch, and Grayling Cross. Her chapter book for adults, What the Cat Dragged In, was short-listed in the International 3-Day Novel Contest and is published by The Asp, an authors' collective based in western Canada.

Gayleen has appeared on Canadian Learning Television's A Total Write-Off, won the second season of the Three Day Novel Contest on BookTelevision, and as a singer-songwriter, showcased at festivals across Canada. She has worked as a radio writer and talk-show host, an advertising creative director, and a communications officer.

A past resident of Saskatoon, Toronto, and northern Saskatchewan, Gayleen now lives in Edmonton with novelist Laird Ryan States in a home that includes dogs, geckos, snakes, monitor lizards, and Marlowe the tegu. When not writing, she can be found kayaking, photographing unsuspecting wildlife, and playing cooperative board games, viciously competitive card games, and tabletop RPGs.

Gayleen can be found on:
Twitter @gayleenfroese
Facebook @GayleenFroeseWriting
And www.gayleenfroese.com

Follow me on BookBub

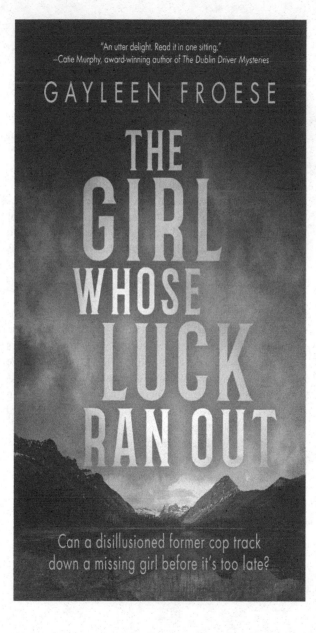

"An utter delight. Read it in one sitting."
—Catie Murphy, award-winning author of *The Dublin Driver Mysteries*

GAYLEEN FROESE

THE GIRL WHOSE LUCK RAN OUT

Can a disillusioned former cop track
down a missing girl before it's too late?

A Ben Ames Case File

Can a disillusioned former cop track down a missing girl before it's too late?

Seven years ago, criminologist Ben Ames thought he'd change a big city police force from the inside. He failed. Now he's a private detective trailing insurance frauds and cheating spouses through the foothills of the Rocky Mountains. Like police work, the job would be easier if he didn't have a conscience.

When university student Kimberly Moy goes missing, her sister begs Ben to take the case. But before Ben can follow up on any leads—What does the Fibonacci series have to do with Kim's disappearance? What do her disaffected friends know? And where is her car?—chance and bad timing drop his unexpected ex, Jesse, into the mix.

Ben doesn't have time to train Jesse into the junior PI he seems determined to become. Amateur sleuths are always trouble. Unfortunately, this is turning out to be the kind of case that requires backup, and his intuition is telling him Kim's story may not have a happy ending...

www.dsppublications.com

For more
great fiction
from

DSP PUBLICATIONS

visit us online.
WWW.DSPPUBLICATIONS.COM